BEYOND BABYLON

BEYOND BABYLON

Igiaba Scego

Translated from Italian by Aaron Robertson

TWO LINES
PRESS

Originally published as: *Oltre Babilonia*
Copyright © 2008 by Igiaba Scego
Translation © 2019 by Aaron Robertson
Introduction copyright © 2019 by Jhumpa Lahiri
All rights reserved.

The quote on page v is from: Isabella Ducrot, *La stoffa a quadri*. Rome: Quodlibet, 2018. Translation by Jhumpa Lahiri.

Two Lines Press
582 Market Street, Suite 700, San Francisco, CA 94104
www.twolinespress.com

ISBN 978-1-978-1-931883-83-2

Cover design by Gabriele Wilson
Cover photo by Sophie Harris Taylor / Millennium Images, UK
Typeset by Sloane | Samuel

Printed in the United States of America

Library of Congress Cataloging-in-Publication Data
Names: Scego, Igiaba, 1974- author. | Robertson, Aaron, 1994- translator.
Title: Beyond Babylon / by Igiaba Scego ; translated from the Italian by
Aaron Robertson.
Other titles: Oltre Babilonia. English
Description: San Francisco, CA : Two Lines Press, 2019
Identifiers: LCCN 2018057428 (print) | LCCN 2019003056 (ebook)
ISBN 9781931883849 (e-book) | ISBN 9781931883832 (hardcover)
Subjects: LCSH: Children of immigrants--Italy--Fiction.
Somalis--Italy--Fiction. | Immigrants--Italy--Fiction.
Multiculturalism--Italy--Fiction. | Rome (Italy)--Fiction.
Classification: LCC PQ4919.C373 (ebook) | LCC PQ4919.C373 O4813 2019 (print)
DDC 853/.92--dc23
LC record available at https://lccn.loc.gov/2018057428

1 3 5 7 9 10 8 6 4 2

This book is supported in part by a PEN/Heim Translation Fund Grant and an award from the National Endowment for the Arts.

ART WORKS.
arts.gov

INTRODUCTION
Jhumpa Lahiri

The epic quest that sets *Beyond Babylon* in motion is not for a place, or a sacred animal, or a precious object. What has been lost and must be found, what must be regained in order to set things right, is something far more elemental, also more elusive, given that it is something most people readily "see" and therefore don't have to go looking for. The quest, in this case, is for color, and for one shade in particular: red. Zuhra, one of the novel's two central female protagonists, has been deprived of her ability to experience, perceive, or distinguish color. Sexually molested as a child, this young Roman woman doesn't see a red stain on her underpants when she menstruates, but gray. Her blood, representative of her fertility, her physiological female identity, has been visually muted, altered, literally drained of significance. While her loss of innocence at the hands of a predator can never be restituted, her second loss, represented by a state of exile from the multihued world, imbues her with a heroic mission.

Beyond Babylon is a variegated tapestry that unfurls over more than four hundred pages and weaves together myriad stories, voices, settings, and time periods. But red and gray, and the contradictory realms they symbolize, are the two dominant threads. Red: a primary color on the spectrum, representative of life and death, of anger and love, of communism, of Catholic cardinals, of brides in the East. Gray, on the other hand, is absent from the color wheel. A singular shade that has no opposite, it is the color of in-betweenness, of imprecision, of shadows. A mixture of black and white, gray may be seen as a compromise, as ambiguity, as a meeting point between extremes. Gray is the color of cities, of asphalt and cement. Of sobriety but also impurity, given that it is not an independent tone, but a meeting point of both.

Colors have always been freighted with meaning: political, aesthetic, psychological, emotional. They are linked, in almost every culture, to rites of passage and to ceremonies of all kinds. In the Middle Ages, when each panel of a fresco told a separate story, each color had a value. Color, in this sense, stands for language itself. And of course there are the colors that we human beings are born with: the various shades of our skin, distinctive and indelible, that also tell a story, that indicate our genetic heritage and mark us from birth to death.

Beyond Babylon is a novel that interrogates language, race, and identity from beginning to end. Both Zuhra and Mar—the other central protagonist in the novel—are Italian women who are black. Zuhra is of Somali origin. Mar is half Somali and half Argentine. Both deal with color as a marker of race. Both struggle with what it means for them. As black women in a predominantly white country, they stand out and also feel invisible. If the inability to see colors is a source of frustration for Zuhra, her spirited telling of the story—in a series of red notebooks, she makes a point of saying—opens the reader's eyes to what it means to be a black Italian woman: an element of Italian society that few see clearly, and some don't recognize at all.

Like most literary quests, the search to regain color involves a journey, in this case, from Rome to Tunisia, where Mar and Zuhra have been sent to learn classical Arabic. This destination is itself described as a sort of "gray" in both the geographic and cultural sense, a nether-zone between Italy and Africa. But nearly everything in this novel is the product of mixture, of convergence, of hybridity, also of doubling. Everything is itself and also its counterpart. Mar and Zuhra are two sisters. They have two mothers. The two pairs of women occupy the center of two stories that themselves intersect in the novel. Interestingly, there is only one principle male figure, and he is connected, albeit in absentia, to all four of these women. If, as the writer Michela Murgia says, everything that is unique can be regarded as fascist, the novel declines male power politically, a power that also stands for Italy's colonial past under fascism: its imperial aggression and conquest, in Africa, under Mussolini. *Beyond Babylon* is a novel that insists upon miscegenation and multifariousness, on blending and blurring, on the freedom to *not* be a certain way. It resists the unifying force of fascism, and rejects the ideal of having only one identity, whether it be national, cultural, sexual, or otherwise.

The novel is steeped in bodily imagery and thick with bodily traumas. In Rome, a city known for its appreciation of the *quinto quarto*—the parts of the animal most people ignore, prized in Roman cooking—this focus on the body and its functions, its innards, its mysterious and occult workings, its cramps and urges, is particularly resonant. This is a novel that talks openly about defecating, menstruating, vomiting, fornicating, and evacuating—not just urine and feces and uterine linings, but also life itself, in the course of an abortion. It can claim Rabelais as an ancestor, and Boccaccio. It elevates what society tells us to keep to a private sphere, and makes it the subject for literature.

The female body as a locus of sexuality, of autonomous pleasure and freedom, is most brutally negated in the act of cliterodectomy, which this novel also talks about. This brutal act of mutilation, designed to erase a woman's pleasure, to silence it, brings us to the myth of Procne and Philomela, among the bloodiest in Greek mythology, which strikes me as *Beyond Babylon*'s literary point of origin. The key elements in that myth are two sisters, violence, and language. And the salient plot points, as recounted in Ovid's *Metamorphoses*, are these: Philomela's tongue is cut out by her brother-in-law, Tereus, King of Thrace, to keep her from telling people that he raped her. She resorts to identifying him anyway, by weaving the story into a tapestry. When her sister Procne learns the truth, she kills Itys, her son with Tereus, and secretly feeds him to his father. When Tereus realizes what his wife has done, he attempts to kill both women. All three are transformed, in the end, into birds.

The distressing moral of the story: a powerful man's desire is claimed through violence; a woman's right to condemn that violence is violently cut away. But if read carefully, Procne and Philomela's tragedy is as much about female empowerment as it is about victimization, with willful communication as the fulcrum. In Ovid's version, the tool with which Tereus extracts Philomela's tongue is a pair of forceps: an implement connected, also in modern civilization, to difficult births, also to abortions. But her severed tongue is described as having a soul. It is transformed into a nightingale, a creature known for its exquisite nocturnal singing. It is only the male nightingale that is able to produce song. The female of the species, like Philomela, has no voice. Incidentally, John Keats, who wrote his celebrated ode to that bird, lies buried in Scego's city.

Fortunately, the fates of Mar and Zuhra are not as tragic as their mythological predecessors. *Beyond Babylon*, ironic, ebullient, and melancholic in turns, is more comic than tragic, clamorous in spirit as opposed to a lament. Yet the points of connection between this novel and that myth are numerous, even down to a repulsive act of cannibalism, albeit in the animal kingdom, unforgettably described: a pigeon that devours chicken, at Rome's Termini train station. In some sense the real protagonist of *Beyond Babylon*, beyond the two sisters themselves, is a specific part of them: their tongue, *lingua* in Italian, the same word for *language*. Language, in this novel, is a central plot point and an ongoing theme. The story revolves repeatedly around what it means to acquire a foreign tongue, to lack an authoritative tongue, to navigate the plethora of languages that both distinguish and divide the human race. It is about seeking the language of our ancestors while simultaneously ingesting the language of our surroundings. It is about the collision, and also the coherence, brought about by the intersection of two contrasting strands.

The act of weaving, in Greek mythology, gave many women a way to subvert the power dynamic in a male-dominated world. In Italian, *trama* is the word both for plot and for the weave of fabric brought about by the intersection of warp and weft. The artist and writer Isabella Ducrot reminds us that Ferdinand de Saussure, the founder of modern linguistics, analyzes language in terms of a weaving formed by a weft of words—syntagmas—around a warp of rules, or paradigms. Ducrot observes that while the weft has been associated, since Plato, with masculine power, the realm of the warp belongs to female narration, which is inherited, unbroken, and ongoing: "The uninterrupted flow of memories and recollections of oral tradition was certainly kept alive by grandmothers, nannies and mothers who, while rocking infants and performing their eternal daily tasks to the rhythm of songs, nursery rhymes and lullabies, have woven the history that women have lived."

The principal languages in this book are Italian, the language in which it is written and in which the main characters speak, and classical Arabic, which both sisters are studying. But Spanish, Roman, Somali, and English are also mixed in. The book interrogates language both as a charged aspect of identity as well as a fleshy part of our body, rooted in our mouths, allowing us to speak and taste, to give and receive pleasure. Given that the book asks the question—What is language for?—the book also answers: Language is for telling, for revealing. The book celebrates diverse modes of telling, singing, speaking, and writing. It documents histories and herstories, preserved and handed down, especially between women.

Language is freedom, but language is also a system, a form of authority that can also oppress. The epilogue to *Beyond Babylon* is an eloquent and rousing manifesto for anyone who has lived among and between languages, and who therefore cannot claim to have an unadulterated or exclusive relationship with any one tongue. It speaks to all who feel linguistically compromised, crippled, mutilated, who experience the shame and alienation of this. If being deprived from the governance of a mother tongue amounts to a form of linguistic nomadism, *Beyond Babylon* reminds us that this is also a form of freedom. It asserts the authority of an alternate system that is mongrel as opposed to noble and pure. As Zuhra succinctly puts it, "I don't speak, I mix." This is her definitive overturning of linguistic patriarchy. Her hymn to all that converges and combines. Her anthem to languages that grow out of the cracks, and stem from unsanctioned sources.

In invoking Babylon in the title—a real place on earth, with religious and historical import, Scego confounds past and present. Babylon is perhaps a container for all the places in the book: an ancient Mesopotamian city, once a flourishing kingdom that fell into ruin, now part of Iraq and the Arab world. Babylon was a city destroyed and rebuilt, that contained one of the seven wonders of the ancient world. A counterpart to Rome, it represents past glory, ruin, confusion, commercialism, and corruption. Like Rome, a river once ran through the middle of it. And like Rome, it is a city associated with, or likened to, a prostitute.

Scego's Babylon also refers to the resonance that city has in Rastafarian religion, and in Bob Marley's celebrated song of protest: "So let the words of our mouth / and the meditations of our hearts / be acceptable in thy sight." Based on Psalm 137, it is a song of tormentors and captors, of suffering at the hands of the merciless, the courage to sing in a foreign land. Music, of wide-ranging genres, is central to *Beyond Babylon*. It is a song by Tinariwen, musicians from Northern Mali, heard on her iPod, whose words elude her but whose meaning she nevertheless appreciates, that prompts Zuhra to write her story, thanks, she says, to a "rhythm that transports me into a cosmic chaos that appears to be my own." But nested within Babylon is the name of another biblical place: Babel, legendary for its tower, and its lesson: our plurilingual condition, meant to punish the human race.

Scego's novel is both a tower, constructed layer by layer, and also a great sprawl. It is in fact neatly organized into five chapters with eight alternating sections always in the same order. The prose is distinctive for its terse energy, its staccato rhythm, all the more interesting given that *Beyond Babylon* is a porous, maximalist torrent that seems to overflow its margins. Geographically it roams from Rome to Buenos Aires to memories of Mogadishu. It straddles different time periods, different story lines and points of view. Its register, lyrical and slang, effusive and abbreviated, tender and acerbic, brims with highs and lows. It is hip and irreverent and it is also baroque in sensibility, another element that ties the book to Rome. Those who read this novel will come to know, intimately, a Rome beyond the conventional, beyond the stereotypes. It is a Rome full of immigrants, full of people who contain different worlds within them.

Beyond Babylon is novel both rooted and rootless, original but clearly stemming from others. In addition to Ovid and the epic quest, it grows out of novels like Hanif Kureishi's *The Buddha of Suburbia*, Zadie Smith's *White Teeth*, Danzy Senna's *Caucasia*: urban, coming-of-age novels written by young writers (*Beyond Babylon* was published when its Roman-born author was thirty-four) growing up with double perspectives, with the challenge of constructing a hybrid identity, of asserting the validity, also the authenticity, of being culturally and/or racially "mixed." It is about the anguish of not being white or of not being black enough, about being Italian and not being accepted as Italian. It is about falling short, feeling excluded from conventional identities, feeling at once enriched and annihilated by the intersection of elements. Another frame of reference is an overtly feminist one, as explored in the novels of Margaret Atwood, the poetry of Anne Sexton, the stream of consciousness narration experimented with by Virginia Woolf. A third source is distinctly Roman: Pier Paolo Pasolini, who had an outsider's perspective and represented the underrepresented of the city, and Elsa Morante, who wrote with a similar force and range—novels of "grande respiro" as it's said in Italian—and wrote with particular insight about the fraught relationships between mothers and daughters, one of the most moving themes in *Beyond Babylon*, which pays careful attention to the experience of daughters who do not resemble their mothers, who feel estranged from their mothers, and who insist, in spite of such gaps and obstacles, upon a vital connection with the women who gave them life.

There is no better time than now to bring this novel into English. Now, when women's voices are being heard in a new way, when the silence surrounding sexual abuse is being shattered, articulated, exposed. Now, when the question of Italy's identity in relation to the rest of Europe is increasingly in peril because of growing populism, growing xenophobia, and racially motivated crimes. Now, when those in power in Italy call to keep out foreigners and close its borders—an attitude unfortunately mirrored in other parts of the word—is the moment to read *Beyond Babylon*, a book that insists on all that is open and flowing, coalescent and coexistent. For the babel of plurilingualism, far from a condemnation, is in fact what enriches and ennobles our natural state. This is a novel not only about the importance of living astride more than one language, but about a woman writing herself, with her own words, and thus her own language, into being. The word *babel* has come to mean "incoherence" in English, but it is Hebrew for "confusion." And Scego has written a novel that takes the act of confusion—literally, the melding together of disparate elements—to its highest and most articulate level.

The myth of Procne and Philomela was revisited by Shakespeare in *Titus Andronicus*, one of his bloodiest plays. In that version, in order to tell her story, Philomela, renamed Lavinia, unable to speak out loud, holds a stick in her mouth and writes the names of her assailants in the ground. Scego, too, has gotten it out, written it down. She gives voice to multiple lives, experiences, and emotions either silenced or ignored by history. In taking this work beyond Italian and rendering it into English, Aaron Robertson has reproduced, with remarkable sensitivity, precision, and elegance, a novel—smart, strident, subversive—that resembles no other Italian novel to have migrated thus far into English.

BEYOND BABYLON

Sólo quiero que comprendan
el valor que representa
el coraje de querer.

"Cuesta abajo"
— Carlos Gardel & Alfredo Le Pera

Caloosheyda waxaa marahaya jidka…jidka heshiika.
Sulla mia pancia passa la linea…la linea della pace.
The line runs over my belly…the line of peace.

"Jidka"
— Saba Anglana

PROLOGUE

I've always pitied Spain. It's a beautiful country, but it makes me so sad, *wallahi billahi*, I swear. And if I say *wallahi billahi* you must believe me. Alice says that I've gone mad and that she's never heard such a thing. "Spain is life," she says. Then she makes a list of all Spain's marvels. A compelling list, full of splendid things, but the pity remains. It's an odd feeling. At first I thought it was because of the civil war they'd had over there. An awful war that saw every man for himself, in the thirties. But the war in Spain has been over for quite a while (not like ours in Somalia, which has lasted for centuries). Now they have Zapatero and gay marriage. Real cool, apparently. Then, all of a sudden, I remembered this pity stuff was Ranieri's fault, my batty art history professor. How could anyone forget those Thursday afternoons when she dragged her classes, me included, through the streets of Rome? What a woman. Her chestnut hair was wrapped in a beguine's bun. It gave the impression of ugliness, but she was gorgeous. She had the eyes of a sly cat and full, soft lips. Whenever she wore her strange puffy miniskirts, it made the boys hard.

Ranieri made us walk for hours around Rome. Far and wide around Rome. Sideways across Rome. She said that by walking we would stumble upon color. "Rome is full of colors," she said, "and everyone has their own, always remember that." It was Ranieri

who made me feel this absurd pity for Spain. We were at the Villa
Borghese gardens on one of her Thursdays, three classes of seniors.
The sun was hot and high for March. *Wallahi billahi*, it was searing, and if I say *wallahi billahi* you must believe me. The clouds
formed rabbits and larks out of the psychedelic air. Children eyed
fat American tourists in their tight bermuda shorts. Everyone's
hormones were in turmoil. Except mine. Back then they were frozen. In that absentminded bedlam, Ranieri jolted souls from their
inertia. No words. Only a gesture. A finger, to be exact. The index,
more specifically. Ranieri indicated a point equidistant from her
and from us, the entire senior class. A timeworn bench that had
seen better days. "See that blue ocean there?" I didn't see anything,
wallahi billahi, nothing at all. Only a poorly built bench. "That's
where he wrote," she said solemnly. "That's where he cried. In exile, alone. Rafael Alberti, the great Spanish poet."

Poet or not, there was no way of seeing the blue the professor was going on about. Instead, I saw everything as washed out.
Pity had taken hold of me by then. That Rafael who was exiled to
Rome, and all of Spain, reminded me too much of my exile from
myself—something unfinished. I dammed my tears so they would
overflow later, when I would be alone at home in the intimacy of
my bathroom. Then I wept, stifling my shouts and realizing only
then that I no longer had colors, I had lost them all around the
city. But how could that happen? And how did I not realize it until
that moment?

Later, I forgot this business about colors. I went on with
my life this way, almost without realizing it. Pale worlds, glassy
eyes, treacherous transparency. It continued like this for a decade,
maybe slightly longer.

Alice says it was because of my virginity. And in fact I'm
still a virgin, sadly, *wallahi billahi*, I swear to Christ and Shiva,
to Buddha and all the souls of purgatory and nirvana—I would
never lie about a thing like that. Virgin like the Madonna who
cries tomato blood, virgin like a baby girl in her mother's stomach,

wallahi, virgin, *wallahi billahi*, and if I say *wallahi billahi* you must believe me. I have to be careful with strong emotions. I could snap, and then who would put me back together? I am colorless. Defenseless. Virgin. Alone. Alice says I should hurry and find a man to fuck me. It's already been nine years since I finished school and there can't be virgins at my age, they don't exist anymore. "You're not in the nineteenth century, sweetheart," Alice says.

I'm a bit embarrassed. Virgins seem a little faded, and pretty uptight, too. I'd like to find myself a boyfriend. I'd really like to see colors again, but it's not as simple as going to the supermarket and picking up a color or a boy. It's somewhat more complicated. I'm certain that, of the girls from my fifth grade class, I'm the only one who still has her heart's hymen intact. Of the eight of us, I'm the only one still in this ridiculous state. Only I have a membrane sewn inside my heart. The first to give herself to someone was Erica. She always said she'd go for it. They told me she did it in a restroom with Enzo, the janitor, but perhaps that was only a rumor. Then, after Erica, the others followed: Deborah, Enrica, Valeria, Cristina, Bilqis. Even Anna, the little yapper, got lucky. She called me a few nights ago to tell me. She said something like, "It happened" or "I did it." And I asked, "Did you like it?" She didn't answer.

Actually, I was acquainted with sex well before them. It's love I've never known. This is my problem. I've never been in tune with the times. I was in elementary school, a boarding school, and we had a janitor that we called Uncle. He had flaky, repugnant skin. Uncle gave me unsolicited lessons about sex. Uncle isn't the right word. For Somalis, all people are uncles and aunts, even the white janitors who look after the children they send away to boarding school. It was like being in a fucking Walt Disney cartoon, and in the end you no longer understood anything, you didn't know if someone was your actual uncle, a distant relative, or someone it was better not to have near you. Well, one afternoon, while I'm going over our lesson on the Etruscans, this uncle who wasn't really one pulls out his thing from the flap of his pants and begins rubbing himself on my shoulders.

So began five difficult years. I washed my thighs with soap every day, meticulously. And that acrid taste? I couldn't get it out of my mouth with a thousand rinsings. I was eight years old the first time. Then I was nine. Then ten. Eleven. When I was twelve, somebody decided that nightmares were only real if they lasted briefly and put an end to my hell. I stopped brushing my teeth so much, only the top row. Mom told me they thrashed him. I'm not sure. I only know that I left through the door of that school never to return. I don't recall his face anymore. I know he did everything to me, and left me a virgin. Away, gone, disappeared. The thing is...that uncle took all my colors, every single one. He took them for himself, and it's not fair. He'd already taken one part of me. Couldn't he at least have left the colors?

That's why I'm searching for them now like a madwoman in Rome. Ranieri said you can find colors here. I found yellow idly dozing in Veio Park. *Wallahi billahi*, it was sleeping like a dopey sloth. And green? It had quite the adventure! It had gotten lost in the Piazza Vittorio bazaar, between the spinach and the Argentinian *mate*, but I snatched it back. Where did it think it was going? I also salvaged every hue of black. Calmly, I filled my sack with colors. When I have them all back, I'll be ready to make love to a man. A man I adore. You can't make love without colors. It would come out all twisted. And I'm fed up with crooked things, *wallahi billahi*, sick and tired, and if I say *wallahi billahi* you must believe me. I want pleasant odors, sweet words, complicit looks, wonders. And, yes, maybe someone with a beard.

Only red is missing from the sack now. I brushed past it once. Right here, in fact, where I find myself now on Via Tomacelli. I'm sure that sooner or later it'll come through again. I lie in wait until then. I take three shifts a day, one in the morning, the second in the late afternoon, and the third at night between ten and eleven. I know everything about this anonymous road by now. Every corner, every shop window, every human being in transit. Via Tomacelli is unusual, it doesn't seem like the historic center. It doesn't seem like anything, to be frank. *Wallahi*, it seems like nothing. The Ferrari store window stands out like an elephant, then a handful of bars, an antique bookstore, a Benetton megastore. Capitalism, money, luxury. But then, at the core, you find a working-class spirit made of old, tried-and-true communist comrades, their newspaper, their potential utopias. Though apparently, the comrades are relocating…they're leaving. I think a part of them will always be here, attached to this road. A profusion of red: the Ferrari, the tried-and-true comrades of the "manifesto," the jackets with pom-poms displayed for sale. My red was different, though. It covered the hair of a man in dirty chestnut boots. It had come out of a door, one of thousands on that umbilical cord mistaken for a street. A short-lived moment. A cigarette rolled during a break in a lifetime. A thick, full beard, a tired gaze, curved shoulders, lively eyes, a shoulder bag like students have. Maybe he studies. He doesn't seem like a bank clerk. He could be a singer. Or a DJ. A poet. A roving nomad. Or who knows, a bum. A lutist. A perfect idiot. Someone in trouble. Myself mirrored in a man. My joy, maybe. My love, my *habibi*. Or nothing. Maybe he's just a pilgrim. Rome is, after all, their city. My pilgrim lifts his eyes. He looks at me. Smiles. Goes back to his cigarette. Smokes it. Time's up. He goes away. He is fading. He turns, sees me. Smiles again. He is *charmant*. He disappears for good, leaving an aura of red. And if love in Rome is that way? An undertone of red?

Now I'm here, making the rounds, three a day—just two on Sundays and holidays. I'm waiting for the pilgrim to return. I tried looking for him at Benetton, in the spaces between the Ferraris, among the comrades, amid the packages scattered from their move. I searched for him at restaurants, on illicit balconies, between designer handbags. I searched in cafes, in all those cafes where the baristas are afraid of their dreams. I looked for him everywhere. But now I'm waiting on Via Tomacelli. I hope he comes.

Then we'll make love. And I'll have put on pretty red lingerie.

Doctor Ross told me she isn't convinced about this waiting thing. Doctor Ross is my therapist. I've always called her that— like George Clooney's character on *ER*. It isn't a coincidence. Even though she's a woman, she's kind of like George. She has his same maternal smile. Even the same dimple. People think Clooney is a sexy ladies' man, but to me he's motherly, hospitable. He has the face of someone you know will never hurt you. Sure, he might go for other women, but he doesn't strike me as an abuser. No, George doesn't assault women, he's not like the flaky-skinned uncle. He's not a believable bad boy. A little like Cary Grant, he has the trademark of Good, of someone who brings you warm milk in bed. Someone who tucks the blanket under your chin, who strokes your head and tends to you. In real life it doesn't matter if one person is a ladies' man and the other is gay.

I jibe well with gay men. They're kind and they're the only ones who tell you exactly how to fuck. If it weren't for them, I might not have known a damn thing about the male body. My friend Lionello, for instance, he's a godsend when it comes to sex. But Doctor Ross doesn't like that I wait for my red pilgrim here on Via Tomacelli. She's like a mother, Doctor Ross, she worries. She doesn't give me orders though. She doesn't tell me don't do this and do that. She doesn't tell me anything. She worries, but she doesn't say a thing. Free will exists and I have to do what I feel, she says, though (and she knows this) I don't feel much. I'm too rational and don't listen to my gut. It's because of the colors. If you don't have colors, you don't even have the stomach to feel emotions. It's a dreadful thing to lose colors, it really is.

Doctor Ross told me to do something while I wait. Well, it's not that she told me, exactly, she guided me to that decision. I was the one who convinced myself that I couldn't stay there propped up like a rake. I could've drawn attention, and with my skin color, in these times, that won't do. It doesn't take much to be confused for a dangerous subversive. A single moment to become a terrorist. All you need is a beard, tattered clothing, an idea in your head. And if you're black, you're always the first suspect. You are suspected of everything, even of living. I didn't feel like drawing attention. I took Doctor Ross's advice and did something.

I moved and went to sit at Ara Pacis. At predetermined hours, I move again and return to Via Tomacelli to seek out my pilgrim. It's barely a five-second walk. When I was small, Ara Pacis was different. Unadorned. Now it's like a spaceship, missing only androids and Venusians. The skaters make up for it. They're very fond of Ara Pacis, where they do their pretty spins. I'm not sure if I like it. It's an odd place. It's like it can never quite take off, feeling envious because the Piazza di Spagna is just around the corner, real life, the glamorous and coveted Rome. I wouldn't want that Rome. Take Via Condotti, for example. What would anyone crave on such a contrived street? It makes me anxious. Too many shopping bags and bodyguards and tailor-made happiness. It's an infectious fiction. This morning while I was walking, for instance, I saw a homeless woman. She was looking into the Cartier store window, crying. A ridiculous scene.

Good for a novel, admittedly. Yes, a book with thick, heavy pages where the punctuation is there for a reason and the silences are imagined. I told myself that perhaps I could write a novel while waiting for my red pilgrim. I bought a graph-ruled notebook. I write better with the little squares. They're less restrictive than lines, more rebellious. Naturally, I bought this notebook with a red cover. I don't really know if it's red, but I said to the sales rep, "Give me a graph-paper notebook with a red cover" and he gave me one with a weird elephant design. I made sure it actually had a red cover before paying. I asked a blonde girl in line behind me. She made a strange face, but she responded. Not with words, with her head. She swung it forward affirmatively. Good enough for me. I had to be sure. I still can't see red, and I only want to write my novel in red notebooks. It wouldn't make sense in another color. It would be crippled. And I'm sick of crippled things, *wallahi billahi*, sick and tired. And if I say *wallahi billahi* you must believe me. I paid and left. Then I bought other notebooks, each of them red, and I filled them with words. Seven in total. I'd like to get to ten. Ten is a round number, it makes you think of something constructed and whole. And ten is the number on Diego Armando Maradona's jersey. I'm a big Diego Armando fan. He's kind of a dorky rebel. Although he's a man, Maradona looks a lot like me. He looks like an angel when it shits.

I wrote constantly in the red notebooks. A few stories. Doctor Ross told me writing was a great idea and it would help bring out the woman in me. I didn't understand. I don't think I grasped the concept. Usually when Doctor Ross talks, I get it. She speaks very simply. She repeats things countless times until I comprehend them, until they're firmly in my brain. She has a lot of patience. But sometimes she says certain things only she knows, as an expert in her field. And when she does, I'm lost. Or maybe I understand *too* well. Usually I shiver and fold my arms, then she looks at me and goes, "Ohhh! See those arms?" I look and see that they're folded. Like a convict in the electric chair I'm closed, stiff. I know it's not a good thing, and that if I want to be well and make love with my pilgrim, I need to open up. Yes, like a rose.

But Doctor Ross—who is, all things considered, still a woman—loved the writing stuff, for the sake of that woman who needs to break free. I never understood it, though. Woman? Why, isn't it obvious that I'm a woman? I have a mandolin-shaped ass, tits, even if they're small, a pussy, hair that a man could never have, a heart-shaped mouth. What else am I missing to prove it? And then, once every twenty-eight days, I menstruate. I love saying that, menstruation. It's a medical term, normal, hygienic. People give you strange looks if you use the real, authentic term. I like it. To me saying that is a purely renegade act. I don't like referring to my "cycle." I don't like saying "I'm indisposed," or talking about "my business." The Trastevere people in Rome would speak of a certain monthly visitor, a marquess dressed in red, and in

Somalia, my home country, you got your *godude*. Americans, now, they bring aunts into it, going on about *Aunt* Flow, *Aunt* Rosie, *Aunt* Martha. In Mexico, they make it gothic and call it a flood of *vampiritos*, little vampires that suck you—but can't they just say "sanitary pads?" The Finnish are the most creative. I wouldn't be so imaginative in the middle of all that ice, but the Finnish are. They call them "cranberry days."

People fear the word *menstruation*. Leads to total panic. They're terrified when something is too real. It used to petrify me, too, before I started seeing Doctor Ross. I didn't say a thing. I didn't have a name for it. I deluded myself into thinking that by not naming it, it would disappear from my life forever. I dreamed of everlasting menopause. I don't hate it, but not too long ago I kind of did. Meaning, quite a lot. Not because it hurts. Everyone hates it for that reason. Now that I think about it, maybe I should've hated it for that too. I get unbelievable cramps in my lower abdomen and migraines that move from my neck to the top of my skull. I can't bear the pain. The migraines are intolerable and always come with horrendous nausea. And then you feel like someone's eating your intestines, or worse, twirling them like fettuccine al ragù. It's not great. But the pain isn't why I didn't give it a name, at least not the physical kind. It was another pain that did it. Whenever I menstruated, each time I saw my soiled underwear, I would despair. It was stronger than me, I'd despair. I stared at my underwear, the toilet paper, and I'd despair. I watched it for hours, standing there frozen, hoping something would happen. Usually absolutely nothing would.

They told me that menses is the color of blood, that it was blood. It isn't really. It looks like it, but it isn't. I remember this from a lecture Professor Gentili gave on human anatomy. She taught us a lot so that we'd know our bodies well, how they work and what they're for. "Don't ignore your bodies!" she'd say. I happened to see her again on a bus when I was in my third year of college. She was smiling into the void. She was always very smiley, perhaps because she didn't neglect herself. In hindsight, menses does look a little like blood. It's red.

I only know this through hearsay. When I look at what's on my underwear I only see a speck of gray. I've asked around, "Is it actually red?" They look at me sympathetically. They all thought I was color-blind. I made them believe I was. It would take too long to explain that I lost colors. I'd like to see that trickle of red flowing down my legs. Something flows, I know, since I get cramps. But I still can't see red. I've only seen it on that pilgrim's head. Ah, what I'd give to watch it run down my legs from my pussy. I would feel almighty. Doctor Ross is enthusiastic about the writing. She says it'll make menstruating less painful. "It's stress, dear." She says I accumulate too much.

Viscous moisture. A heat spray. I'm burning up, sweating. The temperature isn't extreme, but it casts a devious wind, the kind that makes you catch an off-season cold. A violent gust blows, *wallahi billahi*, a vicious gust. And if I say *wallahi billahi* you must believe me. I'm hot, I'm sweltering. The humidity increases, I'm drenched…drenched in myself. It's too early for me to be menstruating. My period is knocking at the door well in advance. I hectically rummage through my bag. No pad, no panty liner, not even some nasty tissues. Just my luck! In a little while I'll ruin these wonderful slacks I bought from Momento. They cost me an arm and a leg. That's how I am with pants, I prefer buying them large, comfortable, sort of trendy. If you want comfort, they make you pay for it. Otherwise, they cling to you and you try your best to fit into an anorexic's pants.

I'm not anorexic. But I was bulimic. I eat normally now. I don't eat Montebovi donuts early in the morning anymore. When I was a teenager I adored those donuts. One morning I made myself a big, fat grilled steak. At the time there was no mad cow disease, *no nada de vaca loca, nada de vida loca,* so grilled steaks were plentiful. I'd found a nice juicy one in the fridge. It was enormous. I had to go to school. I looked at the clock. I had a good two hours to figure this mess out. The morning was just starting off and I could still finish it. I grabbed a frying pan and cooked a fabulous steak, placing a nice egg beside it. I ate every single bit. Five minutes later, I went to the toilet and vomited every single bit. I brushed my teeth and went to school. During the physics lesson on vectors I realized vomiting such an expensive steak wasn't a very nice thing to do. Actually, it was a dick move. I stopped being bulimic that day. Then I started eating sloppily, or I forgot to eat. For the duration of college, and even now since I work part-time, I can get by on breakfast alone.

Doctor Ross says it's all owing to the lack of colors. But now I'm damp; I feel bloody, coagulated scabs along my inner thighs. I'll ruin my pants. And it'll bother me because I don't like anorexic pants. I'm slim, but I have an African behind. I want to be comfortable. I like the pants I'm wearing now. I don't want them to get ruined.

I want a pad. I search frantically. I look insane. I dig through my purse as though a miracle is waiting for me there. I look and look again. Then I realize mine is just any old bag, somewhat banal, black with tit-shaped pockets, medium size—I like carrying my world at my side like the nomads. But it's mid-size, nothing like Mary Poppins's bag. All I know is that I'd like a pad, and I don't have one. I'm getting damper, stickier, sweatier.

A girl next to me smiles. Her hair is curly, black, and wild like mine. She's similar to me in other respects—nose, mouth, and butt. Her face is more relaxed, her back straighter. Her eyes are illuminated by a glimmering frame of Swarovski jewelry. There's an exaggerated coolness about her. She looks me in the eye. She's not afraid of confrontation. Her gaze is glue. It follows me everywhere and won't let me breathe. She's a vigilant, curious girl. We even have the same skin tone.

I should ask for help. She's offering it freely. Yes, I should tell her something, anything, some bullshit, a thought. I'm not sure. I'm reluctant. Why should I tell her something so intimate?

I mean, do I even know her? Does the fact that we have the same skin color automatically make us sisters? She does look a lot like me, to be fair. She's always touching her wild hair and smiling. She has an open book on her lap. I try reading the title but can barely see. The cover is blue, I can see that. It's only red I don't see anymore. The blue book has many pages, and it seems engaging, judging by the girl's posture. She has earbuds in. I can't hear a damn thing or tell what the music is. She stops staring at me like she was before. She's gone back to her book. I'm becoming more moist. The pants are screwed. Can you imagine if the pilgrim came now? He'd see me immersed in my own menstrual blood. Immersed in liquids, damp, sticky, sweaty. I only see gray, though. My menstrual blood flows, but I don't see brilliant red like everyone else. Only a speck of gray, goddamn it.

The girl is rocking. The music must be great. Maybe she's in heaven. I shouldn't disturb her. Now that she's not looking at me, I wish she would. I wish she'd bother me with her womanliness. Perhaps when Doctor Ross speaks of the feminine, she means the vitality that girl exudes. I wouldn't know. She's not looking at me anymore and it's tearing me apart. Look at me, damn it, I'm here, I'm here, don't you see me? I'm here, look at me, please. I need your eyes. I need you and your gaze. Take your eyes off the book. I don't know if it's telepathy or coincidence. She looks up and plants her eyes on me. It's a beautiful feeling. It makes me feel alive.

"Do you have a pad?" I ask her.

"I have a tampon, is that okay?"

I say yes, that would be fine, it's all the same. But I've never put in a tampon in my life.

She gives me two. I go in the restroom in Ara Pacis. It's clean, not too bad. Public restrooms are hell on earth. Dirt, visceral liquids, festering feces, assorted filth. This one had only a vague odor of use. You could smell the cleaning personnel's air freshener. I'm shaking. I don't even know where to begin. Why didn't I look for a drugstore? Then I'd have a nice pack of convenient pads that I'd know how to use. But I'd have soiled myself before reaching that phantom pharmacy, I know it. And now? I have this thing in my hand. I kept the other one in my purse, in case this attempt fails. It's in my hand. I observe what seems like a surgeon's tool to me. There's something vaguely threatening about it. The girl gave me the instruction sheet. I grabbed it, muttering a hushed thank you. She shouted from a distance, "I'm here, if you need me." Yeah, she knows I've never used a tampon in my life. How embarrassing. Does she know about the colors too? Did she understand that I can't see red?

The instruction sheet frightens me. There's a drawing of a chick nonchalantly stretching her vagina with two fingers. The drawing makes the vagina out like a monster. I don't like it. There's writing in every language saying I need to remain calm. *Antes de empezar, relájate. Não fiques nervosa. Prenez votre temps et détendez-vous. Rilassati. Rilassati.* Relax. It's written everywhere. A mantra. They say that if you're tense, your muscles stiffen and the tampon doesn't enter, the body won't allow it. But if you shut your eyes and stop acting like a baby, if you begin to see yourself as a woman and act naturally, then the tampon dances inside you and you can hardly feel it. It's important to keep the string outside. I was almost starting to believe it would be okay when I read about toxic shock syndrome. I was about to reach nirvana, shit, and now there's TSS? They say it's an allergic syndrome or something like that, that some people, only a handful, may be allergic to the tampon. If you are, you can go into a coma. If you feel unusual discomfort, it's best to remove the tampon. This news about TSS wasn't what I needed. Now I'm tense again. Then I reread the instructions in the more harmless section and it's the same thing as before. It tells me that I need to relax and I can't be tense. It's a bit like making love. The man enters you tenderly and tells you, "My love, I won't hurt you"—in the movies they always tell virgins that. My pilgrim will say it to me. "My love, I won't hurt you." And I'll believe him. They aren't all like that flaky-skinned uncle.

He wanted to see me suffer, to see me hurt. He drowned me in his white scum and laughed like a sadist. My pilgrim, though, will love me, *wallahi* I feel it, he will cherish and respect me. He will drown me in respect, *wallahi*, respect.

Inserting a tampon is a little like making love. I must relax, but I'm so scared. I put it in. Easy. I placed the applicator in my vagina until my fingers touched my body. Then I pushed the plunger, pushed it slowly, with extreme delicacy. Calmly, you might say. I was restless, but love is a restlessness that grants peace. In that moment I made love to myself. I treasured me. I was gentle like the pilgrim will be when he arrives. I pushed. The tampon entered and now it dances inside me.

The girl is sitting in the same place as before, with the book open. She's made progress in her reading. It looks like the book is open to a different page. It must be engrossing, she's completely rapt.

"It's in?" she asked, suddenly looking up.

"Yes," I said. What should I have said?

"It was hard for me, too, the first time. I can tell you were braver."

Should I have said something?

I remained silent.

"Do you know Tinariwen?"

Should I have replied?

I shook my head.

"They're a band from the desert."

She put the earbuds in my ears. Her iPod is a striking shade of blue, matching the book. The girl presses play and a song begins. I understand the first few words. The man who's singing says something like *oualahila*. It sounds like my *wallahi*. Maybe the words are related. People are clapping. The man has a chorus behind him. Guitars underscore the words. Oualahila, he keeps saying. Oualahila, his people say. They're telling a story. It's a story I'd like to hear. I also clap in the emptiness. The rhythm transports me into a cosmic chaos that appears to be my own. I clap my hands, move my shoulders. I see the girl watching me and smiling. My hint of movement becomes frenzy. I look like a lunatic in touch with herself.

The song ends.

"They're good," I say.

"*Oualahila ar tesninam…*," the girl sings.

"What does it mean?"

"What does it mean to you?" she asks.

"I heard the word 'God.'" I don't know what else to add.

"Yes, 'God.' He's saying, 'Oh God, you're unhappy.'"

"But the music is happy," I say clumsily.

"Sadness has many rhythms. Like bliss."

"And will he come out of his sadness?" I ask.

"Yes, by describing it. Through stories, he emerges from sadness."

"And what story are they telling?"

"Yours, I think."

"Mine?" I say, dumbfounded.

"Yes, the one you're writing, the one you've had inside for a while. Why don't you continue?"

"It's too tiring..."

"Keep on going."

"But I don't have time, I'm waiting for…"

"It will wait for you, if it's worth anything. You, on the other hand, must carry on. And stop making excuses."

And that is how I, Zuhra Laamane, opened the first page of red notebook number eight. The pen rolls smoothly over the tiny squares. The tampon, in the meantime, dances happily in my menstrual sea.

ONE

THE NUS-NUS

C'è qualcosa nella morte che assomiglia all'amore.

Spoon River Anthology, page 103, the version sold in kiosks, stuck inside a newspaper. Which one? Mar didn't remember anymore. Parallel text. Mar only bought poems with the originals beside them. She reread the verse in English: *There is something about death like love itself.*

The rhythm was as deep as the pistol barrel inside Patricia's mouth.

She frightened her. Mar was sitting in the middle of nowhere in Villa Borghese. Children played around her, young couples kissed, and drug addicts hoping to score their next fix pickpocketed on the 490 bus.

Life flowed freely around Mar. The sky was limpid as in some German TV series. Aimless clouds. Faltering birds. Nothing pierced that great blue facade. Rome seemed like a movie set, like an MGM lot during the Golden Years. Maybe it was only Cinecittà. At every corner, unexpectedly, Visconti, Magnani, or Alberto Sordi could appear. Or why not, the remarkable Federico Fellini with an Ekberg and a fountain, with a Mastroianni and a showgirl. Federico Fellini shooting his new picture with Mar Ribero Martino. A black girl. Too black. With an Italo-Argentinian-Portuguese white mother. Hers was a family of errors. A family of lunatics.

Mar got her name from a poem by Rafael Alberti, a man who had to flee his own country, Spain. Rafael had come to Rome. Perhaps he'd also sat in Villa Borghese. Mar didn't like the poem. She didn't even like her name. But she respected Rafael. He had suffered more than others.

Mar had to go home. How long had she been sitting there? An hour, an hour and a half? The police eyed her. "They think I'm a prostitute, assholes. Idiots." The girl's legs decided not to move. They weren't very rational. They were disconnected from her reality as a woman.

It had been a month since her life had come undone. Ever since Patricia's funeral, she'd felt scattered, like a broken thing shoddily restored. Patricia's funeral was miserable, and she had been miserable attending it. Everyone dressed soberly and respectfully.

Even the church Pati's parents chose was sober and respectful. Mar had never been in that neighborhood. She and Patricia lived downtown, not in the suburbs. Pietralata was unknown territory, and that church was too, now more than ever.

Pati's mother, a chubby Roman from the Abruzzo, insisted on having her daughter's funeral in that neighborhood, in that church. It's where Pati was baptized, and her mother had always hoped to see her right there as the leading lady of another important ceremony. She dreamed of a wedding, certainly not a suicide's funeral. It was because of this unforeseen and inexplicable pain that her husband, a gangly man from Valencia, supported his wife's decision. It was also the only way to calm her. He was willing to do anything for her, and he'd already done a lot in retrospect. That gangly man from Valencia had moved to Italy for her, he'd ripped up his communist party card for her, he'd sternly disciplined that peculiar girl of theirs for her (though, early on, she'd gone to work in Spain). And for her he'd accepted a funeral for their daughter far from Valencia, where his family had been buried for generations.

The church was built in a tacky modern style but the Gothic-like stained glass was stunning. One could see her own colorful reflection in it. Mar liked the idea of becoming red. She didn't choose red for the funeral, however, but pink. Candy pink, to be precise, a disgusting color like the one used in chemical additives for sweets at the fair. She'd matched this with an equally ugly white purse, a red cloak, and high-heeled pumps. The crowning glory was a wide-brimmed hat, like those seen only at British weddings. Mar never wore hats. It was a funeral, though, Pati's funeral, and that was worth making an exception.

She felt her aching feet. Even on that day her mother had arrived ahead of time. She was always fifteen minutes early. Never ten, never twenty, never five. Always fifteen. For that reason, Mar got in the habit of arriving fifteen minutes late. Never ten, never twenty, never five.

She was late to the funeral, too. She walked in, making noise, causing a scandal with her colors. The priest watched her, exasperated. She'd broken the spell of the seminal moment. Evidently he was reading something truly moving, perhaps one of the salvation stories of the New Testament in which Jesus was handsome, blond, and didn't have a trace of sissy about him. Thirty-three years old and no women. Impossible. Jesus was a sissy, and a little hysterical, frankly: the episode in the temple speaks volumes, doesn't it?

Mar watched those in attendance. There were many people Patricia hated. Pati hated everyone, except Mar herself. She'd also hated their child, which is why Mar had to abort. And so they separated.

She hadn't thought about the abortion in six months. Now however, in the emptiness of Villa Borghese, every scene between her and Patricia resurfaced. The most endearing, the most dreadful, the ones she would never have wanted to film. What a flop that'd be, a movie with her and Patricia as heroines, a forgettable movie. Mar wanted to reshoot most parts of those scenes. Even the beginning. Even that first kiss on La Rambla in Barcelona.

Mar stood up from the bench. The police had been watching her intolerantly, with an air of marked insolence. She got up, since the thought of being groped by a bunch of disgusting cops didn't appeal to her. She headed for the 490 bus stop. She could've hopped on the 495. Either would take her to the Flaminio metro stop. Since Pati died, she couldn't bring herself to ride her metallic green Honda SH anymore. She could still smell the scent of her bottom on the seat. Pati smelled of poppies. Her SH smelled of it also. She waited for the bus. Who knew how long she'd have to wait. She wasn't in a hurry. She didn't give a damn about time. She didn't give a damn about anything anymore. She wanted to spend the entire summer drifting between her dump in Prati and Villa Borghese. Every day, back and forth, there and back. Every day, the eyes of heinous cops stuck to her ass or her large tits. Every day in the nothingness, remembering each moment of Patricia's funeral.

But her mother wouldn't let her suffer in peace. One had to keep doing, doing, doing, always doing things for her. No one's hands could stay still. Everything had to move quickly. Hands, legs, the hairs on your pussy. Everything had to move, in perpetual and inconclusive motion. Suffering, stagnation, death—none were permitted in Miranda's kingdom. She had to move in order to be. Move to exist. Consequently, she was dragging her daughter into her latest act of insanity: studying classical Arabic.

"You'll see, *hija*, Arabic will calm your troubled heart."

No sooner said than done. Miranda, efficient woman that she was, hastened to confirm enrollment for two people at one of the most exclusive Arabic schools in the world. Then a quick stop to the travel agency to guarantee a flight for August 3 to the city of jasmine and, finally, a quick trip to Nima, her favorite bookstore, to purchase postcards and maps of Tunisia.

"Yes, my love, I've been studying Arabic for two years. But you'll see, you'll manage fine. Learning a new alphabet opens up other worlds."

Sheer efficiency. That was Mar's mother. It was no accident that she'd sold thousands of copies of her five poetry books. In one country, Italy, where readers of any kind were in short supply, selling a bunch of poetry was a fool's errand. She was proud of this success, she'd say, "Hard work always pays off in the end."

She was convinced this was also possible for that funny daughter of hers who didn't resemble her at all, physically or spiritually. Or maybe she was her spitting image. She'd failed with her. Now she was doing everything she could to make up for it. It was an act of commiseration over the abortion, that bizarre story.

"Are you gay, my love?"

"No, Mama. I love this woman, but I don't know what I am. I'm trying to be myself."

"But you sleep with her, for God's sake!" she blurted.

Miranda loathed Patricia, a woman she didn't understand. If her daughter was a lesbian, why couldn't she have chosen a better woman? Patricia was too white, too sad, too strange. Then there was that nauseating poppy smell she brought everywhere. A whiff of death that never left her.

Patricia was part Spanish and part Italian, a journalist from Madrid whom they'd sent back to Rome, perhaps because no one could tolerate her in the newsroom. Miranda was convinced her daughter was searching for a mother in the strange Spanish woman. Then that child had come along and complicated their lives.

Mar didn't know why she'd allowed Patricia to sway her. She clearly remembered the day, the month, the hour, the moment that their lives changed. Pati made her Valencian paella that evening. The smell filled the emptiness of Prati, which had been their love nest for five months.

"*Esta noche* a friend of mine is coming to dinner. You'll love him…*mucho, muchísimo.*"

The friend worked for an Italian firm on oil rigs around the world. He'd seen a good number of countries, from Kazakhstan to Turkmenistan. He'd been to Saudi Arabia, Iran, and China. He was off to Venezuela next. He spoke many languages very poorly. In fact, he only guessed at them. Mar didn't find the boy very pleasant. She didn't like the way he chopped zucchini on his plate. She couldn't stand him, he made her claustrophobic. She didn't know how to handle the paella. She scarfed it down joylessly.

After eating, Pati rolled a joint and took out one of her treats, a French chocolate liqueur. Mar sipped the liqueur and thought that once the night was over she'd give her woman a good massage to thank her.

Pati surprised her instead.

"It's time you and I had a kid, Mar. Vincenzo came here to help us."

Mar didn't understand. She looked at her girlfriend flustered and confused.

"Tonight I'm going to my friend Marcela's place. She and her husband went on a trip to Maremma. She left me the keys to her house. I'll be there for *el fin de semana*. You all be good and get to it."

Mar felt the world collapse around her. Her sacred center evaporated.

She made love with Vincenzo all weekend. She was touched, kissed, licked. She was revolted and humiliated. For three days, this unknown man who cut his zucchini terribly had his way with her body. It wasn't the first time she made love with a man, but never with someone so foul. Maybe Patricia had chosen him deliberately because she was afraid Mar would want to go straight again.

She didn't become pregnant in those three days.

"Mar, *querida*, we have to try again."

They called Vincenzo another time. The same Valencian paella, the same joint, the same chocolate liqueur. Patricia left with the same Marcela's keys in her pocket. The same scene. The same kisses, fondlings, licks. The same drilling. The same rehearsed pleasure. The man was savage. It went that way for two months. Then, finally, pregnancy.

Mar was satisfied. She wouldn't have to let herself be touched anymore by that repugnant man. If it were a boy, she would call him Elias, like the father she'd never met. Mama Miranda had only mentioned her father's name, not a comma more.

Instead, Pati made her abort.

"Having a child was a horrendous idea." She gave no other explanation.

That's how it was with Pati: take it or leave it. Being with that woman was some kind of oxymoron.

Mar felt vile. The nausea and everything else was turning her inside out. She woke up frustrated every morning and haphazardly took a bite out of any sweet thing in their pantry. Usually there wasn't much. A few stale crackers and expired plum cake. Mar made do. Only sugar could mollify her. She spent entire days roaming disheveled around the house. She raged wherever she could. There wasn't that much space to walk around, but those few meters inside the house provided the only carefree moments of the day. The rest was people spitting one judgment after another at her. Everyone wanted the last word about her body, about her child. Mar waited to see who would win the contest. Who would it be? She awaited her future with tired impatience. Mama Miranda was enraged. "Are you really throwing this all to the wind? Didn't I teach you anything? Tell me *hija*, anything?" And then, as punctual as a Swiss watch: "Leave that woman. She's hurting you."

Was it true? Was Pati hurting her? Could it be possible? Her, with such white skin? She enjoyed massaging that alabaster skin, which seemed like a cadaver's, but not one that was decaying, no, no. It was the whiteness of eternal death. That's why it was alluring and perilous. Mar had asked herself repeatedly whether blood actually coursed through Patricia's veins. *Does she ever menstruate?* In those months when they couldn't let each other go, she had never seen a Tampax, and she didn't remember seeing a pad in Pati's handbag. Maybe she was a man without a cock. Then that means I'm not a lesbian. *See, Mama, I'm not a lesbian.*

But afterward, when the suicide had already happened, Pati's mother said to her, "My daughter lies in a lake of blood." She'd told her like a newscaster. Pati's mother, with her hair in curled layers, her false smile, her extravagant pain. Patricia's red lake. She wanted to see it for herself. She would've taken some of that blood and touched her forehead, like a Hindu with water from the sacred Benares River.

When the day came, Mar went by herself to the abortion clinic. Pati had an interview with a blogger who'd set the internet on fire. Blogs were her strange friend's final hobby. She wanted to start one of her own. Mar went by herself. It was as she imagined, like she'd seen millions of times in the soap operas that occupied some of her depressing afternoons. Everything was white like Patricia's skin. The walls were white, as were the nurses' clothes and the gurney. She was the exception, black as she was. The machinery was the exception, gray as it was. It made no impression on her. It wasn't as large as she'd thought. Discreet, even. Stainless steel, brute force. Yes, she trusted whatever that thing was. It lifted the weight from her stomach. Everything was over in a heartbeat.

Legs in the air, tears, and then that weird noise. She was like a small girl eating spelt soup. Blowing on the hot spoon, filled to the brim. Blowing hard to cool it. Before she knew it, it was in her mouth, slurped up.

She'd never liked spelt soup.

THE NEGROPOLITAN

"They're heretics a bunch of fucking heretics these Christians."

Abdel Aziz says it without a full stop, in one breathless go. The beardless doll's voice hardens with each vowel. Abdel Aziz's voice is a concentration of terse wrath. It almost scares me. I forget that I'm standing in front of a half-pint and, what's more, I forget the half-pint in question is my cousin.

I'm distressed. His baritone seeps into my neural circuit. It's about to disintegrate.

I beg you, tell me it isn't true. Tell me they haven't returned. Tell me I'm on acid and Abdel Aziz isn't saying what I fear he is, that my ears are boycotting him and I'm not sure I heard him right. Tell me something, anything. I'll even take insults. I'm not an addict, I swear, but today I'd rather be in a drug-fueled delirium. At least then I'd have a rational explanation for what my cousin is babbling on about.

Silence. No one responds. I dialed various numbers. Zeus, Buddha, Shiva, Ra, Zoroaster, Mitra, Saint Paul, Saint Francis, Saint Januarius, Milingo. No one can give me an explanation. No miracle. The sky doesn't open and the waters of the Red Sea don't part.

They have returned. The evidence petrifies me. The Jehovah's Witnesses came back. When Abdel Aziz is in this over-excited state, only they can be the cause. What in the world have they said to make him like this? I'd like to tell them, "Cousins, the First Council of Nicaea happened already. And anyway we're Muslims. If Jesus Christ is spirit, man, God, or insanity, it's none of our business. For us, he's a second-tier prophet, a benchwarmer." But I don't have the strength to say anything. I want my busted sofa. I want to lean my head back for a little while and maybe, yeah, close my eyes for a minute. I don't even have time to sit down. Lucy will be here in less than two hours. I need to get moving. We reserved seats. A chunk of steel on rails heading to "Paleermooo" city.

From there, a steamboat will take us to Tunis. To Africa. I'm not familiar with Africa. And to think that black blood courses through my veins, that I was born there. It's not like knowing it, fundamentally. It really isn't the same thing. Birth can be completely incidental. One is born for the strangest reasons. One lemon vodka too many, a languorous glance, by mistake, for revenge, out of sacrifice and yes, even for love. I was born in Africa and that's all. I emerged from Maryam Laamane's hot uterus, I whined some, they washed me, and then I sucked that sour milk of which I have no memory.

I don't understand why I'm going there now, to Africa. Lucy insisted, I think. And I didn't know how to tell her no, I suppose. I can't say no to (almost) anyone.

"Zuzu, you'll see, it'll be like staying in Miami Beach." For Lucy, Miami Beach is the peak of possible delight. Miami for her means the three *S*'s: sunbathe, squander, screw. There you stretch out like an iguana, you tan, you shop recklessly and then, last but not least, you roll around with some local, brawny stud. Lucy knows all of this because she's seen it on TV. It's no coincidence that her favorite show is *Miami Vice*. That old stuff from the eighties, with those two politically correct cops, a pale-faced adulterer and a deluxe, curly-haired black, who really poured their hearts into the three *S*'s, the last more than the others. Between one piece of ass and the next, the two of them solve a few detective cases, with car chases, shoot-outs, and fake struggles in their strictly 100 percent cotton Armani suits.

Lucy has never been to Miami. I don't think Tunis is like Miami Beach. I don't even know if Miami Beach is like Miami Beach, but Tunis certainly isn't. Everyone I spoke to before this trip told me it's like going to Latina. So let me get this straight, I paid €230 for round-trip train and boat tickets to end up in Latina? A city of fascists? Excuse me, I want my money back.

"And Zuzu, the school is fabulous." Ah, yes, the school. I'd forgotten about it. Lucy and I enrolled in the Arabic school, Bourguiba, renowned and cherished by Arabists the world over. You walk in and after a short stint you're a grammarian versed in the first one hundred years of the Hijrah. And, *insha'allah*, with just a few days of the Bourguiban treatment you'll go to great pains to recognize the voice you had when you'd arrived. Enrollment also includes a complete transplant, at the root, of the larynx. A few lessons and you're finally able to pronounce the infamous *'ayn*, the most hated of Arabic letters.

Damn, it's been ages since I've had thirty straight days of vacation (thirty-two, technically, since I ate into a Saturday and Sunday as well), and where do I go to waste them? A school. No comment. And not just any school—one for Arabic! I'm just saying, why couldn't I have sewing or ceramics as a hobby like a sane person? Did I have to get myself tangled up in classical Arabic? Awful idea, Zuhra, awful. Typical.

I'd regret it as soon as I arrived, my spine was telling me as it began showing callous signs of imbalance. My poor spine throbbed like damnation. Maybe I should've listened to you. You're warning me, aren't you, spine? You're one step ahead. It'll be a catastrophe, I feel it, I'm really, truly afraid.

"I mean, Christians believe in the Trinity…they believe God is in three Persons, an absurdity. God is one. Jesus is the prophesied son of God because he is the primordial spirit, not because the Father gives him a good scolding."

What do I do, stop him? But of course I do. Abdel Aziz is too good to end up in Lucifer's hands, that filthy swine. I fill my lungs with as much air as possible, I hold only what I need, and then let it explode in a shout. What do I shout? *Haram*, obviously. *Haram*, or unclean, not kosher, not halal—the stench of sin, so to speak. Abdel Aziz jerks back. Maybe jerks isn't right, he takes a few steps in reverse, baby steps. My cousin took the hit. He's turning pale. Me, on the other hand, I'm enjoying this and say it again, *haram*, this time putting more emphasis on the *H*. If Bin Laden saw me, he'd recruit me for his cave videos. I can already see myself with my AK-47 from Transnistria—a hole in the earth where, if you've got the dough, you can give the finger to both Bush and Ahmadinejad—and families from the Gulf to the Maghreb whimpering in front of Al Jazeera. My voice would become more famous than Fairuz's, the nightingale of Lebanon.

For now I'm a loser who will miss the train to Latin...oops, Paleermooo, if I don't hurry. First I have to reprimand my little cousin. I need to remind him that we are Muslims and that there are certain things he cannot say, out of respect for the elders (that is, for me) who've gone through the infamous thirty-three days of fasting. It doesn't matter to me if he doesn't say the five prayers (I do, even if only recently. I feel very guilty for the lost time. They didn't teach me very well in elementary school. I know the opening sura, though, that one I do) or do Ramadan, the *zakat*, or the pilgrimage. But he can't talk to me every day about Christian stuff. The Vatican is *not* in my top five. And the Jehovah's Witnesses won't get off my ass. I'd say it's open war between us. Before, I promise, I didn't really give a shit. I saw them on the street, and when they stopped me I smiled, walked faster, passed them gracefully, liberated myself like a goddess. Then one wretched day they found my two cousins, alone at home. Mina was sleeping, and Abdel Aziz offered them tea and cookies. Mine! My beloved chocolate cookies.

"It's a good way to learn Italian, sister," he said to me, "and it's free." My two little cousins had been staying with me for seven months. They came over in a dinghy, and now Italian is a necessity, seeing that their (clandestine) lives will be spent here for a bit. What was I to do? I told him: "OK, if it's for Italian…"

From that moment on, the rat hole I insisted on calling home, contrary to evidence, was bursting at the seams. With what? With magazines from those people obsessed with conversion. I have nothing against the Witnesses, to be clear. I don't hate them, nothing but respect, but they invade my personal space. When I found *The Bible: Word of God or Man?* among my dirty bras, I flipped a shit. The house is covered floor to ceiling with stuff like *Why Read the Bible?* Why? Abdel Aziz hides them everywhere. In the kitchen, between the Caetano Veloso CDs, in the fake gardenias and, lastly, on the bookshelf with texts about Islam. If he puts one of those horrid magazines between the Qurans, I swear I'll kick him out of the house. Stop, stop, stop, it's not what you think, I'm not a damn fundamentalist! But man, give a girl her space. I love Abdel Aziz to death, but his brain is turning into gruyère with this stuff. Or maybe it's the pain of no longer having a homeland that turns our brains to mush?

I take out my burgundy passport. I examine it. Zuhra Laamane. Me, with my mother's last name, though she doesn't use it. I, me myself, in the flesh, meat and bone, tits, pussy, and all. Me, Italian. Me, Italian? The usual doubt assails me. Will the passport be enough to prove it? What if I bring my license, too? And my film society card? Yes, I'll bring that too. And my grocery rewards card? My Arci Solidarietà card? Library card? Yes, all of them, I'll take them all. The gas card as well. It adds up. On each one of these damn cards my name is printed, isn't it? Even my address in the Eternal City. Unfortunately, nowhere is it written that I am Italian, but at least they show that I live here. They reinforce the Italianness of my passport.

I don't want a repeat of what happened to me in Spain. Zapatero wasn't there yet when I went. The right-wingers still seemed to be in power. Not that there's a substantial difference. At least in Italy there's not. They say there's some variation in Spain. Could be, but I live here. In Spain they wanted to arrest me. Not at the airport, where in any case a black Muslim knows these things can happen to her. No, not at the airport. They wanted to arrest me in police headquarters. Members of the *guardia civil* are demented. They thought I went there for them to arrest me. I wanted a non-residence certificate to open a bank account. I was a naïve girl preparing to take her first steps as an exchange student in Valencia, the land of paella and *horchata de chufa*. Just a fucking bank account, nothing out of the ordinary. The one in charge watched me with dumb droopy eyes that hung like the surgically altered breasts of a sixty-year-old woman. He watched me, opening his eyes wide. Then he started fondling my identity card as though it were a porn star's ass. He turned the poor card around as if there weren't at least seventy people behind me in line. Then he shot off with cat-like speed and after two minutes, four brutes who looked like they'd walked out of a marine training camp came to take me away. They were huge, muscular, and carried themselves like men who were about to pulverize your bones. They watched me. One of them made me look at his badge. His friend beside him said, "*Por favor, seguidme.*" I didn't really understand what was happening. I was a nobody, an exchange student. A few vague recollections of movies came to mind. The things that happen in Hitchcock films, when the hero is unjustly accused of a crime. The kind of things that happen to Cary Grant in *North by Northwest*, not beautiful Zuzu. The men brought me to a room, blinded me with a B-movie-style lamp, and interrogated me. God, "interrogate" is a stretch. They obsessively repeated a few main ideas: *Eres clandestina. No eres italiana. Puta. Marica. Falsificadora de papeles.* I was enraged. They let me go after forty-five minutes and a phone call to the embassy in Madrid. Excuses all throughout the precinct. I don't give a fuck about their excuses, *entiendes, amigo?* Those were the most disgusting forty-five minutes of my entire existence, olé.

Since that day, I always leave padded with documents. We black Muslims have to defend ourselves at all costs. Mom says I exaggerate. "You're so light, sweetie." And then she adds, to my great embarrassment, "You're not a negro, you're like Beyoncé, like milk." Mom always uses this word. She always says *negro*. Sometimes I hear *nigger* and my blood freezes. For Mom, a negro is anyone darker than her, someone who has kinky hair, a big nose, prominent buttocks. Beyoncé has the right color, she says. The right mixture of melanin. She likes her color. But she likes mine even more. "You took after your grandmother, who was beautiful and fair." I look at myself in the mirror and ask God (or his deputy, for me it's the same either way) why the hell he didn't give me a big nose. He could've made me a real black woman, a bad bitch. I could've had those beautiful traces of Rasta and taken a joint to my own private sanctum to puff myself up with pride. Instead I have strange soft curls, a tiny Somali nose, and ghostly light skin for a black person. Maybe my father was white. The notion is appalling. Mom never speaks of Papa.

My buttocks are African, though. It's the only thing I didn't want, an African butt. I have a disproportionate ass. Lucy says men always look at me. But men are simpletons. They would look at anything that vaguely resembles an ass.

Oh, Lucy…maybe it's her knocking on the door.

It is.

"What are you doing?"

"Ice skating."

She doesn't laugh at the joke. She doesn't acknowledge it. She walks resolutely toward my suitcase. She screams. Abdel Aziz flinches, and I falter out of fear.

"Why the fuck are you screaming?" I say, shouting myself. I feign amazement, but I'm afraid. She doesn't speak. She takes a pair of shoes out of my bag. Oh God, I already know what she's about to say. I stop her.

"Hey, they're comfortable, you know? Easy to walk in. I know they're hideous, but they fit like…"

Lucy hurls my shoes. She flings them at an imaginary point, maybe a garbage can, like a Yankee pitcher would throw the strike of a lifetime. Then she kneels over my bag. She sticks her hands inside and attacks with the vehemence of a Bulgarian purge.

"And what is this? It looks like a nun's habit! I can't walk around with you dressed like this. Oh, Mother of God, saints of paradise, what made you want to bring this stuff? What is this, a maternity dress? You're kidding me, right?"

Few things were spared in the end. "We'll buy everything there."

I'm afraid. It sounds like a threat. But at least the suitcase is ready. Have a nice trip, *safar salama ya Zuhra.*

THE REAPARECIDA

Long hair, broad shoulders, huge strides, and the number 10 on the winners' white-and-blue shirts. World Cup '78. Argentina on the podium.

The country went insane. Maybe it was, with everyone singing praises to the hippie running brazenly on the field. The newspapers showed people howling with pleasure. Each goal, an orgasm.

The papers only showed the ones howling with pleasure. The other howlers interested no one. In fact, they did not even exist. The others were *desaparecidos* brutally slaughtered offstage. The spotlight was solely for the golden boys and the military junta that had made the horror possible.

Since 1976, or perhaps even earlier, people had been kidnapped, tortured, assassinated. Everything was done in absolute silence. Our ears—and the world's ears—were plugged, our lips sewn, our hands bound. The entirety of Argentina had been lobotomized.

> *Argentina campeón mundial*
> *Argentina, rey del mundo*
> *Campeones gran triunfo argentina*

Hosannas and fanaticism. The headlines all the same.

The hippie, for the record, was Mario Kempes. His friends and enemies called him *El Matador*. Goals and orgasms. Officially, that's how it was. For the soldiers, the press, foreigners. The other howlers didn't count. They weren't official. Foreigners wanted the folklore. The press, heart-pounding excitement. The soldiers, laurel wreaths. Self-congratulation and champagne. A shimmering cup and sharp teeth. Orgasms in technicolor. That World Cup was the first one not shown in black and white.

Legend has it that in the first half Kempes was making an effort, but he didn't score. He sweated, panted, swore, but didn't score. He was dynamic like few others. On the field, he was king. But he didn't score. The whims of destiny denied him glory among strikers. The soldiers didn't like his restraint. Restraint could negate their glory, that same glory with which they wanted to deaden the conscience of us Argentinians. It was an act, a miserable conceit. They pretended to be good and we, on the other hand, pretended to believe in an Argentina that was by then a falsehood. But without Kempes's goals, the scaffolding threatened to collapse. It was up to soccer to do something. It was soccer's task. With crosses, shots on goal, extraordinary saves, it had to hide the heinous crimes the junta was committing against the sensible part of the country. The white-and-blue team was under pressure. There were veiled threats. Menotti—the coach of Argentina '78— had what sports journalists called a stroke of genius. "We've got to be more superstitious. You can't win without a pinch of magic." He ordered the future Matador to shave his famous handlebar moustache. Smooth as a maiden, Kempes took to the field against Poland. It was at the Gigante de Arroyito, a stadium that felt like home. He scored a brace. And for the rest of that World Cup he didn't stop until the end.

When Kempes scarred Poland with that double goal, I'd been out of Buenos Aires for months. I was able to get away.

Many Argentinians rejoiced with the team. Their dutiful orgasms had the trademark of a military government and the blessing of Kempes and Menotti. The state needed imbeciles, and for that they'd put on that sideshow of a championship. Money flowed and blemishes were concealed, like the people who disappeared. Like my brother Ernesto.

Ernesto is now a number. He had a face, hair, beautiful hands. He laughed, sucking up air like a century-old combustion engine. He was a good boy. Better than me. And now he is a number on a list of thirty-thousand *desaparecidos* who never came home. We didn't recover his body. To this day they've unearthed only twenty-thousand human scraps, but none belonged to Ernesto. I wonder how many decayed without the comfort of a grave.

So many disappeared, so many dead, so many in exile. The country's finest, most principled citizens were hard-hit. Along with those boys, girls, friends, new mothers, union workers, priests, and intellectuals, the whole country had disappeared. We were all desaparecidos. We couldn't speak, we couldn't discuss, we couldn't breathe. We could risk the same fate as our husbands and wives, our brothers and sisters and parents and neighbors. Everything was controlled and, out of fear, little by little, everyone began erasing themselves.

In those years the newspapers declared:

Guerilla Efforts Truncated
Eight More Extremists Mowed Down in La Plata
Insurgency Suffers Blows

The violent language of the press chilled my blood. I missed the word "kill." I thought it warmer and more considerate than the words journalists used more frequently. I hated the words "mowed down," for example. It seemed to suggest the human being's desecration. It didn't only imply the taking of life, but dehumanization. It was too much, superfluous. There wasn't a headline that didn't abuse words. Everything was a mowing down of subversives all across the country, 13 in Buenos Aires, 18 in Tucumán, 22 in Córdoba. We accepted the news bulletins of death as though it were banal bureaucracy. We had a high dosage of fatalism, some impassivity even, which was ultimately the other face of fear. We were so terrorized that indolence seemed to be the only form of resistance against barbarism. It isn't so bad, the quiet life. A lot happens to others that doesn't happen to me. And it followed that, without a shot fired, thousands of people were disappeared.

The people rejoiced for Kempes, the hippie Matador, and perhaps in that same moment, they were attaching electrodes to your uncle's ass to make him speak. What then?

They rejoiced for Kempes, El Matador. A nickname in poor taste.

Why am I writing all of this for you, my dear? We are in Tunis and you seem content. Why tell you this old story now? Is there a point, Mar? I don't even know why I'm here, on this beach, writing to you. Because I can't handle the lying anymore? I want some trace of a decent life. I've had a trying one. Lying is exhausting.

I met your father in Rome. Is it that I want to tell you about him? Or is it only a way to unburden my conscience? I'm not sure.

I met your father in Rome.

I was sitting on a green bench, anonymous and alone. Rome was great for running wild. Crowds at every gate. Rome to me was like Patagonia, where your grandfather Alfio lived. He was a solitary man with great heart. He was from Genoa. He'd chosen Patagonia to build himself another life. It was a grueling place. They say your grandmother died of boredom.

I was very beautiful in 1978. A real looker, if you can believe it. I had perky breasts, not this blubber you see now. At the time I would've preferred not having them. Now I'd give my life to go back to the way I was. I didn't want them because they drew attention. I only wanted to be invisible. That's why I went to the villa. I wanted a bench and the greenery around me.

One Sunday in Rome, the children rollicked happily, mindlessly. It was 1978.

Outside, Rome thrived delightedly beneath the light of a cat-shaped moon. The city center was nearby. I could have stretched my hand out and touched the Colosseum, if only I'd longed to do so. That nearness caused me inexplicable anguish. The monument reminded me of the corpse of one of our father's friends, the first dead person I'd laid eyes on. The body reeked of gangrene. So did the Colosseum.

Children were always popping up in the villa like poisonous mushrooms. Then he appeared. He looked like a tall child, but he was just very thin. He was like the Buenos Aires sky. Undefinable. I recognized something in him.

It was your father.

A green windbreaker, black hair, and slit eyes. He seemed to be waiting for me. Not a word came out of him. A gesture of greeting. We were mute. He lit a Marlboro for me. I smoked often back then.

Then I left, I remember. One Marlboro and I was gone.

It was before the hippie, before the number 10 or the goals. My brother was already a desaparecido. My mother already hated me. I'd already done a lot of damage all around. This was before the hippie. Before your father, I mean. It was a villa in Rome. The greenery. An uncertain neighborhood. His thin form standing in front of me.

It was like in that Gardel tango, *Tu sombra fue mi compañera.* In effect, we became friends that year. It was 1978. The World Cup in Argentina. They drove electrodes into your Uncle Ernesto's anus. They put the infamous *capucha* on him. A bag over the head and, beyond that, nothing else planned. A person wouldn't know what they were going to do—you couldn't see and you descended into utter panic. It was sadistic: obstructing the view of your own torture.

Destabilizing.

But sitting in that villa, I wasn't thinking of my brother. My thoughts were all for Carlos. A soldier. A torturer. The man I'd been fucking for three years. Who, I believe, I'd enjoyed myself with for three years.

> *Así aprendí que hay que fingir*
> *para vivir decentemente.*
> *Que amor y fe mentiras son,*
> *y del dolor se ríe la gente*

Gardel was always a source of comfort because in his songs I could see myself again. In his songs was the part of me obscured by failure. I obscenely traced the incisions of memory. Children appeared in the villa. I hated them all. I just wanted a Marlboro.

I'd like one even now, here in Tunis. Instead, I'm writing. I stopped smoking years ago. Ah, that's right. When you were born.

THE PESSOPTIMIST

"You can only clean shit here," the woman told me.

She said it with a strange, nasty voice. She was a mean woman. I remember the first one as the meanest.

"You can only clean shit here."

"That's it?"

"That's it."

"Does the shit smell very bad, ma'am?"

"That depends."

"On what, ma'am?"

"On how hard you pinch your nose."

I pinched my nose hard, my Zuhra. But that stench had already latched onto me. It's why I drowned myself in gin. It was there. I didn't resist. The gin made it so that I couldn't smell the stench anymore. No stench, *wallahi*! Not even the shit.

STOP

STOP

STOP

The woman paused the recording. She wasn't satisfied. She thought her voice sounded stupid.

Her finger angrily mashed the black stop button. She pressed it as though her life depended on it. A creak made the whole re-corder shudder. A 7.0 tremor on the Mercalli scale. For a moment, the woman was worried about the pressure she put on her small, dainty finger. She didn't want to break the recorder (again) which, evidently, was proving useful. She felt obsolete next to that old contraption. Modern life, as they called it, was surging rapidly toward digital networks. People no longer recorded their voices. They broadcast directly to YouTube. They retouched the bad re-cordings a little and enhanced them with effects to make them extraordinary. No one in the third millennium used cassettes and record players anymore. Maryam Laamane could use nothing else. She was like that record player, a piece of the past, a stratum of memory. She felt so mellow that way: curled up in front of the recording box. Doing things the old way didn't upset her at all. It didn't depress her one bit.

The idea of recording her voice came to her fortuitously one afternoon. She was by herself. The same drivel on TV. She'd fin-ished reading a book that upset her stomach. Two days earlier, she'd buried her best friend Howa Rosario. She and the entire Somali community buried Howa. She rose early in the morning to go to Termini Station. From there they had to take the shuttle that would carry everyone to Prima Porta, the cemetery, to bury her. That was a time when Maryam wouldn't set foot inside the station, that gangrenous, pus-infested dump.

All roads lead to Rome. For her, and for all Somalis, all roads led to Termini Station. At least that's how it used to be. Rome's roads, all its alleys, all its arteries, its passages, routes, paths, all of its crossroads, even its stops were oriented toward Termini. Somewhat like prayer toward Mecca.

Then one day, Maryam changed streets and didn't end up there anymore. She met with people at Ottaviano station or, as she called it, Ottopiano. She was never able to pronounce that cursed v. Finally she met up in a real place, as one should.

"Why do you make me come all the way up here? Couldn't

we have met at Amici Bar or Lul's, or at Termini?"

Maryam shook her head. "It hurts my feet," is all she would say.

"Ours too."

"Mine more."

She had a decisive, authoritative tone that called to mind the great orators of the past. A Cicero, a Mao, a Fidel. The others trembled in deference.

They gave in and met her at Ottopiano (not even they knew how to pronounce the *v*). A coffee at Castroni's, a walk on Via Candia, the stalls on Viale Giulio Cesare. A short stroll in the dome's shadow. It was in the heart of Catholic Rome, the Rome that spends and spreads. There were shirtmakers on Cola di Rienzo, American tourists with old Canons strung over their shoulders, children with fantastical ice cream cones. It was different from the Rome she'd known before. A quiet and presentable city. A walkable, respectable place that came out nicely in pictures and drawings. Even the pigeons were more well-mannered. With the point of their beaks they plucked breadcrumbs tossed covertly by the tourists. Their pecking was not violent, no anxiety or rush. With grace and savoir faire.

At Termini, by contrast, the pigeons were obese, inelegant, vermin-eyed. They were something to fear. Their feathered uniforms were worn and their steps uncertain. Everything about them pointed to negligence. Tattered, slovenly, wasting time being nothing. When they found something to devour, the expression in their eyes betrayed their unrest. Inconceivable shrieks suddenly erupted. Yearning, voracity, bulimia. They pecked the earth to exhaustion, ferociously and with a certain rapacious haste. They gorged on everything. The station pigeons made no distinction between breadcrumbs and chicken leftovers. Maryam became sick the first time she saw a pigeon eat one of its own kind. Fried chicken morsels had fallen next to a Peruvian child. Two pigeons advanced. War sounded on their beaks and, in the end, the fatter one struck the wing of the thinner, half-limping contender.

It seized the meager spoil of chicken, tossed it into the air, and guzzled it down. It was a cannibal.

That day, that distant day in an unfamiliar past, Maryam's esophagus brought up the partially dissolved remains of her breakfast—rusk and gin. Was she perhaps like those pigeons? Bulimic and bedraggled? Did she still have dreams? Once, her roads were oriented toward the prayer of Termini. She saw the billboards and dreamed of going back to the start of her journey, in Wardhiigley, her peaceable neighborhood in northern Mogadishu. She dreamed of return, a return with no more promises of departure. That way she wouldn't delude herself again.

It had been a while since Maryam stopped going to see the Termini billboards. She no longer wished to dream the impossible. But her heart knew the station was there, close. She felt it in her blood. She was only ignoring it to survive, yet Termini Station was like a magnet, and sooner or later it charmed its admirers. It was always lurking. How long had it been since she'd gone? Right…since she'd stopped getting wasted on gin first thing in the morning.

Howa was worth the effort. She'd been her best friend, and now she was dead. Maryam and the community had buried her two days ago. Just two days. It was for her sake, then, that Maryam returned to the station. She'd faced her fears for Howa. The hospital had told her Howa was dead. In her wallet, Howa carried a little note that said "In an emergency call Zuhra Laamane or Maryam Laamane" and, beneath that, had their home and mobile numbers. Zuhra, her beloved daughter, like her, was very meticulous. That's why she'd slipped that note in Howa's wallet. She knew Howa's head wasn't where it once was and she often pursued distant phantoms, so she'd also included their home addresses in case she got lost. The hospital was straightforward with Maryam. They told her to come to San Giovanni immediately. She did. The word "immediately" frightened her to no small degree. Once there, they told her the news: her friend Howa, her best and only friend Howa, was dead, defunct, finished. She'd fallen from the No. 8 tram. Her right foot had slipped, her head whipped back, cracked. Then came the grim reaper.

Maryam, stunned, looked at the doctor who was giving her the news. She was waiting to hear her say, "We did all we could" or "She didn't suffer long." They always said that on TV. Instead, the doctor said nothing. She couldn't tell lies. They brought her a body, not a person. So the doctor, a blonde forty-five-year-old, said nothing. Truth be told, she did say one thing, but Maryam could no longer remember what it was. It was something trite. When she saw the face on Howa's cadaver, she wasn't shocked—it closely resembled hers in life. Her crooked nose overshadowed everything else. It was still eccentric. Within a few hours, her nose would change. It would decompose with everything else. But for a little longer she'd remain as Maryam remembered her from a lifetime ago.

On the day of the funeral, Maryam Laamane timorously boarded the train. The cars were empty. The people of Rome had allowed themselves an unexpected jaunt to the sea. Thursday, a weekday, a day of work and stress. But it was summer. An exception to the rules was permitted, a momentary craze. One didn't have to go far to sin. To Ostia, Fregene, Lido dei Pini. The sand was dirty, the sea a tad opaque. What did it matter? It was beautiful just the way it was. The girls were blooming and the men were happy. There was an economic crisis—people were sad by default—but the sun baked beachgoers' skin and people longed to fall in love. The crisis could wait until winter. Now there was sun. Hormones hurtled down highways. The women exposed their stomachs, the men bared their chests. Those who, out of decency, did not wish to show their bodies took on the colors of the rainbow. Fluttering objects, Spanish fans, broadsheets, the hems of scarves. Drops of sweat pearled tired faces and mascara trickled in streams from translucent eyes.

Maryam sat her bulky self down. Peacefully, she began

thinking about her affairs. She had to buy beeswax to send to Nura. Her cousin had recommended it often, saying, "Here in Manchester they sell this lousy oil that doesn't protect your skin. I need beeswax for my wrinkles. Send it—that no good Skandar looks at too many skirts for my taste." Maryam promised: "Of course, I won't forget it." Once she put down the receiver, she had a good laugh at Nura's expense. Even with seventy years under her belt, that old shrew still worried that her Skandar would chase girls. "He's eighty years old!" she'd tell her, but it was useless. Jealousy had no logic, Nura's much less.

Until the end, Maryam had hoped she wouldn't have to go to the station and that she could simply show up at the entrance to Prima Porta.

"Are you out of your mind, Mary? We have many suras to read, and we have to do it together, on the bus."

"Where does the bus leave from, sister?" Maryam asked timidly, despite already knowing the answer.

"Where do you think it leaves from, dummy? From the *stascinka*, yeah?"

She'd figured as much. Somalis always met at the *stascinka*, at Termini, the crux of all roads. They congregated at Amici Bar or at Anna's or track 7 or at the Somali restaurant. There were many places to meet at the station, too many.

"If you get there first look for Fardosa, they'll give you your cappuccino with foam." And so, between suras, coffee, memories, thoughts, she buried her best friend Howa Rosario.

Then, in an instant, she plummeted into her present. Alone at home. The same nonsense on TV. A restless boredom made her chest pound. Under different circumstances, she'd have picked up the phone and arranged to meet Howa. Together they would've spoken of good times when Xamar—Mogadishu—was passionate, beautiful, and sensual. They'd have talked about their youth and dreams and the bad times, too, when Siad Barre seized power and decided, as if in a vile game of chess, to sacrifice all his pawns, all the Somalis. "Wasn't it awful the way people died under Siad Barre, Howa?" After Siad, dying was even worse. But Howa was dead, so there was no one to call, no one she really wanted to talk to. Actually, no, there was someone. Her daughter Zuhra. But it was difficult recounting these things to Zuhra. It was hard explaining her failures as a mother. The gin. Her flight to freedom. Zuhra's father. The fear that had skinned her alive for years.

Talking to Zuhra was difficult.

She'd only been able to do so once, with gestures. It was March 20, 1994. Zuhra had come home with a package. "Marco gave it to me." Marco was a boy she liked and studied with. Maryam had seen him once. He had untidy hair and a goatee. He was a little short and walked like an orangutan, but she had to admit he had a certain charm when he moved his eyes, concealed by folds of white skin. Marco had made something for Zuhra. Meanwhile she, the mother, had forgotten. Birthdays were nothing special to her. In Somalia they were only celebrated for children, not adults.

"I'll open it tomorrow," the girl said.

"Why not now?"

"I don't want to get upset."

Sometimes Maryam couldn't understand her daughter. A gift was opened immediately, not resisted or preserved. One was supposed to consume and absorb. But Zuhra overthought things, and in this way she was exactly like her father, Elias, that reckless man who Maryam missed like air itself.

"*Hooyo*, can you tell me one thing?"

"Yes, dear?" Maryam's voice shook. She felt guilty for forgetting her daughter's birthday. That godless *gaal* creation drove her crazy.

"Did you ever enjoy making love with men...with dad? Did you have fun?"

Maryam felt a piece of herself detach. She wasn't expecting that question. She had no words. Or, she had one in mind, but her daughter beat her to it.

"Don't say *eeb*, please don't say that word…don't just say 'shame.' Please, Mom, I need you to answer me."

She knew her daughter needed it.

Was it for Marco? No, it wasn't for him. It was for something they both feared.

She was about to speak when blood began gushing from the television screen. Red, hot, innocent.

The two women were hypnotized. The blood sullied everything: the camera, people nearby, and the blonde hair of a woman, Ilaria, their Ilaria Alpi. For months she'd been reporting on a foundering Somalia. Maryam and Zuhra watched, transfixed by the little screen, to make sense of the dismaying images. The blood was their problem too, especially theirs. Every breath was stifled. Every word interrupted. Every thought blocked. There was only the screen filled with Ilaria's bloodied hair.

It was March 20, 1994. It was her daughter Zuhra's birthday. She'd forgotten to give her a present. Birthdays were for infidels, and on the screen a woman was dying. Zuhra had a ponytail, beautiful and frothy. Maryam looked at her. She reminded her, God knows why, of Sam Cooke and his sweet alligator demeanor. The beauty of her ponytail distracted her from the blood contrail swelling on the screen. Confusion everywhere. Her daughter was born under the Pisces sign. Astrological statistics said she would be a dreamer. But she, her Zuhra, dreamed with her feet on the ground. She was the daughter of wary dreamers. The strip of blood on the screen was becoming a boundless puddle.

Ilaria, a lacerated shirt, a body wilted upon itself, a stringless puppet.

The puppet was torn apart like a quartered ox. Men around her in their *husgunti*, desperate faces, shaking thighs. The eyes of mother and daughter were glued to the pretty puppet's face, the face of dying Ilaria. They wanted to rush over to her and retie the strings so she could stand and laugh again. "Ilaria, what's happening to Ilaria?" Maryam Laamane asked. Zuhra stood and moved toward her mother. For a moment, an impassioned hug brought the two women together.

That was when Sam Cooke played again in Maryam's head. She and Elias had danced to him on one of the nights he pretended to court her. The truth was that she was courting him, but theirs was an old-fashioned Somalia, the sixties were almost over and women had to play the game without arousing suspicion. Her Elias resembled Sam Cooke in some ways. They were so similar in their bewildered childishness and reptilian lust. Maryam was so wrapped up in her past that she hardly realized her daughter's firm hug was increasingly desperate.

Maryam was still staggered by Zuhra's question. What should she have told her? Did she have to explain how she lived in the sixties? How beautiful she'd been back then? That was when Kwame Nkrumah was saying, *Africa must unite*, the years when all Africans believed that anything was possible. Maryam Laamane had been so beautiful in the sixties. Is that what she should have told Zuhra? Right then, in that moment? Yes, in that very moment, she couldn't waste time. She'd already lost plenty with that sad girl.

When she was pregnant with Zuhra, a bell went off in her head, a shiver under her arms. At first it frightened her. Elias caressed one of her cheeks and whispered, "It's the dream in your head." Then, kissing her softly, "It's embracing you." When Elias entered her, it hurt the first few times. He told her, "They will take that jewel from us and throw it away." She didn't understand. Then he said that inside every woman were bountiful jewels of varying size. God had placed the most precious gem between women's thighs. "And we, my friend, do you know what we do?" Maryam Laamane knew the answer. They'd already cut her below and sutured everything. The first time she peed afterward it hurt severely. In the West the experts called it female genital mutilation. She only knew that it caused great pain and that she'd never get her clitoris back. She knew the gem's fate: buried or tossed in the trash. But the night Zuhra became real, through Elias, Maryam felt a yearning, something she liked.

She liked many things about Elias. Chiefly, his smell. He tasted of bittersweet green mango. She wanted to bite him all over. She wanted to sleep on top of him. When he entered her, she felt his weight, saw his contentedness. But she didn't know what to do. Should she have laughed? Clenched her fists? Cried? Then that evening, her underarms, the tip of her thumb. It was like in that Sam Cooke song when he said, *They're twistin', twistin', everybody's feelin' great.* It was the dream embracing her. That girl who, when she came out, hadn't known love like she deserved. The gin's fault, and Siad Barre, and her head, which didn't know what direction to take her in. That day was different. It had been some time since she'd come back, healed perhaps, waiting only for that moment to arrive. But Ilaria Alpi was dying. Maryam decided then that she would respond to her daughter's question once things were calmer.

Now, however, Howa Rosario was dead. Perhaps she didn't have much time either. She couldn't have known. She didn't want to take a chance. And so that afternoon, Maryam Laamane took out a recorder to tell her story and give her answers. Her daughter, Zuhra, would appreciate the attempt. Maybe Howa Rosario would, too. The story was hers as well, after all.

THE FATHER

I was conceived. And I conceive. I am son and father. But I am a failed son, a failed father. They told me: "You must tell your story so as not to lose it or yourself." It happened on a phone call from a distant place that I once knew. The voice spoke to me and I simply listened. I heard other things. A note of harsh resentment in a once crystalline voice. I thought: she's growing old as well. I hadn't suffered her resentment; I'd left before I could. A scatterbrained deserter with a lurid, soiled conscience. I wasn't needed anymore, so what was I to do? Remain and live in unchecked failure? Maybe I should have, but it takes balls to fail and withstand it. I didn't have enough, not even the two I was guaranteed. I abandoned the voice. In fact, I abandoned many. "*Assalamu aleikum*, brother," the voice thundered. Or so it seemed to me, because that is what I felt beating inside my chest. Though, in truth, the voice was very calm, as always.

She'd gotten my number from Hagi Nur, who does business with the Chinese. He got rich, doesn't know what to do with all his money, and he still lives like a beggar. Hagi Nur, a con man like all merchants. But I liked that he could always take a joke. He used to live like me. We reminisced about how the women in Mogadishu batted their sweet eyes at us and how we were sprightly, young, with every muscle in its proper place. It was once a great thing to be young in Mogadishu. It seemed that anything was possible, that anything could happen from one moment to the next. But now all the young people want to flee. Sixteen long years of accursed war. Oh, merciful Allah, redeem us. Unrelenting shooting eviscerates us. We are all like moldering corpses. There is no longer sweetness in girls' eyes. The girls are afraid in Mogadishu. And they are afraid in Kismayo, in Merca, in Barawa.

The young people dream of the West: polished palaces, throngs of people, opportunities. They don't imagine that life can be challenging there. If you warn them and say, "It's not like you think, child," they laugh in your face. "What do I have to lose, Granddad?" And you, Granddad, you don't know what to say or how to say it. They tell you: "Better to go through the desert than rot in the grip of terror." They leave through Khartoum and Nairobi, they cross the Sahara and then those in Libya and Tunisia try their luck in broken-down boats that will take them toward the gateway to the sun. The prim Mahmud calls it that, *Bab-al-Shams*: Gateway to the Sun. For him the West is *hurreyya*, freedom, the sun. He is only eighteen years old. He wants to realize his dream and become a doctor to heal himself and others. He knows death bides its time in the desert, and that people drink their urine and make pacts with *sheitan*, the wretched red devil. He knows this, but he wishes to leave all the same. He is an adventurer, as are the others. Hagi Nur and I were part of the fortunate generation. Yes, we've been hurt and disappointed, we were cowards and bad men, but at least we can say our youth was plated in gold. We cavorted in ignorance on the streets of Shebelle, our eyes glazed over, our throats savoring life.

The voice told me my daughter was now a woman. I have two daughters. I only know the other one's name. Sometimes I dream of them together. The voice said I must tell my story to these girls, especially the one I had with her. And the other? How would I find her? "Don't worry about it," she told me. "Just do it." I hadn't heard that voice for almost twenty-five years, possibly more. We loved each other once. We were husband and wife. I wondered if any of that fondness was still there. I wanted to ask her, but the connection was bad, there was crackling now and then, she was growing fainter. And if I'm honest, I was ashamed. I hadn't conducted myself properly with that voice, that woman. I said to her: "Yes, I'll tell my story. I'll record it like you're doing and I'll speak Somali slowly." Our daughter, she informed me, doesn't understand it well. "It's time she knew her father," she said.

"It's time." And for an eternity I repeated her words in my mind. She promised she would give me a photo of Zuhra. "She's very beautiful," Maryam Laamane told me, "like the photos of your mother." She's very beautiful, she said. I repeated this as well, over and over again. "But, Elias, she doesn't know it. That's why you have to tell her your story, because beauty without history is mute."

Now I'm sitting here in front of a Chinese gadget Hagi Nur got for me. A red tape recorder. It's the latest kind. He showed me which buttons to press and I picked it up fast. I'm not completely senile. "When you first start you'll feel foolish talking to yourself, but just remember you're doing it for her. That will get you through." And she was right, it has helped me.

Yet how does one begin to tell a story? From the beginning, I think, with the protagonist. But am I the protagonist, or simply the last link in a perplexing chain? And what is the beginning of an individual? It isn't very clear to me. His birth? Or perhaps something that precedes it? Hagi Nur has a theory, he told me as we were sipping our spiced tea the other evening at his house. "Our beginning is the beginning of those who came before us," he said, "and those after us." Listening to Hagi Nur, I realized that life is a circle, a continuous beginning and end. No movement is precise, we cannot quantify, define, specify. The beginning is the sum of all our beginnings, the subtraction of past beginnings. The beginning is utter chaos, in short. So, my Zuhra, to make it easier, I will tell you how I was conceived. And if one day I must meet your sister, I will tell her also.

Here, Zuhra, I am starting my story. It's yours too, in part. I wasn't a father to you. I'm more like a stranger. But listen to me anyway, okay?

While I'm at it, I'll tell you everything as though it weren't my story, but someone else's. It'll hurt less for us. That's what I tell myself.

Am I ready? I don't think...I don't know. What do you say, my big girl? Does conception occur in the mind or in the heart?

Elias's mother first dreamed of the boy when she was twelve years old, but she had to wait six more years before giving birth to him. She did it in a way she never could've imagined.

She was born to a family of fishermen in an age of colonial tyrannies. Her family was odd. They looked everywhere in search of life. The ocean was a threadbare bed. The men left at dawn and the women waited on shore. Sometimes they would catch nothing, not even a miserable sardine, but there were also days when fishing yielded fat tunas. Each tuna was a celebration. The difficulties of the endeavor and the wait were forgotten. People are born, people die, but the one who fishes is sometimes in between. They do not live or die. They wait, but no one knows for what.

The mother, who had a name as mild as a dragonfly, hated the sea. Her city, Brava, was in a small valley and everything revolved around it—marriages, funerals, births, quarrels, breath itself. Famey, as the girl was called, wished instead to breathe the exhaust fumes of those metal heaps they called automobiles. She wanted to inhale them deeply to become an automobile herself. Famey had seen one only once. There were white people inside, the ones rumored to be in charge of the country. The big city was full of automobiles like that. She knew this because her cousin Ruqia had married a soldier in the Italian army, a *dubat*, and was living like a queen in the capital Mogadishu, the red city. When she came to Brava, Ruqia flaunted gorgeous gowns and did nothing but praise her Omar, who "was honored because he'd performed like a hero in Libya." *Libya? What is Libya?* Famey asked herself. *It's probably another place where people have automobiles.* The girl would only speak of that distance place, mysterious Libya, when she was fawning over her cousin and her dear Omar. She dreamed of automobiles every night. Every night she pictured herself as a great woman escorted around Mogadishu. She also dreamed of Libya. She liked how the name sounded.

Brava bored her. The people seemed happy not because they were fortunate, but because they were stupid. "What are these people laughing at?" she asked herself, perplexed. "Don't they see that the ocean is eating us alive?" The sea, in effect, had a price. Human lives. It had swallowed many Bravanese over the years, some literally devoured by sharks—they feared nothing, and the smell of fresh blood drove them recklessly toward the shore. Others paid their sad tribute directly to the water. They drowned and that was it. But the people were happy all the same. The air was temperate, the fish abundant, the sand clean. The women cooked from morning till night. Tuna was served in soup or on skewers, the *mufo*, the bread, accompanied multicolored sauces and the *gallamuddo*, Brava's pasta, made tongues spin in pure pleasure. Famey hated all of it. She was bored and wanted the life Ruqia spoke of, married to a soldier. Her mama shook her head every time she heard her complain. "This will end badly. Maybe it's time you find a good husband."

Famey, I didn't tell you, cut a fine figure. She was a starfish with intense green eyes. That could happen in Brava. Everyone passed through the little Somali valley. Egyptians, ancient Romans (shipwrecked with many togas and *latinorum*), Arabs, Portuguese, Malaysians and, lastly, Benito Mussolini's Italians. In Brava, colors were gradations of a story, an encounter. There were white Bravanese, black Bravanese, curly-haired Bravanese, straight-haired Bravanese. Eyes the color of cobalt, spruce, and charcoal. The noses were a cornucopia of forms. Long, short, chunky, coarse, outlandish, truncated. Something for all tastes. To distinguish themselves from their brothers in the Horn, the Bravanese invented another language. They spoke in Somali and prayed in Arabic, but the language of their hearts was an explosive mix of Swahili, Portuguese, and Arabic. In Bravanese, they sent their children to sleep. In Bravanese, they commemorated the Prophet's *miraj*. In Bravanese, women learned the secrets of wedding nights.

Famey was beautiful and she knew it. Like all beauties, she was a little fanatical. Before ending up in the maws of a shark, her father had made his wife promise she would never impose a husband on Famey. Her mother was an honorable woman and respected her husband more than herself. She said, "Very well," but then thought, *There are other ways to convince a girl.* After much wandering from house to house in search of the perfect match, her mother bumped into Abd-al-Majid. The boy was frail, but he had a full head of black hair and a complexion that reminded her of a baby tuna.

The mother's plan was to make Famey and Majid fall in love. They would naturally come to the point where he was on his knees asking her to marry him. This was in fact what happened, but not in the way the mother had imagined. One day, during the turbulent thirties, word arrived in Brava that one of the many cousins who emigrated to the big city was getting married. The bride was named Nadifa. Everyone knew her. From a young age, she had been a nasty, runny-nosed brat who played pranks on the fishermen and constantly repeated a strange word that no one ever understood. She would say it and run away laughing. The fisherman puzzled over the word at length.

"The word doesn't exist," one of them said. "No, that brat is insulting us." "I think it's a word from the Quran." "No, impossible. It must be something those wretched, kinky-haired *jareer* say." Conjectures, basically. Then Nadifa left with her family for Mogadishu and everyone forgot about her, at least until the announcement of her marriage to a wealthy Somali who worked alongside the country's new masters. The same fate as her cousin Ruqia. Wives of collaborators.

The mother made sure Famey and Majid attended the wedding together and that they'd be alone. She feigned sudden illness and the kids took the shuttle bus. They were both sixteen years old.

The *shitaue*, the shuttle that connected Brava to Mogadishu, hadn't been around for that long. It was the invention of an *Abgaal* who had copied it from India. I don't know why that man was in India. Dark-skinned Africans, in those times, certainly couldn't move freely—not like now, anyway. By comparison, today's dark Africans travel like courageous adventurers. How he ended up down there I couldn't say; even at that time, there were people with the travel bug in their blood. Somalis, you know, could sense commerce anywhere, and India was a stone's throw away. The ocean was all it took to connect it to Somalia. That man set up three transit lines: one from Brava to Mogadishu, another from Merca to Mogadishu, and the last from Galkayo to Mogadishu. Most of the revenue went to the Italians, the country's masters.

Six people were on the shitaue that day: the two unknowingly betrothed cousins, the driver, himself an Abgaal who had the popular name Mohamed, then Muqtar, a merry man who never stopped talking, and finally a couple that was moving to Mogadishu permanently, Jamila and Farah.

The shitaue was half empty. It wasn't the best time for travel. The sky foretold of a storm and burning souls. The new masters thought themselves omnipotent. They had crushed Ethiopia, proclaimed their Empire, and flaunted their manhood. In the thirties, the Italians believed they were gods. Soon enough they would awaken from their demented dream. But at the time, it was best not to run into them outside of Mogadishu. People said horrible things about their excursions.

"Nonsense!" the driver said, "I know my shitaue, we take this route all the time. Nothing has ever happened to me. I'd really like to see…"

His wish was granted. Two jeeps loaded with young white men stopped the defenseless shuttle. "Fresh meat, boys!"

The six passengers were forced to get off. They were divided, women on one side and men on the other. A tall man with a square head and a pentagonal ass walked in front of them, reviewing. Famey thought he must have been important. His uniform was different. He was completely square, even his hands lacked roundness. It was as if he were speaking a language that wasn't Italian. Famey did not know Italian, but this wasn't it. She would swear on her life. She was oblivious, little Famey. The others were wetting themselves in fear, and she was busy examining the shape of the high-ranking soldier. Famey was an attentive observer and had an ear for languages. If someone had paid the slightest attention to her upbringing, she would've undoubtedly become a polyglot.

The man was a lordling from the Lower Saxony who'd molded himself into an SS officer. He and Colonel Guglielmi of the Twentieth Division had made a bet inside the jeep. They would ask the first Somali they encountered who instilled more fear, the Germans or the Italians. Guglielmi, sure of himself, said, "These are a loyal people. They fear us because we're their lords and masters. They don't even know who you are." The German said only this: "They will know who we are," and five minutes later they came upon the shuttle.

The Somali they asked was Muqtar, the long-winded man who wouldn't shut up. He was the only one who spoke Italian. Sometimes, talking excessively was pointless. It didn't help Muqtar and it didn't help the rest of the group either. To Guglielmi's question, instead of responding with "Germans" or "Italians," he said, "The English." Why? To get out of trouble. Fear is a horrid emotion. *If they're asking me that*, he thought to himself, *they may want to hear that they're good and valiant, while the English are scoundrels.* So, hoping to praise the Italians and the Germans, he ended up insulting them both. Muqtar blathered on like a radio. He didn't limit himself to saying, "The English," but went into a detailed account of their ferocity, of how merciless they were with beasts, children, women. He described their bloodthirsty sneers, their wicked salivating. The outcome: Guglielmi shot him right above the brow.

It was the end of the world. All were raped, regardless of sex, thrashed, humiliated. Farah, who was traveling with his wife, had his privates cut off by the German official. They were immediately scooped up by two skulking vultures drawn to the stench of death.

Famey and her cousin suffered the same fate. She was taken by three different men. Two Italians and a German. She lost her voice with the first one, flailed, bit, tried wriggling away. With the second one she could no longer do anything, terrified by her cousin's shouts. She knew very well that these things happened to women. How was it possible that it could befall men as well? She thought the men would annihilate them with their bullets, not their pricks. Who could save her if they were doing the same thing to her cousin? Thus, with the second and third, she was relatively cooperative, so useless was it to resist. No one could save her from that nightmare. From the corner of her eye she saw Guglielmi raping Majid.

They did not say anything to anyone in Mogadishu. The festivities for Nadifa and her rich spouse lasted four days. On the fifth, Majid and Famey announced their engagement.

TWO

THE NUS-NUS

She squeezed into her khaki pants from Aigle, the ones Pati had given her for Christmas. Her favorites. A large pocket in the front, with a convenient top zipper. Without thinking twice, Mar shoved a small volume of poems by Sister Juana Inés de la Cruz inside the pocket, then slowly advanced toward Avenue de la Liberté.

"I'm not waiting for you, *hija*," her mother told her as she still clung to her purple pillow. She never parted ways with it, taking it on every trip. "I have to take the entrance exam. I'm up first. You're lucky, dear, that you don't have to take exams. I wish I could start from the alphabet, too. Lady Luck really does favor the young."

Luck? Who said anything about luck? And what alphabet was she talking about? Ah, yes, the Arabic alphabet. She forgot she was in Tunis, forcibly enrolled in school. What did those absurd puzzles matter to her, those indecipherable signs? Her mother was forcing her to unscramble them, but did she want to? No, of course not. Going to Arabic school—whose fucking idea was that? She didn't give a damn about Arabs, Arabic, Hezbollah, or Bin Laden, and Tunis disagreed with her like a plate of badly fried calamari.

Mar felt something like a clean cut on the jugular. A slicing wound. Vile nostalgia. She pined for Villa Borghese and the shameless policemen staring at her ass. Dragging herself anxiously along, her mind fixated on Patricia. She'd been in that city for only a day and Patricia was already badgering her. The time spent with her, the pain felt for her. Ceaseless memory. She felt like a roach. A nasty, worthless roach.

She was late. Surely she would show up to the lesson after it had already begun. Fifteen minutes later, not a minute before, not a minute after. She was hungry and tired. She wanted to go back. There was no breakfast service in their boarding house, people arranged everything on their own. The people…what people? One day in Tunis had gone by and the only person she'd seen inside was the sister who'd given them their keys. What was her name again? Sister Meditación. She was Argentinian, like her mom. Naturally, such social affinity was forgotten. But those sisters were familiar, and they were practically the only ones isolated in that faux Muslim, faux Western, faux everything city. Their clothes were an intense, deep blue, like the skies in Japanese animes. Sister Meditación gave her and her mother a thorough tour of the place. The atrium, the elevator, the clotheshorse, the washing machine, the kitchen, the terrace, the parlors, the giant blow-up photo of John Paul II, (the Pope was always John Paul, because to many people it was as though he'd never died) with Ben Ali, who looked like an obese transvestite from Pigalle. To even the playing field, there was also a normal-sized photo of His Eminence Pope Benedict XVI. The tour concluded with the bedrooms. She and her mother stayed on separate floors. Mar got lucky with her room. She was on the third floor. Her mother was on the first. The floor between them spoke volumes.

Sister Meditación had the gentle face of an adolescent. She was very young. Looking at her, Mar was convinced that true faith granted great serenity. She herself had faith in nothing and knew she would be eternally damned. "There are no strangers in this place," the sister said. "That is the only rule." Mar wondered if they'd have recognized Patricia. She always stayed there. Wearing that black-striped tee and those awful dark shoes. She didn't know how to dress. It was pathetic. As soon as the sister and her mother went away, Patricia took possession of the bed. "Get away from there," Mar commanded. "You're dead. I'm the one that still has to sleep and wake up every morning." Patricia settled near the room's only window. She curled on the ground in a fetal position. "Leave me alone. The bed is mine!" Mar shouted.

She laid a mat near the window so her lover-friend could lie down, but Patricia had vanished. Mar wondered if she would come back. She'd never believed in ghosts. Patricia, however, was not a ghost. She was part of her, it was different. If she were a ghost, she would've had blood and brain splatters everywhere. An eye socket split in half, the eyeball dangling. If Patricia were a ghost, Mar would've feared her. But she wasn't. She was one of her projections. A macabre fantasy.

Who knows if Sister Meditación would've recognized her. She was such a sweet lady. Though on that point she was inflexible: "No strangers in our *maison*." Was Patricia a stranger?

There was a huge espresso machine in the kitchen that she could use to make coffee. Laziness had gotten the better of her by then. The thought of fiddling around at that hour with an espresso-maker she'd never used didn't appeal to her. She preferred a café. They were downtown, after all, on a cross street of Bourguiba Avenue, the Champs-Élysées of the hapless colonized, the parlor of Tunis. "They clean it every night," her mom told her. "That's all they do, mostly picking up garbage. Bourguiba Avenue has to shine like a mirror." She headed toward that parlor, dragging her feet. She stopped by the currency exchange first and then plopped herself like dead weight in a crowded bar. A man sitting next to Mar watched her, intrigued.

"Are you American? *Vous-êtes français?*"

Mar didn't respond. She lit a cigarette, then ordered a croissant and mint tea. "*Chaud, s'il vous plaît.*" She sucked in the noxious cigarette smoke. She should've quit smoking. She hadn't enjoyed it in years. Patricia would scold her time and again. Her mother didn't lay off that vice either. "Do you want to reduce your lungs to a bacterial clump? You want them to explode like an atomic bomb? Do you want to die in pain?"

Mar *was* dying from pain. She opened the little book of Sister Juana's poems and distractedly read some verses. The words dripped with icy rancor. It couldn't have been easy being trapped in a woman's body during the seventeenth century, in Mexico or anywhere else. It wasn't even easy in the twenty-first. The croissant was nauseating, she didn't like it. As a child, she would've eaten fifteen of those peculiar, buttery croissants in a row. They offered her a sweetness her mother didn't know how to give. She was always lost in her reading, her mother. Mar had gained weight to make her see that she, her daughter, her black daughter, also occupied a space…and what a space. She became all folds and round rolls. Her mother, lost in her readings. She, lost in butter. The poetry, lost in its incommunicability.

Her mother's poems made her sick to her stomach. They were narcissistic delusions, a continuous spewing on defects, power, compromise. The poems were filled with subjects, virtues, struggle, feminism, rights. You could feel the social tension and the weight of responsibility. The closed fist. The ideology. They contained Cuba, Che, Salvador Allende, the unavoidable *desaparecidos*. The contradictions of the USSR. Politics, anti-capitalism, Socialist International. Even Mao was in a poem. China. The proletariat. The shattered ideal of Deng Xiaoping's new direction. Fidel's ambiguity. The European divide. She, the poet's daughter, the one who was too black, she was never there.

"*Eres española?*" The guy wouldn't give up. "Russian?"

He was blabbering like she did at Patricia's funeral. Pure delirium. None of the attendees liked her pink dress. They didn't like her. She'd bought the awful dress a week after the abortion. Then she'd never worn it. The saleswoman told her, "So cute! You're a doll." Sometimes salespeople lie out of mercy. She wanted that dress, and nothing and no one would make her change her mind. Salespeople know when they've got a sucker.

Once she was home she'd made her plate of special cornmeal. Pati loved it. They ate. "*Me ha gustado mucho, nena. Como siempre.*" Mar tidied up, washed, scrubbed. They sat down together to watch a black-and-white film on TV. It was a strange movie with a twenty-two-year-old woman pretending to be an adolescent. It was Ginger Rogers. Mar searched in vain for Fred Astaire in the black and white. She hoped the two would tap dance together. She wanted to be rescued from what she was about to say. Only Fred Astaire could do it, but he wasn't in the movie. Midway through, both of them were fed up. A bit of channel surfing, one woman beside the other, distant. On the screen, a bloated, black-veiled Loredana Bertè appeared. Mar felt vaguely sad. Bertè had always reminded her of Toulouse-Lautrec's pitiable whores. She was singing one of her old hits.

With no bread and butter, you can eat me
Oh oh, oh oh oh

Mar began clapping her hands and dancing like a spinning top.
"*Estás loca? La gente duerme.*"
"*Qué se joda.* Everyone can go fuck themselves. And fuck you too, Patricia Delgrado Ruiz. Tomorrow, leave this house forever."
That she did.
No more Patricia day to day. No more poppy perfume first thing in the morning, no more Fassbinder films, no more Hernandez books, no more stupid cow statuettes spread around the house. No more hair in the spotless sink, no more frizzled toothbrush. Even that four-dollar shampoo and the egg balm were gone. What about those coconut cookies they went crazy for? Nothing. With her gone, they'd lost their taste.
Mar couldn't be with Patricia anymore. Every time she looked at her, she thought of that disgusting spelt soup. She thought about the gray machinery above her black body. She thought of the suction. The disgust she'd felt when that man penetrated her

for the first time. No, she couldn't stay with the poppy-scented woman anymore.

The priest exhorted those who were able to take the Eucharist. Someone wept. Everything was arranged in perfect funerary fashion. The tears, the hardened faces, the flowers, the stench of incense, the sunglasses, the black shawls. Mar rose in her pink dress. Her mother grabbed her by the arm.

"What are you doing? *No puedes, hija…*you're not baptized."

"Fuck you, Mama," and then she moved toward the casket, breaking away from her mother's aggravating grip. Quick, casual, rash.

Mar looked at the others. Their backs, their hairstyles, the rapid movements of their perplexed eyes. They were analyzing her, scrutinizing. They were trying to understand what the hell was happening and what the hell would happen. No one dared break her stride. The deceased's parents were paralyzed, waiting. Mar stroked the casket, *el ataúd.* Then, she leaped on top of it. Her butt struck the rough wood of the coffin and a *thump* sounded throughout the church, astounding everyone.

Her mother, the poet Miranda Ribero Martino Gonçalves, was also paralyzed. She was neither pained nor frightened. She was merely becoming inured to her horror. How many more times did Mar wish to be born? Miranda knew in her heart that Mar didn't belong to her. Her womb refused to acknowledge her. Miranda knew she was an errant mother. She knew she would always have to brace for the worst.

Mar familiarized herself with the coffin's coarse wood. Beguiled, she caressed it before speaking.

"Peter Sellers wasn't actually named Peter, but Richard Henry Sellers," she began.

Buffoons, the dumb stares of buffoons were trained on her. She continued.

"His brother called him Peter. He died a few days after the boy was born. His parents never accepted it. Peter—well, Richard

Henry—would later say they called him Peter from the start, even if he couldn't say why exactly. He was born on September 8, 1925, in Southsea, Hampshire, and died in London at only fifty-four years old, done in by a diseased and overworn heart. He acted in more than fifty films. My favorite is still *The Party*, where he plays an Indian bit actor, Hrundi V. Bakshi, a man of many shades. Before landing a film role, Peter had cut his teeth on pre-show theater performances. Now I'll tell you, in chronological order, every film Sellers shot from 1950 until his death. Write it down. Henry Hathaway's *The Black Rose*, 1950, Great Britain; Tony Young's *Penny Points to Paradise*, 1951, Great Britain; Alan Cullimore's *Let's Go Crazy*, 1951, Great Britain; Maclean Roger's…"

Two men cut her short, one in a dark suit and the other in jeans. She knew them but not very well. They were also Spanish, and journalists. And perhaps also unhappy. Mar realized she had great strength. She resisted the men's attack. The one in jeans tried thwarting her from behind, while the dandy in the dark suit wanted to subdue her from the front. Mar wriggled away. She fought hard, never ceasing her poetic declamation of that queer, sad hero's tragicomic filmography.

She got to Clive Donner's *What's New, Pussycat*, 1965, Great Britain, before they threw her unceremoniously out of the church. She shook off the dust. The pink dress was filthy and her hat had flown away. She'd scraped a knee. Her wrists ached.

But she was finally able to tell Patricia something that mattered to her. She never talked about herself. Peter Sellers was the focus of her research. She was finishing a dissertation on him. Patricia never asked her anything about it. Nothing interested her, nothing beyond herself. Patricia was very self-centered. In her heart, Mar had always known that. She didn't ask her about the spelt soup or the gray machine. She didn't ask Mar how she was doing. She hadn't confided about her suicide plans. "Damn, Pati, I could've come with you. You're so selfish, a damned egotist."

"OK, now I understand, lovely lady...you're British," the young Tunisian blurted.

Mar didn't look at him. Was he a handsome boy? She couldn't see beauty anymore. She stood, left some money on the table, possibly too much, and headed reluctantly toward her first Arabic lesson: the alphabet. *Alif, ba, ta...*

THE NEGROPOLITAN

"What have you decided, my love? What will you do when you're an adult?"

My mother's usual line. She asks me this every now and then. One day she asks and the next day, nothing. Each time she ends a phone call or conversation with me, she asks the same maddening question. At this point it's a tic, it's stronger than her. Mom sometimes forgets that I'm an adult and that I'm closer to menopause than infancy.

I just got off the phone with her. I've been in Palermo for four days. Today I take the boat to Tunis. I miss my mom's caustic voice, and a text message seems like a bland way to communicate. I only felt fondness and jubilation. I felt like Judy Garland singing "Somewhere Over the Rainbow." Swallows fluttered in the sky above. Kids ran happily into the perfect blue sea. I forgot that I was in dusty, summer-scorched Palermo. Despite the sweltering heat, I was strangely tranquil. Then, what a shame, I got the unfortunate idea to call my parent. I went to a rundown call center near my bed-and-breakfast. I dialed her number and waited for the *tuu-tuuu* that gave me the green light.

When I call Mom I'm always somewhat agitated. She's my mother—we've known each other for thirty years. There aren't any huge secrets between us (besides my father's identity) or any significant ongoing crises. It's just that every time I call or talk to her or propose something to her, I feel that I'm not perfect like she wants me to be. It gives me insane performance anxiety. On the phone, my anxiety reaches its apex. I change, I start to act. I play it safe. I list my accomplishments for her. I tell her I'm happy. I tell her my friends adore me. And, yes, I'll find a fantastic man when I really want to. Right now it's more important that I figure out what I want in life, and then, once he notices my self-confidence, he'll love me even more. I don't want to waste my life with slackers. No, thank you. Yes, the man will come. Yes, everyone is enamored of me. *What a beautiful girl*, they tell me. *What a great body. You're so refined.* We're Somali, everyone knows we're beautiful. I praise my neck. My bottom. My skinny waist. "No, Mom, I'm not emaciated. No, I eat enough. Yes, I stopped doing that thing… you know I did." Mom always reminds me of my bulimic past. She doesn't forget anything. I read the pain in her face constantly. She hides the Coca-Cola from me. I used to weigh 175 pounds. Now I weigh 128, I'm fine. Ugh, enough with this, Mom. I've changed. I'm trying at least.

She and I don't talk much. We can't. I thought I was a blabbermouth, but not with her. I read the pain in her face, the guilt for having left me in that school when I was little. That's the way it went, Mom, and it could've been worse. A horrendous thing happened to me at school, but that's enough now, please. I'd like to turn the page. She said, "Okay love, let's turn the page." She always calls me "love," it freaks me out. I'd prefer that she called me by my name more often. Zuhra. She said it so rarely.

Mom demands that I be happy. She doesn't ask for it, she insists. That's why her questions irritate me, I know I won't meet her standards. I know I'll never be as happy as she wants me to be, which enrages me. I feel like a nobody.

Then the offhand remark, the pinnacle of anxiety, the question I never knew how to answer. Why doesn't she lay off me? She tells me exactly why. She doesn't approve of what I'm doing.

She wants me to be a doctor, a gynecologist. "My sister Fardosa is a midwife," she tells me. I don't push back. I don't want to start an argument. Sometimes, though, I bite. "Your sister Fardosa—I can't bring myself to call her Aunt, when do I ever see her?— is a butcher. She cuts the clits of young girls, stitches them up, and stops them from having a good fuck." Anything but a doctor! I spit on gynecology. I mean, I spit on butcher gynecology. No blood on my unblemished gown, *ya ummi*. I want to stay clean. As honest as can be.

Then *ummi*, my mom, bites her lip. She knows her sister is a butcher. And she knows it's all owing to the grace of God that I'm not like her. I earned a degree in Brazilian literature. I like Brazil. One day, once I've earned a pretty sum, I'll live there. I've even chosen the site where I'll build my little house, near a hipster beach on the magical island of Florianopolis. I went three years ago. Never, in any place, have I found such an absence of antagonism. People live their lives and don't think about anything else. They don't think about busting your balls or, worse, disintegrating them. And everyone smiles. I'd be stringing beads for tourists from sunrise to sunset. Then I would dance in honor of my *orixá*. Mine is Iemanjá, queen of the sea. Yes, I'm very close to the sea.

The problem is that Mom can't stand the work I do. I think she's convinced that I distance myself from any baseline of happiness. I sell CDs in an entertainment megastore (you could call it that). It's a dreadful job, I know. Not so much because I'm a sales-clerk, that's all well and good. It's because I'm exploited. At this point, we're all butcher's meat—not only the clits Auntie Fardosa cuts off.

Everyone I know, when I tell them what I do, says to me: "Oh, working in a record store, that's cool! You must be living it up!" Absolutely not. I can't stand it. First of all, I don't work in a cute tiny record shop, but a megastore. Secondly, I'm not living the life. People think it's *High Fidelity*. Three nerds spending their time ranking indie records, pointlessly fantasizing and cooking up disastrous plans. If only. I'd spend all day listening to the songs of Caetano Veloso or the sacred sister Maria Bethânia. Instead, I have to put up with stupid compilations and Britney Spears. Music is blaring in the megastore all day long. Usually it's garbage, not music. No one I know gets it. Megastores are huge. They're enormous, usually two floors. Where I work, there are three. Libla is German, but it's spreading through all of Europe. They have stores throughout Germany, from the Upper Saxony to Bavaria, and it's well established in France, in Benelux, and in Portugal. They're struggling in Great Britain and Spain. Now they're trying to catch on in Italy.

"Libla," our manager Augh says, "was made to kick the asses of those bastards at Fnac, Mondadori, and Feltrinelli." Competition is quite the bogeyman, to the point that manager Augh—Ottavio Cantoni—spent months photographing people who went in and out of those other megastores. Months stationed in front of the Feltrinelli across from the Largo di Torre Argentina, even longer in front of the Mondadori near the Trevi Fountain. There's always a carrot-haired woman avidly smoking a cigarette in the pictures. I wondered if someone was photographing the boss while he photographed them. The redhead is in all his pictures. Who knows? Let's drop the conspiracy theories. I still don't know whether Cantoni is gay or not. I mean at times it seems like he is, with his lurching sashay, and other times he seems riveted by the clientele's tits. It's unusual. If he fucked around some, Boss Cantoni would be better off, that's for sure. He strikes me as someone who's been chaste for millennia. Kind of like me. I've been chaste my whole life. At least I don't take it out on other people. Maybe Cantoni would treat us better if he got laid.

He definitely wouldn't be so obsessed with orifices. Orifices, empty spaces, gaps. An important rule when you work in a megastore is to never let anyone see the gaps. Everything has to be covered with books, DVDs, CDs, cassette tapes, calendars, planners, photos. The megastore is huge, you get the idea? No, huge is reductive. It's an enormous piazza. But—and here's the rub—there are only a few of us to do everything. Sometimes an orifice eludes us. The display wall remains just that, a wall, a hole, a void. If Boss Cantoni doesn't realize it, maybe one of my coworkers comes to save the day. My colleagues are usually dog-tired, though, and might also pass by the gap thousands of times without seeing anything. Boss Cantoni sees it the one thousand and first time. And that's it.

In my first month of work I didn't think a human being could have such a reaction. If they'd have told me, "Zuhra, get ready," well, I'd have laughed. Instead I began changing colors, appearance, essence. I shuddered. My fear was incapacitating. Boss Cantoni doesn't shout, he just makes you feel like a piece of dried-up shit. He takes you to the orifice. You see the yellow wall. He identifies the orifice, menacingly pointing his finger. You keep looking at the yellow wall. He says the word: "hole." Not like we common mortals would, no. His voice becomes metallic. It ricochets. The letters disperse instantly. The *H* seems light years away from the *O* and the same goes for the *L* from the *E*. The sound comes directly from the great beyond. It siphons off your life and energy. You try a remedy, flinging an old Mina record or the *Six Feet Under* box set up on that damn wall. You do something, anything. It doesn't matter if the hole isn't your department's responsibility. It's your fault all the same. You passed by and it was your job to see it, cover it, fix it.

Here's how Libla's three floors are divided. The music department is by the entrance. You'll find everything there, from Celia Cruz's salsa to ABBA ballads. The books are on the lower level: fiction, nonfiction, cookbooks. Films are on the top floor. Everyone in the megastore has a department. When I interviewed they asked me, "What kinds of things do you like, miss?" I remember the question because I was asked by a potato-nosed, tortoiseshell glasses–wearing girl who seemed to be in urgent need of a line of coke. I'm always empathizing with people, this is my biggest problem. "Books," I responded. The tortoiseshell girl said, "What else?" I said, "Film?" The interrogative tone came out of nowhere. The tortoise woman made me doubt myself. Naturally, they placed me in the music department.

Okay, the records are beautiful, they shine like the sun, you can use them to comb your eyebrows, but beyond this what point do they serve? I don't understand anything about them. I tried explaining this to the coke addict. But, *sniff*, and she went into drug-induced shock. Music, what is it? For example, what difference is there between jazz and nu jazz? The fuck do I know? And British pop, how is it any different from Swedish pop? Again, I don't fucking know! The distinction between Brazilian *chorinho* and bossa nova? Huh? Mozart and Salieri? This I do know. Salieri was a scumbag. You have to know music well to sell it. That's how it used to be. Books, though, are something I know well. A lesson on Decadentism? Sure. Aestheticism? Why not? The Generation of '27? *Claro que sí.* How about an annotated reading of Kourouma's *Allah Is Not Obliged?* Goddamn, I can't wait! Even with movies I don't play around. Hell, I was watching Griffith before he became fashionable in Italy and I know all of Fassbinder by heart. I'm not kidding. But music…shit, I'm an amateur.

I'm not always in the music department, so my colleagues don't pay me much mind. They think of me as a kind of prostitute who goes around with anyone. One who isn't faithful to the department or her products. Rita, a big girl who looks like a WWI German tank, told me one day: "You don't deserve to be called a record-seller, you're only a stocker." I'd been working there for two months, and to be stripped of the honorific of record-seller really broke my heart. Rita's face, usually polished and smooth like marble, became grotesque when she said the word "stocker." Her lips suddenly became pendulous, the skin around her nose dried, and her usually curly hair wilted like spaghetti napolitan. Stocker. At Libla it was a repulsive word. Stockers were treated like the untouchables of India. Some tolerated us, others openly displayed their hostility.

The manager never gave us the official title of stockers. He never gave a formal address telling us, "As of today, you are appointed by Libla S.p.A. in the official role of…." No, Cantoni doesn't make speeches. Cantoni acts, and he does it like a bulldozer. He couldn't give two fucks about your feelings. I go back and forth between the records I consider part of my department, then sometimes I go up to the films and other times I cover the kids' section. It's a real mess. I never know how to move things in the kids' section, and when I go there I make a fool of myself. The customers lose their patience and swear at me, which is frustrating. I'm a good worker. I don't deserve offensive words.

Mom doesn't know this side of being a stocker. Otherwise who would bear it anymore? She already thinks I'm unhappy. The phone call with her left a bitter taste in my mouth. I'm going to snack on good cassata. Then I'll shut myself in this cesspit of a room they gave me. I have to take the entrance exam for Arabic school. I have no choice but to study. I'm shitting my pants just thinking about it.

THE REAPARECIDA

I have very large hands. The right one is slightly swollen. They've always been this way: barely feminine, an aesthetic failure. I have reservations talking about my hands. I've been ashamed of them for as long as I can remember. Honest to God, they were dreadful. I say they "were" because I've gotten somewhat (not very) used to their chunkiness. But before, when I was a girl, I wanted to cut them off, those dreadful paws. They unsettled me. They felt like a foreign body light years away from me, from my dreams.

Today I'm an adult. No, what am I saying, I'm old and, come to think of it, I'm still ashamed. The feeling hasn't completely subsided. It's ridiculous. I'm already decaying, certainly my fat hands shouldn't concern me. They should be the last thing on my mind. Instead they're still the first. The years go by, priorities change, and still we suffer from fourteen-year-old bullshit. More than my hands, shouldn't it be my flaccid thighs? My saggy chest? I have wrinkles around my mouth, my forehead is so full of creases that it looks like one of Ikea's mass-produced striped rugs. My hands should be the least of my concerns, *carajo*. I stand in front of my tiny bathroom mirror every morning (the one that reflects my best image) grappling with the passage of time. I saturate myself with creams, salves, elixirs of purportedly everlasting life. I anoint myself with oils as though I were an oven-ready cake. But it's still my hands that vex me.

Maybe it's because I wanted to be a pianist like Rosalyn Tureck. Not too many people remember her, but she was a goddess. I wanted to play the piano like her. I wanted to soar on those ebony and ivory keys like a deranged tightrope walker. My fingers would've danced vehemently and perhaps what would've come out was a symphony or a motif to be sung softly between one thing and the next. I dreamed fancifully of exquisite nails and oblong fingers, like a vampire's. One hand able to caress and remediate. One miraculous hand, the hand of a saint. Things turned out differently. I had a truck driver's hands. My parents didn't have the money to pay for piano lessons. Ernesto was already taking them. Mother said: "You've got no future with those giant hands," and she wasn't just talking about the piano. I was useless to Mother. My dream was in shambles. Goodbye Rosalyn Tureck.

My fingers were thick, square, massive. Mother made sure I knew it every day. She scolded my imperfections. She wanted a daughter who resembled her in both charm and malice. Instead, she got me. She never did abide it, and if it wasn't Mother making me notice the defects of those stubby fingers, some especially odious companion would think to do it. My nails were so thick they made you think of exertion, manual labor, the plebs. My hands were not of noble stock. They were adapted to hard work—southern hands, like those of my parents. They were wide, but not extraordinarily long. Compared to the rest of my body, my hands were ridiculously big. They were broad and used to holding objects. They looked like spheres more than anything.

By contrast, Ernesto had beautiful hands. He knew how to play the piano. He skipped between the black and white keys like a grasshopper. When he played, he was happy. Ernesto was always happy.

I didn't become a pianist. I didn't follow in Rosalyn Tureck's footsteps. I didn't follow in anyone's footsteps, actually. For a little while I was a goalkeeper. Don't laugh, I'm serious. A goalie like

Zamora, Bacigalupo, Jašin, Zoff, Banks, *el pato* Fillol. I wasn't half bad. If my vagina weren't an obstacle, I could've lifted a world cup in the air. To play soccer, and certainly to make money off it, one needed a penis. It was unjust. Think about it, today someone could've had an old poster of me hanging in their back shop. Maradona and me. Instead, no penis, no poster. Just a vagina that has brought me a great deal of trouble. And it's not me on the wall, but Maradona, still skinny in his Naples jersey.

Even my papa had one of those posters in his backroom. Of course, it wasn't of Diego Armando Maradona. In his time, people doted over Di Stefano, that player with the face of a sad accountant. Di Stefano was one of the greats, and among the most humble. The man on Papa's poster, however, was Amadeo Raúl Carrizo. He was with River. A man who revolutionized what it meant to be in the goal. They should've treated soccer like Western history—a BC and an AC, before Carrizo, after Carrizo. Before him, players used to block with their bare hands; they'd scratched each other while the ball slipped away like silk. The risk of doing serious damage to one's own team, letting a ball get away into the goal, wasn't that remote. Amadeo Raúl wore gloves, he was the first. Genius idea. He was also unquestionably the first who left the penalty area to defend the goal with his teammates, not to mention the first to kick from one end of the field as a means of attack. He was a teammate and friend to Di Stefano. Yes, that sad accountant who brought glory to Real Madrid.

Maybe it's because of the poster that I also rooted for River Plate. Mother was, as expected, with Boca Juniors. Ernesto too. Mother would say to me, "River is a pompous team. You're just one of the rabble. Like Boca." It was true. I denied it. I had feelings of grandeur. With an aristocrat's body and a laborer's hands. I was ashamed of myself. River let me dream. I felt different, cleaner, cheering for River. It gave me the illusion that my station in life would improve, that I wouldn't always be confined to the slums where Mother thought I would flail. Plus I loved the team colors.

They were taken from Saint George's flag, a red cross on a white background. The red was like blood and the white was like a kind of milk you could swim in, where you could exist (or resist?). It was the Genoese coat of arms, from Papa's city. Many of River's founders came from the port city. That's why I listen to De André nowadays. I like everything that comes from there. Papa didn't speak much of Genoa, but when he did, I was awestruck. I was with River for Papa and for Amadeo Raúl Carrizo. Papa wasn't a fan of River. He didn't root for anyone. He was perpetually tired. I wonder if Carrizo had ended up in the store's supply room accidentally.

It was my hands that got the attention of the boys on the Santiago field. The day was more humid than usual in Buenos Aires. High humidity was one thing *porteños* were used to from the cradle. It exceeded human imagination, seeped inside you, the bastard heat, down to the marrow. Five-year-olds already stricken with rheumatism. The boys of Santiago field asked me to be the goalie for their ragtag team. They were missing one Ruiz Hernández Blasetti. He had chicken pox and that was the main challenge for the brawny kids of Pepe Rinaldo corner, which wasn't a neighborhood, but a residential courtyard that just so happened to be called that. The matches took place between either end of the courtyard. The team names were randomly assigned, too. One day you were from Santiago and two weeks later you came from Pepe Rinaldo, then after a month the cards would be reshuffled and you'd end up on Claudio Ramírez. There were classics that lasted for years, others that disappeared after a day. My first team was Santiago and so was my last.

Because of my hands, they didn't realize I was a girl right away. I was on my way home. I had to do homework at my friend Ana Franca's house but she was running a fever and Doña Rosalba, her mother, gave me a piece of pie and said, "Go straight home, *hija*, and don't stop for any reason. Tomorrow you have your history exam." Ana Franca and I had to study. I enjoyed history;

I wasn't worried. The pie was great, especially the browned crust. Ana Franca's mom had a way with sweets. I ate very well at my classmate's house. At my house, there was only disgusting salted fish and bread. Every now and then someone would indulge in *asados*, but no sweets, not even a miserable stale cookie. Mother wasn't a great cook. In general, she wasn't anything special on other domestic fronts either. Our clothes were drab, almost completely faded.

I didn't listen to Doña Rosalba's advice. It was Alfredo's fault. He was a little guy with a pockmarked face, distended like a rat's. He had a kind spirit, though. He looked shorter than me, but if he really straightened out his shoulders he surpassed me by a few centimeters. His face contorted in the effort. He gnashed his teeth. Then he said something to me like, "I think you'd make a great goalkeeper" or "We're short a goalkeeper." I don't know the exact words, but I do know they recruited me. I'd never seriously played soccer before that game. I don't know why I agreed. Because I liked a challenge? The team introduced themselves. There was Chico, El Brujo, Mono, Lorenzo García, all boys my age or older. When they asked what my name was I said Ernesto. And that was that, pats on the back all around. From Alfredo, only a flick on the cheek. They were very affectionate boys. They had *esprit de corps*. I was inexperienced. I'd had a little fun with Ernesto doing a few crosses from time to time, but Lord, I'd never stood in goal. I recklessly accepted, since my desire to belong to a group was stronger than my fear of making a fool of myself. I simply threw myself into a new adventure. I also did it because I didn't have many friends. Ana Franca, sure, but besides her there was basically no one. I was bashful and everyone teased me because of my hands. I couldn't endure it and I shut up like a clam. Those boys, though, wanted me *because* of my hands. I played well and made two decent saves. I had good luck with games, any game. I could intuit my opponent's moves when they entered my zone. I knew how to beat them. I got dirty. Returning home, I got an earful from my mother. I didn't tell her about the soccer. She gave me a good scolding.

I lasted for six games on Santiago before I was unmasked. Betrayed, I should say. I'd been followed. She became suspicious because of the filthy clothes. I had a habit of stealing Ernesto's shorts. Then I'd artfully place them in his dirty laundry. She knew Ernesto couldn't sully his shorts like that. And everything smelled like me. Feminine, like menstrual blood.

I was splendid in my improvised athletic wear. I'd cobbled together a pair of kneepads. I lined my hips with rags to soften the falls and I wore a real pro's hat. I didn't make many saves in that game. We were better than our opponents. I fired up my teammates. Then, I don't know when, Mother appeared. She stood in the middle of the field. No one dared say anything to her. She came toward me and, as in the worst comic strips, took me by the ear. She pulled me away saying, "Haven't you realized she's a girl?"

What a shame, I liked being the goalkeeper, holding that ball between my hands. It gave me a sense of power. My hands were beautiful when they held a ball.

All of Santiago ended up in Esma. Everyone, no exceptions. Even Ana Franca was kidnapped. She's still a *desaparecida*. But she wasn't taken to Esma. I forgot where. Years later I saw Alfredo Díaz again, the one who'd recruited me. His gaze was lost in the nothingness.

Do you see? I can't be consistent or chronological. I tell you things haphazardly, as they happen. That's not what I wanted. You know, I let the inspiration of the moment take me away. I'm here, on Carthage Amilcar beach, and they're scrimmaging in front of me. I'm reminded of myself, of the Carrizo poster, of Ana Franca and her mother who made stupendous pies, of Santiago. When boys play they are beautiful, careless, happy. Who could've thought about Esma with a ball between their feet?

They also put your uncle Ernesto in Esma. Here we are again. I've told you this thousands of times already. I'd like to retie the strings of the matter. That's why I repeat myself. But I'd also like to get lost along the way. Retying frightens me, yet I must do it.

Esma. I hope you never forget this name. Write it in your diary. Tattoo it on your body. Repeat it dozens of times. Mark it on whatever post-it notes you've got. Teach it to your dearest friends. Add it to your cellphone memos. Do not forget. Your uncle ended up in there. All of Santiago ended up in there. You can't forget it. It would be like killing them again.

For a while I tried forgetting that accursed name. I tried to forget I had a brother named Ernesto. At night, though, I dreamed of Jesus Christ using the *picana* on him, that awful instrument of torture whose name no one in Argentina wanted to hear anymore. Thinking of it makes me want to vomit.

I only learned who had been detained in Esma afterward. We discovered many things afterward. Before, nobody knew, they suspected. Rather, we all pretended not to know. They kidnapped our neighbors and we covered our ears as forcefully as we could. The soldiers turned the radio volume up. You couldn't overthink if one day you didn't see Veronica again, who always went to buy bread for her mother. Beautiful smile, eighteen years old, a baby bump, her whole life ahead of her. Then suddenly, no more Veronica, no more bread for her mother, and her child perhaps adopted by assassins. These were recurring things in Argentina. One couldn't fret about it. An entire country was desaparecido. Everyone pretended like things were fine. You went grocery shopping, you planned parties, you watched the World Cup. When someone you knew was swallowed up, *chupado*, as they say now, you thanked the on-duty military for turning the volume up. Hearing a man scream like slaughtered veal did not sit well with anyone, and it ruined your digestion.

Anyway, I knew nothing about Esma. We knew other things about Ernesto, like how they took him, for instance. Only Mother tried learning more. She was the only one who never stopped knowing. I had no cognition of anything. Where, why, what.

Where they had taken him, why him, what he did. I constantly asked myself, Why? For what? And above all: Where? Where? Where?

I didn't know they were torturing him so close to our home. We're from the northern part of Buenos Aires. Esma, too, is in the North, in an area flattened east to west by myriad streets and alleyways. Avenida Comodoro, Avenida Rivadavia, Avenida Lugones, Avenida del Libertador, Avenida…

Today, Esma is a memorial museum. In that putrid detention center, they celebrate the finest Argentinian youth exterminated by the military in the '70s.

I wonder if there's a point in having a museum there now, in that way. Well, I shouldn't really be talking. I'm the last one to say anything. I wasn't much better than the torturers, since I was a vulgar accomplice to the system. A parasite. They say that because of memory, Nunca Más will take effect in all parts of the world. But we know that torture often still happens. It happens at Guantanamo, it happens at Abu Ghraib.

I'm glad schoolchildren now visit the torture rooms, see the horrific sites, *capucha* after *capucha*, and the equipment required to apply the picana to the detainees' genitals. There's another purpose, too. We Argentinians can no longer fully rejoice. I would say that we human beings can no longer fully rejoice. Memory cannot be enclosed by four walls, even if those are Esma's walls. Memory shouldn't be politically correct, much less a destination for a humanitarian vacation. I can see it already, the moral crusader-tourist who, after Chiapas, Cuba, and Santiago Bernabéu Stadium, arrives in Buenos Aires at 8200 Avenido del Libertador, at Esma. Armed with good intentions—not to mention a digital camera— in search of uncomplicated emotions. I imagine the tourist immortalizing farcical poses in that building. I see him months later, in his bland and tranquil house in the Global North, explaining the powerful sensations of that horrible tour to his friends. Bona fide tourists, pretty photographs, enthusiastic comments from his buddies, someone thinking of going the next year. But I wonder, does any of this help Argentina?

We Argentinians snicker and think: "It's done." We are thoroughly, sincerely convinced that with humanitarian tourism and a few institutional ceremonies we'll get through it. We think that period is closed forever and we can finally look to the future. Maybe that's true. The museum makes sense only if memory becomes flesh, if memory is active. Does it make any sense if the criminals go unpunished? If the criminals are honored? And the reasons behind the extermination left unexamined? What sense is there? Today it's worse. The country lives in an immense cultural and moral void. Neoliberal politicians make us into slaves. When Menem was still in charge, everyone reinvented something about themselves. Their nose, their breasts, a new chunk of fat on their buttocks. It was the country where plastic surgeons made the most money. Then what happened? The illusion of being rich and white went away. In our hearts we returned to the Third World, and the old wounds of the past reopened. In fact, they had never closed.

Esma, Escuela de Mecánica de la Armada. It was enormous. So many trees. Like a playground, a park for martyrs. Your uncle was tortured there before being "transferred," that is, killed. I don't know how long they kept him. Maybe six months, perhaps a year or two. But not three. He was still alive when the World Cup was going on. His girlfriend told me that. They probably gave him an injection like all the others and tossed him from a plane. He would have been smashed. Dispersed, in scraps, dissolved by the stomach acids of some flesh-eater. I hope they ate him right away. I think an animal's stomach is a good tomb, better than putrefying in the open air.

At that point we didn't know anything. We waited for our swallowed-up loved ones. The mothers waited more than anyone. Your grandmother waited, her hopes never faded. I never believed he'd return. Mother hated me for that. She spit on me and called me *traidora*. She was right. I was, in a certain sense.

She was a particular woman, your grandmother Renata. She'd adopted the Portuguese grit from her father and the Spanish stubbornness from her mother. She knew how to cook salted codfish like few others on this earth. But if you asked her to cook something else, she poisoned you. She was not a fantastic cook. She would knit, singing fado. She may have made love singing fado. I still remember those inconsolable songs. There was one I liked a lot. It spoke of the fear of eternity. Mother sang that calming, melancholy song whenever you were with her.

We threw many parties. Ernesto was like mother. He sang, but with a modern twist. He liked Dylan, as well as the Beatles and the Rolling Stones. He never believed in the rivalry between the two bands. He was right. He loved fado most of all. Sometimes he would grab his guitar and accompany Mother in one of her ballads of betrayal, jealousy, and death. He mixed Portuguese with the Lunfardo of tango. Mother and Ernesto's styles blended. They were fantastic. They would drag your intestines out from the sarcophagus of your bones. I shivered for weeks whenever I listened to those Portuguese words I barely understood. They hit me straight on like a fist.

"I'm Maria Severa's heir," Mother told everyone. No one in Buenos Aires knew about Maria Severa. My father, the son of Italians, at best knew of Caruso. No one had ever heard anyone speak of Maria. I took a survey once among my peers. "*Loca*," was the response I got. Mother stood, statuesque with her immense chest, and repeated that name infinitely, Maria. Then, solemnly, she said her last name too: Severa. On those occasions, my father became as small as a Dachshund puppy. Only his moustache stayed upright on a face otherwise made invisible. It was obvious that he would die soon. When Ernesto was kidnapped, he'd been dead for more than three years. It was a blessing. At least he believed we were happy.

Then I learned who Maria Severa was—a prostitute. She sang in the slums of an alcoholic Lisbon. Mother was also from the slums. She put fish under salt in the mornings and might have let herself have some in the evenings. She never told us anything about her, about her past life, about Portugal. She sang, but never reminisced. I don't know how she came to Argentina. It's almost as though her life began with her love for my father, that dark Italian who reeked of misery and humor. They were a stunning couple.

I couldn't say the same of Carlos and I. I was very Italian. I'd inherited that skittishness and ruggedness from my father. I don't believe I inherited anything from the Portuguese. Another kind of ruggedness, perhaps. Carlos, though, he was perfection. His colors never clashed. He was pastel-hued. I think of the soldier's water hazing rituals when he, with his pastel colors, had entered naval school. I imagine water sliding delicately over his soldierly body. It doesn't drench him, it doesn't disturb the perfection of his military colors. Carlos had studied at Esma. It was a school. A school with desks and pencils. On one side, there were those who studied, the professors who gave lessons. On the other, there was an area designated for torture. Carlos was there before, at Esma. He'd gotten in by working like a mule. Then he returned later. He put the picana on people's testicles. He didn't tell me these things when we went to bed together, at first. He often fucked me from behind. I rarely looked him in the eyes. If I did, I might have seen the capuchas of the people who went through his hands. He applied the picana to people's testicles. I learned it after we were together for some time.

My mother also knew. One evening, she slapped me and said: "*No mereces que te llame puta.*" It was a slap without fury. Something like an observation. She had been a *puta*. She knew that all whores retained a shred of dignity. I'd gambled that away. I let myself get fucked from behind by someone who may have tortured my brother.

I should tell you about Ernesto, though I don't know what to say. He was a brother like any other, perhaps better than others. He ran himself into the ground at the *villas miserias*. He wasn't a politician. He only believed that humanity had to help itself out. They took him along with his betrothed. They called her *Flaca* because she was skeletal, a stalk. Her real name was Rosa Benassi. She also had an Italian father. She, however, was not unrefined. She had a face from the Renaissance, like one of Leonardo's Madonnas. With none of the ruddiness, though. She was too thin.

I met her in Rome five days after meeting your father.

I'd like to tell you about her. That's why I'm writing.

THE PESSOPTIMIST

The bundle was ready. The year was 1975. The mother began telling her daughter about her first departure from Mogadishu, when she left everything to follow her man, her daughter's father. "Everybody came to see me off and you were so small, Zuhra." A sob caught in her throat. Maryam Laamane found herself crying again. She had always been quick to cry. She didn't know how to refuse the past. She restarted the recorder many times. She pressed stop and then record and then stop once more and then went back to hear herself again, forward to get past herself, then she pressed record again. She was having a good time. The two-colored buttons were like a toy piano to her. They rekindled her childish spirit, which was never completely dormant. She had fun. The buttons were a distraction but her voice didn't entertain her at all. It was serious and solemn. No, Maryam, what are you doing? That won't do. You're too composed. Do you want that poor girl to die of boredom? Of course, Zuhra wasn't a little girl anymore, but an exquisite, thirty-year-old big girl. She was a woman. Yet she saw her as a child. She had wanted more than anything to overwhelm her with cuddles and hugs. But people didn't do that in Somalia, people didn't touch one another that much. *Eeb*, a shame. Because of that, people tried loving each other without touching excessively. And those who were touched hid behind some wall.

Maryam rewound the tape and began relating the time when she'd prepared her luggage and took a plane to join her husband, Elias, in his Italian exile. "I don't know why I'm starting from the middle," the woman said, "I've never been good at respecting the order of time and words. Howa Rosario complained about it all the time. She said that my stories had no rhyme or reason, you couldn't understand anything, it was hard keeping up. But you do, Zuzu, you keep up with Mama. I'm trying to piece together all the fragments of us."

In the middle of Maryam Laamane's story was the journey. Before that, an image of her nostalgia: her neighborhood, her tribe come to say farewell on that day in 1975. Maryam, a young woman at the time, had a heavy heart. She knew she wasn't leaving for vacation. They knew it too. The whole neighborhood, the entire tribe. Everyone had a thousand requests.

"If you see Nur, can you bring him this handmade *otka*? Nur loves meat. He stirs it with rice. Don't forget, Maryam. Nur loves it so much." And if it wasn't otka for Nur, it was some other devilry to take to the land of the whites. In the end Maryam was weighed down with bags. Farewells and bags from those who had loved ones overseas.

"I can't take anything else, I'm sorry. Maximum is twenty kilos of luggage, they told me. Otherwise they'll throw everything away," she explained to her neighbors. "Friends, please, I can't…" They were not offended. Some, however, kept insisting, because you never know. Maybe at customs the police would turn a blind eye, and besides, Maryam was so beautiful, certainly she would be able to add a little something. Everyone knew that customs officers let attractive girls add a tiny bit more. She only needed to try, to take a chance. "But here, my dear. It doesn't weigh anything. My package is light, see? It won't cost you a thing to take it. That way you can make Nur happy. Poor boy, he's so homesick. When he calls me he always speaks of our fat, fragrant grapefruits. Who knows what he would give for a good taste of sweet grapefruit.

Where he is, and where you're going, my dear, the grapefruits are sour. They burn your stomach. They make you cry. May God curse Barre and his progeny. Ah, all our children go away. They want to light a fire under my Nur's ass, you know? Because he thinks, Nur's someone who thinks a lot. Day and night. Would you bring my Nur some grapefruits? They don't weigh much, I swear! Squeeze them in there, right there…on the side. They don't take up space, you see? It's so easy. My Nur thinks. He needs some sweet grapefruits to be able to keep doing it."

The people insisted. Maryam felt guilty for not being able to help everyone. Those were deplorable years. Barre came to power on October 21, 1969. He lit fires under everyone's asses. With communism as an excuse, he said that everyone was equal, but that he was more equal than others and was entitled to more because the country couldn't do without him. Maryam committed his speeches to memory. She studied his words so that she could use them one day in the chamber of an international tribunal. Those words were written with the blood of Somalis, those who stood in opposition, those who dreamed of a true democracy, those who wanted to live a dignified life.

Even the common people couldn't stomach Siad's lies. They knew he would never defend them, the story he told on every radio show and in every official speech about the Ethiopian enemy at the borders was a scam, and the nation's only enemy was the man himself. Many decided to leave Somalia, "for a little while, at least until he kicks the bucket. Until democracy returns."

It was the seventies and people still believed in the future. No one at the time thought, however, that their escape would become an eternal destiny for Somalis, an ineluctable karma. No one imagined that twenty years later a war would break out between brothers, between Somalis, to divide the blood-soaked power that tyrant Barre left behind. A hemorrhage of people, ceaseless, shameless, everlasting. Somalis began leaving in the seventies because of politics and continued in the eighties because of famine, in the nineties because of civil war, and so forth, without interruption, in 2000, 2001, 2002, 2003, and today, at this exact moment, all the time. There is always fleeing, a notorious and nearly unavoidable fate for Somalis. First there was Barre the communist, who requested a glass of blood every morning, and meanwhile people left arm-in-arm with the Americans and the thieves of the Italian Socialist Party. The war was left to others, those with strange names and startling hunger.

"Would you bring some grapefruits to my Nur? Allah will repay you. Allah is sure to repay the generous."

Maryam was about to join her husband. She felt good because soon she would kiss Elias on the mouth. She dreamed of his breathing every night. She took the sack of grapefruits and tucked them in the side of her bundle, squashing them a bit. "Nur lives in Milan," they explained. *What is Milan?* Maryam Laamane wondered. She was only familiar with Termini Station. They'd told her to go there and make no detours because that was where people reimagined their dreams. That was where people found all the Somalis again. She knew that because Elias was at the station and he'd written her a letter. What was Milan? Was it far, this Milan? Could you walk there from Termini Station? Would the grapefruits last until then?

A kiss on the right cheek. One on the left. The third on the forehead. From everyone. A hug. Another hug. For everyone. A tear. For her. Busy as she was with packages and grapefruits, Maryam almost didn't notice her auntie's shadow. The shadow was quite menacing, partly because her auntie never hugged anyone. Usually, as everyone knew, she opened her mouth only to reprove. Sometimes she gave advice, but only in front of her *burjiko*, her coal-fired oven. She was a mature auntie, aging with few pleasures. Maryam shuddered. She was leaving. All she wanted was hugs, not nerves.

The woman came to give her a hug. Maryam felt suffocated, like she was dying. Her auntie didn't want others to see that she was hurting from this departure, and so she hid her face in her niece's wide bosom. Maryam was astounded. Despite wanting the old woman's affection, she hadn't expected it. The *shaash* barely covered her auntie's head. She looked like a spinster who didn't know how to behave in front of people. Her scarf slid indecently down her neck. Maryam tried readjusting it some, indiscriminately. She thought about how things never stayed put on her beloved auntie's head. A pointless task, the hand slow, the fall swift. Hair to the wind, her auntie was like a virgin. No one noticed the hair. No one was scandalized. Her niece noticed, though. She saw that her auntie had an intricate white forest on her head. The smell of ginger mixed slightly with that of mildew. It was the odor of experience, a good smell, of someone who sees the world for what it is.

Her auntie knew the ways of the world very well. Maryam had always known this. She knew it even though she'd never left Somalia. "Take this money," she said to her niece, "it will help you over there in Italy." Italy —that was where the girl was going. Italy. Termini Station. It was big money. Ancient. Maryam looked it over. It was like nothing she'd seen before. She didn't say a word. She accepted the gift, folded the enormous banknotes and stuck them in her bra, as though they were rarities, as though someone would actually want to steal them. The bundle was ready. "Niece, go and write me. Tell me whether there are women with three breasts in Italy like they told me."

Yes, Auntie, I'll tell you, the niece thought, *I'll tell you about the three breasts and the five mouths and, yes, I'll tell you about the holes in the Colosseum, but let me go now, let me go because I have a long journey ahead.* Her aunt held her tightly by the arm.

"You will miss this land, girl. You will miss it, you know that?"

After that she gave her, in addition to the money, a small sack filled with sand. "I took it at Seguunda Lido early this morning. Smell it when you feel bad."

Maryam placed the sack in her handbag. Too bad her bra

was already occupied by those oversized bills. The sack contained something genuinely precious. She would make Elias smell it, too, as soon as she arrived at her destination, by her lover's side.

Auntie Salado, as the staid woman was called, had said she'd slept with an Italian during the years when the fascists were Somalia's masters.

She grabbed Maryam by the arm. "Remember to get a good look at the three-breasted women!"

"Yes, Auntie Salado, I'll tell you about the women with three breasts and five mouths, I'll tell you about the holes in the Colosseum. I'll tell you everything. Let me go now. Otherwise I'll miss the flight. Let me go." The aunt reluctantly let go of her arm. It was the last time they saw one another. *Auntie Salado, tell me, were you in love with the Italian who made you his?*

"It's a shame you never met Auntie Salado, my Zuhra. She made the best *sanbusi*." Maryam's recording meandered aimlessly. That's how it was when she began telling a story from the middle, everything seemed permissible. Going forward, doubling back, stopping, losing oneself. Maryam was reminded of two days earlier. She was at Termini, about to board the train that would take her to Prima Porta to bury Howa Rosario, and she ran into that idiot Gor Gor. Oh, how she hated that man. The Vulture, everyone called him. An old Somali drunk who begged for spare change to buy shots. And if you didn't give it to him there was hell to pay. He called you *sharmuta* in all the languages of the world. If you didn't give it to him you were a whore, *sharmuta, puttana, putain, puta*. Maryam Laamane didn't like that imbecile at all. She didn't like drunks in general. They reminded her too much of herself when she was one of them, when she was seduced by the translucence of gin in the early morning. She'd been like Gor Gor. She begged for change for a few drops of gin and people, not just Somalis, laughed behind her back, repulsed. Gor Gor was also obsessed with Mussolini. He thought himself a fascist. Ridiculous, a black fascist!

The morning she went to bury Howa Rosario, Gor Gor was declaiming the Duce's words. The year 1936, the imperial year. Maryam told her daughter this in the recording. She emphasized the word "imperial" with a quiver of indignation in her voice. There was nothing imperial about puny little Italy; it was merely a clump of voracious people who didn't know how to ask for forgiveness. Gor Gor's words bounced brazenly off the walls. Those words still hurt Maryam, who was curled up in front of the recorder in the middle of her living room. She tried not making a big deal of it. The words were sharpened like a porcupine's quills. It was difficult not to feel them, they stung. She wouldn't die, but they opened wounds nonetheless. Maryam didn't like remembering that year. 1936. Her wrath was depleted by the violence inflicted upon her family. It was the year her father died.

He died, they'd told her, on Graziani's southern front. She didn't remember much about that man who died at the Battle of the Ogaden. She didn't know anything about him except that he had very large hands and had gone to conquer the empire for the Italians. He was ruddy, this she remembered well, and his skin was almost diaphanous. Not white, but something close to it. There was a photograph of her father that circulated in the family. He was wrapped in white fabric and a turban. Her papa was a *dubat* and he'd gone to fight the Ethiopians in Abyssinia, to invade them, in a sense. It wasn't a pretty thing. He was coerced, like many others, and forced to kill people. He wasn't particularly upset with his Ethiopian neighbors. They were *gaalo*, but who cared. They would have to answer to Allah about their infidelity, it wasn't his job to convert them. In fact, he didn't really think about them at all. But he happened to be summoned. They took him from the street, forced him to leave his job, made him wear two strips of white fabric, and sent him to bring ruin to other blacks like himself. To his brethren, the people of the Horn.

Her father was involved in many battles but didn't die in one. It was an Italian, theoretically on the same side, who killed him. He was cleaning his weapon when a shot inadvertently fired. Even today many argue over "inadvertently." Some of his companions-in-arms maintain that the Italian was a complete swine and that Maryam Laamane's father said something the swine didn't like. Shot fired, father gone, truth uncertain. Her mother died shortly after of a broken heart. Maryam had always lived with her aunts and grandmother.

It was nice living with her aunts, including Auntie Salado, the strictest of them all. They were good to her. Of course, she gave them a lot to deal with when she was small, but the same wasn't true of her brothers. In exchange, they didn't control her too much. Maryam had quite a bit of space for herself in the city. She mostly used it to run. She liked following the flights of falcons from the ground. Maryam yearned to fly all day and find herself a bed on top of a star. Maryam Laamane ran. She ran happily. Her father died on Graziani's southern front, her mother died of a broken heart, but her aunties filled her with sweet words so that she wouldn't think, so that she wouldn't cry. One day as she was running she saw a group of boys. She knew one of them, he was always fighting with her brothers. She passed them as she ran.

"Hey, little girl, I know you, where you going so fast?"

"Nowhere."

"Everyone goes somewhere. Going nowhere's not possible."

The little girl considered this. And, truthfully, she didn't know where she was headed. "You're right. I don't know where I'm going."

"I know where *I'm* going," the boy said proudly. "Soon I'm going to Italy to visit my father."

"Your father lives that far away?"

"My father, little girl, is from that far. He's Italian. He's beautiful like the sun, he has hair like the sun and glass eyes. Kind of like mine, but his are see-through glass, you can see into his soul. My father's name is Alessandro and he's waiting for me. When he sees me, he'll smother me with kisses and presents. Then I'll become an important man, understand? You can do that over there. Not like here. Here you're nothing. You roll over in the sand. You crawl. I don't want to crawl."

The little girl looked at the boy. She didn't know his name, she knew only that he'd brawled with her brothers. She did notice, though, that he was light-skinned. Could he have been one of the *mission*—those half-blood bastards people whispered about from time to time? *Ugly people, the mission*, they said in passing. You couldn't trust them, they had the invader's blood; they were primed for betrayal. That's why her brothers fought them, because you couldn't trust their kind, they had the blood of too many people mixed within them. And mixtures, everyone knows, are explosive. They do damage. But to Maryam, this mission, this half-blood, was kind. He was amusing and spoke quickly. Sometimes he inserted strange sounds between his words like some kind of baboon. A baboon that favored white.

"I don't like Italians," Maryam said.

She recounted the incident with her father, about Graziani's southern front and the accidental shot.

"The Italians gave your father money. You should be grateful for what you have now. It doesn't look like your family is against the Italians anyway. Seems to me your Aunt Salado was in love with one of them."

In love? The little girl ran. She left the boy without saying goodbye. In love? With an Italian? Auntie Salado? Did Italians even know how to love? If they did, why did they allow her good father to die so senselessly on Graziani's southern front?

No, Auntie Salado was a spinster. She couldn't love an Italian. She was a spinster, a spinster, a spinster. That's what everyone said about her. She didn't like men and people knew she preferred helping her sisters with children. In love with an Italian who was transparent like glass? The Italians Maryam saw on the street terrified her. Their skin was flushed red and oozed liquids. Everyone said these weren't the ones that came before, they weren't rulers—they were helping them become free. Not everyone agreed on this point. Cousin Hibado, for one, didn't agree at all. She said the Somali Youth League would liberate them soon and that those dirty Italians didn't have good intentions. She said the AFIS, the Italian Trusteeship Administration, was a nasty trick. In Maryam's eyes the trusteeship was a huge blunder on the Italians' part, the ones helping them become free. She agreed with Cousin Hibado. No one helps you become free, you either are or you aren't. Some things you can't learn, you simply feel. The adults told her as much. Except Hibado, who told her the exact opposite. She'd been taught that since she was small, she had to believe the adults. Which adult was right? She couldn't make heads or tails of anything anymore. Adults said too many things, all of them confusing. She felt dazed. Howa Rosario hadn't come along yet to bring light into her life and explain that it is often the young who truly understand the way the world works. She didn't yet have her most special friend. She was still rather lonely running behind the falcons. It was the fifties. Soon they would be freed.

The water in the pot boiled, oil in the frying pan. Auntie Salado in front of the burjiko like a captain at the wheel. Auntie Salado at the burjiko was fast. She pirouetted like a firefly, spreading a pleasant fragrance that no one was immune to.

Chaos in the Middle East, guerilla warfare on the frontier. Guerilla warfare of ideas, chaos of emotions. Serene Auntie Salado in front of the burjiko, encased in her aromas. Maryam Laamane short of breath. Chasing falcons was strenuous.

"Auntie, *habaryar*, there's a boy that says you were in love with an Italian." As soon as she said it, Maryam bit her tongue. She should've greeted her first, settled in. Maryam felt like she'd made a huge mistake. Maybe she should've waited to eat first. The smell was so good! Now she risked losing it. Auntie Salado had made meat and rice. You could smell it from afar. Every Thursday night she made meat and rice, both at once, because the day after was Good Friday and it was only right to mark that day with a little cheer. She also smelled potatoes and carrots. Then, alongside that, distant but powerful, was green coconut *bisbas*. Ooh, coconut, what paradise! She liked its sweet aftertaste of crystal and sand. She would forfeit the coconut because of her irreverent tongue. Surely Auntie Salado would get angry and tell her it wasn't good for little girls to talk about adult things. God's angels, the ones everyone carries on their shoulders, the ones that record our sins, would sew her mouth shut because she, Maryam Laamane, was a bad girl. That the angels would sew her mouth shut didn't matter to her so much, but losing the wonderful food did. She would regret it, mostly because of the coconut. "Ah, my stupid big mouth," the girl whimpered. She made a penitent face to try and move that marble-hard relative to pity.

Auntie Salado looked at her from where she stood. She did nothing else for a while. She didn't comment on what was said. She looked at her and that was all. Her face betrayed no emotion. Then she returned to the food frying over the fire. She couldn't burn it. The girl sat on a *gember* and awaited her punishment. She couldn't leave as if nothing had happened. She had to wait for her aunt to get angry and tell her decisively, "No dinner. Go to bed." So she waited on the gember. Out of boredom, Maryam twiddled her thumbs. Soon she had enough of that and started watching the flaky ceiling. There was a lizard and an orange butterfly. They were dancing. The lizard wheeled around the butterfly. The latter had no fear. It orbited, challenging the lizard, which didn't even want to do it harm. Maryam wondered whether they would marry after their dance.

"Hey, little girl, what are you looking at?"

"Don't you think that lizard is gorgeous, Auntie?"

"Yes, you're right. I think it's because it's searching for something to make it warm inside."

"Why, because it's cold?"

"Yes, all reptiles are cold. Like us, dear. Men and women, we're also cold if we don't find heat somewhere."

"The lizard is looking for heat in the butterfly?"

"Right now, yes, dear, don't you see how it's spinning?"

"Will it find it there?" the girl asked skeptically.

"No. The heat is inside its own stomach. The butterfly has no heat to give, it will die in a few hours. When the lizard learns how to warm itself, then it will also know how to love. It won't dance that agonizing dance anymore."

The girl watched her auntie. She was very tall. She had a *shaash* on her head, like a bride, though she'd never been one. It sat lopsided and precarious. A stunning spiced aroma rose from the burjiko. It was freezing inside the lizard's stomach. And inside her auntie's?

Little Maryam placed an ear to her auntie's stomach. She burned herself. Her auntie was warm, boiling.

Days later, Cousin Hibado dragged the girl and old woman onto the city streets. "You can't stay at home and watch. You two have to step into history as well."

Maryam found Cousin Hibado sort of curious with her white dresses and black belts. Politics was constantly on her mind.

"We'll free ourselves. You'll see. We'll free ourselves. Even if these apologists for the Italians still want to be slaves, the people are no longer with them. From now on, they believe in those of us with the League."

The family was in awe of that enthusiastic girl. She put her feet on the table and shouted verses to her soon-to-be homeland, free and united Somalia.

Those years were fleeting. After the war that ravaged the world on account of the piggish North, the South had decided that it was no longer the era of slavery and that it could live differently. Certainly it could be said that the piggish North had tired of colonialism, that by then it no longer benefited them to own and support their territories in the South directly, that there were more frugal ways of controlling and taking advantage of the people. After the great war, the second one, the piggish North told the poor South: "Do whatever you like, we won't stop you." But it wasn't really like that. The North still decided who got to be free, when, and by what means. Somalia was to be supervised, it had been decided. Not all Somalis agreed. There was the League. There were people like Cousin Hibado.

"Where are you dragging us off to, Hibado? Where are you taking us? Where are you taking this little girl and old woman?"

"We're going to demonstrate and protest for our freedom. For the rights of bodies and souls. That's where I'm taking the little girl and old woman."

The streets were full of people packed along the curbs like stockfish. Or schoolchildren. Men and women workers. The people. They stood, waiting on the roadsides. For what? The Italian Trusteeship Administration. That was what would govern them for ten years and teach these ignorant Somalis democracy, so it was decreed in a faraway country. In New York. In a palace made entirely of glass.

Everyone was lining the streets. The Italian administrator was about to arrive. They had to welcome him. The administrator arrived by car, looking out the windows. He saw nothing but the people's backs. Asses and backs, necks and hair. He saw only the rear, never the front. The people turned and faced the other way as he passed. They were rejecting him.

Hibado squeezed the hands of the little girl and the old woman. Maryam understood that this wasn't a game, but an adult matter, perhaps the history that Hibado was always going on about.

On their way home, her auntie told her about the Italian. It was not a nice story because the Italian never made her laugh.

"Elias made me laugh a lot," Maryam told her daughter, who didn't know that she would be the future owner of those cassettes. That said, the woman pressed the stop button. That was enough for one day.

THE FATHER

It had been a long time since the rain fell that hard.

My old soccer field was covered in green. My old field—I scored so many goals there. Your sister's mother was a goalkeeper when she was younger. She also played on a field like this. She was from Buenos Aires. Beautiful, exceedingly so, but she didn't know it. I loved her very much. We kept one another company during a terrible period. I do hope your sister is like her, at least somewhat, with her grit if nothing else. And you, Zuhra, are you like Maryam? She didn't love soccer, she liked to go to the movies. She went crazy for them. She was only a girl when I married her. She spoke to me for hours of cowboys and long-braided Indians, the Indians that she loved and who were called *alibesten* in Somalia. I never understood why. Now my old soccer field is full of little kids with AK-47s, their cheeks packed with that hallucinogen they all chew, that damned *qat*. It was different when I played there. We were carefree. Now the children have empty stares. Occasionally, though, when there's a brief respite from the war, rarely, someone brings an old deflated ball. I watch them make a few passes. Sometimes they're pretty good.

The world turned its back on these kids, but behind the world's back they still play, unaware of having already grown up.

Who knows if they dream of making a goal like Maradona's

at the Mexican World Cup in '86 and holding a trophy in the air. Eleven touches of the ball. Eleven magical touches, starting from midfield and going straight to the goal. The older kids are trying it, eleven touches aren't much. Their adversaries fall like bowling pins. The cup is close, poverty far away.

They dream behind the world's back. Even I, old now and worn, maybe I dream, too.

The fields are green and we wait for a carnival that will not come. Perhaps it will come and take us away with its festiveness. It gets dark early in the neighborhood. The elderly sing an old ditty and I prepare to revisit our past again.

Elias was born in Mogadishu, or Xamar, as Somalis like to call it. Xamar is an Arabic name, deriving from *ahmar*, meaning "red."

The name was serendipitous. His mother, Famey, didn't even have a chance to give it to him. She never saw him. She died before hearing his first wail. She was brain dead. Body intact, but the brain dead. The name, his aunts said, was given to him by his father. On the day he was born, they recalled. No one remembers, though, what the hell the weather was like. Aunt Nadifa maintains that there was a powerful wind, Aunt Zahra spoke of a battering rain, while Aunt Mariam remembers an intolerable heat. Only Aunt Binti shrugs and says, "I don't have time to recall such a silly thing."

Majid wasn't present at the birth. Everyone said he'd changed with marriage. They'd noticed the strange crease around his mouth and the eyes that permanently looked elsewhere.

"Ah, marriage changes the spirit. Look at how serious Majid has become. No, he's no longer a boy now."

All the remarks sounded the same. The words used most often were *responsible, wise, conscientious*, and *adult*. In everyone's eyes, Majid was no longer a boy. Goodbye to the crying, the thrills, the fistfights, the laughs. People knew Majid didn't laugh anymore. His lips were hardly ever upturned, and rarely did he show teeth.

The few times he did, it was Famey who made him do it.

Famey… She never lost her will to live. When the Italian and German troops left them suffering and humiliated in the sand, she took his hands between her own and let them rest on her bloody garments. He couldn't look her in the eye.

"Cousin, I am not a man anymore."

"You'll be my man if that's what you want, if you want me."

She taught him to love her again one day at a time, without asking for anything in return. Merely a smile every once in a while. Famey felt sharp pains in her lower abdomen. At night she saw those white men's eyes. "The last one was so small." The little rapist vomited milk on her. Sometimes she would wake in a sweat. Then she would look at Majid, and every night he'd remember that she was the strong one. He didn't know about her nightmares, and he couldn't have consoled her anyway. He felt injured in his humanity and dignity. Maybe he could've run a hand through her hair, as one does with a child. But no, Majid couldn't even do that. After two years of chaste marriage, Famey said to him one night, "We have to." He understood, and they made love as if it were the world's cruelest torture. Rain decided to visit Mogadishu and owls beset the night with tireless verses. He couldn't imagine how to approach that generous woman's body. He got on top of her because it seemed natural to him. He struggled. He held onto her breasts and hurt her. She didn't get wet and he didn't have an erection. They stopped. She caressed his forehead. "We'll try again tomorrow." Every night he grabbed onto her breasts and every night he hurt her. No wetness, no erection. Famey was exhausted. They had to have a child but they didn't have the strength. They had to, so as not to give rise to rumors. People noted the unsteady progress of their marriage. They had to make a child. They had to do it together. "One day we'll get better," Famey said to herself.

One day. It seemed so far away, though.

During those two years in Mogadishu, she learned how to be a seamstress and her husband found work as a cook in an Italian household. It was difficult for them to see men with pale skin. Each time, their faces cracked with fear. Their hands shook as their horror resurfaced. Famey felt her stomach swell and fill with gas. For days afterward, she couldn't eat anything. They only learned later that not all men with pale skin were dangerous.

In Mogadishu, Famey also saw her beloved jalopies again. They thrilled her at first, especially the smoke and horns. Then she began getting used to them and they no longer seemed like such extraordinary things.

It was Mogadishu's colors she found extraordinary. The city was engulfed in white, an immense expanse of complexes as white as snow, like Famey had never seen. The white prevented the sun's heat from entering the homes, someone explained to her. It was a sort of protection from the tremendous equatorial swelter. So different from the brown huts they carried on their backs in the bush. The nomads never had houses. In the bush, they made a provisional space. That space was their house for a little while. They moved their huts, prayed to God, and ate whatever they could find. Then another drought and a new place to seek out and explore. Very different from her city of fishermen, made of a duller white. In Brava, the waves dirtied everything when they moved. In the big city everything was fixed, stable. People found houses in precise locations and didn't move.

In the big city, she and her husband lived with an aunt and a multitude of people from their *qabila*. They had a lovely room, and she put a wicker mat and two chairs inside. One day her husband brought netting and a mattress. "Lugale told me you're supposed to sleep on this. Lugale said we should no longer sleep like the bush people by the sea, we're city folk now." She didn't like the bed that much. The hard wicker mat felt more real. On that so-called mattress they bobbed like a camel's tongue. She felt strange on it. She did like the bed's color, though. It was flame red. Mogadishans loved colors very much, maybe because they lived perennially in white houses. Women and men surrounded themselves with green, azure, pink, fuchsia. She herself bought a chromatic *shaash* to match the masses.

Then one day she got pregnant. She hadn't bled in three months when she told her husband. She only said, "I'm expecting." He didn't react. Famey was upset. Wasn't that what they had been waiting for all that time? Wasn't it the end of their nightmares? Majid had become catatonic. He hardly spoke to anyone. He said only essential words. Good morning, good evening. What should I cook today? Did you buy meat? See you tomorrow. How are you? Goodnight. Only functional words came out of his mouth. Nothing superfluous, nothing wasted.

In the evenings at home, when he wasn't too tired after cooking for the others, he sat on the wicker mat after prayer and unburdened himself of the rosary hanging from his *futah*. The auntie who hosted them was scandalized seeing him at the *burjiko* like a woman. She was scandalized seeing him slice zucchinis, peel potatoes, weigh the rice. She was scandalized seeing him scrape, clean, and clean again. She was scandalized seeing him boil, put things in the fridge, sauté. She was scandalized when she saw him prepare, decorate, garnish. She was scandalized when she put the food in her mouth and found it marvelous. Despite the rosary, the five prayers, the silence born of modesty, the auntie considered her nephew the devil incarnate. Iblis in the flesh. He was too much of a woman to be pure.

Famey knew it was that auntie who instigated the disparaging rumors about her husband's worth. No one would've noticed his effeminate step had she not planted suspicion in the fools. The child she was carrying was necessary. For him, especially for him. Why wasn't he excited? Why didn't his behavior suggest even minimal interest? She was doing it for him, dammit! Only for him. It didn't matter to her whether she had kids or not. She felt empty. All she wanted was to expend the little energy she had left. From that day forward, Famey had a feeling she'd be dead soon. Perhaps she already was, but she refused to admit it. *Idiot, don't you see I'm doing this for you?* she reproved him with her eyes. He didn't look at her, as though the matter didn't concern him at all.

When she went into the throes of labor, Famey knew she wouldn't survive the pain. She was submersed in her blood, drowning in it. The midwife was exhausted and the aunties around her despaired. That was one moment. In the next, Famey was gone.

No one attended to the child. No one looked in the direction of the bundle that was Elias. They thought he was dead, rotting meat. Majid unobtrusively walked into the room of his wife's ordeal. It is said that he merely glanced in the mother's direction and knew. Then he looked at it, the bundle carelessly tossed aside. He approached it, placed a hand on its forehead. They say a person remembers nothing of their own birth, but I know Elias remembers his father's hand on his tiny forehead. A small hand, with tapered fingers that would've been ready to seize life if his dignity hadn't been shattered without warning.

The hand was warm. The same temperature as Elias's heart, the only living thing in that child. The hand warmed the rest of the body. Elias suddenly shivered. His body ignited with a strange light, what they call life. He let out a long, deep cry. The aunties were shaken from their pain and realized that Elias was a lifeless bundle no more.

Majid looked at him and said, "We will call him Elias Hayat."

Hayat, his middle name, a woman's name.

Hayat, Life.

THREE

THE NUS-NUS

"Why is your mom white?"

It was the question everyone asked Mar sooner or later, always, everywhere. It was the through line of every conversation. They asked others about their names, and Mar about her color. White. A color she despised. A color she depended on. A color she sought out like a maniac. Mama was white. Patricia was beyond white.

Antonio Lorenzetti was the first to ask her. She'll never forget the first time. It was in third grade. She'd gone to London with her mom right before. Her mother was obsessed with Virginia Woolf and they'd traced her footsteps around Bloomsbury for a little while. Her mother transformed into Mrs. Dalloway and forgot she had a child. When they returned to Italy, she was in the third grade with Antonio Lorenzetti.

"Why are you black if your mom's white?"

"Exactly, why am I black?"

"No, you have to tell me. Why?"

"I don't know."

"Your mom didn't pass on any of her color to you?"

"Nope, none."

"Your hair is hideous, you know that?"

"What?"

"Disgusting, Mar. Ugly as shit."

"Are you saying I'm a turd?"

"You're black. A nigger like the Africans."

"What are Africans?"

"Poor people. They don't even have shoes on their feet."

"But I have shoes. And I have socks, too."

"When your mom found you, you didn't have them. You were naked. Your mom is white, she has money, she bought you those shoes. And she bought you socks, too."

"What?"

"Africans die of hunger, their bones are outside their bodies they're so skinny. They're kind of gross. Yeah, really gross. They stink, they stink a lot. They never clean themselves."

"Why?"

"Because soap costs a lot. Africans don't even have money for bread. Luckily sometimes they can climb up trees to eat some bananas. Africans are like monkeys, they eat a lot of bananas."

"Bananas are good. I like them."

"Because you're a monkey. Don't you see that you're the same as a monkey?"

"What?"

"Yeah, you are. If I was your mom I would put you in the washing machine. I'd use the bleach from that old lady in the commercials who's always saying, 'Without Straappp.' That way even your irises would be white."

"But white eyes aren't pretty. I don't want white eyes. I'd scare people."

"You still scare people. I know you're a girl, but everyone else doesn't. When people see you they'll scream. No one likes black. It's like the dark. I'm afraid of the dark."

"I like it."

"I know, you're like the dark. Isn't your mom upset you came out black? Didn't she ask the stork to take you back? Or at least to bleach you?"

"No...why?"

Mar always wondered where that reprobate Antonio Lorenzetti ended up. Maybe he sided with New Force.

Mar looked around. The Arabic professor was a fat woman with an endearing face. Each time she wrote a letter on the board, her maternal bottom rocked from right to left. She had one of those berets that was cool in '68 and a chic revolutionary's hair. Mar liked the way she rotated her hand when she wrote a letter. Real art. She didn't write, she painted. She'd written many letters. The *alif*, the *ba*, the *ta*. She liked how she painted the *saad*. The *saad* was a beautiful letter. Mar felt like Michelangelo. She looked at her peers. They were Rembrandt, Raphael, Picasso, Dalí—each of them artists. Everyone was enthralled.

Mar turned away from the board for a moment. She took a survey of the room. Entire continents. In this one room there was Asia, America, Europe, Oceania and, yes, Africa. No one there would've asked her, "Why is your mom white?"

She returned to her piece of paper. She mimicked the professor's gestures and felt like Leonardo da Vinci come to life again. She looked at the *saad* she'd traced in her notebook. Yes, it was beautiful. An honest-to-God Mona Lisa. Mar smiled. For now, Patricia had given her a break.

THE NEGROPOLITAN

Othman Al Bahri. It sounds like the name of someone who lived long ago, someone from the distant past. We only met him six hours ago. Just six hours, clocked, lived. Othman Al Bahri is permanently relegated to my past now. The present began the moment this green cup full of slop—I can't bring myself to call it coffee, it's more like diarrhea—splintered and set a hairy cockroach loose.

Othman Al Bahri. A pretentious name, pompous and grating. It was the name of an important person, no doubt. He's a pain in the ass, now almost more than last night. Who are you, Othman Al Bahri?

"I know," Malick told us. He smiled at us with a certain Dolce & Gabbana charm. An ambiguous smile that persuaded both me and Lucy. We believed him right away, even if Lucy did a little more. His smile was irresistible and, like all irresistible things, treacherous. Malick showed his moon-white teeth, stretching his lips as wide as possible, and we pranced at his feet. I don't know if I'd call it a smile, really. It was a smirk. That was enough for us. We saw it and imitated the way he stretched his lips to show our friendship. The effort caused facial paralysis. Lucy, however, was calm. The fact of the matter was that Malick lied to us. He didn't know Othman. After a few hours, in fact, not even Othman Al Bahri's shadow appeared.

Who is Othman Al Bahri? More importantly, who the hell is Malick?

Meanwhile, I find myself face-to-face with the fattest cockroach I've ever seen in my life. Remarkably, I'm not screaming. I'm not flipping out. I'm not doing anything you'd expect me to do. I'm less of a sissy than I thought. I watch it. It disgusts me. I sip the peculiar drink I've got in the cup, which I won't call coffee. Then I lift my heels, gracefully. My thoughts are still completely absorbed by Othman Al Bahri and last night.

Who are you, Othman? A bloody warlord, a crazy malefactor, a religious pain-in-the-ass, a charming pirate, or a coincidence? Are you tall? Fat? Pock-marked? What are your eyes like, Othman Al Bahri? And your nose? The rest of you? Do you exist? Why did they name this filthy street after you? No one knows where it is, did you know that? We tried finding it for hours. It felt like an eternity, a petty, cheap eternity. Maybe you were never worth much, Othman Al Bahri.

Malick smiled at us last night. Or, he smiled at Lucy and said, "I'll think about it," and then told her what no human being, endowed with even the most minuscule trace of life, should ever say: "You don't need to worry about anything."

I should've started worrying when Malick began eyeing Lucy. We were on a boat. What a lousy idea to travel to Tunis on a boat. Lucy told me we'd have fun. Instead I learned that I can't handle the sea. It's horrible. It makes me want to throw up, but I held back whatever was roiling inside me. An ex-bulimic would stick nails in her stomach to stop herself from vomiting. I'd rather be sick as a dog, but the toilet will never again have the satisfaction of seeing my partially digested food. I don't want to feel that burning sensation tearing me in half. No, never again.

The waves dance a restless tip-tap on my guts. I'm shaking in a cold sweat. Wouldn't it have been better, my dear Lucy, to take a plane? Instead, you wanted to dally in Palermo. "It's a beautiful city." End of conversation. Take it or leave it. I took it, my friend. Oh, Lucy, she thinks she's an expert. A little like Maryam. Only Maryam always digressed, steering clear of love. Away from me, my father, Howa Rosario. At some point, who knows when, she started believing that love was a shifty thing that couldn't even be seen in the light of day. So she strayed. She moved in the opposite direction of the emotion she felt, the opposite direction of me. Maryam was always a snake, elusive, or she pretended to be a snake because her nature is unlike the rest of ours. I sense it from her half-smiles, her smooth skin, her sweet eyes, her aroma of mature papaya.

Lucy didn't avoid love, she delighted in it. She avoided time. She wanted it to stop. She lollygagged, trying not to think about it, trying not to look in the mirror and see wrinkles digging grooves into the corners of her mouth. If she had to visit an auntie in one place, Lucy would surely jump from grid to grid like in a game of Battleship. With Lucy you disregard grids, schedules, people, meetings. You disregard the predetermined, the indeterminable, the certain, the uncertain.

But you never get bored with her. I mean never, *abadan*. Her way of spinning things is marvelous. She leaves with her head held high and new shoes on her feet, kind of like Carrie Bradshaw in *Sex and the City*: "I'm never without my Manolo Blahniks." Think of how many *Sex and the City* box sets we could sell at Libla! Women go crazy for those four jaded Americans who fuck from sunrise to sundown. Whatever happened to the lovely TV movies from before, with morals, family, married life, a pet, and the American constitution? Give us back *Bewitched*. In any case, Samantha, who fucks like a man, is my favorite.

Upon arriving in Tunis, I had the shock of a wearying wait. Two hours in line at passport control. I hate lines. Libla's customers, who become furious if someone doesn't serve them immediately, turned me off of them. In the Tunisian port everything was slow. We were in Africa, after all, and life went at a different pace.

Why run, why accelerate death? They told me: "No wild scenes, you get used to it with time." I tried, but in the second hour I fervently yearned for Switzerland. Some idea to study classical Arabic! Unhealthy. Thrusting oneself among idling Arabs. I ached for chocolate, clocks, banks, efficiency. Of course, immigrants aren't treated well in Switzerland—they consider you a parasite—but no one deprives you of a pleasant *Guten Morgen*. In Tunis, though— and this is clear as soon as you step foot on the pier—men give you a full-body X-ray. I can't stand their stares. They undress you with their eyes and some try making love to you with their pupils. I don't like this staring game. I'm afraid of the obscene.

Now I'm here in front of a cup and a cockroach. In a little while I'll take the school's placement exam. I don't want to end up with the novices; I have to defend my honor. Yesterday I tried reviewing irregular weak verbs on the boat. Terrible idea. In the end I didn't know whether it was the sea that made me sick as a dog or those absurdly conjugated Arabic verbs. Then I closed the book and shouted, "Sadists!" I got up and went to some unidenti- fied point on that old heap, blaspheming the sick grammarians of the classical period.

Do I really have the entrance exam already? It seems like just yesterday that I left Rome. This is coming from someone who felt like she'd spent an eternity in bed. I was only curled up for six hours. Lucy is still sleeping. I'll wake her up in the next twenty minutes or so. Or no, thirty. My star sleeps so well, like a child.

Malick has a moustache. He looks like Omar Sharif from *Funny Girl*, perhaps less elegant and skinnier. He has a penetrat- ing stare. Lucy caught it without any effort. She glued her right eye to his and did the same with her left. After that, she didn't unstick again. She stayed like that, having a grand time. Lucy and Malick, the world champion of gazes, reveled together. She knows how to do it. She's taken men on before. The Tunisian squirt could do nothing but offer us his services as an escort. He was under her spell.

"We don't know him, Lucy, what if he gets some idea in his head?"

"Don't worry about it. He's a human being, what can you do? We'll tear him apart if he tries anything."

Malick turned out to be a real lifesaver. We got lost with him, but thankfully he knew the language. Not that he did a lot, but at least he was a somewhat friendly face. The boy was very distracted, though. We waited in line for two hours at passport control. It's not like we were entering Israel with a terrorist's suitcase. In those two hours, I prayed to anything I could for a bed. I was a mess. Vomit stirred inside me. The sea hadn't left me on solid ground.

Malick also looked exhausted. How old was he? Lucy was right: he was a human being. At most, he was twenty-two years old. Lucy was studying him. Hardly a maternal gaze. Very lewd. *But…but…Lucy, you can't! You can't really marry him. Yes, I get it, he's nice…and yes, I know, he's really something…look at that ass! How thoughtful of God…yes, but…it's not ethical, Lucy, you can't do it! This is a poor country, we come from the wealthy West (even I—a black woman—am a wealthy westerner here) and they are African. No, but what are you saying? Of course I'm not a racist. Excuse me, I'm colored too, but I'll acknowledge that there's an economic disparity. I buy Manolo Blahniks for myself. And what about him? Have you seen how he's dressed? His T-shirt is from two World Cups ago, it's ridiculous. He's not doing well, dear. Look, Lucy, how old are you now? Thirty-five? So, let me get this straight, will you always be thirty-five? Won't you change? Aren't you approaching the big four-oh? No? Am I wrong? Of course, you also have the right to your share of happiness. You say he isn't poor? But, he might…*

In the meantime, the little squirt had stopped a taxi. He negotiated the price. I thought I might have heard *khasma*, five, or maybe *khamseen*, fifty. Malick was getting pissed during the exchange and his skin was changing color. He turned violet. His veins bulged and the hairs of his moustache stood on end. It frightened me. Then we got in, dead tired. The seats were riddled with holes. They told me even the taxis in Mogadishu were once this shabby. Now there are no more taxis. There isn't even any Mogadishu.

Malick looked at the driver and repeated the name of the street, our destination, the finish line, the coveted bed. Othman Al Bahri. Yes, the one and only. The taxi started going in circles. Once, twice, three times. Even though we didn't understand a word of the conversation between our squirt and the cabby, it was immediately clear to me and Lucy that the street wouldn't be found. It wasn't the usual trick to run the meter, especially since we'd negotiated the price and there wasn't a meter in the car. Only the banal tragedy of a street that couldn't be found. I wanted to cry. My bed, my rest, was moving further away from me.

Malick was losing his patience. He turned from violet to yellow. He said something forcefully to the cabby—it was full of 'ayn, the nefarious Arabic letter that all students hated. I also picked out some al, a few bi, a handful of 'ala. "I'm screwed," I thought. "It takes me forever to recognize one preposition. They're going to put me in the first level with the kids, idiots, and horses." Despite my exhaustion, the thought of the entrance exam concerned me more than the street that couldn't be found. Maybe it was better to study Arabic at Centocelle; it's also full of Tunisians because there's a mosque. I would've been spared the seasickness, the money for the tickets, and the panic. The next month off they give me at Libla, I'm putting myself in a huge resort at Centocelle.

It was pitch black. I could barely see my hands. The taxi entered an industrial neighborhood. Everything was closed and funereal. "It can't be this place," I said to myself. I looked at Lucy earnestly, but she was distracted. Her hand was resting on the squirt's back. In his ear she was whispering a poem by Nizar Qabbani, the poet of women. No! We're lost and that's what you do? Recite poems in a stranger's ear? Lucy, wake up, we're with two strangers in an industrial park! It's like that film on the Circeo massacre, *The Herd*. They'll stuff us in their luggage. I'm scared!

But our cabby, a guy with a very sweet face, kicked his brain into gear. He had an epiphany. One of his uncles, who was married to an Algerian, lived in the area. "He'll know!" and then he said, "I think he lives on Via Othman." We trusted him (did we have a choice?). Basically, the uncle lived on *a* Via Othman, but it wasn't the one we were looking for. The uncle also had an epiphany. I was concerned. The story was prolonged yet again, for almost another hour.

After wandering endlessly, we saw a mirage: a blonde girl with a short skirt. "She's an angel," I said to myself, worn out by then. "She could show us the way to paradise." She was a Norwegian, and I learned later that her name was Michi. She showed us that we had been near Via Othman Al Bahri for hours. We'd just gotten turned around.

When I saw the cottage that was destined to be our home for a month, I grew worried. Shouldn't there be rooms like in a hotel? Lucy and I had each asked for a single. As soon as we entered, a handful of shocked faces watched us curiously. They were all seated around a table like in *The Last Supper*. There was even someone who looked like Jesus Christ. Among the women, many could've played Mary Magdalene's part. Dan Brown. The Holy Grail. The sacred feminine. I was going mad. Fuck, give me a bed, any bed. I'm beat, destroyed, and I reek. I smell like rodent crap. Help!

A lanky blonde came to meet us. There was a hint of Russian about her. She said something to us in Arabic, then switched promptly to English. She seemed to have come from Oxford. A pristine, noble accent. I was bowled over. My senses came back for a few seconds, but my exhaustion was greater. I was taken in by that Made in Serbia blondness. The lanky woman accompanied us to our room (it should've been a single but it was a triple) and tried explaining something to us. Who could understand her? She gave us some bars of soap and sent us to bed. A woman in the room was snoring loudly.

I just woke up. Coffee, cockroach, and general stupidity. Soon I'll go take the placement test.

Ahlan wa sahlan. Hello, little girl, this is Tunis. Welcome to an unknown place.

THE REAPARECIDA

Enrico Calamai has given me a passport to leave Argentina in half
an hour—not a minute more or less. I'd gone to the Italian consulate in Buenos Aires with one of my brother Ernesto's friends.
Her name was Clara. She was pretty, one of those marvelously
pure girls who it would be good to marry. Clara's face was spotted
with freckles and her eyes were huge. All of her fear was in those
eyes. She was also a political activist. Like my brother, like Flaca
and so many others, she'd turned her back in the *villas miserias*
of the suburbs. Her politics consisted of giving a hopeful smile
to those who had less in life. Clara wasn't Argentinian. She was
Uruguayan. It was obvious. She was more pragmatic and sensible than us. She calculated the incalculable. We didn't know how
to do this. Things happen and overwhelm us without warning.
We Argentinians always have an astonished smirk painted on our
faces. We grope around like newborns in the dark of life. Clara
had moved to Buenos Aires for good, and for a while it was going
well for her. Her story was uplifting. It was suitable for the vita
of a martyred saint. She'd met her husband, Miguel, in a *cantegril*
near Montevideo. They were happy. They made plans. They wanted
to open a school for the underserved, and she would graduate with
a degree in philosophy. But there was no time to plan that now,
nor any for philosophy.

Miguel was taken early. He remains a *desaparecido* to this day. Clara wasn't with her husband when he was kidnapped in a Ford Falcon without a license plate. She was warned. They told her: "Don't come back home if you want to save your neck." For months she lived in hiding. By chance, I met her on a road in the Boca quarter. I remember that it was one of those cobblestone streets. The Italians had laid them down. Now, in many neighborhoods, they've been ripped back up. If you happen to go there one day, *hija*, maybe you can see them in San Telmo or Barracas.

I didn't recognize her right away. She'd lost weight. She spoke gibberish and reeked of menstrual blood. She had been reduced to a larva. What could I do? It was a strange time for me. I'd left Carlos six days earlier. I spat in his face, shouted my frustration at him, my hate for him—for his smell, his uniform. I shouted what I hadn't been able to say for three years. I said the unsayable and took pleasure in his injured pride. I spat and screamed for hours. He was motionless in his uniform, indifferent, chilly. His coldness threw me off. I'd been his lover for three years. He'd stuck his crooked penis in every orifice, he'd rested against my chest countless times, and now he didn't say one word to me?

Oh, Hija, how I long to tell you that my behavior, the decision to leave Carlos and insult him, was due to a metamorphosis, an honest rediscovery of my political path, an awareness of the terrible Argentinian situation. Oh, how I long to tell you that, finally, my pride as a sister, citizen, daughter, and woman was rebelling against the system. I long to tell you that I finally understood that man was depraved, an assassin, that he was merely an infamous swine. I long to tell you many things, hija, but unfortunately I cannot. It wouldn't be true. I'm ashamed to admit the true reason behind my separation from Carlos. Still today, after many years, I feel dirty. Yes, Carlos was what he made me feel: filthy. I felt at home in his slime. I'm afraid I even liked it.

Jealousy was the real reason. He betrayed his wife with me, and me with numerous other women. I knew I didn't have Carlos's body exclusively. I wasn't the only one to tickle his genitals and sink in his liquids. In Buenos Aires there was a long list of hens he'd been entertaining himself with. I certainly shared him with the tortured. Inflicting torture on the *montoneros* was the activity that excited him most, absolutely. He told me one evening. He loved using the *picana* on the kidnapped. He felt his intimate parts tingle every time those poor bodies sizzled. He felt a sensation that went beyond a mere orgasm. He felt ecstasy and lust.

"Torturing," he told me one night, "makes me feel like God." From that night on, he always lit a cigarette after sex like they do in bad B-movies. He'd tell me about his day at Esma. It was odd hearing him talk about torture. He used the same benign tone housewives use when they prepare the grocery list aloud. I wondered why he told me about his business. He had a military ban. He wasn't supposed to leak anything. He told me, sparing no detail, about every second in that house of horrors. I know the building's layout, the names of the "greens"—the soldiers—and those they captured. He told me many names. I unconsciously listened for Ernesto. I wanted to help my brother, and I don't know why I allowed myself to be taken from behind like a mule. I was bewitched. I'm not sure if I can call it love. Carlos didn't deserve to live. He believed he was loved. I felt squalid beside him.

And yet in those first six days of separation, I felt his loss like oxygen. I also felt the loss of his voice zealously singing *Oh, juremos con gloria morir* as he made me his. I walked to avoid thinking. Buenos Aires is a city that's dead inside, but it comforts me nonetheless. Its beauty soothes the flurries of my heart. I met Clara during one of my Buenos Aires pilgrimages. I couldn't bring her home, it was too dangerous. I advised her to hide. I would bring her something to eat later. She squeezed my arm. I was shocked, I remember. She was weaker than a child. With deceit and quick adjustments, we were able to clean her up a little. It wouldn't last long, I knew. Esma was around the corner, and if it wasn't Esma, it would be El Banco or Olimpo—torture centers spread across the country. Sometimes I had dreams that I ended up in there. I embraced Ernesto again and confronted Carlos with his picana. He would've tortured, perhaps even killed me. But I would've left unchanged. I felt dirty and lousy. I missed Carlos. I was ashamed for not thinking more of Ernesto. My mother was right when she said, "*No mereces que te llame puta.*" I had no dignity. A good whore at least keeps that. What did I have?

Calamai was the perfect solution. The Italian vice-counsel was a handsome man. He had a Mediterranean charm that made him more desirable for a late evening date. He must've been very gentlemanly with women. Despite his timidity, it was clear that he'd had many. For a moment, the young thirty-something man made me forget the rotten apple I'd gone to bed with for three years. His reticence, the elegance of his gestures, let me glimpse another world for the first time. Until then, I'd revolved around Carlos. After that day at the consulate I knew that I should've revolved around myself. It was a eureka moment. All it took was looking a clean person in the eye. It was like taking an injection. In little more than thirty minutes, we had our beautiful Italian passports.

I remember nothing of the trip. I only recall the end. Clara and I said a warm goodbye at the Leonardo da Vinci airport. I never saw her again. I wonder if she's happy today.

In Rome, I went to live with the Martino Brezzi family. They were distant cousins of my father. They welcomed me like a daughter. They knew about Ernesto. They were scared for me. My mother hadn't tarnished my reputation for the rest of the family, but she should have. When I think about the Martino Brezzis, my stomach aches, not just my heart. The Martino Brezzis were legitimate communists. They believed in human rights, they railed against injustice. There were five of them: Leonardo, the head of the family; his wife, Marta; and their kids, Liliana, Luciana, and Lorenzo. All of them were little. I slept in the same room as Liliana, a very diligent girl. I had ghastly nightmares and feared contaminating an innocent fifteen-year-old with the wickedness that engulfed me.

The Martino Brezzis lived in a popular neighborhood of Rome, San Lorenzo. To avoid thinking about *mis pesadillas*, my nightmares, I went strolling in the Verano. That monumental cemetery was my salvation in those first months in Rome. I didn't want to see the glory and splendor of the city. No Forum, no Piazza Navona, no Colosseum. The pomp reminded me of Videla. When I passed by, I closed my eyes. I traversed Piazza Venezia like someone blindfolded—Benito Mussolini had spoken from that balcony; I couldn't stand it. I thought of Carlos and his corruption, Ernesto and his purity. Only in that cemetery was I able to be myself. I'd choose a tomb at random, then I'd start shouting as though I were possessed. I yelled, I cried and thrashed. It was only appropriate that people should lose hope. I'd thank the deceased in the grave I'd borrowed. It helped me like nothing else did.

San Lorenzo was fundamental to my survival. On one street in that neighborhood, Argentina came back to me in unexpected ways. I came across Pablo Santana. He was one of Ernesto's group. They'd gone to school together, worked in the villas miserias together, fought for the same things together. I don't know why, but I had taken his kidnapping for granted. Never, ever would I have imagined meeting him on Via dei Sabelli with a bag of groceries in his hand. My *Hola* was a whisper, nearly a sob. He threw his bag on the ground and crushed me in an embrace as wide as that of Christ the Redeemer. He held me tightly. A couple of people thought he and I were in love, crazy for one another. It was merely the pain of being Argentinian that united us. On Via dei Sabelli he gave me the lay of his new life. He explained that he too had left thanks to Calamai, and said, "They nearly caught me. I still don't know how I got away from the Ford. It was parked right there waiting for me." As we spoke, he sometimes disengaged. In those semi-dark moments, he was remembering Ernesto and all those who were no longer there. "I wasn't able to save Pilar. They took her at a friend's house. She was four months pregnant. Our child would've been born by now." When he spoke of Pilar, he didn't wish to think of her as dead. I said little or nothing. I made him talk. We set an appointment for the next day at Cafra, on Via dei Serpenti. "I have a surprise for you," he added.

I didn't return to Via dei Serpenti again until just a few months ago. It was my base in Rome at the end of the seventies. I was always there. Later, I tried to forget that street. Too many layers of pain. I went back for a dinner with my editor. I might have invited you to come with me, I don't remember. There's a good Indian restaurant there. The samosas are spectacular.

In the late seventies, Via dei Serpenti was the meeting place for Argentinian exiles. We were sad ghosts. Cafra was there, the anti-fascist Argentinian center. We denounced the crimes of Videla and his lackeys. From there, the exiles sought to show the world—and especially Italy—what was happening. It was a world of many colors teeming with intellectuals, activists, and students. Videla would've classified it as a den of subversives, and perhaps some Italian political parties would've tried making us appear that way. But we were united. There were some magazines circulating in that period. I liked *El Debate*, a Marxist magazine.

We were strange subversives. From our perspective, no one could call us Marxists or communists. Those were the Years of Lead in Italy. People who challenged the system also challenged bourgeois garb. Ripped suits, preposterously long hair, record-length beards and moustaches, women's bodies on display. In Argentina we were different. Sober. Chaste. No parka. No lace-up boots. No bangs. No miniskirt. We were ladies and gentlemen. Ties, jackets, a few bowties, skirts below the knees, short hair. Ernesto was like this, with never a hair out of place. He had a briefcase, too, which made him look serious, like a businessman. "What a model," I hooted. "You look like a Wall Street CEO instead of a bum." He smiled with his eyes and said, "That's exactly what I want, to be like someone on Wall Street." A lot of people thought like

Ernesto. Opposition wasn't a suit to be worn, but a way of life. Ernesto wanted to do it, not show it.

Even in exile no one lost this habit. They were exceedingly serious on Via dei Serpenti. No excesses, no colors, nothing extravagant. Entering that hole-in-the-wall on Via dei Serpenti, I realized how much suffering had been caused by those medal-decorated soldiers. Everyone had tense, long, tired faces.

I didn't see Pablo on the first day. I looked for him. I asked for his whereabouts. A twenty-two-year-old boy told me where I could find him. He was cute. He had the same obligatory crease on his forehead. He was tense like the others and stood in a corner with a guitar. He had very short hair, and you could already discern his eventual baldness. Neither of us lingered on pleasantries. He didn't ask for my first or last name, nor did I ask him. He did show me a photograph, though. There he was, a little younger, around fifteen, with four other people. One girl and three boys. He told me their names. I remember them still. Osvaldo, Roberto, Raúl, and Sofia. He didn't know anything about them anymore. They were his siblings. He said nothing else to me, only that despised word. *Chupados*. The swallowed up. Osvaldo, Roberto, Raúl, and Sofia, vanished, probably dead without a burial, without a tomb, without a last goodbye. He showed me the photo, then he started to sing. It was typical in those years to show photos. It happened all the time. At every meeting, every party, every outing, at funerals, baptisms, marriages, birthdays, at parent-teacher conferences, at passport appointments. Everyone went around with a stack of photos to show other exiles. They looked at old faces in black and white and sobbed in silence. I remember telling someone about my strolls to the Verano. A couple of girls followed suit. I ran into them every Wednesday afternoon. Every time we saw one another, we shook hands. Our hands were always freezing, even in August.

That first day on Via dei Serpenti I remember singing Bob Dylan with the sad boy. We made a mash-up, which lightened our moods. Since that day, I've become a fan of old Bob.

I loved tango the most, though. Gardel was the only master of my heart. I liked his discretion. In Buenos Aires, they said he never took advantage of his conquests or betrayed people's trust. A real man, a good soul. Mother, though, liked Ignacio Corsini. It was the same story as River and Boca. She was with Boca in response to me, while I rooted for River. Likewise for Corsini. She sang, mixing his songs with her fado to spite me since I loved Gardel very much. Corsini was one of the greats, but not like Gardel. I perceived human limitations in Corsini's voice that Carlos didn't have. Corsini was also a charismatic man full of pathos. It pains me to think that I spoke ill of his melodious voice. Mother made me lose my temper. She would never admit that I, her daughter, had good taste. When she thought no one was listening, I heard her croon Gardel's "Cuesta abajo." She was like that with me. She wore a stone mask.

Tango was my first love, but not my only one. On Via dei Serpenti I was introduced to Dylan. I didn't know then that he'd be the craze of a lifetime. I would find out soon enough.

And yes, Flaca comes into the picture.

In the late sixties, Dylan had an ugly infatuation with country music. His fans couldn't stand him anymore. He became vapid. He made albums that didn't leave a mark and a few were passé. His fans wanted the moxie of his early years, the roughness, his stand-offish relationship with power. No one had the courage to tell him. Dylan's face, which was always somewhat sulky, scared people. He wanted to play his music. He didn't care about his fans. *Crucify me, it doesn't make any difference.* The boy was stubborn. I happened to hear him in Milan some time ago. I no longer recognized the songs. Dylan was a part of me. I'd become honest because of his songs. I wanted to sing them and remember my voice from a former time, purify it, maybe. Robert Allen Zimmerman did his own thing. He hadn't become Bob Dylan for nothing. A little guy of about twenty looked at me wryly. He may have noticed my disconsolate face. "Bob never sings them the same," he told me. "He changes everything live. He doesn't repeat the message like a half-wit. Every concert is an event. Different and the same as itself. Pure coherence, goddamn!" The twenty-year-old was exalted. His eyes were red from nervous anticipation. He was like a mystic at his first sacrament.

The country binge ended with the sixties. It made sense. Everything is a parenthetical in life. Robert Allen Zimmerman started frequenting Greenwich Village again. He realized the Big Apple, that fanciful city, was his true inspiration.

You also like Dylan. When you were a child, I raised you on the notes of "Mr. Tambourine Man." I inherited my lovely voice from my mother. Of course I can't sing fado, but I'm not so far from it. I draw on ancient sources. De Gregori (another one you like) says that, with his singing, Dylan reaches Homeric heights. I only want him to reach you.

That's where Flaca comes in.

Flaca, my brother's fiancée, the perfect girl, the woman whom my mother loved more than me. Flaca. Rosa Benassi. Daughter of Italians. I saw her a few days after that first encounter in Rome with Pablo Santana, on an anonymous Roman street. She was singing "Hurricane." A Dylan song from *Desire*, 1976.

I discovered that Ernesto had given her that album for her birthday. They weren't ever able to listen to it together. He was kidnapped before she had a chance to unwrap it.

She liked Dylan. She liked Mercedes Sosa and Baez, too.

And I'll tell you one thing, Man, she danced to them.

THE PESSOPTIMIST

Ever since she was a little girl, Howa Rosario had a long luminous black braid. It was perhaps the first memory Maryam had of her friend. A luminous braid. The second memory was of her nose. Quite a strange nasal orifice. It stole the scene like an old star at La Scala. She had a precious face. The eyes of a gazelle, the mouth of a filly and, in the middle of those assorted perfections, an enormous, gargantuan twisted vortex. It was tiresome trying to identify it as a nose. It was like a work of baroque architecture. To the point that Maryam, years later, seeing the dome of the Church of Saint-Yves, said, *Wa assaga!* There it is. She meant Howa's nose. That coiled dome had the same purity as her friend's nose. The same virginal candor. Maryam was moved by it.

Most people, however, thought the eccentricity in the middle of Howa's face was a disgrace. Curiously, not everyone noticed it right away. First, people looked admiringly at Howa. With mouth agape, they delighted in the thousand perfections with which Allah had endowed her. Pure, ascetic ardor was in their expressions. Then, unfailingly, their faith dwindled because of her damaged nose. They stared for a few moments, but that was often all it took to make them shake their heads and murmur, "*Kasaro, kasaro.*" Tragedy, a tragedy. Sometimes people shouted *kasaro* at her just to share their private pain.

The reason that nasal appendage was so, let's say, *original*, was an accident. There are conflicting accounts as to when it happened. Was she six years old? Ten? No more than twelve, whatever the case. Nearly everyone knew how it happened. The girl had confronted a *jinn* with her rosary, the people said. The jinn wanted to dishonor her, and she was defending herself. Flickers of the rosary. A flurry of *acuudu billahi mina sheydhani rajimi*. The devil moved back. It was a mean, atrocious, libidinous jinn without scruples. Having been unable to savor her innocence, it cruelly decided to disfigure her forever. That was why it bit her nose. It sank its grubby, monstrous canines into her pretty, delicate little nose, for which the family had received many compliments. Her beauty vanished forever without leaving a trace, not one memory. A nice treatment the jinn had given her, and a lasting one at that. "I want to see if she can find a husband with that trunk." And it ran away, hair to the wind, laughing uproariously. A truly sadistic jinn. "This is why she carries the rosary like an old woman," people said, wanting to find an explanation for her unusual juvenile devotion. That's why the story of the jinn seems plausible to most people, otherwise how does one explain the rosary? Her attentiveness to religion and the prophets? To prayer? "You need to enjoy yourself," the world shouted. Instead, she hugged the rosary to her chest like an anchor of salvation. Maryam had always had serious doubts about the story of the jinn. Howa's nose certainly was ugly. Horrible, frankly. But blaming it on the jinn was carrying it too far. "I think she just fell out of a tree."

They knew much earlier that they would become close friends. Both were from Skuraran and their houses faced the same open lot. They said the ceremonious *Assalamu aleikum* multiple times a day, and if it wasn't peace be with you, it was a *wanaagsan* something, a good something. Good afternoon, good evening, many good blessings upon you. Wanaagsan at every hour of the day. It was a lullaby. One hardly looked at the other when saying the exceedingly courteous word. They were like fine-tuned machines with conditioned gestures. Howa let her rosary dangle, and Maryam fidgeted with her hands.

Skuraran was so distant, a remote past that bordered on legend. Skuraran, their neighborhood, among the first to disappear. It wasn't the warlords' civil war that turned it into a heap of ruins. It was much earlier than that, because of one soldier's longing for power. The *caudillo* Siad Barre razed it to the ground. With one sweeping motion, he made Skuraran vanish. It was the same gesture Mussolini made when he ordered Borgo's destruction to make room for the anonymous Via della Conciliazione. In Skuraran, there were secret passages, balconies, wells, tunnels, alleys, arches, hiding places. Like the stripes on a reptile's body, confused but elegant. Skuraran. Maryam Laamane had walked so many paths there.

The gazelle-like Maryam Laamane didn't run anymore. She was now a woman, sitting in her living room in Rome, intent on recording her own life. Or trying to. Her posture in front of the recorder had become more balanced. Her axis was straight and her head didn't sway uncontrollably from side to side. Maryam was calmer. Her hands didn't sweat anymore. She was getting used to untangling knots. Her own, and the disordered knots of history.

She dearly missed Howa, her lifelong friend, who was also like their neighborhood Skuraran: distant, cold, gone forever. A past that bordered on legend. "May God have mercy on her and on all of us," Maryam whispered softly into the recorder. Howa Rosario, dead. No more rosary dangling at her side, no more laughs, no more nostalgia.

Maryam Laamane was alone. Was it true? No, no it wasn't. Zuhra was there. Yes, thanks be to God, Zuhra was there.

She and Howa were only in a few photos together, but those few were important. Maryam's favorite was the one where she was with Howa Rosario and little Zuhra in front of the Hotel Archimede, near Termini Station. They were leaning sleepily against an earth-colored Beetle. Zuhra had confused, curly hair, her arms were folded, and she wore a short dress that made her into a worker bee, a triumph of yellow and black. It was the handiwork of her crazy father. Maryam liked this photo. It was taken on the day she found Howa Rosario again. Siad Barre's regime was to blame for them falling out of touch. In the picture, Howa no longer had her black braid. It was covered by a sea-blue scarf. It was beautiful. Her crooked nose lit up like a neon lamp.

"Your dress is beautiful!" she'd said before hugging her.

"Your husband made it."

She knew that. She recognized her tailor husband's surreal style. She might've even noticed the dress before Howa's proboscis.

They found themselves again on Via dei Mille. It was from there, years later, that Howa's funeral procession began.

Howa Rosario was lovely. One almost didn't notice her crooked nose.

Skuraran, a long-lost epoch. They had spoken of it for the first time in 1960. They'd become friends in those nine glorious years of democracy. Then they lost each other. Life, difficulties. They found one another again only in 1978. And in 2006, Maryam buried her.

On that day in 1960, she didn't suspect their friendship would last so long.

Aunt Ruqia ordered her to "go get a bit of *ageen* from *Hajiedda* Saida." Ageen, the buttery dough that smelled like home.

It was a day of preparations. A wedding day. Who was getting married? All of Somalia. It was the much longed-for independence day. The next day, July 1, 1960, they would be a free and independent state, a country that could have its say and stand on equal footing with the others. No more masters, no more Italians, no more Englishmen. No more dogs tarnishing their homes. They would finally be free. They would shout their joy to the world. And they would hoist their flag in the wind, under the sun. A blue background and a star. The sky. The same sky that made her happy every night.

The country was in a state of great anxiety. People prepared speeches, dances, songs. The women cooked fragrant meals. Everyone on that strange eve dreamed about the celebration that would marry Somalia to liberty. The five points of the white star. The five territories that made up the land of aromas and beauties. Missing from the roll call were Djibouti, the North Eastern Province, and Ogaden. They still didn't know that there would never be total reunification and that, on the contrary, the territory would be sold in pieces to the highest bidder. But in 1960 people were ambitious. It was the year of Somalia and all of Africa.

Maryam wasn't thinking about border problems then. She only had the next day's festivities in mind. She set out toward Hajiedda Saida's house. It was always like this. In the end, they always sent her to Hajiedda Saida's place. "You're the smallest. The ageen is your responsibility." The compact ball of yeast dough stunk. The more it stunk, the better the *injera* would be. Why did she have to be the one to endure that vile stench for such a long way? Hajiedda Saida's house was sad. First there was that beefy husband of hers, her second, who ranted from morning till evening. An ugly thing to see. She didn't like how he looked at her with darting eyes, as though he'd never seen a young girl before. Howa Rosario's braid was also there, and that did much to reassure her. There were many braids in that house. Only Howa Rosario had one so beautiful. Then, abruptly, the beefy man died, and she disliked going to that house a little less, even though Hajiedda Saida herself was still rather unnerving.

Everyone called her Hajiedda because she had gone to Mecca, so she deserved honor and respect. There weren't many women then who could afford a pilgrimage to the Sacred City. Hajiedda Saida had gotten rich through her first husband. He was a *dubat*, someone who fought alongside the Italians. Maryam's father was as well. The hajiedda's husband had beheaded many people. Sometimes Maryam wondered if her father also carried out massacres. He'd worked for every hard-earned cent. It was right, in Hajiedda Saida's eyes, to make good use of that hard work.

What was better than a lovely trip to Mecca? Someone warily pointed out to the great woman that it was dirty money. "Your husband killed innocents, and he did it for the whites." Spitting on the ground, she said, "He killed infidels, *gaalo.*" At that point talk was useless. It was useless telling her that not all Ethiopians were *gaalo* and that Libyans most certainly weren't. "But, Hajiedda, they were human beings, weren't they?" Talking was useless since she instilled a reverential dread that made your bowels run.

What scared Maryam, though, wasn't the bulky woman or her stature as a pilgrim to Mecca, but her unmoving eyes. She was indecently fat and had eyes that didn't move in their sockets. They were threateningly fixed. If there weren't all that womanly meat to prove it, Maryam would've mistaken the hajiedda for a chicken. The same unmoving eyes. The same threat. Maryam couldn't stand chickens. They disturbed her. She felt overwhelmed by the world's anxieties and something else as well. Aunt Ruqia made fun of her: "Look at how big and fat she is, and she's afraid of a stupid animal."

"It's not stupid, *Habaryar*, you can see hell in their eyes."

"Oh, come now, what are you saying! It's one of Allah's creatures, like any other. No, a little dumber, but it's good, Maryam. It's also very tasty."

Maryam didn't eat chickens and she tried never to cross paths with one, much less meet their gaze. She avoided it like the plague. She had a small coop at her house but tried ignoring it the same way she tried ignoring the day her aunt decided to wrench one of the stupid creatures' necks and cook it for dinner. It was far worse seeing them killed. The body moved without the head. It ran deliriously as though still clinging to a pale illusion of life. Only that once had she seen her aunt yank a chicken's neck. Atrocious. Never again, *abadan.* The animal's body raced the hundred-meter dash, quick as lightning, while the face was stuck in a grimace of contracted pain. The eyes, however, were as fixed as they had been in life. Perhaps in life it was already a corpse. She was terrified. She didn't eat chicken anymore.

She moved past the wooden door. "*Hodi! Hodi!* Anyone there?"

She saw plaited hair arranged around a trunk and a black Buddha with a brown scarf on her head. The Buddha was immobile. Her plaits, however, vibrated like the sound waves coming from a black saucepan nearby. She could hear the Quran being read aloud. It was about time for the evening prayer. Families were getting ready to eat and many were busy preparing for the following day's ceremony. "Somalia is getting married. Oh, dear friends, Mogadishu and the nation are marrying, they're marrying liberty. Independence! Independence!"

July 1 seemed far away to her. First she had to retrieve the ageen and then confront this fat woman.

Clack, clack, clack. Her small feet rapped against the ground. *Clack, clack, clack.* A gentle percussion.

"Good evening to you, Hajiedda Saida, my aunt would like a little ageen for tomorrow."

"Howa is taking ageen to the *signorina.*" She said *signorina* in Italian. "It's a party, a grand party, I suppose. And do you know why?"

Yes, she was right to be afraid. That dead chicken's cadaverous eyes were glued to her and didn't let go for a second. The woman's eyes and immensity demanded a response. Maryam felt lost. She wanted to escape, vanish. She wanted to be invisible but realized that probably wouldn't happen. She had rather long legs and a distinguished chin, a wide forehead and rebellious hair. Her lips bound her to the earth. Her chest bound her to her increasingly apparent femininity.

"*Sai perché, bella signorina?*" asked the black Buddha.

Maryam felt afire. She bubbled over with fear and sweated from her scalp. In her mind that *perché* the woman uttered resounded like a curse. It shouldn't have been asked. The reason for the celebration was clear to everyone. There was no need for explanations. Everyone was happy, were they not? The *perché* was a fracture. In one blow, Maryam felt her certainty crumble. *Could this woman not be happy?* She didn't understand. *Are you not Somali? Then you must be happy today. It's our day.* She wanted to tell her this, or something of the sort. She wanted to draw the shape of their land with a fine point, to dance so as to make her part of the event and perhaps hug her to make her feel among friends. *You don't ask the reason for a birthright*, she wanted to tell her. But she said nothing. Nothing came to mind, in fact. In response to the *perché*, she whispered discontentedly. She countered with a banal, practical explanation. An obvious truth.

The black Buddha looked at her condescendingly. She wasn't satisfied. Maryam could see it in the way her cheeks moved arhythmically in disappointment. The Buddha was indignant and made it clear. To Maryam it seemed almost as though the woman's size had tripled. She occupied more space around her.

Maryam felt like she was choking, an absurd inkling of death.

The big woman took the girl's hands between her own. Maryam noticed that her hand was frigid. It repulsed her nearly as much as the chicken's fixed eyes. They remained like that for a while, until Maryam almost started liking this unexpected cooling sensation in the overabundant heat of Mogadishu. Then the big woman spoke and all the fear Maryam thought was gone came full circle. Everything about the woman frightened her. Her bulk, her stare, the soft way she said, "You are all wrong. You, the people in this house, the people pampered by our politicians, the whole world." Wickedly sneering, she said, "We're only good for obeying. We serve no other purpose."

The big woman began singing an old fascist war hymn. Maryam didn't know how to say the words, but the rhythm had a combative style that she sort of enjoyed. One two, one two, one two.

The black Buddha projected beams of light. She was at the height of ecstasy.

In that moment Howa appeared. She struck her mother with

her trademark rosary, held firmly in her right hand. She struck her, whispering an exorcism.

"Silence, wicked woman. *Na ga amus*. Be still. Be still," the crooked-nosed girl shouted.

The woman Buddha remained seated on the wicker mat. She sniggered. At her daughter's every *a'udhu billahi*, away Satan, she chuckled more cruelly.

She jerked and seized the girl's rosary, pulling the young body to herself with inconceivable force.

She looked at her disdainfully. "You can't even defend yourself from an old woman like me. You're worthless. This little necklace has never helped you. It's never saved you."

The girl shook free from the bulky Buddha as if from a mass of annoying ants.

"Tomorrow is independence day, my dear friend," Howa Rosario said to Maryam with a smile. Maryam was disoriented. She didn't understand what had happened between the two women, but she thought it all very strange. Howa smiled. "I'll see you tomorrow," she said. And so it was.

THE FATHER

Majid knew where to find her: in front of the theater. He was joined by the white family's driver, a young kinky-haired *geerer* named Hussein.

The whites had gone to hunt big game in the North and would return in five days. Mogadishu was layered with a fine, pink dust that promised fertility to the women and nightly bliss to the men.

"When you get there, do you want to be alone?" the geerer asked conspiratorially.

"If you don't mind," Majid said.

They were putting on an amusing comedy at the theater. The plot was in the title. *Sirrey*—Deceiver. A conventional story: a mother swindles a poor business owner by making him marry the ugliest of her daughters. The audience's laughter could be heard outside and Hussein, despite not understanding a word, joined in the general mirth, shaking and laughing like a madman. Majid did not laugh. He never did.

"Where do men take women nowadays?" he asked.

"You've never taken one out?"

"No. My wife, God have mercy on her soul, was my child-hood friend."

"They go to Ferzal's. The Indian. The one with the turban on his head, the Sikh. He doesn't care who comes in. He doesn't ask questions. Even the Italians bring their *sharameet* there."

"But she isn't a *sharmuta*, even if…"

"Even if?"

"Nothing. She's not a whore. That's all."

The people began exiting. Everyone had a cheerful air about them. For a short time, the *riwaayad* and the hijinks of the mother and ugly daughter had one-upped reality. Life was difficult, but that fiction made it more bearable.

"Murid is such an idiot," one girl said.

"Yeah, a nitwit," another echoed. "He's so stupid, making a fool of himself like that. A life with that ugly Fadum… I feel sorry for him."

"Oh poor, idiotic Murid," a nearsighted boy chortled.

It was all maligning and badmouthing. They laughed about Murid, the mother, and the ugly girl. The riwaayad was becoming a daily reality. The mother was taking the shape of a real mother, a fat one who had a fish banquet in Xamarweyne. "Come on, the one who spits every time she says the word 'sea.' Come on, you don't remember? The one who has the daughter with the big messed-up teeth." The comedy was transforming into real life, and the badmouthing into gossip.

Majid was struck by the scents those people gave off. A blend of jasmine, sweat, and raw onions. They had worked hard and would probably go back to working hard shortly. The smell was also his own. In the white people's kitchen he smelled a little like jasmine, a little like sweat, and a little like raw onion. He smelled like offal, eggplant, mango, roasted coffee, and almond, too. Sometimes he reeked of garlic, other times of fresh tomatoes. In the white people's kitchen his odor was strong and absolute. In the kitchen, he melded with and overcame the air. In front of the neighborhood theater, his odor was a trifle lost in an olfactory paradise.

Then he smelled an emanation he'd never known.

"It's like milk," Majid said to himself. He was pleased and

smiled demurely. Only then was he able to laugh. Maybe it was because the sun did not shine its light on him.

It wasn't milk, however. It was Bushra. Bushra, his sister-in-law, or as she was called more often, *Ebleey*, the libertine. Bushra was lovely. She wore a green habit that didn't do justice to her figure, and her gait was unpretentious, hardly noticeable. People walked briskly around her, everyone rushing to get away, to disappear. She, on the other hand, wallowed in her feelings after the comedy. She was the only one who didn't laugh. Her gaze was lost in a remote, fraudulent universe.

The sky was clear in Mogadishu, the night hot and the stars large like watermelons. Pink studded the clear blue of the equatorial city with dazzling beams.

"I'm going to go now," Hussein said. "I'll be back in a half hour. Is that enough time for you?"

"That'll be enough. Go on now, she's coming."

Hussein split without him having to say it twice. His shadow disappeared swiftly in the moon's direction.

Majid was alone with his thoughts. In a minute she would be next to him. In one minute. No, now fifty-nine seconds. Fifty-eight. Fifty-seven. Not much time separated him from her. He'd gone there with a purpose. He had to intercept her...and then? Then what? He'd forgotten everything. He'd had a plan before leaving the white people's home. A precise design, without excuses, no vacillation. He pictured the scene. He knew how he would wave her down. His hand would cut delicately through the air so there would be no offense, no vulgar pat on the back. He didn't want to touch her, deprive her of respect, violate her. He only wished to stop her, get her attention, speak to her. His gesture would move the air just enough to put a few goosebumps on her arms. The woman would shiver and lift her head. Her gazelle's gaze meeting the eyes of a man. He would make the speech that he'd prepared more than ten days before. He would ask for her hand and she would cry from joy. Bushra would be his. All according to plan.

It was easy, the only thing he had to do was make the right moves, say the right words. The rest would follow. The rest was Bushra's tears, Bushra's happiness, Bushra's gratefulness.

The rest was his chest expanding proudly. He would feel a little like a man that evening and maybe even sleep some. He slept so little as it was, and that little was troubled by nightmares. In his nocturnal deliriums he saw the face of the fascist who split him in two. He felt the boiling sensation that had pierced his anus. He felt that terrible, wet heat, the foam inside him, and the rhythmic pounding of the fascist's penis inside him. Then he felt shame. In that obscene moment he felt the loss of his virility. He saw his unfortunate travel companions. Most unforgettably, he saw the body of the poor wretch who was killed. While the fascist bore through him, Majid thought, "How I wish I were dead like him."

But the thought of proposing made him the happiest man on earth. There had been no need for a declaration with Famey. They were united by an unspeakable pain. It made sense to become one. She wouldn't have expectations, and neither would he. They would continue their chaste marriage forever, and he lacked nothing. He worked and misfortune kept him company. Sometimes it was hard to move on, but the kitchen placated his baleful memories, as did Famey and the heat of her embrace. He wasn't affectionate with her, however. He couldn't hug or kiss her, he couldn't even talk to her. He didn't like to talk anymore. Prior to that cursed bus, he had been a fun, irreverent chatterbox. Nothing was the same afterward. There was no longer anything worth living for, and so nothing to laugh for. He became serious, lifeless, a catatonic vegetable.

There was the child. He didn't want to think about it during the boy's inception. "It's not my business," he said to himself. Of course he had inserted a part of his body into his wife's, but he wasn't there. Only his organ was moving, not his will. He hadn't moved that much inside her. He'd made some minor circular movements and then came immediately. It was hard enough getting the organ up. Asking him to enjoy himself was too much. His wife didn't like her conjugal duty either. They'd done it a handful of times and she became pregnant.

"It's not my business," he said to himself until the day of the delivery.

Majid didn't want it. He wasn't mean, but he was a destroyed man, almost mortally wounded. He decided to wait out his life. He didn't have a great longing to go on, but strangely, he didn't have much of a desire to die either. When he saw his little son covered in his wife's blood and when he lightly touched his skin, he knew right away that his life still had some purpose, because that boy was, in fact, completely his business.

He was there for the boy, fifteen seconds away from Bushra. It was for the boy that he'd memorized his speech to ask for Bushra's hand. He did it for Elias, Zuhra. He loved that unwanted child immensely. He wanted a simple life for his son, without obstacles or humiliations.

He didn't want any possibility of Elias, his son, becoming an object in the hands of a sadistic white man. He taught him from the beginning: "Defending yourself is the most important thing you can do." He wanted autonomy and strength for Elias. He was his child, he could not deny it. He didn't want to deny it.

But a small child was in need of a mother, Majid said one day. He had only the burden of choice. The women were all ready to take care of the son of poor, young, unfortunate Sister Famey. They were ready to show Majid that handsome Elias would be happier with them instead of another. The women began squabbling and making threats. Insults flew. Binti and Zahra threw a few blows beneath the belt. Auntie Bushra didn't get caught up in those disputes. She said, "Not me, I'm staying out of it." For that reason, she seemed the most fitting to Majid.

Bushra was a widow. She'd gotten married and two months later her husband Hakim had croaked, severed cleanly by one of the vehicles Famey enjoyed so much. His body was collected in pieces from various locations. His arms were detached, sent in two different directions. His torso was flattened into the sand and his head ended up in one of those whites-only restaurants that were common in downtown Mogadishu. Hakim had liked women very much, and according to his aunt it wasn't a coincidence that they recovered him from the lap of a blonde *gaal* with a generous bosom. "Your uncle's head ended up right in the woman's cleavage." He could smell her scent: Ater Nurra, the most popular perfume in Mogadishu. Auntie Bushra swears she glimpsed a roguish simper on her dead husband's face. Even the fact that his penis was erect wasn't entirely lost on her. He'd always been a backstabbing traitor. She tried putting the pieces back together as best she could. Some parts were missing. Maybe they were already eaten by worms or nibbled on carelessly by the goats. The search for his nose was in vain, and for his right eye. The essentials were restored. The mischievous head, the torso, the pelvis, the legs, the neck, the arms, the erect prick. They were cleaned, tended to, perfumed. They were wrapped in shrouds and buried with the honor befitting his kind nature. He was very nice, Uncle Hakim. He told witty tall tales that would surely have made you smile, Zuhra. Everyone cried at the funeral. There was moaning and chest-beating in a doleful procession. They had come from the bush to mourn him, mostly women that your uncle had given himself to throughout his short life. A couple of *gaalo* were there also, which surprised most of the attendees. They all cried, in various forms. Reserved, inconsolable, melancholic, pained, berserk, nostalgic. Only your aunt didn't cry. She didn't shed a single tear. They say she laughed instead, uproariously. To be sure, she did spill two tears, but it was because she couldn't hold back the force of her laughter. Today people still wonder why your aunt behaved that way. It wasn't decent for a widow. "Poor thing," someone said, "the pain has gone to her head." And that was true. In the neighborhood they say your aunt laughed uninterrupted for a month and a half. Then she stopped and didn't laugh again. For the people in the neighborhood, it was still discomfiting. They had grown accustomed to the crystalline cascade that rose from the unusual woman's throat. It was so beautiful when she laughed, so graceful.

In the fourth month of pregnancy, the neighborhood received the news. Bushra was with child. By the fifth month, Bushra knew that the creature in her womb would not be long for this world. When it was born, she gave him her husband's name. The gesture was appreciated. The child, however, was born with a serious defect. He was taken to shamans and even one of the white people's doctors. No one could figure it out. Bushra resigned herself to seeing the creature die. She caressed its head and whispered words that were wineskins full of sweetness. When the child died, it was full of milk. Liters of milk had drained from her breast, as during the monsoon.

Her maternal milk had stimulated Majid's nose. This milk would be given to his little Elias. Within seconds, he and Bushra would be standing next to each other. Majid wanted milk for his son. He was set on marrying the woman. He did not fear her. She was so lovely and agreeable.

"Don't fool yourself, Majid," his cousin Warsama advised him, "she has five hundred lives. She can transform herself into a woman, but at night, remember, she is a scorpion who makes our strength idle, our penises dormant. Be careful, Majid. She is a witch. She will sever your testicles and steep herself in some dirty concoction. She wants to steal your soul, Majid. Stay away from her, God damn her."

The sky was clouding over. Perhaps the first rain of the season would lift their spirits with solid and abundant drops. Minutes passed, and then they were together. He had to talk to her immediately, make no delay. Nothing but emptiness around them. The crowd from the comedy had thinned. It was only him and her. A man and a woman. In between them, a declaration. A child.

He had to do it for the boy.

"Do you want to marry me, Bushra?"

He didn't greet her. He didn't say hello, good afternoon, good evening, how are you. He skipped the pleasantries and every minimal standard of decency. He didn't give her time to breathe or think.

"Did you think this through?" she asked, astonished.

"Yes. It's the only solution." He said it with much conviction.

"Do you know what they say about me?"

"Yes, I do."

"Do you believe it?"

"Do you?"

"Me?" She was baffled by the question. "Do I what, cousin?"

"Do you believe the rumors about you?"

"Don't be ridiculous."

"There you have it. Don't be ridiculous."

"They call me *Falley*, the sorceress. They say that I killed my child. Do you understand? They say I was a monster because I didn't lie with my husband, Hakim, but with a demon. He was the one who went with other women, always, even two gaalo. And I'm the adulterer. They find me guilty of *zina*, convict me of having had relations outside of marriage, which I never thought to do. Stone me, I said at the market, if you're sure that I lie with a demon. Prove it. Everyone stopped talking. But their words are still killing me. They will never end. If I marry, they will speak ill of you too. Will you be able to stand it?"

"Yes, I want a mother for my boy and I want serenity."

"Okay, cousin."

And that, Zuhra, is how Bushra became my new mama.

FOUR

THE NUS-NUS

Smoke gurgled in the iron hookah. Mar took a long pull. The taste of tobacco and the scent of apple made her sentimental. She felt downy and soft, taken to a parallel dimension. A shame not to have good weed. Smoking that would've been a thousand times more powerful.

Her smoking buddies were sweethearts. A Swiss named Thomas had proposed their sudden excursion. They'd taken the TGM, the historic Tunisian tram, to Sidi Bou Said. "There's a splendid terrace!" the Swiss said. "And the *shisha* should be smoked somewhere nice." The blond knew his stuff. He'd been in Egypt for a year and a half, he was a prolific smoker. Mar found him amusing. He was a handsome boy, the kind you could really fall for. If it weren't for Pati, that thorn, maybe she would've let loose. She had only been in the country for a short time and already felt her senses unraveling. She thought Thomas was gorgeous. That was something. It had been a while since she'd thought anyone was beautiful. He made her laugh. He was silly, especially when he spoke of Egypt. Every time he pronounced the word Egypt, the Swiss carried himself like a statesman. His chest expanded, his eyebrows rose, his voice grew deeper. It was like the beginning of a legend: "One time in Egypt, an iguana..." And if it weren't an iguana, it was a fat merchant, a pure prostitute, an indecisive bride.

People suddenly became icons, full of grand importance. In addition to Thomas, there was a German girl with teal-colored hair, a couple of Norwegians, and a cordial group of Italians from the North. Many of them lived in her dorm, so they became friends. In her class there was only one half-crazed English woman, who was pretending to study on that lovely day. Everyone else had an easier time with Arabic than she did, but it didn't matter to her. They would be the ones doing the ordering.

She asked for a *citronade*. Someone told her it was good for the stomach and would thwart the diarrhea that was sure to come. It was an awful time to think of diarrhea. The place was so nice, with the sea, the white terrace, the people sitting in intimate groups. The thought of her stomach was maddening, and she certainly couldn't be bothered with it at the time. Patricia had been attuned to her own body and its physiological functions. She could talk for hours about how her crap floated in the toilet. Disgusting.

Sometimes Mar forced herself to remember why she liked that woman so much. Patricia wasn't pretty. She dressed terribly. She wore jeans and T-shirts, strange dark shoes, and used a poppy-scented perfume that Mar couldn't stand. Her hair was stringy, straight spaghetti. Her prominent bangs made her look like a junkyard mannequin. She had very white skin, so similar to that of Mar's mother.

Mama, where did Mama end up? She'd seen her at the bar that morning hanging out with a tall, scrawny black girl, like herself. Short hair, she noted, and a particular elegance in her movements. It was weird seeing her mom with another black girl. It was almost as though she were with Mar, notwithstanding a few substantial differences. Her mother laughed, she was relaxed, and the black girl was laughing carelessly, too. When Mar was with her mother, Miranda never laughed. Mar didn't either.

Everyone told her having a mother like that was a blessing. "How wonderful, Mar, to have a writer for a mother. Aren't you proud of her?" Proud? She never understood the meaning of the word. What did it mean? What should it have meant in the geo-politics of her existence?

To understand her mother, one had to read her. And even doing that, one wouldn't understand that much. She had read her first book, *Calle Corrientes*, to glean something of her past in Argentina. There was nothing at all meaningful in those poems. Only abstract images of a pain she did not wish to share. For years, Mar had searched those poems for dates, loves, hurts, fears, night-mares. Instead, she found herself in front of a surrealist painting, everything interpreted and perhaps nothing understood. She'd never tried asking her mother about it, not even as an adolescent. She knew about her *desaparecido* uncle. She knew they'd taken him away in a Ford. The soldiers had been given vehicles and a mountain of arms by the powerful Uncle Sam. Mama didn't tell her about her friends from that time, the music she listened to, the films she watched. She didn't tell her about what she did for fun or what clothes she wore. She never spoke to Mar about her grand-parents. Her grandfather died before her uncle was loaded into a Ford, and her grandmother passed away after. Mar was sixteen years old when someone called their house to give her mother the news. The only thing she said was, "*La abuela se murió.*" Her facial expression never changed. She was stunned. Her grandmother's case was closed. No one spoke of it after that. Mar remembered a picture of her *abuela*. She had a regal nose and eyebrows that were far apart. She didn't know anything else about her grandmother. Everything was a fucking mystery, like the rest of the bunch. She hated the word that everyone abused: *family*. What did it mean for her? Her family was her mother. Her shapely face was the extent of it. Her family had also been Patricia, briefly. Her father was a Don Juan who disappeared to Lord knows where, her uncle was tortured by the military, and her grandmother had eyebrows that were far apart. It didn't take much to make a family.

Mar took in her surroundings. The café was a little off. People were arranged so that their eyes met. The terrace was where people went to see and be seen. It was a game, seasoned with shisha and mint tea. There were normal couples, young people who'd returned from France (or Italy?), marriage-ready girls joined by their older brothers, tourists in kitschy attire, businessmen from some other Arab country, a few African delegates. Everyone looked where they weren't supposed to. Those with husbands looked at the other men, as did those with wives. They played with fire without burning themselves. There was the self-righteous man with expensive clothes, lacy scarves, shoes made in Italy. Those transgressive, desirous stares cost virtually nothing. The men threw themselves on smug unaccompanied tourists. They were brazen, bordering on obscene. It wasn't a café, it was a stage. Everyone acted according to his or her role.

She sipped the citronade. A moment of calamity's absence, which felt like happiness.

Then three kids arrived. Patricia was with them. A Patricia in flesh, bones, blood, and brain matter. A Patricia white like cream. Her name was Katrina, like the hurricane that wiped out New Orleans.

The vacation changed course.

THE NEGROPOLITAN

Today I met Miranda. A super-mega-ultra-freakin' sensational woman. Extraordinary, phenomenal!

OK, OK. I'm out of breath, I'm excited. I'm going to end up vomiting the kebab I ate for lunch. I still don't really understand all that's happened to me. This whole day was out of the ordinary. I don't tend to meet people like that at Libla. To be honest, I don't often run across a Miranda type outside of Libla either. This marvelous human lives in my city, in Rome, and I've never met or even walked by her. Just saying Miranda doesn't do her justice. The red-headed diva from *Sex and the City* is also named Miranda, but this one is completely different. She's a serious, real woman. Saying her full name is the way to do it: Miranda Ribero Martino Gonçalves. No diminutives. She looked at me with those green eyes of hers and said, "Call me Miranda, *nena*." Her voice is like honey, a sweet lullaby that cradles those who hear it. Part of it is because she's Argentinian, from Buenos Aires. All Argentinians sound like singers to me. They don't talk, they hop between notes. The Argentinians are nice people.

She sat near me during the placement exam.

The Bourguiba School is a big deal. The placement test is a big deal. The people there are insane: the ones who put in the effort, the ones who stress out, the ones who get lost in all that exposed skin. I greeted Lucy at the entrance. Her test was on the first floor. Mine was on the third, Room 19. I walked to the staircase. The scene was like a procession into Our Lady of Mount Carmel. We went at a snail's pace. It took me an eternity to walk up three flights of stairs. They were all crooked and warped, slippery, too. If people hadn't been there to cushion me, I would've fallen as usual.

I noticed the worried faces as soon as I entered Room 19. Mine also became troubled and drooped slightly. I mean, I had to take an exam, right? I'm scared shitless by tests. I remember the hardest one I took was in linguistics. I didn't understand anything about Saussure and I was taking a course on the Basilicata dialect. It was a torment worthy of the Spanish Inquisition. Commotion in my mind and stomach. I left a mess in the toilet. In the end I scored a hundred on the exam, but I still don't know a thing about Saussure.

I threw myself like ballast on a rickety chair and waited for something to happen. I was alone in the room. I had no one to talk to. Everywhere around me, Japanese people bustled about with their cellphones as others buried their noses in books. I felt very much like a prehistoric woman: I only had a ballpoint pen and a pitiful notepad. No sign of my Arabic grammar book. Prehistoric, and a bit moronic. They'd send me back to studying the alphabet, I thought, with the children and novices.

Then she entered, wearing a burgundy Gypsy skirt and a white chemise with red glitter in the center. Simple. I looked at her undyed hair. *Cool*, I thought. *She's not afraid of her age.* My mom is constantly dying her hair. "Put the veil on, Mom, why do you torture yourself?" Mom looks at me as though I'm stark mad and rebuffs me when I touch her hair. It is sacred. Her Majesty is wronged as soon as you make a negative comment. Mom doesn't trust me when it comes to aesthetics. "You would let your hair grow out if you cared about yourself as a woman." Mom can't stand my perpetually short hair. "I'm comfortable, Ma," I tell her.

She shakes her head. She doesn't believe it. I don't believe it. She knows me well, she knows I'd be happier with longer hair. She knows I'm afraid of being a woman sometimes. It's because of what happened to me at school when I was little. They made me feel grimy in that hellhole. Mom knows it, that's why she'd like me to grow out my hair. So that faith in the woman I have inside myself will be restored. Doctor Ross agrees with my mom about the hair. She says that underneath, however, is a little girl suffocating the woman I became. The little girl wants love, but I offer none. How many people am I made of? Many, Doctor Ross says. I must believe it.

Miranda's hair is very long, though, straight and tousled. The out of place hairs give her character. You can tell she's a rebel. She sat next to me, looked over, and said, "*Sabah el kheer. Buongiorno.*" I didn't say anything, I didn't respond. I made an *O* shape with my mouth: wonder. I had to say something, I know, I know. At least try to respond. I said to myself, "Now she'll think I'm stupid," but it was only my heart beating three thousand miles an hour. I knew this woman with the straight hair well, Miranda Ribero Martino Gonçalves. I knew her before she opened her mouth and looked at me. The picture on her books shows her as young, beautiful, athletic. The original that I had in front of me didn't deviate much. At home, in Rome, I had all five of her poetry books.

I know her *Calle Corrientes*, my favorite, by heart.

Miranda is great with Arabic. She knows the ten Arabic verb forms very well, while I barely know five. I think they'll put her in the third level. I don't know where they'll put me. I hope it's not with the Japanese people who only talk on their phones. I have nothing against the Japanese, in general. Great people! I adore Haruki Murakami. Nothing but respect. But the ones in my class are an alienating mob. I don't want to become like that. Miranda says they're just guarded. Maybe she's right and I'm stupid. They'll make me start again from the alphabet. Arabic is a real headache, and cursed is the day I decided to study it. I like it, but it throws me off. I'm no longer sure of anything. The grammar is a sadist's creation. Certain things don't get through to me. It's a bona fide scourge. Though, when it comes to individual words, I know many. I get it, it doesn't count, Somali has many Arabic words. But damn, that has to count for something, right? I mean, no one in the world speaks it, I'll never do anything with it, but at least it helps me understand a smattering of Arabic words and a handful of swears. They murmur curse words on the streets here. Someone approached me once. He whispered a hieroglyph in my ear. Had he taken me for a whore? The men seem starved of women. They look at you, they undress and seduce you. It's scary. I've never enjoyed being looked at by men as though I were some kind of cream puff. I don't like the idea that, later, they might try to eat me.

After the test, Miranda and I went to a kababery. We found one near the synagogue on Avenue de la Liberté, on a traffic-plagued corner. I'd seen it as I walked past in the mornings and said to myself, "Never here." Miranda explained to me that the sleaziness of the locale meant nothing. "Everything here is a bit dingy. It's good, you'll see." I approached the server. I told him, "Shawarma, please." I didn't know how to say much else. My tongue was stuck. He shoved everything he could in the flat bread. Greens, onions, yellow sauces, spicy sauces, multicolored sauces, meat and, lastly, French fries. I felt bad. *I can't eat whatever that is, filled with fat and fries. I'll fall right on my ass.* I thought about my large, round African buttocks. *I don't want to make the situation worse.* My expression was grim. *What can I do? Tell him no thanks, I don't want it, or pay and then toss it?* Behind me, a line of the famished had formed. The kebaber gave me a dirty look. Fearful, I took out my purse. I was in a tizzy searching for coins. I looked at them. Problem: I didn't recognize them. I looked again. Nothing. I didn't understand what he wanted from me, what the heck I was supposed to give him. He muttered something in Arabic, then something in French. I don't know which language is worse. I gave him a random banknote out of desperation. A girl with a violet *hijab* and eyes outlined with kohl looked at me and sneered. Maybe I gave him too much money. What the hell did he say? I didn't understand. I didn't even know what I was about to eat.

Then came Miranda's turn. I took notes. Miranda had been in Tunis for five days. She arrived early to spend a few days by the sea. She'd already been to La Marsa and Sidi Bou Said's terrace. "We have to go together," she informed me with a slightly foreboding tone. I looked at her and jotted down note after note. I was learning the art. Me, the lowly disciple. Miranda stared Mr. Kebab in the eyes without fear, *sin miedo*. She said the magic word, *bila*. I repeated it internally like a mantra. *Bila, bila, bila*. It's a little Arabic word that is fundamental for surviving here in Tunisia. It means "without." Miranda looked at him and pointed to the food. She said *bila basal*, without onions, *bila sauce*, without sauces, *bila fil fil*, without pepper, *bila fried*, without fries. In the end, her kebab wasn't obese like mine. It was simple. Inside it was *khadrawat*, veggies, and meat. The requirements for a balanced meal. Then we went back to Bourguiba. Miranda convinced me to take the afternoon Tunisian dialect lesson. I was tired, but I consented. I'd just scarfed down my oversized kebab. My stomach couldn't handle it. There I was, sitting in the lesson, belly bulging with riotous gas.

Miranda and I didn't find spots near one another. She sat beside a big watery-eyed German. I'm near a girl who is all curls. Her name is Agata. She seems very diligent. She already bought the dialect book. She's skimming. She has pants with red flowers and an orange undershirt. Her curls are insurgent and welcoming. She smiles at me. There are lines on her forehead. That smile of hers doesn't come easy. "I'm from Padua, you know?" she says, as if justifying herself. "We have a sense of duty over there. Too much, if you ask me." She reminds me of Shirley Temple, but she told me she used to be a hothead. "Remind me to tell you about Chiapas." Shirley Temple mixed with Subcomandante Marcos? I'm curious. I want to pull her out of this muggy room and take her to a coffee shop to get a mint tea with pine nuts. This country's tea is perfect for loafing around and chatting. *Agata, let's get out of here. The lesson hasn't started and it's already dragging.*

I don't manage to tell her in time. A gaudy lady sits down and starts reciting a list.

Eighteen people are in the class. There are a handful of Japanese students, some Spaniards, and many other nationalities. There are Italians, obviously. I don't understand why they say Italy has zero population growth. You find Italians everywhere in the world, each with an Invicta watch, a cellphone, and that attitude of "I'm dying, give me a coffee" etched on their faces.

"*Sabah el kheer.*" Good afternoon, the lady says to us. I'm in the second row. I see that she has beautiful eyes.

"Sabah el kheer," she repeats. She points to someone in front of her. The professor shakes her head. She shakes it harder, violently. The person in front of her is a little old French lady. I can tell from her Jeanne Moreau hairdo. How old is she? Seventy? Older? She is wizened, thin, with a long neck. Fuck, making yourself study Arabic at that age takes guts. The Frenchwoman understands that she is to repeat the teacher's words. One by one, we repeat *Sabah el kheer.* How lovely, I say to myself. I feel like I'm in kindergarten. We repeat good afternoon. Then she makes us repeat good evening. How are you? I'm well, thank you. And then, how is your family? How's your aunt, your hightailing cousin Berta, Lassie who's on her way back home, and why not, Oum Kalthoum's hamster. Oum Kalthoum is one of the reasons why I study Arabic. Her voice burrows inside you and pelts your heart. It makes me weep. She's like Roy Orbison with Moira Orfei's hair, but her voice…it's heaven.

This feels like a lesson for barbarians from the Pleistocene period. None of the eighteen in the room are interested in merely repeating the obvious. Agata puts her heart into it. I'm fed up, like hightailing Berta.

Recess. I'm a little girl. I sprint out of the room and stand alone in a corner. Agata, the Paduan, stays behind to study. Someone is approaching—a boy with the hint of a moustache. He's cute.

"*Soy Luis*," he tells me. "*Soy cubano…he oído que hablas español.*"

Modestly: "I speak everything, my Latin American brother." He talks to me about Cuba. I forget about Tunisia.

"*Mañana si quieres vamos a la playa,*" and I almost burst out singing Righeira, but I restrain myself.

Do I tell him yes? This is no ordinary school. Everybody invites you somewhere. Everyone makes friends. I say yes. He cashes in with a big smile. The Cuban is handsome. He has amber skin, large eyes, curly hair. He's tall. It would be nice to fall in love with someone like that. It would be healthy. I never fall in love in a healthy way. Usually I tie myself to other people's dilemmas. Smiles frighten me, I know there could be something behind them later. Happiness, possibly, or muddied serenity. I'm attracted to the mysteriousness of faces. The things I can never make change are faces, walls, and mules. I'm positive. No sex, it's a no-go. I'm thirty years old and still afraid of sex. I haven't looked at my pussy in ages. There might be cobwebs.

I look for Miranda. "Let's go to the ocean tomorrow." It's not a question. She doesn't respond. It sounds like an order. She says to me, "I hope my daughter can come too." She has a daughter? What I'd give to be in her shoes.

Among the eighteen people at the Tunisian Arabic lesson, there's one unusual boy. He has an extremely long face and a great wall around his heart. He needs help, I can tell. I feel affection for him right away. The Cuban—his positivity, his smile—is wiped away. I lose my bearings in this other whirlpool. Tonight I'll dream of him. He will suckle at my breast. Mine, his mama's. I search for Miranda. I want to be rescued from my pesky infatuation. I look for her. I want to forget about the Cuban sucking my breast.

I look for Lucy. I need to be rescued. I don't want that boy suckling me. I'll either fall in love with the Cuban or somebody else. I know how it ends if I get attached to these problematic types. It ends with me suffering and hurt, feeling like a dump and strangulating the little girl inside of me who can't seem to become a woman.

Lucy, my friend, where are you?

I see her surrounded by a group of old blond fogeys. I catch and drag her away. I have to show her the boy who stilled my heart with his long face.

"Where are you taking me, for the love of God! Careful, you're rumpling my dress. Malick is outside, you know? He's waiting for me. He says he'll tutor me in Tunisian."

Malick, still? He's an animal! I don't say it. I only say, "I'm not wrinkling your dress, but you know…" I don't finish the sentence. She reads my mind.

"Oh, Holy Child of Love Divine. You're in love again! Make sure this one isn't a fag. I'm begging you, please."

"A fag? Quit it, Lucy…"

"Quit? Have you forgotten your great love Leonardo Pietrosi? Or as he demands to be called now, Priscilla, Queen of the Desert?"

"Actually, he goes by Cher."

"If you have to wrinkle my dress, at least let me see a good show. A real man. One fag was more than enough for me!"

I don't like when Lucy calls Leonardo a "fag." You know, it was tough with him. She reminds me constantly that the love of my life turned out to be gay. I know, I messed up, but in the beginning he'd assured me that…of course I could see the meandering gait, but he was always hurting his leg, he did Latin American dance in the evenings. He used too much violet perfume, I can't argue with that, but even authentic *celoduro* machos in Tunisian salsa use an assortment of perfumes. And yet it seems that they like women quite a bit. He could've told me this from the get-go. He could've spared me a year by his side. I dubbed so many CDs for him. He wrote me letters. We went out so little. Then he confessed of having known a guy named Rodolfo. Rodolfo was a fag's name. I should've known he wasn't just a friend.

No, he's not a fag, Lucy. Come look in his eyes. And then, Lucy, tomorrow we'll go to the sea with a Cuban and an Argentinian. I'm more or less on solid ground. Believe me, Lucy. Watch us and see, he's not a fag. Only a wall. I don't want to be his mama. I don't want to protect him. I don't want to hurt myself. I don't want to suffocate the girl inside me again with a demented love.

I want to feel protected, Lucy.

Help me so I don't suffocate the little girl. Lucy, I beg you, help me save her.

THE REAPARECIDA

I lived the years between the godforsaken World Cup and the Malvinas War like an invalid, leaning on Pablo Santana. I felt a love for him that knew no limit. Knight Pablo, unknown friend. He stung me with his disregard.

We never made love. One evening he told me why: "You are contaminated." That night I found out he knew about Carlos. When I'd seen him on Via dei Sabelli, with the bag of groceries, I was merely the sister of Ernesto, a *compañero*, so I was also a *compañera*.

I didn't see him at Cafra. We met on a street in Prati. The buildings in that neighborhood faced away from the Vatican. The Piedmontese built them in the years after unification. Prati was supposed to be a residential neighborhood for the capital's new government. It was also a slap in the Pope's face. I wonder if Pablo knew this story.

He and Flaca sold their wooden ducks there. The duck was supposedly a symbol of the freedom struggle. Perhaps it was really a symbol of misery. I saw the duck first, then Flaca's outfit.

About ten years later, on July 8, 1989, I was alone at home. You were little, Mar. We still lived together. I don't know where exactly. We might have been living at a friend's house. We had been there for one year. I didn't like the neighborhood. It was full of fascists, but the house was full of light. *It's the price you pay for light*, I thought, *the price for being flooded with it*. I made a few friends in the neighborhood. I remember that unfortunate day. Menem took office as the Argentinian president. Alfonsín agreed with him—the country had to move forward. I felt an acute pain in my heart. The Radio One newscast was a dagger in my chest. The country was done for. It had reached the end of the line. It had to change, and this seemed like a step backward. Twenty-thousand steps backward. That man had *una sonrisa norteamericana que no me gustaba, carajo*. It was fake, the shit-faced smile planted on his face. He wouldn't do anything good for my beloved Argentina. Nothing good for me. By then I was considered an intellectual. People would ask for my opinion. I only wanted to cry. I felt impotent. If only I'd been there in Buenos Aires, I could demonstrate with *las madres y las abuelitas de Plaza de Mayo*. I knew about their meeting on Thursdays at 3:30 around the Pirámide de Mayo, with white scarves on their heads, conjoined one to the other in an embrace. Yes, I would've been there, alive, and I wouldn't have been crying with a half-empty bottle of double malt whiskey in front of me. My nerves turned to pulp that evening. I called Pablo. I don't know if he understood my words, mumbled with buried pain. I do know that half an hour later, he was at my house. He rang the intercom incessantly. I came after a few minutes. I slithered on the ground, too drunk to walk. Too drunk to have dignity.

When I opened the door, I shouted, "Shit!" It was the only time he hugged me after our encounter on Via dei Sabelli.

Me, Pablo, the mothers of Plaza de Mayo, any Argentinian endowed with a brain and heart, we knew what a farce that man was staging for us. In the months that followed, everything became tremendously clear. Menem pardoned hundreds of officials tried for human rights violations. Among them were the infamous *carapintadas* who had made life difficult for Alfonsín, and those responsible for the Malvinas defeat. The worst was yet to come. It came in time for Christmas. Pardons were granted to Videla,

Viola, Massera, Suárez Masón, Camps. Pablo called me that day. "They did it," he said, "*hijos de puta.*"

Those who stained their hands with the blood of our sons, our daughters, our loves, our closest ties, are now free, I thought. I didn't celebrate Christmas. I told you nothing, Mar. I should've said something to you from the beginning. I should've summarized, cataloged all of my errors, all my incongruities. I wasn't ready yet.

Forgive me. I can't retie the threads of my strange life in chronological order. I have difficulties with time. Habit makes me unwind the wool of time, unstring the cloth, weave it again, find the knots, unstring it again to undo the knots. I don't want imperfections. In my case it's a futile wish. I hope that one day, when I'm no longer here, you won't learn things about me that you dislike. I don't want you to think that your mother was a *mentirosa* maggot. I was a maggot, I don't want to justify myself, I know I was a *chica mala*. But never a liar, not with you. I didn't tell you, that's true, but I did not lie to you, ever.

The day I met Pablo and Flaca, I walked around Prati. I probably had an interview. That was my main activity at the time. I wanted to become independent, take up my studies in sociology again and leave the Martino Brezzis. I was uncomfortable in their house. They were pure. I was scared of blighting these diligent people with my traitorous disease. I'd bonded with Liliana. She had a good head on her. She had dreams. She didn't act like a fifteen-year-old and was very mature. Every evening she read Gramsci's *Letters from Prison*. She cried. One evening she said to me, "He was very loved." Even so, I wanted to leave them. I liked Liliana and the rest of the family as well, but I wanted to create a new Miranda in that gigantic city. I wanted to be reborn, like Venus from the froth of the sea.

Pablo and Flaca were bizarre. I saw the duck first, then Flaca's white outfit. The duck was fat and looked like it had indigestion from *dulce de leche*. Yet the face was kind. Its beak was like that of *el pato* Donald, Donald Duck in miniature. Its maternal girth moved me. It reminded me of my mother. She was often on my mind in those years. I'd left and hadn't said goodbye to her. I didn't want her to spit in my face. I wouldn't be able to endure her telling me, *"No mereces que te llame puta."* It was the unbearable truth. I ignored it.

Adversity was my chaperone and also my present. The duck, however, looked happy. There was a glint in its drawn eyes. Then I could see that the glint wasn't coming from the duck, but from the white background. I raised my eyes slowly. Things revealed themselves to me piecemeal. The whiteness was a cloth, the cloth a dress, that dress a woman, the woman Marilyn Monroe. It was a Marilyn without breasts, the dress from *The Seven Year Itch*, blonde hair, perhaps a wig. Her makeup was garish, caked-on, laborious, a triumph of rainbow dust that didn't quite make sense. She was like a Picasso painting, painful to look at. At the same time, I was entranced by this crude draft of a woman. *Why would she dress like that?* As soon as I'd formed the thought, I heard a man's voice tell me in Spanish, *"Hay que quitarse el sombrero delante de ella."* I touched my head. I had a beanie on. I snatched it off. The Picassan Marilyn struck a pose, performed a jazz dance step that might've only been a bumbling strut. *Is she thanking me?* I bowed my head in return. I felt stupid on that Roman stage. The voice chimed in. "Do you really not recognize her? Don't you remember her anymore, Miranda?"

I looked at her more closely and glanced at the duck. I think I was hoping for an epiphany. I didn't know who that ridiculous woman was. I turned toward the voice and saw that it was Pablo Santana. He told me the ridiculous woman was Flaca, born Rosa Benassi, daughter of Italians. Rosa had deteriorated into a drooling fool. I cried. In the seventies, I didn't know how to do anything else.

What was I doing in those years exactly? I can't precisely say. I was traipsing around a city called Buenos Aires, a city that still has that name, though I don't believe it's the same anymore. There is a before, a moment in which the irreversible has not yet happened, when the soul hasn't been lost. I lost mine, but I'm not the only one. There were many who pretended that everything was proceeding as normal. The slogan was *No te metas*, don't meddle. So we stuffed cotton in our ears. As if that weren't enough, we drew from our dark sides. I think of that despicable statement, "There must be a good reason they disappeared." A good reason? What would that be? Tell me. Integrity in ruins. People in ruins. Our conscience was swamp water. We were reprobates. Me, us, everyone. We didn't lift a finger. We all ate popcorn and watched the *Videla Horror Picture Show*. The front row was packed with moronic smiles.

They took Ernesto in the seventies, toward the end of the decade. At the start, however, there was excitement all around. In years past there had been banana dictatorships. Years when, little by little, people took power and wore the country down like a termite wears down wood. We young people waited for Perón. The old folks, too, waited for Perón. We were duped into thinking that the man who had aroused such excitement with his aplomb and his beautiful wife—his first wife, Evita, who Argentinians considered the *only* one—could solve all our problems. We believed he was God instead of a man. Perhaps a specter. We believed in him when the decade began.

I lost hope only after his first speech at the Casa Rosada. Yes, from the moment of his first political act after eighteen years in exile. He was elected president with sixty-two percent of the vote, his largest electoral triumph. He presented himself on the balcony with his nutty four-dollar slut, Isabel Martínez, whose real name was María Estela. The idiot was named vice president. You could see her mock Evita with every breath of her mucus-filled lungs. She didn't deserve the prestige. Why marry such a mediocre woman after Evita? I remember the speech. I'd gone to hear it with Ernesto. It was one of the few things we did together. Perón was decked in full regalia and seemed younger, at least that's the sense I got from afar. I remember trying to hear the *viejo*'s words, but I couldn't make anything out. Someone handed me a pamphlet and I read it. I didn't understand. Ernesto explained that the pamphlet announced Perón's Armed Revolutionary Forces and the Montoneros had joined forces.

I remember being alarmed by the bulletproof glass Perón had erected as a barrier between him and us. It wasn't like before anymore, even the viejo had sold out to power. I felt a throb at the opening of my stomach. I wasn't very well read in politics. I liked tango and soccer. I thought politics was complicated, too many acronyms and changes I didn't understand. On that day, though, I understood the glass. It represented something no Argentinian could ignore. The idolized leader was afraid of the fucking activists. That September, Perón's fear materialized as bulletproof glass, which would defend him from the people, his people. In '74, they became an unwieldy furor.

On May 1, 1974, Flaca and I found ourselves again at the Plaza de Mayo. Ernesto and my mother weren't in the city. They'd gone to Patagonia to do something that I don't now recall. Something to do with Grandpa Alfio's house. One day I'll show you Grandpa Alfio's house, I'll show you all of Patagonia. It seems like hell, *hija*, but really it is paradise, and not only because of the silence. There it seems that life finally decided to call a truce. That suspension of pain was so gratifying. It seems incomprehensible, I know, and it's not easy to imagine if you don't experience it. But I swear, dear, that's what the land makes you feel.

They were away. I was alone. I hadn't met Carlos. I would meet him soon after. That day I was still pure and virginal.

Flaca had snug jeans, her hair in a braid, one hand covered with gray metal rings. She might have been stylish, but the braid was outdated. She looked like my grandfather's grandmother. She'd come to visit me at home. I was alone, as I told you, reading an important book by Jean-Paul Sartre. I'd found it in a library. It was titled, simply, *Antisemitism*. I want to die when I think of it now. Perhaps that book was trying to warn me about the future, but I was never good at reading signs. So I set the book down and went to open the door. It was her, Rosa, with her unfashionable plait.

"Will you come with me to Plaza de Mayo?" she asked, tilting her head. I watched the braid twirl. I told her yes. It was hard to say no to that girl. She was so lovely and pure.

There was mass hysteria in Plaza de Mayo. Many people were young. They all looked very fair. In those years, my hormones were running a thousand miles per hour. I wanted to sweat on top of another human being. I wanted someone else's saliva in my interstices. I didn't know it yet, but this was the *saudade* of having given birth. I felt incomplete. Alone, I was no longer enough for myself. I wanted to enter the bloodstream of the universal spirit. To give, receive, share, lavish. I was about to go crazy. Yes, crazily, madly in love. I would come to love everything. And yet, stupid as I am, I forgot to love myself. I hardly loved myself at all. I felt like a roach, or something worse.

Flaca loved me dearly, though. She read between my lines, you understand?

"Hey, girlie," she said, "we came here for Perón, not cute boys. Remember?"

I grimaced in mock horror. We cackled. My mouth wide. Hers, wider. I scoped my surroundings. The boys were striking, as were the girls. We were a beautiful generation. That was a volatile time politically, but generative. People debated everything, from films to plays. The city was a riot of movie clubs, theaters, off-Broadway shows. Unconventional years. Trailblazers and dimwits. A beautiful generation. Sensitive, healthy, altruistic. A generation of dreamers. I can't believe it was fractured. Those who didn't die in the concentration camps—230 of them throughout Argentina—were consumed by fear and cowardice. Many left the country and were never really seen again. Today in Argentina, everyone is either a therapist or in therapy. We were lost thanks to a bunch of sleazy brutes.

What agony, what ancient pains I'm calling forth. I must, dear. I've been keeping you in the dark. I'm not proud of it. I couldn't do it earlier, understand? You might not. Something inside me has changed. Could it be this place on the Mediterranean? I believe so. The dictatorship in Tunis boggles the mind. It's breathtaking. It's what brought the pain out. I don't remember what Perón said, not even from that time I heard him. His words, which once inflamed souls, sounded false and hypocritical, and not only to me. Gardel came to mind. His slicked back hair, his droopy hat, his frank stare. I don't know why I sang. It was absurd and irreverent.

> *Así aprendí que hay que fingir*
> *para vivir decentemente.*
> *Que amor y fe mentiras son,*
> *y del dolor se ríe la gente.*

"You heard him too, right?" Flaca asked me.

After a few moments, everyone was making noise. No one listened to the old man anymore. Then the ear-piercing chorus: *How is it, how is it, how is it, General, that the people's government is full of criminals?* It was true. The evidence was overwhelming. I wasn't the only one who thought so. Before Perón could make a final point in his speech, we left the piazza along with everyone else. It was a pointless speech, and quite possibly malevolent. It wasn't worth listening to. When Perón reached the end, there wasn't a living soul in Plaza de Mayo. The dead souls were sickened.

Flaca and I slipped into a cinema. They were showing an old movie with Marilyn Monroe. It was Billy Wilder's *The Seven Year Itch*. Flaca knew the gags by heart. When Marilyn's dress lifted in the subway gust, crowning the erotic dream of the Middle American male, all Flaca could say was "Poor Norma Jeane."

I don't know why, but I kissed her on the mouth.

THE PESSOPTIMIST

Maryam enjoyed recording her voice. She felt like one of those good surround speakers whose sound one could feel in the heart. She no longer pushed the buttons anxiously. She didn't rewind the tape anymore. Her gestures were sure, her hand firm. Her voice did not fluctuate.

"Zuhra, sometimes I feel like Howa is sitting next to me. This thought helps me a lot. Because I have a fickle memory, I never remember minor details. She wove the thread of time for us both. She kept every genealogy in mind. But now, sitting with this recorder, everything is so clear to me, like the noontime sun. I think she's the one whispering the past in my ears."

Maryam's thoughts wandered back once again to Termini Station and Howa's funeral. It was where everyone had gathered to leave for Prima Porta, on the fringe of the city where Howa would lounge for eternity. Needless to say, everyone was late. Typical of Somalis. The only Swiss, right on time, was Maryam. It was her turn to wait, though not for that long. Better than usual. Maryam analyzed her surroundings. Termini's walls were covered with papers. Flyers of all kinds, some very large, others small, had been stuck everywhere. They all shouted. All were urgent. They advertised social events, restaurants, buses to Eastern Europe, black hairdressers, refugee welcome centers, Italian language schools.

The walls in the capital station were so different from the walls of the small village where she once lived.

The woman thought of Primavalle and its infinite walled paths. *What was Primavalle crying out for?* she wondered. She realized uneasily that Primavalle was covered almost exclusively in real estate ads. There wasn't the same phantasmagoria of paper that inundated Termini.

Termini's walls permitted obscenities to the point of tastelessness. Nude women in lewd poses caught the attention of rich white men with fuchsia-colored numbers to call. Every announcement was written in at least two languages, Italian and English or Italian and Third World-ese. Maryam, simply to kill time, took a survey of the languages used in the little, poorly tacked flyers. There were more than fifty, she determined, with no trace of pride.

The Somalis still hadn't arrived, not even those who should've come early. Had she gotten the days mixed up? *Perhaps,* the woman thought happily. *Maybe Howa Rosario isn't dead and you came here by accident.* Maryam clung to this silly illusion for a moment. Good sense didn't allow for daydreams. Howa Rosario was dead, dead as a rock, finished. Howa Rosario was in the arms of angels. She was going away, didn't Maryam understand this?

Yes, Maryam understood.

To distract herself from her new pain, she turned fully toward the walls. She looked at the ads like children look at Christmas gifts, with suspect curiosity. She read the notices, interpreted them, laughed at some. Then in the confusion of meaningless words and subliminal images, she saw her: Norma Jeane Baker. She was stunned. It was a photo from early in her career. A picture in which Norma Jeane's evolution into Marilyn Monroe hadn't completely happened yet. Her face was sweet and her sensuality was not pernicious. Norma/Marilyn was like a fearful newborn. Norma reminded Maryam of panna cotta on ice cream. Abundant, frothy, soft. It was so good you had to eat it right away in a single bite. The panna wasn't destined to last. Pure consumption. Pure indulgence. Norma was also consumed. The first time Marilyn Monroe thought of consuming her, Norma hid. Then came the universe's turn. Maryam wondered what would've come of Norma Jeane if Gladys Pearl Monroe, her mother, had hugged her as a child. Sometimes Maryam Laamane thought she might be Gladys. She wasn't convinced that she carried out her motherly duties as well as she could have

"Zuhra, I should've hugged you more. The *jinn* in the glass got the better of me." Maryam Laamane had a theory on alcoholic pathology. "It's the jinn's fault, my dear, when I was like that, when I wasn't the mama I wanted to be." Jinn: little demons contained in a cherry-flavored drink. They cheated her.

Maryam wasn't surprised to see Norma Jeane in Termini. "It was predictable seeing her stuck there," she said into the recorder. Norma popped up in her life at unexpected moments, as she had the first time, on July 1, 1960.

They'd risen at dawn. There were things to get ready for the party. They had to make something to eat for everyone, for those who'd fought in the past and those who would soon pour out of their homes, including their own. That's the way things were in 1960, in Mogadishu. Houses were wide open. Intimacy was an alien notion. Neighbors were members of the same big community, the same *umma*. Everyone was family. They gave of themselves merrily, especially that day, in a constant give and take. They filled their mouths with *halwa*, hot dumplings, fragrant *injera*, spiced rice, stew. Everything was gulped down with *shai* and ginger coffee. There were also colorful drinks being passed around, and the children argued briefly over sugared *bur*.

Everywhere she went, Maryam gorged. She ate five times that day. She was so thin that everything slid off her without consequence. It was late, after the afternoon prayer, when her aunt called to her. "Take these sweets to *Hajiedda* Saida."

The girl didn't like this very much. "Send Leila, please. I went yesterday and…"

183

Her aunt wouldn't hear it. "Maryam, don't act like you normally do. I don't want to punish you today. It's a celebration, Somalia's celebration. Don't make me. Obey and come back quickly." Having said that, her aunt put the bundle of sweets in her lap.

Maryam was terrified. Until that moment, everything had been perfect. The sweets, the laughter with her friends, the air of festivity and happiness. Then this assignment, the last thing she wanted to be doing. The previous night seemed like a hundred years ago. Maryam wanted to create some mental distance. She hadn't understood anything of what happened between Hajiedda Saida and her daughter, but she guessed it had to have been serious. The woman scared her to death. She shivered when she thought of the dead chicken eye.

If she didn't go, she would be punished, and she didn't want that. For the rest of her life, she'd regret missing the celebration, which was for the entire country. Maryam couldn't say why, but her absence would be an unforgivable crime. She wasn't sure that in the future there'd be anything like it in the Horn, which Allah had given to Africa.

She entered Hajiedda Saida's house. The big woman wasn't there. The wicker mat on which that enormous mass sat the night before was folded so that jinn and demons wouldn't dirty the prayer fabric with their vile feet. The house seemed abandoned. It was ghostly.

"*Hodi! Hodi!*" the girl said. "Is anyone there?"

She repeated *hodi, hodi* for a bit. Then, tired of a wait that was straining her young nerves, she decided to leave. That was when Howa Rosario appeared.

"Everyone went to feast on sweets. I'm the only one here," Howa said.

"Oh, yeah. Hi."

Howa Rosario smiled. The quivering little girl in front of her made her laugh.

"We agreed to meet at the celebration, remember? I can see from the junk you're wearing that you decided not to wait for me."

Maryam was embarrassed. It was true, she'd promised the pretty girl with the crooked nose that she'd wait for her, that she'd make the rounds of the houses with her and taste that heavenly bounty together with her. Maryam wasn't good with promises when food was in the equation.

"Yes, I'm sorry. I tasted a few things…but now I'll go with you. I brought you this." She handed over the bundle her aunt had prepared.

"No, Maryam, don't worry. We'll still walk around and maybe we can go to the cinema. I'll ask your auntie for permission."

The news made greedy Maryam's slender body jump. Infantile enthusiasm.

"First I have to pray the Maghrib. Skipping the sunset prayer isn't good. That's when the angels change places."

"They change places?"

"Yes, dear. The angels never stay still."

Maryam thought about the angels. It seemed like a beautiful thing that they never stayed still. Neither did she.

"Howa, would you teach me how to pray?" the girl asked timidly.

Howa Rosario smiled. "Of course. Do you know how to say the *fatiha*?"

"Yes," Maryam Laamane said proudly.

"Okay, my friend, then you know how to pray."

The film she saw with Howa Rosario that day was *Some Like It Hot*.

She laughed a lot with Howa that night. Howa had straight, bright white teeth like those in drawings. Before Marilyn, before that strange story of cross-dressing men, the two girls were nearly beaten up and left in tears.

They'd said the evening prayer, then the *dua'a* rite—a thought for those who were no longer there and another for those who were alive but doing badly. Twelve times they recited the *ikh-las*, the sincerity sura, then the fatiha, the opening sura, another twelve times. Their hands bowled over their faces to filter impurities of thought. They were ready. They made tribute to Allah, the Tenderly Merciful, the Clement—praises and thanks. They'd done the duty of good faithfuls. After prayer, it was time to go out together. The two girls, Howa with her braid and Maryam with her mirth, were ready to conquer Mogadishu.

The city wouldn't sleep that night. There were parties everywhere. Fireworks cut through the equatorial sky and animals joyfully yipped in cryptic verses. Maryam would give her life (or at least half of it) to have King Solomon's ability to understand the beasts of the earth. She would've liked more than anything to know how to decipher birdsong. But she was a little girl, not King Solomon. A little girl happy to have a special friend, one with such a luminous braid. There were films in Mogadishu that night, as well as theatrical comedies, traditional dances, patriotic songs. The country's elite gathered at the National Theater for a show called *Tradition and Folklore*, which retraced the homeland's history through dance. The elite were dressed in the finest Somali fabrics. Tailors had been working for weeks to create a surfeit of colors. The two of them were merely a small child and a young girl. One dressed in red and the other in blue, their best clothes. They were happy.

"Let's go to Cinema Shebelle. I heard they're showing a good film with chase scenes."

That sounded good to Maryam. She'd never gone to the cinema. She responded to her friend's proposal with an enthusiastic yes.

"First, dear, let's go tell your auntie you're staying with me tonight."

Her aunt gave the green light. She knew Howa. Besides, her hair was spellbinding.

"The girl will drive you crazy," her aunt told Howa. "You have my permission to smack her!"

Maryam Laamane cowered.

"There's no need, ma'am," Howa Rosario replied. "Maryam is sweet."

Maryam's eyes filled with tears. Her gratitude for Allah al-Kareem, the Generous One, had enabled her to meet this most special friend.

In the middle of their journey, the two ran into Fauzia Ahmed and her five-girl posse.

"Where do you think you're going?" Fauzia snapped.

Howa Rosario responded unfazed. "To the cinema."

"Hear that, sisters? This one thinks she can go to the cinema," Fauzia said, enraged, and then spat in her face.

Howa took a kerchief that she had in her skirt, cleaned herself well, then grabbed hold of Maryam and started to leave.

"Darling, where do you think you're going now?" Fauzia asked, getting more worked up.

"To the cinema," Howa Rosario said again.

"You're a coward like your father. I spat in your face, if you didn't realize. You have to do something," Fauzia said.

"Yeah, you gotta do something," the five henchwomen echoed.

"Exactly, I'm going to the cinema," and with this Howa Rosario hoped to end the matter.

Maryam Laamane couldn't tolerate that impossible woman's pronged tongue insulting her special friend.

"Shut up, fool," she said. The words came out with unusual ease.

"You brought a little pest with you, I see?" Fauzia said.

"I'm not a pest. I am Maryam Laamane Abdi. You don't have permission to insult my friend Howa, got it?"

Howa squeezed Maryam's hand. She hoped to keep her quiet. In vain. Maryam kept talking.

"Did you catch that, friends?" Fauzia Ahmed said. "Another traitor." She faced Maryam. "You're not allowed to celebrate. This party is for those of us who've earned it. You're a traitor, like your friend with the bulbous nose. Your father and his father were soldiers for the Italians. They killed, they were prideful, and they got rich off the labor of honest Somalis."

"Hush, you idiot." This time it was Howa speaking. "Leave the girl alone."

"You don't tell me to shut up. You're a lowly bitch."

Silence. The night's pleasant air became suddenly tense and chilly, the trees threatening, and the animals nervous. Fauzia's five companions held their breath and Maryam Laamane panicked.

Howa had steely nerves. She didn't want to get into it with this fool on a festive night, but she knew she had no other choice.

Fauzia laid it on. "Look at her, a cheap little slut…"

Fauzia's smile was a malicious sneer, her voice three octaves higher. A group started forming around the contenders. Years later, when Muhammad Ali went to Africa to fight the rematch of all rematches, Maryam would remember Fauzia and Howa Rosario and that senseless combat.

Fauzia railed with insults. She flung mud. She didn't know why. She smiled, too, wanting the crowd to cheer her on. She wanted to ingratiate herself with the jury. She repeated the word "slut" a million times. After the millionth, Howa Rosario couldn't hold back anymore and slapped her vehemently. It sounded like a bomb.

"Your mother should've beaten you more, fool."

Onlookers waited restlessly for Fauzia Ahmed's reaction. The mob grew vastly. The tussle between the girls briefly overshadowed their much coveted independence.

No reaction from Fauzia. Only ice cold words.

"The truth hurts, yeah? If you take it so personally, it means you really are a slut. Else you wouldn't have reacted like that."

Fauzia scored a point. Howa didn't know what to say. The fool was making her do what she didn't want to do. She had to defend her reputation. Now she couldn't simply ignore it and walk away. She had to show the others that it wasn't true, that she wasn't a slut. She was an intact, sewn-up maiden, as God hoped she would be.

"Stupid Fauzia Ahmed, I hate you, I hate you," Howa Rosario said to herself.

In a case of contested reputation, tradition demanded that the accused had to challenge the one who insulted her in a test of virginity. She had to defend her honor by showing her vagina to a group of female volunteers. These impartial judges would determine the truth. Howa was tempted not to stoop to that debased compromise. She was devoted to Allah, she said her five prayers, she adhered to Ramadan. Why did she have to submit herself to a rite that had nothing to do with Islam? Doctor Jumaale had explained it to her. He was a good man. He'd told her many things. He'd explained how to cook healthily. He'd advised eating papaya when her stomach refused to do what it was supposed to do and he'd also told her that "The *gudnisho* isn't something written in the Quran." She didn't like this. Her infibulation had made her ill. She still remembered when it happened. Four women held her down as the fifth cut the flap of skin that hung from her vagina. They didn't just cut that, but much of the stuff around it too. She only realized this afterward. She remembered the blood on her thighs, the needle penetrating her skin. And her first pee, an indescribable pain. "Had I known you earlier, Doctor Jumaale, I wouldn't have let myself go through such a painful thing, which God never asked of me."

The people around her were ferocious. They would massacre her with jeers. She'd made plans, she wanted to work, be independent, leave the fat monster that was her mother. Instead, she was lost. Everyone would find out that…

She had to throw down the gauntlet. *Fauzia Ahmed, cursed is the day you came into the world. May the wrath of Allah crash down upon you, daughter of Iblis.*

"I challenge you," Howa said. Her voice did not break.

Maryam Laamane, meanwhile, was trembling. She was scared for her new friend.

"Come to my house," one woman proposed. "You'll be examined there."

Many women, volunteers from the crowd, went with the girls. They would inspect the girls' privates.

Howa prayed in the stillness of her mind.

"Howa, you were offended first. And so you must undress first," the mistress of the house said, pointing to a wicker mat beside her.

Howa Rosario obeyed without protesting. What else could she do?

She lay down on the wicker mat, arms crossed above her head, eyes on the ceiling. She mechanically opened her legs, keeping her knees bent and nearly touching her head. Her thighs were wide, as though in offering. Someone brought an oil lamp to see more clearly. The women approached, curious and uncomfortable. A crowd soon formed around the girl with her knees up.

"What is this!" one of the women from the group shouted.

"It's white," another said.

"Very white," a third echoed.

"What could it be?" a perplexed pair asked.

"It's tough," someone with a tottering scarf on her head said.

"We want some, too," the jurors yammered.

Howa didn't understand. She only felt the cold wicker mat irritating her ribs.

She pulled herself up in astonishment, but with the dignity that had always distinguished her.

"Excuse me, ladies, what is happening?"

Maryam Laamane explained the mystery. None of these women had seen underwear in their lives. Howa Rosario was thankful for the distraction. She'd forgotten to remove them. She was also grateful to the seamstress Bushra, who taught her that secret. "Drafts and sand can't slip in with these on." That was basically true. She would go thank her the next day. Although, when she thought about it more, the idea weighed on her. There was unfinished business with Bushra.

THE FATHER

Before Mickaël Kra's jewels, Marianne Fassler's leopard skins, Alphadi's perfumes, Pathe'O's gaudy shirts, before all of them, great pioneers of African style, inestimable designers, dear Zuhra, I was there in Africa. Before the sub-Saharan *sapeur* posed as stars, before Papa Wemba wore Ferré, before Mobutu made everyone don the Maoist *abacost*, before this and anything else, before everything and everyone, I was there. I was one of the most famous African designers. I was sought after, my patterns worn everywhere. For me it was art, but also mundanity. I remember Mrs. Zeinab Moallim, who requested a traditional *garees* gown in the form of a moon because she didn't want to feel alone after her husband married another woman. And Shukri, who asked for different colors as he got older, or Mr. Omar Tenenti, who was going on a business trip in Mauritania

It's strange, dear. I never thought of making money. It was enough for me to make people beautiful and be paid the proper amount. Who was thinking of a boutique in front of the Ritz? In my eyes, the Ritz, Paris, the Champs-Élysées were science fiction. Rome, where you live now, the Rome that colonized and forgot us—that was also science fiction. The only reality that could contain me was Africa. I was among the greatest, they say. Hagi Nur showed me one of my photos in a book one day, an arresting

picture. I was next to Sékou Touré. I'd made him a nice *mise*.
Kwame Nkrumah hadn't died yet—Nixon and the English hadn't
yet played poker with his life—and Sékou Touré wanted a suit
to welcome an old battle companion. I made clothes for important people, the ones you see in history books. Without Bushra,
I wouldn't have been anything. She was the one who taught me,
shaped me. She was more than a mother. She was the very essence of life.

Where was I? Right, when Bushra became my new mama.
The mama of little Elias Majid. Elias was a beneficent child swad-
dled in goodness and closed in the embrace of a thousand hands.
It wasn't only his aunts who loved him, but also the neighbors, the
cats, strangers. Every song, every word and every thought was for
Elias. Everyone searched inside him for something that was no
longer there. The truth is that everyone was looking for Famey.
The child was her emanation. They all deluded themselves into
thinking that death hadn't come for that slight, strong girl. Death
hadn't taken her away in a bath of blood and placenta. The child
was the miniature of the small mother with the same big eyes, the
same infantile bliss, the same perfect gentleness. By loving Elias,
one made fair tribute to the sister, neighbor, mistress. Majid was
respected by all. The people knew that his seed, his collaboration
had been needed to make that puppy boy. They often ignored him,
though. Only the mother mattered to the world. Her expelled
placenta, her scattered blood, her screams from the outer edges
of death. She had sacrificed herself for the child. It was fitting to
consider it hers alone.

In truth, the sacrifice had been greater. No one else could
imagine it. The shout of Famey dying was the shout of Famey
raped, the echo of Majid raped. It was trampled dignity. Their
wounded pride, their despondent love. It was her. It was him. She
who gathered the clothes soaked with blood and sperm, furiously
wrung them out and threw the sand of the wildlands on top of
them. And it was he who stood up and fell back down. It was she

who went to him, rubbed sand on his backside, massaged him. She who whispered the words of a soft lullaby in his ear. He who stopped her hand. He who tried to massage his pride. His sex. He who pulled up his fallen trousers. He who cried. She who was not allowed to hug him.

Majid was respected. He was a worthy husband for Famey, though perhaps too skittish for the people's liking. Not even the jinn, they whispered, tempted him with their boorish wisecracks. He seemed immune to joy. A mask. Children feared him, but he was considered a man deserving of most people's trust.

They considered the only flaw, more like a misdeed, to be his rushed marriage to Bushra. Your aunts (and others) were very upset by Majid's choice.

"Why does it have to be *her*?" Aunt Ruqia asked.

"Why the witch?" others echoed.

If Majid had married a jinn they wouldn't have been so bothered. Somalia was full of men who married jinn. But men who married villainous witches, well, this was open to debate.

The old wives' tales about Majid's marriage didn't end with domestic uproar. The neighbors, acquaintances, pets, strangers, and everyone else wanted their say. Cheerful gossips were unleashed, as were blossoming maidens, back alley bachelors, sly shoe shiners, retailers, *qat* pushers, charming soothsayers, conformists, contrarians. They slandered and badmouthed those two as though it were the only subject worthy of conversation on the planet.

The question that played over and over on everyone's lips was why her exactly, with all the women there were in the glorious land of Punt?

Yes, she's pretty, but what else? Okay, she's also intelligent, but then, tell me, what more? Certainly she knows how to run a house like no other, but then, come on, then what? In bed they say that…but then, excuse me, what else?

It was as though Bushra had to show that she was faultless,

immaculate. Hers was a strange fate, having to prove that she was herself.

The women openly envied her. They considered her an oaf, a social climber, something of a slut. The men derided her in public so as to dream of her more lucidly at night. Her gazelle eyes stood out in people's minds. They say her fame reached distant moorlands, where only the name of Bilqis, the queen of Saba, was eminent. In those lands she was compared to the queen for her beauty.

In their first month together, the couple gained no respite—words, words, words.

"She twists you down there," asserted Omar, vendor of *zaytun* and other assorted fruits. "She twists you so much that you don't know what's going on and can't use it well with women anymore. You get so twisted that it almost doesn't go through their sewn slits. It's as if you turn into a woman."

"Majid strikes me as womanly, don't you think, friends?" quipped the jackass Muqtar.

"Be quiet, friend," Yousuf chastised. "Don't let those words touch your lips. You're a believer, and it's not right to offend your neighbor. Even though I think you're right, it's because Famey died that he wavers so uncertainly."

"Quiet, snakes. Majid is a good man, God-fearing and blessed with a beautiful son. He wavers because he is hurting. According to his poor, late wife, no one should doubt his virility. The women chatter among themselves and Famey once told my woman that he never let her rest, ever. The man has appetites to satisfy, if you get my meaning."

"So now he'll find a worthy opponent, the good Majid! They say that woman, that witch Bushra, is very greedy," Ahmed squawked.

"Yes, that's exactly what they say," everyone said in chorus.

"Yeah," added Hamid, Mrs. Ferrarotti's valet, "I heard she stupefies men with potions that..."

"That what?!" Mahmoud shouted, torn between libidinous

curiosity and measured disgust.

Precisely "what" was never answered. The climax came only with the final revelation:

"I heard from my second wife," Libaan said, "that the witch has meat swinging between her legs. She's not sewn like our women."

"What are you saying?" the chorus asked, aghast.

"I'm saying," Libaan repeated, "what I just said, that she has meat hanging between her legs. She still has *that thing which must be cut*. Oh, don't make me say the damned word."

"The word?" Othman said. "Don't tell me that…"

"That's right…" was Libaan's reply.

"Poor Majid. They say the meat hanging from women's parts can kill our virility. How does that happen?" Othman asked, dismayed.

"I don't know," Libaan said. He sounded defensive. "I do know that the Arabs and Italians who live on our land say they're not afraid of the hanging meat, that it's actually better. But how? If it kills our virility, how can it be better?"

"Ask me, friends, ask me. Over here." It was a stranger who no one had ever seen in the neighborhood.

"Who might you be?" asked the chorus, vexed by the intrusion.

"I am me, and that's enough. I've traveled. I've been with women who have the hanging meat. There is an island, countless kilometers away from here, where the women wear colored gowns and massage your feet. Women who smell of cocoa and incense. Women who are like the evening sun. After offering you seafood and sweat and tears, they offer themselves. They lay down nude and you spread yourself on top of them. They all still have their *kintirka*, and so they're happy."

The intrigued men wanted to ask more but were too scared.

The stranger continued his story. "They sigh beneath the weight of a man, they stir and enjoy themselves like us. Sometimes even more."

"A woman, enjoying it?" the chorus asked. "Isn't it against nature?"

The stranger shook his head. "Your friend Majid is lucky. He'll savor a meal that you can't even imagine, fools that you are. Cutting that splendid addition to the woman is an incredible disservice to ourselves, as well as to them. Oh, the thought of not seeing my beautiful mistresses anymore, setting suns! Here in this arid land, your fear makes the women arid too. It's an unrightable wrong!" The stranger hit himself on the head a thousand times in a show of pain.

"Ah, you're a foreigner," one of the chorus said, a man who worked for customs in Mogadishu. "What do you know about our women? Bushra is a witch. Her hunger befits a witch and her hanging meat is a witch's. She could very well be the daughter of Iblis's daughter."

Bushra had fun. In the first month of marriage, she entertained herself by going around listening to hearsay. There was always someone who didn't know her and went to her to report the latest on Bushra the witch and that dunce Majid. If she had known the alphabet and the magic of writing, beautiful Bushra would've kept a journal. She didn't know how to write, so when she got an idea in her head, she would transfer it to fabric. The truth of that first month was written in those weavings. People lined up to acquire a *bulgi* dress or a ceremonial *dirah* made by the sorceress designer Bushra. Aware of her success, she raised the prices a little. She ran a good business, despite having to take care of the little one.

Those canvases told stories of desire and perdition. In the fabrics there was only a frustrated love and a love repaid. The marriage was a contract, nothing more. Majid, adhering to Muslim tradition, bore the burden of his new wife—her sustenance and her good conduct. She, on the other hand, as written in the prenuptial, occupied herself entirely with the little one. She gave him her milk and her love.

The wedding was a formality. They didn't throw a party, they didn't call friends, they didn't eat delicacies. After the wedding, Majid went to work. She simply began sewing. From that moment on, Bushra had an adjunct. A tender dumpling of a child.

Elias had the discerning gaze of one born ready for the troubles of our ephemeral existence. He moved his hands and tiny feet round and round, as though he were rushing to stand, walk, and gallivant through the streets of the world. He cried as needed but knew how to respect his new mama's time. She cradled him in her arms, intoning the traditional poems of her grandmother Medina. They were praise songs to the rain, to nature, to the simple purity of nomadic life. In Bushra's voice, one discovered the granularity of sand, the sweetness of noble camels, the unequalled ferociousness of raiding hyenas, the infinite tumult of an eternal love. Her poems were lovingly perceptive, their hearts bathed in blood and adoration.

The first night, Majid came home tired. She gave him a massage. He fell asleep hoping to maintain a certain distance from his wife's body.

He wants to save himself for when he has more strength, the naïve woman thought.

The second night, Majid came back even more tired. The bags under his eyes had excavated his face to the bone. He was like a ghost, something to fear. But Bushra desired him. She massaged him vigorously. "I have to give strength to these drained muscles." She ran oil over every patch of skin. Feet, calves, thighs. She noted proudly that her spouse, still unfamiliar to her, had a beautiful back and promising buttocks, which she heartily rubbed down. The bed (the same one Majid had shared with Famey, may Allah have mercy on her bedeviled soul) wobbled like a blind crane beneath the enamored woman's passion. Bushra was truly in love. She had always respected Majid. She'd been his sister-in-law, and only because of that had she rid herself of iniquitous thoughts. And anyways she'd been married to a man who'd made her into a full-fledged woman, despite the dreadful pain that came with being a virgin. After Majid's diffident marriage proposal, her respect for the first husband gave way to gratitude for the second.

"He isn't afraid of me," Bushra said to the other Bushra, the insecure, small one that lived inside her, which the people call *nafs*, soul. "He doesn't think of me as a witch, or the daughter of Iblis's daughter."

Gratitude quickly became love, which muddied the waters. Bushra sewed herself a stunning dress for the lonely wedding. She found an orange material that she wrapped herself in like a pearl. He was too tired to recognize her efforts.

The first week passed without any fuss. Bushra was faithful, in love. She massaged her unfamiliar man and, secretly, also massaged herself. She wanted to offer herself with ready, firm thighs. She massaged her breasts, which were like pulp-heavy papayas. And she massaged her sex and the hanging meat that had been her bane. They hadn't cut her like they did the other sisters.

It had happened by chance. No one realized she wasn't present at the infibulation with the others. There were many that day, and people were tired. The floods had just come. There were dead to bury, livestock to attend, plans to review. Everything was chaotic and unforeseen. The truth is that they forgot her. And so the meat still dangled from her vagina. She was good at concealing it from her sisters. She never undressed in front of them. She never allowed her vagina to be seen. Bushra had seen the state her sisters came home in. Immense pain, terrible pees, horror. Anima had died from the operation. It seemed absurd to Bushra. "Why do something God does not want?" a young imam asked her one day. The people took and threw stones at him, insulted him. But the young imam said, "You are fools for cutting what Allah has created." Bushra impressed those words on her heart and permitted no one to touch her anymore. Even her first husband was silenced. He tried rebelling to show her that he was the master. She said, "Try me and see." He never complained about the swinging meat. In fact…

But that's a legend and now, my Zuhra, I don't have time for asides. I want to talk about Bushra, Majid, and their bridal bed.

Twelve days after the wedding, Bushra realized how their marriage would proceed. Majid returned earlier than usual. There was almost nothing on the stove. She was breastfeeding Elias when her husband entered.

"Our Elias is feeding well." Was it an affirmation or a question? Bushra didn't know. She was about to lay the child down to make him a cup of tea even though he hadn't asked anything of her.

"Finish with Elias," he said, "he has to grow and support his parents. Feed him. I'll make dinner."

Her husband was a cook for rich whites. They said he was the best and that there was no one better than him at the *burjiko*. Meats softened at his touch and the rice was never overcooked. People spoke of marvels. Until then, Bushra hadn't tried any of her spouse's cooking, not even boiled water.

She heard him bustling about with provisions. The burjiko resounded rhythmically like a cowbell. The child laughed. She did as well. The smell was good. Everything was ready by the sunset prayer. They prayed together and then ate. The meal was huge, one of their most pleasant. There was a flower in the middle near the rice, a white mountain encircled by mounds of goodness. Green vegetables, white onions, red meat, yellow bananas. Some sultana for flavor. In a glass in the center, a coconut and pepper sauce. The rice wasn't the kind she used. It was long-grained and smelled delicious. And the meat? It was tender, mixing with her saliva as though it had been destined for it. One piece of bread was enough to hearten them. Sweet cinnamon tea to wash it all down.

Bushra balled up some rice and meat in her right hand. Most people used three fingers to pick up food. She used four. In amazement at all the good food, she was in danger of biting the fourth finger. She took a handful at first. Then she took a liking to it and the small quantity became medium, then large. Majid didn't touch a thing. Bushra finished the entire plate. All the rice, meat, and greens went to keep her stomach acids company. Everything was inside her. She even finished the pitcher of sweet tea. She was astonished. She'd never eaten so much in her life. Would she die? she wondered. She felt strangely light. She would gladly start eating again, from the crown of her days to the soles.

She belched, then realized that Majid, her spouse—the Majid whose thighs she massaged every night, the Majid she desired more than herself—she realized he was looking at her. *Who knows what my husband will think of me now*, and she began crying. She'd eaten everything without decorum, discretion, or limit. He would insult and possibly denounce her. Everyone would say, "The witch lost her marriage with a burp and a fistful of rice." Majid watched her. She read reproval in his face. *How could I be such a simpleton? I should've said no, I will cook, husband. He tested me and I failed.*

"Why are you crying, Bushra?" Majid asked with a look of shock.

"It was so good I finished it all." She felt stupid for saying the obvious.

"I'm glad."

"Glad?" she was dumbstruck.

"Yes, you're nurturing our son."

Ours. Had he said ours?

"And if you want, I'll prepare it for you every night. But don't ask anything else of me, understand?"

Bushra quickly said yes. She massaged him well that evening. She shook him out like dusty fabric. *Don't ask anything else of me, understand?* She'd said yes, unfortunately. Majid fell asleep away from his wife's body. Bushra dreamed of being his. In her dreams she broke her promise, but it was clear that they would never make love.

FIVE

THE NUS-NUS

The bell rang hysterically. One long trill, two short. Recess. Mar noticed how studying classical Arabic made adults into children again. They had waited nearly two hours for the liberating ring. Perhaps the hysteria was due to exhaustion. Studying Arabic required great effort. Dragging oneself out of bed in the morning and then diving into a language that demanded more than most others wasn't sustainable, at least not for her. They toiled endlessly at every stage. Some were on the alphabet, some on irregular verbs, some on complex medieval treatises. They left the classrooms with sweat-soaked clothes and steam coming out of their ears. You can recognize an Arabic student from the heap of alphabetic scribbles spilling from their ears. The trill made them happy. It brought back the sense of wellness one felt in elementary school. Back then, it was arithmetic or grammar that wore them out. The trill is the only thought, the secret dream. the chocolate candy bar Mommy put in the lunch box. Right then, though, Mar didn't dream about chocolate, but the two Camel Lights positioned strategically in the right pocket of her Sahara. She was no longer a little girl. Neither were the other students. No more candy bars, only Camels. And maybe a coffee. That school had everyone: twenty-year-old college students, forty-year-old businessmen, fifty-year-old spinsters, sixty-year-old retired professors, and then thirty-year-olds like her. They were there hoping for a job in some company, dreaming of a university teaching post or at least a publication, and many were attending out of senseless passion. She was the only one there by imposition. It was a divine dictate, that in August 2006 she be brought to that patch of North Africa.

The break was twenty-five minutes. It seems like a long time, but a closer look shows it to be very brief. Five minutes were spent walking down the stairs. It wasn't a descent, but a procession worthy of *Semana Santa* in Seville. People were stuck in line, twitching in anticipation of cigarettes and sweets. There were two floors, the classrooms packed, the space restricted, the atrium filled. Everyone made plans in the atrium and no one met up again.

Mar also had plans, but not in the atrium. She and her date had settled on a different spot for Camels and sweets, the entrance to the coffee shop in front of the school. Her date was Elisa Mercadante. She was Italian, like Mar. A journalist. She looked like Björk's twin sister. They'd met in the school hallway on the second day. Elisa knew Arabic pretty well. She'd also written a book on Arabic journalists on satellite news channels. Elisa Mercadante had contacts everywhere. Sometimes her byline graced the magazine *Alias*, the Saturday insert of *Il Manifesto*. If Mar had read her resumé she might have detested her: Bachelor's and master's degrees, global experience, publications. She would've thought, *Here's someone who'll kick you to the curb*. She would've imagined her as the classic career woman. Complete with Gucci, an attaché case, a string of black pearls, a Rolex, and a jet-black cellphone in a designer handbag. If she'd read her resumé, Mar would've envisioned a bun on her head with red locks framing an oval face, small eyes, a mouth enlarged by Yves Saint Laurent fire-red lipstick. She would've thought of a woman who reads financial magazines, who goes to the gym and does pilates to distract herself. Then she would've imagined the chill LPs orderly arranged on the shelf in her studio. Luckily, Mar never read Elisa Mercadante's resumé. She didn't have time to form misconceptions. A Camel

Light brought them together. Mar had forgotten her pack at the nuns' place. By recess, she was already in withdrawal. Elisa was in front of her. She reached out to this other person and asked for the most important thing to her next to oxygen.

Mar thought Elisa was kind. A simple girl, much different from the ones she knew. Much different from Pati and Mama Miranda. Elisa wore ripped jeans, bobbed black hair, and a vividly colored flared tee. She looked like a drive-in waitress, not a serious professional journalist. But she was. Anyone could see that after exchanging a few words with her. She knew about the crises of the globalized world. She could tell you the trends, controversies, perversities, and bullshit. She knew six languages and wanted to add another one, standard Arabic, to the resumé, the one Mar luckily hadn't read.

"I don't want to learn how to speak Arabic. No one can really know how to speak classical Arabic well, not even native Arabs. I just want to understand Al Jazeera." That was her goal, to understand Al Jazeera and, maybe, why not, a couple of dialects—Syrian and Egyptian—the most common in the Arab world. Did she, Mar Ribero Martino Gonçalves, have goals? Probably not. She only wanted to survive the summer. Everything would be reevaluated after that.

"I'm late, sorry," Mar said. "There were people everywhere."

"It's okay, sister, the barbarian hordes haven't descended here yet. Let's get in line. We have time to sit down for a nice tea."

Mar didn't order tea. She ordered a caffè latte to spice things up. And at Elisa Mercadante's suggestion, she got a pastry.

"They're good here."

Mar took a bite while they waited for their hot drinks. On the first bite, she didn't get what was so great about the pastry. On the second, she thought it was too sugary. She didn't like excessively sweet foods. In that way, she was exactly like her mother.

The waiter came over. He had a white shirt and a moustache that reminded Mar of a nineteenth-century bandit. He wasn't a boy, but a grown man. He looked at them both. His staring began to annoy Mar. All the men looked at her like that here, with obscenity and innocence. He opened his mouth. "*Enti arusa,*" he said, "*enti gemila giddan ya hubbi.*"

"Ehhh?" Mar intoned. Elisa laughed enthusiastically.

"What did he say to me? What'd he say? Come on, Elisa, don't laugh. Tell me."

"He said," the voice came from behind them, "that you look like a bride and are very beautiful, my love."

Mar turned slowly. The voice was warm and comforting, a Linus blanket to wrap around oneself and fall asleep in forever. She didn't often like men's voices. Usually they disgusted her. This one, however, was warm. She was astounded when she saw that the voice's owner was a gangly Chinese man no older than twenty-five.

"My name is Guu Chang Yang, but you can call me JK. It's my nickname."

She, Elisa Mercadante, and JK had breakfast together.

JK was a Semitic philology student at the University of Rome. He was twenty-three years old and hoped, one day, to continue studying what he was born for: "I'm going to write a book that will revolutionize Semitic studies." First he had to graduate. He wasn't far from being an expert. Afterward, he'd be free to do what he wanted. He worked in his parents' restaurant to get by. They weren't on the same page. They wanted him to continue in business. Accounts to balance, clients to serve. "If you don't like the restaurant, you could try apparel," and if it wasn't apparel it would be some other nonsense. He was fed up with that life. The Chinese weren't only about trade and profit. They were a people gifted with sensibility and flair. Refined sculptors, splendid painters, exquisite philosophers, illustrious poets. China was a multi-millennial empire. Not just weapons and money, but culture as well. It seemed the world had forgotten that such a huge country wasn't merely a conglomerate of people, but a legion of ideas as well.

Mar sipped her latte slowly. Drinking the insipid sludge repulsed her, but she needed coffee to survive two more hours of class. The beautiful voice of their new friend JK wrapped them in a spiral of joy. She watched Elisa and saw that she was also delighting in JK.

"Let's go to the medina district after school?" Elisa proposed. "We'll eat kebabs and get lost in a bunch of random junk. Sound good?"

Mar and JK happily agreed. No one had had time to go there yet. They decided to meet in front of the bar when lessons were over.

I almost want to tell Mom, Mar thought with a surge of affection.

She left her friends and went to search for her mother. She went into bathrooms, her classroom, the faculty lounge, the little garden. No trace of Mama Miranda. Mar was disappointed. She'd really wanted to tell her mother. The bell rang again, less insistently, almost cheerful. For the next two hours, Mar thought of how happy she'd be with her two friends. *If only I'd seen Mom earlier.* The thought of not finding her brought a cloud over Mar.

When the bell rang the end of lessons, Mar dashed from the classroom like a restive little girl. That was when she ran across her mother. They hadn't seen each other at all that morning. She'd stayed in bed while her mother was probably already sitting at her first row desk like a diligent student.

"*Buenas tardes, Mamá. ¿Qué tal?* You all right?"

Mar used a hospitable tone, which was never the case in exchanges with her mother, who was pleased and cheerful. Mar made her proposal. *She'll never accept. Mama never accepts anything from me.* Her predictions were wrong. Miranda accepted joyously. To emphasize that joy, she hugged her. Mar thought Tunisia was doing a lot of good for her mother. She responded to the hug by squeezing tightly. Tunisia was also doing a lot of good for Mar.

"I know a great place. Do you trust me?"

They'd reached an agreement. Elisa Mercadante's prodding was rewarded.

"Sweet, you'll start salivating from how good it is!"

The kebabery was like thousands of others in that city of the Maghreb, though this one had special bread. It was an Indian *chapati*, soft and made right there in front of the hypnotized clientele. The toppings were like everywhere else, but the bread made everything softer and flakier.

They took their stuffed chapati and sat like four adolescents on the top floor.

"Kids," said Elisa, "did you know I'm in withdrawal?"

Miranda was smiling, but Mar grew worried.

"Me too," JK commented.

Miranda bit off a piece of her chapati.

Mar didn't understand. She took a sip of water. She saw Elisa's finger pointing at her. It was threatening, neurotic. Mar feared it. She didn't want to come off like a fool. She expected her new friend to elaborate on the vague warnings.

"Mar, you're not saying anything? Don't you miss alcohol?"

Ah, that's what they were talking about. Liquor. She calmed down.

"No, I'm straight-edge like you, remember?"

"Since when?" her mother asked.

"You know since when, Mom," the girl said bluntly.

Miranda thought of nipping that conversation in the bud, which would inevitably lead to a skirmish. She shifted the focus of her words.

"I heard that you can drink pretty well in the hotels here." She said it like a public service announcement.

"Yeah," JK confirmed, "the hotels have everything. If you're a foreigner you can buy alcohol at the supermarket, but I can't really remember…there's some kind of restriction."

"Yes, yes," Elisa Mercadante said, "I know all about it. There are times when you can't buy it, Thursday and Friday evenings.

People told me they overcharge you at the hotels, but fuck it. I'm going tonight. I need a damn beer."

"This chapati is good. Well done, Elisa," Miranda commended.

They spoke of many things. The political situation in the Middle East, the fashion trends in New York, the time when every Chinese person would have a car, the World Cup that had just happened.

"Where did you all watch the game?" Elisa Mercadante asked.

"I saw it at some friends' place," JK replied.

"I caught it at Circus Maximus," Miranda said. "When Cannavaro lifted the cup, it was like the world was ending. I had a blast."

"I didn't see it actually, I don't like soccer. Mom is the soccer expert in the family. Didn't you play goalie when you were little?" It was one of the few things her mother had told her about Argentina. She couldn't see her as a goalie. She couldn't imagine her mother in Argentina. She had no image of the country in mind.

"Yes, but it was a long time ago," Miranda said, shaking her head.

"Come on! Don't keep us in the dark."

"I was the goalie for a neighborhood team. It was called Santiago. I was good, but nobody knew I was a girl. I played six games." Miranda offered a half-hearted smile.

"Did anyone from Santiago go pro?" Elisa Mercadante blurted. "Did you play with anyone famous?"

Miranda's expression changed. She put her chapati on the plate.

"You don't like it, Mom?" Mar was concerned.

"No, I have to get back now…it's just that, after a while my stomach…all this bread."

"I completely get it," Elisa Mercadante nodded. "I remember the day my Grandma Rita…"

Lost in the anecdote about Grandma Rita, no one remembered

to revisit the question about Santiago. Miranda's appetite returned. The bread hadn't nauseated her at all. Only the memories were indigestible.

Distribute, bicker, jostle, wink, bargain. This is the medina. The souq. *Market of dreams.*

I, a lonely merchant, love you already. I meet your eyes and already I love you.

Will you let me, señorita? *I sell trinkets by day and night. May I? May I show them to you? Here are the beauties of the African land. Hammocks, lampposts, hookah, fake carpets, real Persians, oil extracts, myrrh, incense, (black-market) beer, ashtrays, the hands of Fatima.*

Will you let me? What language do you speak? From your bearing, I would say you are…? Yes, you are…? We understand one another, señorita, eh? Did I wink at you? I don't think so, I would never, señorita, I am a gentleman. I am Arab and noble. A shopkeeper. I don't make uncouth gestures. Your hand is not used to these tourist vulgarities. You are the daughter of the children of the world's nobles, deserving of sapphires and diamonds. Ah, if I were your husband I would cover you in emeralds. I would take you riding on my camel and perfume you with oils in a pavilion. I would make myself yours…yes, yours, completely yours. Your slave, your devoted lover. We would love each other and live in joy and prosperity with the aid of Allah, architect of man and creation. But we were born on two continents, into two worlds. Into two opposing ideas. In between there is a sea. You are busy. I am as well. Love was not made to wound. I thank the Clement and the Merciful for allowing a poor sinner to rest his eyes on so great a beauty. And as the poet says:

> *Mild the afternoon on which you were born, friend.*
> *Mild the day you became a woman.*
> *Mild the hour in which your light kissed me.*
> *Drunk on you, I shall die contented.*

Now, between you and I, pearl of my heart, are these wares. Vile money. Rummage. Look, shatter, touch. Afterward, in solitude, I will inhale your scent. And, drunk, I will dream of the Lord's virgins. Oh, were you but one of them.

Take what you will. I will not make you pay much. I cannot donate it. I would offend you. I must negotiate. I do not want serpents jeopardizing your purity.

You, woman, patron. And me, merchant. This is all the multitudes must know. Neither jinn *nor man need know of the love spoken only by our eyes.*

The medina was a fever dream. If they couldn't swindle you with merchandise, the merchants swindled you with promises of love. Whatever it took to sell a measly lighter.

"It's wild. They name prices while reciting Nizar Qabbani," Elisa Mercadante said.

"Who is Nizar Qabbani?" Mar asked. She was ashamed of her ignorance.

"*Hija*, he is the poet of women. Some guy with a henna-red beard recited him to me a little while back."

"You can't even escape the elderly. Old sleazebags, these Tunisians," Elisa Mercadante said.

"I would just say great businessmen."

They'd gone there to take a leisurely walk and already the day was full of bags and knickknacks. Mar didn't want to buy anything, but the colors, and the courtesies, got the better of her. She loaded up on key rings, vases, oils. She smiled like a simpleton.

Her companions were thrilled. Elisa and JK were full of life, and her mother had blossomed again. It was the first time in years they'd spent a moment together without snapping at each other's throats.

The commotion was driving Pati back. Mar was pushing her lover down into the circle of the damned, where she'd put herself voluntarily with a pistol shot in the mouth. Even the Pati lookalike, the girl who, in Mar's eyes, resembled her dead lover, had vanished. Maybe it had been a hallucination from too much *shisha*. Mar finally felt whole, a girl with the blood of the North and South commingled. For the first time, she could think of nothing bad about herself. This sense of peace reminded her of when her mother sang Víctor Jara's "Alfonsina y el mar." It was her favorite. Miranda had a voice filled with *dolor*, like the Alfonsina of the song, dressed in the Sea. Her arms were waves. An ancient voice *de viento y sal*.

She didn't sing that song for Mar very often. She preferred singing Dylan, it was easier. But every time Mar would throw a tantrum and shout "Alfonsina!" beating her fists on the ground, Miranda would give in. Sometimes she grabbed the guitar. Her voice was mellifluous, de viento y sal.

"Mama, why don't you tell me what happened in Argentina?"

While she was lost in her thoughts, she saw the girl who resembled Patricia as if she were a drop from the same pond. The same white skin. The same lost stare. Mar said goodbye to her friends and mother. She decided to follow the captivating girl. She wanted to get to the bottom of this. In that very moment, the girl decided to run. She was alone. Her stringy hair fluttered as she dashed through the hordes of bartering jackals. Mar was behind her. She thanked the heavens that she'd put on her gym shoes that morning.

THE NEGROPOLITAN

I want the black man. Yes, I want him, I want him, I want him, until death do us part and beyond.

I want to fall in love with a man whose skin is the same color as mine. I want his muscles, his joy, his intelligence. He might love me briefly, but at least he would love me. He wouldn't make me feel inadequate. No, he wouldn't make me feel like an idiot. My black man, the only one, the essential. Me, his black woman, the only one, the essential. United forever in melanin.

Enough with the *gaalo*. I don't want to hear any more about white-skinned dolls. White *no pasará, nunca pasará*, it will never, ever do. Enough with dairy products and their derivatives. The ivory creature is a thing of the past. You stripped my land, you will never strip me. I want to give myself to my skin brother. The man who knows my natural pH is no one to spurn. I am the sister of Cam, in Cam, for Cam. I am full of black pride and that's that.

A beautiful speech infused with wisdom about black pride and black promises. Calibrated words. *Ivory creature*. My goodness, it sounds so dignified! I repeat it a couple of times. I taste the sound. I'm euphoric, it's a marvelous phrase. Dante must've used it, certainly. I'm delighted by my genius.

I repeat the speech countless times, from Tunis Bahria Station all the way to Carthage Amilcar. I have to internalize and start to believe it. I cannot fall in love with a white man again. I don't want to. Whites do nothing for me. They mock me or, heaven knows, think of me as some exotic animal. That, or they're gay like the last one. I have to stay away from white men. I don't like suffering. I have to be reflected in the man I love. White blinds me. I can't see myself in it.

Whites are set on wronging black people anyways. Granted, Lucy is white, but she doesn't destroy, she's a woman, an exception. White people usually demolish. You have to keep a hundred eyes on the lookout. Defend yourself. I have to get it through my skull: they've got the colonial vice. Then they have the gall to say: "We did it to civilize you."

I repeat my speech. I have to imprint it on my memory. One, two, three, repeat. I have some time. I'm on the train connecting Tunis proper with its seaside surroundings. I'm with friends. The train is exactly the same as the one to Ostia Lido, down to the very passengers. The kids are more boisterous. They open the doors of the moving train to look tough, rebel against the man. Miranda knows French. She exchanges a few words with them. They snicker and tease her some. They tell her they'll visit her and give her "the caresses and kisses your husband doesn't give you anymore." They make maps of their family trees. Tunisians have relatives all over the world: in Italy, France, Spain. Somalis also have thousands of relatives, everywhere. The boys tell Miranda they'll soon join their relatives in the other branches of the family tree. "I'm going to make a ton of money," one boy named Yousef tells us. With both his hands, he exhibits his future abundance. "A ton of money like this," opening his arms as wide as they'll go. "Then I'll come back here and marry Uarda. She knows. She's waiting for me." Dreams, so many dreams. They have nothing else. This is a country that pretends to be rich although it is incredibly poor. I know why the boys open the train doors. For a second, pitching themselves from a moving train seems like the only option. This lasts only a moment. The urge to play prevails.

Thoughts of jumping recede as the train pushes onward.

Black man, I want you. Black man, I need you. Black man, where are you?

I'd like the black man to rescue me from my mistakes.

Maybe you, Black Man, could have saved me from being raped.

A large white man raped me in my school's bathroom. My little girl underwear was smeared with dishonor. Where were you, black man? Why didn't you come for me?

Sometimes I want to ask Maryam Laamane for my father's name. If he were with me, he would've stopped her from taking me to school. Maryam, I love you, but why did you put me in that place? Why, Mom?

We arrive at the beach.

I see someone else. The black man doesn't show up and I'm about to lose myself again in milk. The black man isn't here and I'm sad. I'm going to make another mistake. My black pride is becoming farcical. Am I a traitor?

Here he is. I recognize him, the one who got me excited the other day in front of the Bourguiba School, the guy with the drooping face. A beautiful little man who is in the same Tunisian dialect class as me. He seems cool, though it may be too good to be true. The guys I like have the skin every girl wants, but it turns out they're all depressed. God knows how much I need lightheartedness. I want to make a frank declaration of love. I don't know your name, white man. What does it matter? You're tearing me apart. Surely you'll make me suffer. You're acting strange. Peach-pink flesh, smooth as a pig, hairy like a turkey, a tad chubby, shaved, deodorized. Downcast eyes and an ambiguous smile. Irony or shame? You're not wearing swimming trunks like everyone else, but a 1950s-style blue speedo.

You wear a speedo, but you close your thighs like a boarding school girl. You're sitting on a towel with a Donald Duck print by Andy Warhol. Pop art kills me too, gringo. We should put your towel on display at the Guggenheim Bilbao. It's a relic. And if we displayed you, gringo? You'd be perfect in a museum exhibit case. Isolated and self-contained. Honey, you'd clamp your thighs tighter than you already do. You're consumed by panic. Don't be afraid of us, we're just four elegant young girls. Valeria, Manuela, Miranda, and myself. Between us four, I'm the most harmless. We're all from the same place, the same *mabit*. We've caught up with the others from the mabit. I barely know anyone. I don't know you. Are you from our mabit? I don't think you are. It's *maktoub, maktoub*, already written. Fucking destiny, in other words. The Cuban, who I do know, is also there. A shame I'm not into him anymore. I think it'd be healthier to have a fling with him. There are a lot of boys, a few gaunt girls. I see a Chinese man, too. You rule above them all, gaal *halouf*, incredulous, clamp-thighed piglet. Peach man, I feel like you'll be one of my worst downfalls. You're not a fag, are you? You never want your man to be a fag, you know?

He's peeling, I think, *he's peeling! He's melting in front of us.* I've never seen anyone so pink in my life. It's a bit disconcerting. Some people are very pale, very white and evanescent, though I've never met anyone peach pink. Where did he come from? A Japanese manga? He has manga eyes. Huge, ball-shaped eyes the color of a murky lake. You could see the little stars. He could be Candy Candy's twin. His hair is straight, a little white, a little yellow, clearly neglected. It makes him look like an enterprising intellectual. He's probably a bookworm. He definitely is. I recognize bookworms. The library types are my specialty. I bet he goes to his city's Libla.

Why isn't there a handsome Senegalese man around? The ones with long bones, a frank stare, a bold way with words. I know I'd be happy with one of them. I wouldn't wear too many masks. They would say to me "sister" and I would say "brother." "Gimme five" and "Black power." I would dare to sing "Redemption Song," even if it was out of tune. I'd pretend to be a griot for my Senegalese brother. Our skin would unite us and Bob Marley would, too, the Prophet, glory unto him.

But the pale-faced halouf? What do I have in common with him? Beats me. My heart doesn't want to face itself. I hate when it's pounding in my chest like this.

The men I've chosen up to this point have been walls. Doctor Ross says it's my fear of the penis. I don't want one inside me. She says I won't let anyone in. In my circle there are only innocuous people with their own problems, with whom I can't build anything. They have nothing to do with walls, and that's why I chose them, that's why I keep bumping into them. She says the walls represent my fear of violence. The fear that it'll happen to me again. Doctor Ross also says I'm afraid of building a relationship with a man. She says I'm afraid of trusting myself again. "Evil wasn't only done to your body," she says, "but to your soul." My soul is fabric, permeable to pain. It absorbs and withholds, not always permitting things to leave.

How do I let it out? I can't live like this anymore. I want someone to bring back my stolen dreams. I had so many before. I had colors. I don't know where they are anymore. I want all my colors back, all my dreams, no exceptions. I close my eyes. When I open them again, it's still too dark.

"Ciao." The word is spoken by a chorus of refined young women.

They're my friends. I'm with them on a beach a few kilometers from Tunis proper. *Ciao* is the only Italian word they also say in Arabic.

"*Sabah el kheer*," someone responds in Tunisian, chewing on every vowel of classical Arabic.

The girls and I get undressed. That's when I know. I can sense it, fuck. Everyone is looking at us.

Generally, I don't like being watched. It's a horror show. Tunisians make me feel like a whore. We're only taking off our jeans, keeping on our swimsuits and sarongs. I shouldn't be surprised. We're all from the same parish. Mosque, I mean. Sort of. The Maliki school in Tunisia is going strong. Somalis are Shafi'i. I never understood the difference. My mother barely taught me the fatiha. I'm trying to make up for lost time. I recently learned to pray. Mom is always on my ass about religion, but she should've taught me. I'm fine. I put on shorts—hardly a thong. I wear shorts at the beach in Rome, too. They still look at me, but not as much. I'm properly dressed for a Tunisian beach, like the other girls from around here. *Stop looking.* Maybe they're not looking at you because of your exposed body (mine can hardly be called that), but because you're different. Unfamiliar.

The Tunisian men on the beach have something obscene in their stares. From fifty-year-olds to little boys with baby teeth. All of them. The women aren't much better. Women seem discrete on the surface but analyze you from afar. Jesus, it's embarrassing! I see love nests in their stares, pubic hair, sweat, ejaculate. If you'd told me that the men here undress you with a look and the women stick you in a lab phial to analyze you under their microscopes, I would've hightailed it out of there on a ship to *Roma Caput Mundi.*

Lucy is soaking it up. "Don't you feel more like a woman here? At least they appreciate the goods, not like our gutless men." I don't want to feel like merchandise. I don't care much for being treated like a commodity. "Holier than thou," she says to me and laughs. She has a beautiful smile. After school, I invited her to the beach. She told me: "No, thank you, I'm going with Malick, we're going to Hammamet." As if to console me, she added, "Tomorrow, though, I'm all yours, let's go shop in the medina." Damn, I was hoping she'd forget. The shopping threat has been looming over me since Palermo. She'll make me buy horrible, uncomfortable high heels and hooker's clothes, I know she will. I don't want to succumb to shopping. I love my coveralls, jeans, and large pearl-gray pants. Let's hope Malick asks her to do something else.

These guys aren't even looking. I wouldn't be that upset if they were. I'm used to ribald glances. It happens in Rome, you bet. I'm upset because their stares go beyond the skin. X-rays of the torso, legs, and back. They count your vertebrae, watch the blood flow in your arteries, push against your spleen with desirous eyes. No, I'm not here. My spleen is mine and I alone command it. Look at how these brazen boys study Valeria's left tit, to say nothing of Manuela's ass. She's powerless. Poor thing, she's got nun's bloomers on, too. Show a little respect, fuck!

Our group seems to have descended directly from Mars. It's not a tourist beach, I know. Only locals here. I don't care if they look at us, it's normal. I'll get used to it. Besides, we're being noisy. We're making a racket, speaking a thousand tongues, inserting Arabic words, laughing and singing. We draw stares like magnets. Those who speak Arabic are halouf. Some in the group speak it excellently.

The curiosity goes both ways. Valeria and Manuela stare in disbelief. "So what, do these women come to the beach fully dressed?" They have clothes on, skirts, shawls, and everything. Some go into the water with sunglasses and faux-Vuitton handbags brought by their émigré brothers who came over on Alitalia. They dine in the water, they drink tea. Men and women become friendly, flirt, hide. The water is the only place where boys and girls can meet. It is the only place, besides the cinema, where love is born.

My mother says that in Somalia she also went into the ocean clothed. "Isn't it uncomfortable?" I asked her once. "It depends," she said. She thought men's careful analyses of her backside were more uncomfortable. "I never went in the ocean with an overcoat on. Not even a jacket or hat. I wore shorts." Good idea, Mom. I copied her. I put on shorts before coming here and tied a sarong around my waist. They look at me, but they don't count my vertebrae and, most importantly, they don't fixate on my ass like poor Manuela.

It's strange being watched all of a sudden. At Libla, no one ever watches me. I'm invisible to the customers, otherworldly, like an elf.

The thing is, at Libla, I'm mistaken for the cleaning lady. That's why I'm otherworldly. No one ever asks the cleaning lady for information, *abadan*. It's like she doesn't exist. The equation says that black is equal to maid, never to saleswoman. At least for some people. Hell, don't you see it? Don't you see this phosphorescent yellow card with my first and last name, my badge number? Why do you think I have it? It has nothing to do with a residency permit. Wrong answer. It'll seem strange to you, but I'm a citizen of the Republic, this republic, and I believe in the Constitution of '48 and its values (I know that for certain lunatics it's out of style). This awful sweater that makes me look like a hot-air balloon on a Segway, why the hell do you think I put it on? The color is disgusting, shit green. Do you really think I have such horrible taste? Understand this, Libla customers: like it or not, the Eternal City is changing around you. We are also here. I've been here for more than twenty years, which is no small feat. There are others older than me. Your panic is belated, customer. You should've shit your pants thirty years ago. Too late now.

I've seen some pitiful things! Sometimes I watched Libla customers wandering anxiously, looking for a sales rep. Some white man or woman who could assure them, who could show them the shelf with the De André CDs or the Deutsche Grammophon box set with the divine Mozart arias. They walked around me. I was invisible despite my nametag and sweater. Once they lost every hope of finding pale skin, they'd indignantly start, "Really! Where are all the salespeople? It's a disgrace!" Whereupon suspicion was born. In the early days, I brandished Mozart like a weapon to show that I was the saleswoman, but I got tired of it, and now I limit myself to casting the evil eye at vapid customers. Their faces are always so eloquent. *What is Mozart doing in this Zulu's hand?*

In the off-hours, there is *only* this Zulu! I'm a stocker and, as such, I have the worst shifts. It lasts until eleven on Saturdays and Sundays, which amounts to me having basically zero social life. My friends on the outside say to me, "Lucky you, living in Rome." Of course, all my friends go to the movies, see Ascanio Celestini—powerful stuff—attend jazz concerts and lectures, exhibitions, festivals. All in all, people have fun in Rome. They make money. Tourists come. The metro falls to pieces, but in the end the balance is positive. The Colosseum wasn't built by accident, after all. It's a city hungry for glory and glorification. It sucks being outside it all. With my hours, sometimes I can't even catch a movie. All these cultural events and I can't make it to a single one.

In Tunis, though, my social life is a dream. Everyone seeks me out, everyone wants me. I almost don't have time to study. Almost. I'm trying to make up for lost time here on the beach. I'm lying down and doing my best to read a children's fairytale in Arabic. Every six words, I open the dictionary. Every sixth word is a recalcitrant verb. It's a cute story about a Chinese emperor, a nightingale, and a girl, a *bint jamila*, a beautiful girl. I feel like I'm reading a Harmony romance. What'll happen next? Will the opulent emperor marry the poor, beautiful little girl? At the pace of six-words-then-dictionary, who knows? I'll find out in a hundred years. The slow pace calms me. I reflect on my thought process.

Luckily, Miranda is with me. She's beautiful in her swimwear. She's secured a sarong around her waist. The Tunisian boys stare at her suggestively. They've gone to mush in the sun, held in check by their desire for golden skin. Only Miranda and I are beneath the umbrella. She's under it because she's too white. "I'll burn in the sun," she says. And I, as a good black girl, don't want to become charcoal. I announce it to the world: black people, Muslims and non-Muslims, tan. Yes, *noir*, dark, black becomes *plus noir*, darker, blacker. So much so that, in response, they invented that trashy whitener. My mom and I agree that it's junk. Fardosa, my older cousin who lives in Manchester, applies it heavily. She puts the ointment on like a woman obsessed. She waits thirty minutes. She transforms from a black Muslim into an off-white Muslim. Impressive. I read somewhere that the stuff causes skin cancer. Fardosa doesn't want to believe it. She's on her own.

Miranda has a lovely voice. In our group, I'm the only one who knows she's a celebrity. She's won prizes all over the world.

She writes in every language. Her native Spanish is mixed with all her other belongings. Echoes of Catalan, Italian, Portuguese, English, French. There are also Arabic words and, unexpectedly, Somali. That's why I know of her. One of her poems is entitled "Return to Mogadishu." The poem bowled me over. Now that I have her in front of me, talking about her poems is embarrassing. Maybe it bothers her. I don't want to bore her now that we've started becoming friends.

I want an aunt like her. Her skin caresses the sand like a flower petal. One night she'll take me to a beautiful place beside the sea. She'll offer me a bit of *mate* and tell me of her Argentina. You can see she has the temperament of a heroine. Perhaps she is one.

Halouf—the pink man—got into the water. He hasn't said a word to me. His skin is revolting. I can't imagine someone like that taking me by the hand, kissing me, embracing me. His skin is offensive. It's like pork. I wonder if you're not supposed to waste any part of him either. Peach skin. It'll be useful for party favors. He got in the water twenty minutes ago, he might get out soon. He looked pained when he stepped in the ocean, the water touching his porky flesh. He's scary. I'm scared for him. I don't know what his name is, but I pity him. I should only be concerned about myself. I should take care of me. I never knew how.

THE REAPARECIDA

I have always been duped by appearances. I fall for them. I'm a dolt. *A ragin' idiot,* my butcher would say. His name is Davide. He's a kind man of slight stature, born here in Pigneto. Actually, now Pigneto is over there, across the Mediterranean. Sometimes I forget I'm on a crowded beach in another country, with a notepad and thoughts lost in chronological chaos. When I think about Pigneto, Mar, I think about my newly bought, well-lit apartment and the sounds my neighbors make. The thoughts make me happy. I feel at home. I'm glad I moved. Pigneto is comparable to San Lorenzo. History conceals itself in quaint nooks and crannies. Davide says that when he was little his mother took him to Piazza Vittorio to see Rome. For Davide, Rome began there at that strange crossroads which, for many people today, means the future, degradation, culture clash, too much stuff for one piazza alone. It depends on one's point of view. Davide's Rome began amid the fake Piedmontese porticos of a rustic piazza. "All the men in Pigneto died from heroin," he tells me. "Ragin' idiots, all of 'em. They gambled with their lives, ma'am." He found his brother Giorgio, three years his elder, in a bathroom with the syringe still in his arm, his mouth foaming with hot saliva. He wasn't even twenty.

Davide gives me good meat. I never ask about the price. I

don't think he's an honest butcher, but with the state of the euro, who is? Who can afford to be honest these days? I know Davide doesn't care. I think he was tipped off about my origins, about me being Argentinian and having a certain fondness for meat. Despite the fact that my mother cured fish, I've got to say I get by pretty well with meat. It's a shame you're vegetarian, otherwise I would've made you my specialty: Venetian-style liver. Papa went crazy for it and I made it all the time. I'm from Venice, you know? Oh, Mar, you have so many cities within you. You represent Venice and also Genoa, Lisbon, Buenos Aires, Mogadishu, Rome. And who knows how many others, hija. What absurd journeys your ancestors made to be able to create you, star of my sky. Perhaps even Davide the butcher isn't only from Pigneto, even though he tells everyone he was born and bred there. It's very important to him: "I'm from Pigneto. Right around these parts. Not like the polished dandies, those educated artists who've come to live in this neighborhood. It's only a pretense, ma'am."

I, too, am only a pretense in Pigneto. I am a pretense everywhere. I'm attracted by pretenses, every flicker seduces me. It doesn't take much to trick me. A nice tie, a cocksure step, a fancy perfume, Italian shoes. Since childhood actually—we haven't talked about this—I've been completely subjugated, a serf. A bare-faced slave to pretenses. That's why I rooted for River Plate when I was in Argentina. That soccer team was a front. The players gave the impression of prosperity, despite being born of poor, penniless immigrants. Boca was more carnal, truer, alive, but I liked the ties, the smooth hands, the traitorous stares. I liked the salmon, the caviar, the evening joyrides in hurtling vans. That's why I let myself be taken from behind by Carlos. His uniform enchanted me, as well as his authoritative behavior. I felt a man inside me. Now I know he was only a frigid rabbit.

I'd thought of Carlos as the type of man in perfume ads, the man who never needs to ask for anything. He took me without warning, without asking, without foreplay. He put his penis where he wished, as he decided, when he wanted. He entered and exited at his leisure. He splattered me with sperm, sometimes forcing me to swallow it. Then he would lie on his side in silence or, if he was in a rush, he'd run to put on pants. I remember the stickiness he left me with. Usually he doused my face in semen. I don't know why it excited him to death. Stopping me from spitting out his mess was another thing that got him going. It was like glue, the kind that makes even the impossible stick. With no other man have I felt this way. His fluids dribbled down my skin. They made me feel greasy.

I didn't enjoy myself with him. It was all about obedience, a perpetual *sir, yessir*. I never orgasmed with Carlos. With Elias, your father, yes. The first and only time. Elias was kind. He knew where to touch me, what to do, what to say. It was so unusual for me to be treated like a person that I had multiple orgasms out of joy. I don't know why I let Carlos do those things to me. After making love with your father, I knew that another Miranda was possible. Another way was allowed. When I think about it, Carlos and I never even had a nice conversation. Yes, he was handsome, very handsome, but was that enough for me? His colors were subdued, different from my own. Carlos was pastel, not olive like me. He was the pretense I was searching for. The pretense that, in a certain sense, I wanted to imitate. I'd watch as he got dressed. He was slow and meticulous. Each article of clothing was a ritual. In private he sprayed everything on you, but the public had to see him as an honest, upright man without perversions. To satisfy those, he had my dumb ass and the *desaparecidos* whose suffering gave him pleasure as they roasted from the *picana*. The desaparecidos and I, complementary, interchangeable.

Carlos died, someone told me, in forgettable fashion. An accident. A car cut him off on the street. They say he died on impact. He didn't suffer. There was no justice. The news left me indifferent.

After all, he didn't look me in the eye when he stuck his penis in my ass.

Flaca, though, was someone who looked you in the eye. She recognized you well before picking up your scent. She loved you even before you looked for her. I loved her. As a sister, as a friend, a woman, and a lover. We weren't actually lovers. I only gave her that one kiss at the movies. She responded by opening her mouth and sticking out her tongue. It was dark. No one saw us. The moviegoers were more interested in the late Marilyn Monroe's breasts. I still wonder why she responded to the kiss. We never spoke about it. Two days later, Ernesto asked us, "So, what have you done, liars?" Flaca tenderly took his hand and said, "We gave each other a kiss." My blood froze. Ernesto laughed amiably. "You're becoming good friends."

Flaca didn't know how to lie. Ernesto, on the other hand, rarely picked up on low blows. He was too pure to think his sister was in love with the woman he intended to marry. It didn't register with him that women could love other women. I, however, didn't love all women, only Flaca. She was and is my only great love. The only one I've truly had. The only one Ernesto truly had.

How silly my brother was, from the time he started loving that girl. He was peculiar in a harmonious way, with dissonances that concluded in logic. He blushed, trembled, stammered. Perfectly in love, with its clear, unmistakable symptoms. He was delicate with her, sometimes too delicate. Ernesto was afraid of breaking her, his Flaca. He believed she was angelic, incorporeal, barely human. He touched her tenderly and cautiously. She was the most important string of his guitar, the string which kept the entire melody of life alive. His Flaca, *su mujer, ahí, qué lindo vivir junto a ella.* Her fragile, compact, tiny essence. A flash of light in his beautiful, boyish eyes.

I loved watching those two. They gave me hope. They were in love, happy, and reckless. They made love in hidden alcoves. Their sighs elided with those of nocturnal animals. Ernesto was big, giant, muscular; Flaca, small, delicate, impalpable. In the end that small woman didn't die at Esma like her muscular man. She survived the torture and everything else. The picana, the insults, the humiliations, the beatings, the spit, the threats, the agony. She, slight and fragile, had made it. She was a survivor, a dragonfly held up by her pain. Oh, if only it had been that way for Ernesto. He was too good to survive, too much of a man to make others less fortunate than him take his place.

I will die in your place, companions. Me, friends. Go on with your lives, I beg you. Laugh, eat, amuse yourselves, make love. I will take your place in death's carriage. I am tired of smiling while they burn my testicles. Tired of resisting. I don't want these scum to see me cry. I am thinking about my mother when she sang while trying to wash clothes. Ah, Ma, you were never good at cleaning. You weren't cut out to be a housewife. You always had the foibles of a diva. And Ma, you have beautiful hands. One wouldn't know you salted fish for half your life. You should've been singing your fados in some smoky place, in your adored Lisbon, not washing our soiled underwear. It's a shame I never saw Lisbon, Ma. Sometimes I dream of it in this prison.

I enjoyed hearing you sing, Ma. I accompanied you, clumsy with the notes I didn't know how to make sense of. No one sings here, Ma. Here, all anybody does is cry and groan. Most of the time we stay silent. Ma...

Not him, Mar. He didn't make it. He was broken, insulted, and mistreated. I don't know where he died. Without a burial, without the comfort of a visit, yours or mine.

Desaparecido, one of many. A number, not a goodbye.

The end was only a distraction for him. The sedative injection and the drop toward Río de la Plata, perhaps not the relief he was expecting. I can't imagine my brother in there. I can't imagine anyone in there. I've read many books over the years. Testimonials, fiction, reconstructions. I've read confounding details, prosaic details, details of details. I've read and tried to understand, I've tried putting myself in those people's shoes. I've gone mad in the attempt. And I've written. Mar, I still don't understand anything. They tell you things, many things. But deep down you don't really understand. How can one conceive of such horror? How can one enter into another's pain? You can't. You can do anything, try any road, but the truth is that you won't enter it. The road is blocked. You can approach it if you'd like, become acquainted, help others become acquainted with it. We can't understand the pain of the desaparecidos. We can't understand anyone's pain, but we don't have to forget. That's why I write, why I try.

I had no memory of the ludicrous Rome of the late seventies. I didn't try remembering it either. I lived in the present with annoying interferences from the past. Finding Flaca again warmed my heart. I was happy to see her, happy to chat with Pablo and relive the Buenos Aires of the time when I was still pure. Flaca bore on her body the signs of something I didn't want to think about. She was of unsound mind. She no longer thought the way she used to. No irony, no wordplay, nothing. Emptiness. She never took off her white Marilyn Monroe dress. There was no way to make her take it off. Sometimes, to take a bit of the stench away, she rubbed dry soap over herself. Flaca reeked. She reeked of memories, fears, and cauliflower. She reeked and I wept.

One day I came to the little room in San Lorenzo with a plan. I wanted to motivate her. I wanted to reclaim my friend from a time long since past.

"Go clean up, Rosa, we're leaving."

She wasn't speaking much anymore. Pablo explained that whenever she did grunt some small word, it was barely audible. Her muteness had begun in Europe.

"With every journey, one word less."

In Rome, Rosa exhausted her stockpile of words. She still sang, even if it was always that one Dylan song. She went to wash up and I swapped out her dress. I'd found a theatrical costume seller near Piazza Cavour who had a lot of Marilyn garb. The owner was a heavyset man, chatty and stylish. He gave me an honest price that bled me dry. I was so poor in those days. It was a sacrifice that I made freely for Flaca. I would've prostituted myself for her. Anything for her.

The shower gave me time to fill Pablo in on my plans.

"I want to see her dance one more time."

Pablo shook his head. "She won't do it."

I will never forgive myself for bringing her to that place. I led her to a horrible fate. But how could I have known? How…? I wanted to do her some good, give her a shock, just a little one. I forgot that at Esma she'd had plenty. I was a fool for trying to elicit a simple emotion.

I was full of ideas at the time. Pure effervescence. Maybe you, Mar, were the one who pumped so much enthusiasm into my life? I'd slept with your father. I was already pregnant. Everything happened very quickly. Our meeting up again, our distracted loving, piecing ourselves back together. I needed warmth and I needed him. Your father was worn down—a man in exile. He wanted to feel like a human being. I did too. We hugged each other. A joke, an aside.

When I brought Flaca to the dance studio, no one knew about my pregnancy except me, Elias and, of course, you, my daughter. I was never able to hide things from him. I respected him. Likewise, he respected me. It may have been the most stable relationship I've ever had. Men always used me, hija, and took me for a fool.

I was obsessed with dancing in those days, especially the dancers themselves. I was obsessed with Flaca and her lost dance. Did you know she was a wonderful ballerina? A promise for Argentina. Do you know what they did? They broke her points. Those bastards struck her on her legs, her future. They flattened her feet. Many years later, after Flaca was gone, one of her prison mates told me that a "green," a soldier named Ruiz, would pull her big toe until it bled. He enjoyed watching her bleed.

I wanted to do something for her, Mar, the only woman who was my friend, whom I loved more than a sister, more than my mother. I only wanted to see her dance. She was gorgeous when she did. Everything seemed possible, the entire universe was manageable. I didn't want to hurt her. I didn't imagine that fate…

I thought about her and Buenos Aires. Buenos Aires for me was Rosa dancing happily, not the cemetery that the soldiers had made it into. Dancing Rosa. I wanted to see her dance in Rome. That's all. I wasn't trying to be selfish.

I'm skipping the context, the characters, the lives. First I should tell you who Rosa was in Buenos Aires, but I haven't been doing that. Rosa was beautiful. I don't know what else to tell you. She wasn't like the dancers now who dance for applause and glory. She danced for the dance itself, for the music. She was a go-getter who put her heart into whatever she did. She didn't want to show the world that she was the greatest. Flaca danced because she had no other choice. It was like breathing. "I want to be music," she told me, "I want to transform into a note." When she soared toward heaven, you believed that she was a note, she was music. Rosa worked hard. Ernesto griped about her fastidiousness, her overzealousness. "She never thinks of me." In this regard, Ernesto was an idiot like all men. She took a step and everyone fell silent, even him. He adored seeing her dance. Rosa was technical in her training, to a fault. She tried and tried again. She sweated like a ram and was happy when she performed a step as she'd envisioned it. "It's the only way I can free myself." That was her favorite thing to say. Her teacher Igor Ivanovič, who had trained the greats, instructed her properly. She wanted to memorize the techniques and moves, then forget them when the dance began. She wanted to play with the dance, improvise, discover herself. She performed as anyone, any woman. With her steps she was a queen and a whore, a saint and a sinner, a leper and a prisoner. She was Carmen, Odette, Juliette, Manon. She was Rosa. She was Buenos Aires. She was the person I didn't know I could be.

That day in Rome, each of her movements was a ritual. She wore her consecrated white dress that afternoon, as one wears a tunic for a secret rite. She was the vestal Norma Jeane Baker, the priestess of a lost memory. I had on a brown dress that I'd bought the week before at Porta Portese. I spoke in rapid bursts about something or other. I was like a radio gone haywire. She was mute beside me. We were a strange couple.

The dance school was downtown on Via dei Giubbonari, in a condominium built before the *ventennio*. The plaster was falling to pieces, everything was flaking off. I went in warily. I didn't know what I would've done to protect myself. I was met by a woman with sunken cheeks. You could see in her face the effort it took to be someone she wasn't. She opened the door and said, "Good evening, Argentinian friends." *Una sonrisa norteamericana que no me gustaba, carajo.* The woman smiled too much, it was strained.

"Which one of you is Rosa?"

Flaca stepped forward. It was a graceful dance step, a gift. The sunken-cheeked woman looked at her disdainfully. I didn't see it at first. I thought it was admiration. No. This was pure hatred, dark envy.

"We don't dance here, miss. We do that later, in the gym. Didn't they ever teach you discipline?"

The word made me shiver.

Had I perhaps brought my Flaca back to Esma? Instead of Videla and his minions, who was there now? This ugly woman, that's who. An ugly, sunken-cheeked woman in leggings.

I wanted to take my Rosa away from there, but something held me back. A charge in the air, I think. A charge with a face, a name: Elsa. For her, it was worth resisting, breathing.

A woman formed in miniature. A perfect woman. A bundle of muscles and efficiency.

"Don't mind Barbara," she told us. "She's jealous by nature. She can't stomach other people's talents."

The woman with the sonrisa norteamericana retreated with her tail between her legs. She looked like she might retch.

"Barbara is a perfectionist. Don't pay her any mind."

"Does she know it?" I asked stupidly.

"Of course she knows, otherwise she wouldn't come here to let me insult her and be my helper. She's sadistic and thinks that makes her stronger. Besides saying it, what can I do?"

Elsa was Hungarian. She'd been deported to Auschwitz, and at that point she no longer had any reservations. Barbara, however, doesn't come back into our story again. She was kind, despite everything, especially when she spoke about her Fiat 500. Thinking about it makes me sad. She didn't have anything that was truly hers, except her perfectionism.

You should remember another name. Alberto Tatti. A man I met in a stairwell who worked for a local radio station. I think it was fate. Ah, why did I bring her there?

THE PESSOPTIMIST

Somalia now is only its war.

"The people know nothing else, Zuhra. They know that there is dying in Mogadishu, but they don't know much else. They don't even know where we are on the map. Once, a lady asked me if Fidel Castro was the leader of Somalia. I laughed, but Zuhra, I should've cried. It's the Italians' fault we're doing badly today and they don't even know how to point us out on their garish maps."

For Maryam Laamane, Somalia wasn't only its war, but also the most beautiful peace. That's why she remembered the way it was before. The age of independence, when the Horn had hopes and beautiful dreams.

July 1, 1960. It was Africa's year. Everyone believed it was Africa's year, and not only because of independence. Africans especially believed it. Those from the North, the South, the East, the West. The islanders, too.

Muslims and Christians believed it. And Jews with them. And animists with them. And atheists, too, along with the communists. Some anarchists believed it as well. Those who didn't believe in anything started believing it.

It was because of their ebullient dreams and willpower. People rooted for those who were not yet free, like Algeria two years later. The cheering was unbridled, bordering on indecency.

They shouted that name, *Algeria*, lifting their arms in the air. They lifted their arms to pray, fight, rejoice, and hope. *Algeria!* Africa shouted and rose up. A grand contest between the oppressed and the oppressor.

1960 was Africa's year because Africans dreamed, their hearts beat, their minds were stimulated, their stomachs never begged. It was a good year.

Then it was over. There were mistakes afterward. An array of nightmares. Delusions, cruelties, foolishness. Many realized that nothing changed. They had become the Third World. It was somewhat like being a colony. They still depended on others. Their leaders, champions of liberty, were corrupt. Those who weren't were assassinated. Military powers, sacred powers, bureaucratic powers, depraved powers. All the powers in the limelight, excepting one. That of the people.

The year passed. 1960, the people's year, lasted for a single beautiful moment.

Maryam Laamane remembered that she was young in 1960. She was young and tender like a growing calf.

"Yes, my Zuhra, like a beautiful calf."

That day, the people hadn't realized anything. They knew it was an important day, but no one could have imagined how much. The people knew little. They only knew that it was a day of festivity and that they were free and finally had a flag. A large, magnificent flag. They didn't know anything else.

Not even Maryam understood. At the time, she didn't understand many things about the world. She dreamed and walked the streets without a care. She wasn't a fool. She knew this was a special day, one she'd remember. But in the moment she didn't make much of it. Maryam was easily distracted. That, for her, would be remembered as the day she became Howa Rosario's friend.

They went to the movies to see Marilyn Monroe, a plump white girl with a big chest, light hair, a full mouth, and a funny face. Maryam was disppointed when she saw the film poster out-side the theater.

"Are there Indians with feathers—*alibesten*—in this movie?" she asked her new friend.

"I don't think so," Howa replied, ever spare with her words.

"That's too bad. I like the alibesten. I always cheer for them. I don't like the cowboys. They have hideous blue clothes and nasty hair. The alibesten have long black hair that they braid. They're very beautiful."

"Now then, little girl, have you lied to me?" Howa asked with false reproach.

"I don't tell lies," Maryam declared indignantly.

"You told me you've never been to the cinema! Now I find out you know all there is to know about alibesten and cowboys."

"No, Howa, I told you the truth," the girl whined.

"Come now, don't cry," Howa said. "I don't like seeing people cry. Stop that."

Maryam was frightened by her new friend's tone. Her sweet voice had distorted into something severe and unpleasant.

"My cousin Jamila told me everything. She's slick. She tells her mother she's going to run some errands, but you know what she really does? She escapes and sees ten minutes of a movie every day."

"And how does your cousin pay for the ticket?"

"Well," the little girl stammered, "well, she says men pay for her. All she has to do is smile a bit and they pay for everything. I mean…"

"Never do like her. It will end badly."

For the second time in the span of a few minutes, Maryam was afraid of her. "I won't," she said quickly. She didn't try salvaging her cousin's honor. The little girl knew the battle was lost.

The audience members around them clamored. Some chatted calmly about their business. Those who understood the film's Italian tried explaining to the ignorant what was going on.

Maryam Laamane watched images in motion for the first time. It was so strange seeing people move across the white cloth.

"Howa, do they come out of the cloth? Will they come say 'hi' to us?" she asked earnestly.

"You're really daft. This is the cinema, not one of those theater comedies, those *riwaayado*."

"What's the difference?" Maryam asked.

"There's a big difference. With film, the actors can be everywhere at any time."

"The woman with the big chest is everywhere?" Maryam asked, increasingly dismayed. "Isn't God the only one who is everywhere?"

"You're crazy, Maryam Laamane, really crazy. What does God have to do with it?" Howa laughed, shedding her hardness for the first time.

"I don't know, God always has something to do with it," the girl said hesitantly.

Maryam stopped asking questions. She concentrated on those men who ran away dressed as women. They were goofy in skirts and heels. The woman with the big chest was also silly, with her girlish smirks. It was a shame there weren't alibesten in the film.

"The alibesten won't come on at all? Not even accidentally?" Maryam asked.

"No, there are only thieves here, and then there's Marilyn," Howa clarified. She was almost as aloof as an Englishman.

"Marywhat?"

"Marilyn Monroe, the blonde woman who's singing now," a voice said from behind them.

The girls turned around, frightened by this unrivaled, commanding tone. The voice was coarse like the rind of an unripe fruit. A voice that, at some angles, revealed glimmers of sweetness. Maryam shivered. It wasn't fear, but deference, quite like devotion. Maryam had a blasphemous thought. She thought the voice belonged to God incarnate. Maybe he wanted to punish her for wickedly taking his name in vain a moment before. Maybe it was because of what made itself known to the ears before the eyes. He'd wanted to catch her by surprise. Maryam turned with her eyes closed, too scared of the punishment. She knew that Iblis himself dealt with foolish girls like her. She was sorry she hadn't said goodbye to anyone, seeing as she'd be dead in a moment. At least she'd say goodbye to her new friend Howa. Suddenly, she grabbed her hand. When she opened her eyes, she saw that, luckily, God had decided to forgive her. In His place was only a woman with a red *shaash* and a drawn expression. She was tense as a clothesline.

"Maryam, this is Bushra, the seamstress."

"It's a pleasure, ma'am," she said. "Is it really her, Howa? The one who sewed your—" Howa Rosario punched her on the thigh before she could finish her sentence. She didn't even manage to say "underwear." The little girl's bestial cry resounded throughout the theater. The pain burned like chili pepper. Bushra didn't laugh.

"Ma'am, kindly, we have to go. The girl wants to see an al-ibesten movie."

Maryam's new friend relieved her of a heavy weight by yanking her away at the speed of light. She didn't have time to utter a single word, complain, ask, negotiate, or understand. Only when they were far from the theater did Howa attempt an explanation.

"Forgive me, Maryam, but that woman wants me to marry her son. And I don't want to."

Maryam didn't know what to say. The arm Howa had grabbed to pull her away hurt. Everything hurt. She didn't understand why Howa wouldn't want to get married. All women wanted that.

Howa began running and screaming, "I don't want to, I don't want to!"

People took her for crazy. She ran away from Maryam, from everyone. She went far but came back after a few minutes. She'd been crying. Maryam was pleased to see that her expression had returned to calm.

"If we run," Howa said, "we can get to Missione Theater. I know for certain that they show cowboy and Indian films there and at Elgab. It's not like here at Shebelle, which only shows lovey-dovey things." The little girl felt the hope of seeing the alibesten burgeon inside her. She didn't say a word to her friend. She limited herself to waiting for an explanation. Right on time, Howa said, "The show at Missione is the same at Elgab, but it starts later. When the first show ends at Elgab, they take the film canister to Missione. I know because one of my cousins does it, he has a bike and runs fast."

"Faster than us?"

"No, not faster than us."

They got to Missione Theater exhausted. Maryam was happy. They showed a good movie with the alibesten. She was the only one cheering for them in the cinema. At the end of the film, Maryam promised her most special friend that she would marry the seamstress's son in her place. Maryam placed her hand over her heart and swore. Strange tears appeared on the edges of Howa's eyes. She stroked her little friend's head. For the first time, the crooked-nosed girl felt loved.

THE FATHER

I should tell you about myself, about what I did, what I dreamed. It's time for me to speak. But I think you should hear about Majid and Bushra first. About how much they suffered and how much, despite appearances, they loved each other.

Marriage, many people were saying, had mellowed Bushra. She was fuller, more cheerful, more carefree. She had a good word for anyone, including those who had fiercely attacked and insulted her. She harbored no bitterness toward anyone, not even the worst offenders. She smiled peacefully and the world responded in kind. People did still whisper, though, especially the gallant men.

"Eh, that Majid, who knows what he does to women…," they elbowed each other knowingly.

The truth was decidedly different. Bushra and Majid, as you know, had a chaste marriage. She sprinkled herself with unguents to seduce him but he turned away, ignoring her every night. Many nights he didn't come home. He would sleep in the house of the white masters.

Days went by without a purpose in the city of Mogadishu. Those were transitional years when people awaited a future radically different from the past. Years dominated by the masters. Others arrived to replace the old ones with a new language, new divisions, new practices. The people didn't much lament losing the ones from before—the pale Italians—and happily began speaking garbled English. English tutelage lasted a short time, however. Someone in a high place, some palace of glass in a city across the ocean, decided to bring back the former masters.

The glass palace was replete with preposterous women and men. It pretended to contain the world. They smiled with lips of varying sizes. Often the smiles were false. Each person had a fistful of them in their pocket to paste on their mugs when the moment was right. They were winning, classy, becoming smiles. Nothing was excessive in the glass palace except the decisions. These, more than being excessive, were cumbersome and sometimes utterly idiotic.

And so, some of the many preposterous people in the palace decided that the Italians should return to Somalia.

"They're fortunate," someone mumbled.

"Yes, very much so," somebody else said.

Maybe they were thinking about pasta with tomato sauce and basil. Somalis hate pasta. They hate pizza, too. Their dream was flat bread dipped in meat sauce, perhaps with a sweet banana and a sugary *shay* as sides. A helping of *bisbas*, naturally. If the food wasn't spicy, it didn't make sense to the people of the Horn. You couldn't put bisbas in pasta. It was too tough for their bittersweet taste buds. They also hated the Italians. They'd been tyrannized by them for years. Colonialism spilled from their ears. The hate was understandable and legitimate.

"Why do they have to come back?" the people shouted.

"Because you are not ready," came the response from the glass palace (always very respectably).

"We're not ready? For what? Explain to us and you'll see that we are."

Then an uncomfortable, suppressed cough from the glass palace. They knew very well that Somalis had long been prepared for their independence. They also knew they had to satisfy Italians like Alcide De Gasperi, that ranting psychopath.

Behind De Gasperi stood everyone else, people like him, founding fathers. They had fought against Mussolini and fascism. Valorous people. But on the colonial question, once they had risen to power, they behaved exactly like the Duce. From Nenni to Togliatti, in fact, everyone prayed that eastern Africa would be firmly in Italian hands. The uniform didn't matter, whether black or red, blue or green, all of them were imperialists to the core. The alibi for their revanchism was the economy, the explanation for every global malady, and secondly, the population "surge." False Mussolinian myths that persisted and which were meant to slake the idiots.

In the glass palace, some shook their heads. The French and English most of all.

"Italians, my goodness. They don't change much, do they?"

"*Bien sûr. Les italiens…*" The French hated their cousins and always managed to throw in some impropriety hardly passable under censorship.

No one thought highly of the Italians. Take Churchill, who saw the boot as a "den of lurid communists." Even still, he couldn't refuse the people who had helped wipe out Adolf Hitler. And anyway, the English, that exemplary clan, were making a big mess of borders and territory redistribution in half the world. It couldn't go worse than Palestine, right?

The United Nations gave Italy—a country that surfaced from a twenty-year fascist regime and a world war with broken bones, having lost the war and a pile of money on top of that, a country whose soul was destroyed—the United Nations gave to that very country the responsibility of guiding Somalia toward independence.

"Now you must teach those Zulus democracy," they decreed from the respectable palace.

Ten years of Italian fiduciary administration in Somalia. It was mandated. Signed, sealed, and applauded. The infamous AFIS, the Italian Trusteeship Administration, was beginning.

There was jubilee in Italy. Neocolonial magazines—*Africana, Oltremare, Riconquista*—published special issues in which the civilizing role of the Italian race was exalted. They were overjoyed in the Ministry of Foreign Affairs. The glass palace offered rivers of champagne to everyone for an unexpected victory. One must remember that many of Alcide's collaborators were in the ministry. They were previously paid by the fascist regime. Those in the Ministry of Foreign Affairs were the same ones in the Ministry of Italian Africa. As in many sectors, from the university to the economy, all that mattered was that the crafty devils hadn't been embroiled in the disaster of Salò. Afterward, in the constitutional republic, they were automatically pure, as though they'd never had an affair with fascism. Moreover, there were veterans' interests to safeguard. A clean sweep, then.

But how was the news received in Somalia? And by Majid, your grandfather?

The question everyone asked was: "Can one truly teach democracy?" Somalis preferred the English to the Italians. Partly because pasta nauseated everyone, and partly because you could reason with the English. Abdullahi Issa, a young intellectual and leader of the Somali Youth League, said in those confusing days, "The English are perhaps worse colonists than the Italians, but with them, you work in freedom. With the Italians this is impossible. They don't look for competent people, only gullible fools." It was wise not to trust the English on the issue of borders, however. They sold you for chump change, and Churchill wanted to save the world from the red danger of global communism at all costs. In good Winston's nightmares, the cigar disappeared and Stalin's moustache obscured the boot until it was engulfed. It only took a second for the Englishman to abandon the young Somali leaders to their own troubles. Furthermore, those in the Somali League began irritating His Majesty's Foreign Office. They were too forthright and radical for British tastes. First there were interests in Kenya to defend and then there was the hot button of

Palestine. They decided to sacrifice the SYL in favor of full coop-eration with Italy.

That was a strange time for Somalia, which in hindsight could've produced better results. Somalis believed in their inde-pendence. Years of foment, dreams, anti-Italian demonstrations. But in the end even the League capitulated. The message of the global community was clear: go with the Italians or forget inde-pendence. The Somali League and the other parties began work-ing assiduously with the trusteeship administrators.

Our country, Zuhra, had a thousand things wrong with it: im-poverished, divided by clans in eternal war, lacking infrastructure worthy of the name. There was so much work to be done. They had to build a ruling class and a base of discerning bureaucrats ready to confront the entanglements of the future and, at the very least, find a solution to the border problems with Kenya and Ethiopia.

On paper, Italy promised they would do this and more. In reality, however, the objective was different. This was the era of the Christian Democrats, when Italy benefited from the plan and cor-ruption became political praxis. Once on African soil, Italy taught what it knew best: corruption. A strong Somali political class wasn't useful to the *Bel Paese*. The goal, if anything, was to rear a needy and corruptible political class. Though it wasn't always the case, most seeds sown at the time were pernicious poisons. Almost all Somali leaders had done apprenticeships in Italy. Some, like the future dictator Siad Barre (who impacted our lives, Zuhra), were monitored directly by the Italian secret service. AFIS lasted from 1950 to 1960. In those ten years, infrastructure didn't exist Public administration came to a standstill.

Elias grew up during the anti-Italian struggle and the first years of AFIS. First he had Bushra's milk from her generous chest, then Bushra's food right out of her magnanimous hands, and fi-nally Bushra's words pouring copiously from her modest lips. Black skin, white teeth.

Bushra gathered small pieces of cloth for the child to play

with and had him tie them in whimsical curlicues. He was bombarded with color at a young age. When he was older, she taught him how to stitch hems and attach buttons. Bushra didn't know she was steering him toward her own profession. To her it was a way of letting him while away the time, a game like any other.

While Elias knew Bushra's world of needles, hems, fringes, buttons, fabrics, and colors very well, Majid's world was alien to him. Majid himself was completely alien, even in his own eyes. Famey was the only one who knew him and shared his secrets. But she had died giving life to the child. She drowned in her blood.

Sometimes, when he was sure no one was spying on him, Majid stretched his arms out in search of Elias, as Elias had done that first time when he made clear his will to live. It would last for a moment, a short-lived oblivion. The hideousness of life took away the dream. His tense arms became feeble, his ardent desire a weak flame.

Because of this, he decided to work on a semi-permanent basis at the house of the gaalo he cooked for. Majid's white employers were the Pasquinellis. Mr. Antonio and his wife, Magda Pasquinelli, formerly Remotti. The Pasquinellis were a family made up of father, mother, mother-in-law, three children, and a cousin. They came from a region near Padua, though Magda insisted that her father was Venetian. They'd been in East Africa before Mussolini. He had, at least. Africa was his hobby, and a lucrative one at that. Magda met him during an afternoon tea at her Aunt Marta's house. The aunt was a jovial woman who enjoyed spending time with the family's beautiful young people. Magda and Antonio were cousins, in fact, though distant. The tea was a blind date. He was just passing through, but she was dreamy-eyed. After a while, trunks and luggage were on their way to Benito's empire.

Magda didn't like Africa very much, but she tried tolerating it because that was just how things were. She did everything she could to transform her corner of the city into a scaled-down

Padua. She missed the porticos, Scrovegni Chapel, the unsmiling people. In that city, in Mogadishu, everything was wanton. Too much color in the clothes, too much exuberance in the gestures. And she hated the beautiful women. How many of them had her Antonio sampled? How many had he fooled around with? She knew he had. It was no secret that Italian men got into shenanigans with the locals. "The sluts don't turn them away."

In this lurid city of negros, she only liked the cook. She had chosen him. He was a taciturn boy, hardly excitable, well-mannered. He cooked like a god. Of course, she had to make some slight revisions. For example, that fetish he had for putting spice in everything, she put an end to that vice. Apart from minor details, she was very satisfied with her cook.

Majid, however, felt nothing toward the woman or her family. It was only work for him. They didn't respect Somalis. They still believed they were masters, but he was fine with that. He didn't want to think too much. He followed orders and kept his mouth shut. Work's only purpose was to make him forget.

He cooked meals calmly. Everyone told him, "Bravo!" Sometimes Antonio Pasquinelli added a "Superb!" He didn't react. He didn't show appreciation for anything, not even the glowing compliments. When they had guests, the Pasquinellis usually showed him off. They dressed him in European wear. They denied him the *futah* he found most helpful in the kitchen, and they placed a flower in his shirt pocket. Magda Pasquinelli told him: "Comb your hair, Majid. You look like a beggar." He had curly, intricate hair that he'd stopped combing ages ago. He sprinkled two dashes of water on his hair in the mornings and left in the same way he'd woken. It was the only defect the Pasquinellis could find in the superb cook.

Vittoria Pasquinelli's fifteenth birthday arrived. She was the oldest of Antonio and Magda's children.

"Prepare your usual, dear," the woman said to her trusted cook. Majid liked cooking rice. It reminded him of his Famey's smell.

Maybe it was the cardamom or the cinnamon. He felt inspired that day. He made a delicious rice dish. It smelled like a woman.

He thought of Bushra. The roundness of her bottom, her delicate face, those immense eyes. He thought of her velvet skin and the scent of oils on her soft body. The kindling of desire lit in his groin. A lonely erection in the kitchen was normal. Every day at that hour he thought of Bushra and her perfect body. He cared for her more than himself. He desired her as no man had ever desired a woman. Was he still a man? Could he admit his shame to her? He preferred dreaming of her instead…

No. It wasn't enough for him to dream about her. If she hugged him in her arms that night, he would relish her scent. Yes, that's what he would do. He was her husband after all. Was it wrong if he hugged her a little bit?

"Mommy wants you to serve today," a girl's voice stirred the man from his thoughts. "Mommy says Yousef is too dirty and we have to host important guests."

Majid was annoyed. He didn't like being the waiter. He put a clean white tunic on top of his apron; he wet the rebellious curls on his head and pretended to comb them with two fingers. Then he washed his hands. He waited for the call. When he heard the bell sound, he carried his masterpiece to the table.

They were all seated. Vittoria was captivating in her lilac dress. She was kind, the only one in that house who smiled at him without giving too many orders. There were two other heads. One blonde and one almost completely white. Majid didn't like white heads. They brought back irrational fears.

He placed the rice on the table and got ready to serve it. Then his heart jerked. For a moment he felt like he was dying. The white head was similar to one seen too closely years ago, on that terrible afternoon with Famey and the other sad wretches from the shuttle. Could it have been Guglielmi's head? He focused for a moment. The same mean eyes. The same unsightly moustache.

"Majid," Mrs. Pasquinelli lilted, "a plentiful portion for my

Uncle Alberto. He's a soldier and needs to eat."

The uncle smiled. Majid thought he was losing his mind.

Then he remembered that he had a son. Elias would avenge him. He had to run home and tell him.

SIX

THE NUS-NUS

The girl had a video camera in her hands. She was swinging it from side to side in the same swaying motion as her straggly hair.

Mar observed from afar like a bloodhound watching its prey. She didn't want to get caught. When she'd seen the girl in that serpentine coil of people that was the medina of Tunis, she decided on pure impulse to follow her. But stalking the unknown Patricia lookalike was putting her on edge. She had fun until she saw her wavy hair cleave through the air. Before, she was with friends, chatting, bargaining. Now she was alone, following a ghost she'd wanted to forget.

When would she ever again gorge on *chapati shawarma* with Björk's clone and a Chinese man who aspired to be a philologist? They weren't people you found on every street corner. They made her laugh. It had been a long time since she'd laughed with all thirty-two of her teeth. Only Peter Solloro, with his depressed dementedness, occasionally managed to uncover a few shining teeth. For everyone else her mouth was hermetically sealed in disconsolate pain. And what to say of Miranda and the two of them together on that strange, happy afternoon? Miranda was different. That's all Mar could say. It was hard to believe. Each time she said it aloud reinforced its reality. There was a light around her mother that wasn't usually there.

Miranda, Mar knew well, was used to lights, especially the limelight. She was a famous writer, translated into more than twenty languages, comprised of a thousand souls. She wrote columns all around the world, entertained important people and artists, was invited to every film premiere. On those occasions, the light passed through her, giving her slim figure the soul-soothing tones of an Irish forest. Her mother wore green to present herself to the world. Teal, light green, forest green, soup green, dark green. Mar hated green. She couldn't stand it. For her it wasn't the color of hope, but of oppression. She didn't like the wall of trees her mother had placed between them. She was her daughter, and it seemed as though she were any other stranger. Mar envied her mother's readers, even the most miserable. They understood her, and she put in a tremendous effort for them. She'd read every damned poem. She'd read them with a magnifying glass to take them in better. It couldn't be done. She couldn't see her mama, her Miranda, in the verses. Sometimes she felt like she was missing the substance of those blood-scrawled words. It was as if the Miranda of the poems wasn't the Miranda from real life. Her existence was divorced from Mar's. She didn't like her first three poetry books. She'd never confessed this to her mother. She wouldn't have done it under torture. She liked her mother's later books more. She began adoring her simple, unembellished style. She always talked about politics, never about herself. Always going on about Argentina, but constantly cryptic. One could understand her better there, nearly enough to comprehend. Nearly. There was inevitably a black hole waiting on the next page. Mar still envied the readers. They cried when the poet cried. They sighed when she sighed. Everyone was perfectly symbiotic. Only she, Mar, remained on the outside of her mother's chorus and heart. This was another thing she couldn't tell Miranda, though she didn't know why. Perhaps the reasons were unnameable.

Mar wondered if her mother knew she'd written poems, particularly the early ones, far removed from her reality. The streets of

Buenos Aires didn't belong to her as she thought, nor did the pain belong to her as she believed. Mar wondered if her mother, the great Miranda Ribero Martino Gonçalves, had ever understood that more layers existed within her. Living next to her was hell, but also the sweetest of paradises.

They'd been happy that afternoon. She, the daughter, with her mother. It wasn't the distant, haughty Miranda. Or the genteel, reasoning Miranda. It was only her mother. Simply a woman. Her mouth full of chapati shawarma, meat and scattered bits of onion. She was a mother who had fun with her daughter and who grumbled with her mouth full. She was a more relaxed mother. More human. That was what scared Mar. Oftentimes Miranda didn't seem human. Her face looked like that of Christ carrying his mortal cross.

The afternoon was past perfect, but she'd left her lovely group to pursue a mirage, the strange girl with the video camera. Mar knew she was like Miranda in this regard. She was also a Christ carrying her woman's cross.

The girl with the video camera was moving quickly, like a camel between dunes. She was swift but graceful. Occasionally Mar saw the glint of her glasses coruscate in the distance, a green and violet flickering. Mar thought the girl dressed peculiarly. In that way, they were alike. Ripped jeans, prison-striped blouse, orange clogs with purple buckles. She carried her backpack on her stomach. Someone had evidently notified her of the preferred pastime at the medina: slyly pilfering tourists' fat wallets. Everything had to be done speedily. Thieves had a difficult life in Tunis.

The police were on alert and it was the overseer Ben Ali himself who wanted nothing bad happening to the tourists. Tourists were money, international prestige, and one of the reasons the great master-father of the country was tolerated by the West. Mar didn't like his chubby face. It was redundant, obsessive, brutal. A senseless replica. Every shop, every corner in the house, every hotel, every public restroom, every hole was papered with that man's fat face. On her first day in Tunis, Mar had mistaken him for a comic actor. That face encrusted with rouge, mascara, and foundation made her laugh. Like a good Argentinian, her mother explained that by no means did this man make others laugh. Many people in the country had disappeared under mysterious circumstances, and in Tunis the story was the same: *desaparecidos*, torture, heartache. Her mother never spoke of desaparecidos. She never spoke to Mar about the past. The portrait of the African dictator upset her stomach.

The spindly girl didn't buy anything from the bazaar. She stole images with the ravenous contraption in her hands. People in the souq didn't like being filmed. The women put their hands over their faces. The men glowered. The spindly girl was unconcerned. Only the motions of the famished video camera mattered.

They walked many of the medina's byroads. They passed the great mosque of Al-Zaytuna and, still running, the spindly girl ventured onto the side streets Mar had named for the baskets that lined them. Recently, seemingly moments before, JK had explained that these baskets were used for weddings. "Women and guests perfume themselves at the weddings. The baskets are for the oils." They looked like cradles to Mar. The lace handles, the delicate lining. She thought a newborn would fit nicely in one. Hers would. Sometimes, in her dreams, she saw her child. He grew, teethed, took his first steps, smiled, made funny faces. Pati was never in the dreams. Miranda was. She was the one who cradled him when he was tired. She sang "Alfonsina y el mar" with her windy voice. The child in her dreams was always a boy. His name was Ernesto like her desaparecido uncle. She didn't want to name him Elias, like the man to whom she owed her life. She didn't know him. She didn't know if he was worthy of respect. She'd discovered Ernesto in her mom's fifth book. He was real for her. The son in her dreams was always Ernesto, like her uncle, like Guevara. But people wake up and dreams dissipate. Mar awoke each time bathed in sweat. She remembered the gray machinery that had guzzled her child.

She remembered the spelt soup she'd hated as a kid. She remembered the frightening suction that plunged her into chaos. She remembered Patricia, who made her abort.

Each time she thought of the child—lost for nothing—she wanted to hate Patricia. Why had she humiliated her like that? Why? She had loved her too much. She'd put her on a high pedestal. Mar had forgotten herself, for her. Why had Patricia repaid her with a forced abortion and suicide? Why not take her along in death?

The video camera girl's hair elicited strange notions of extinction. A different death with every swing. Sliced veins, makeshift nooses, dives from nonexistent buildings, leaps onto the subway, the more standard colored pills. Tunis no longer seemed like the restorative place it was before.

Mar's eyes settled on a chessboard. The checkered table appeared beautiful, at once unique and manifold to her eyes. She was mesmerized. She forgot she was following the girl. The chessboard was a tacky souvenir. Something was written on the side in orientalesque Latin characters—a banal, touristy saying. The board was made of reddish faux wood. It opened like a box of assorted chocolates, and there were other games inside: checkers, dominoes. Mar's staring turned into action. She opened the chessboard like a lunatic. This shade of red bewitched her. She needed to absorb the color, the essence of life. Two meaty men approached her. It didn't take a Sherlock to understand that they were the bazaar owners.

"*Bonjour,*" they said to her. "Do you speak English?"

"Italian," she said tersely.

"Of course, miss, beautiful Italy. Parmessssan," one of them said in false Bolognese.

The other one nodded.

"How much for the chessboard?" she asked somewhat brusquely. She didn't like bargaining.

"For you, miss, only forty-five dinars."

Too much. She was tired. JK had told her that everything was negotiated in the souq. One couldn't give a merchant the satisfaction. Some struggle was necessary, for dignity if nothing else. She was about to say okay when a voice from behind her said, "*Khamsat 'ashar faqat,* fifteen dinars."

The two merchants looked in the voice's direction. She did as well, more out of instinct than curiosity. She started when she saw the profile of the girl with the video camera. Like the hurricane whose name she bore, Katrina, she swept away the merchants' absurd pretenses.

"Forty-five dinars, it's too much, *demasiado, nena,*" she whispered in Mar's ear.

Nena? Had she heard right? Was the spindly girl speaking Spanish? Had she called her *nena?* Only Pati called her *nena,* with an inkling of resentment in her voice. This girl, however, had a blaring voice. No resentment. Maybe it was happy. Yes, she had said *nena.* Mar was delusional for a moment. She looked at the girl's face more closely. It was relaxed, plain, devoid of resentment or torment.

"*Demasiado?*" Mar said, the corners of her mouth partially puckered.

"Yes, *demasiado.*"

Then followed a dizzying boxing match in Arabic. The guttural sounds chased one another confusedly in *D* flat. The numbers were aligned on a scale along which they rose and fell depending on the whims of battle. The fatter of the two merchants didn't intend to give away his chessboard cheaply. His companion, however, watched Mar rapturously. The girl with the video camera showed off her Arabic skills. Mar was the only one doing nothing, breathing absentmindedly.

The younger man moved closer to the girls.

"Are you virgin?" he asked Mar in mutilated English.

Virgin? Mar didn't understand. What did that mean? "*Virgin?*" she repeated like a malfunctioning android.

"Yeaah. No man in you…no man…in…" his mouth became a dirty, pornographic fold.

Mar didn't understand. She responded. His face fell. All pornography disappeared from his expression. Mar realized that he was young, probably the bazaar owner's son. His forehead was wide and curious. His eyes were submerged in pockets of sincerity. The sign of a good person. Would he have been that way under such a stifling regime? Or would he have raped a woman just to show that she was worth nothing in the chain of power? Ben Ali smiled triumphantly from a filthy corner. In the distance, a muezzin called to prayer from an 18-inch TV.

Tunisia was in dress rehearsal for civil war.

"You good girl, *ya ukhti*," the young man said.

Mar smiled stupidly. The chessboard was purchased for nine dollars.

"Come back soon, *presto, presto*," father and son said in unison.

Mar wondered what the young man had asked her. She wasn't sure she gave the right answer.

Katrina, in the meantime, was planning the future.

"*Hay una fiesta*…a party in my *mabit…mañana por la tarde. Hay cerveza, también.*"

"*Cerveza?*" Mar asked. She knew the word: beer. She remembered that drinking was difficult in this country, only permissible in hotels and dive bars. She envied her mother, who wasn't a teetotaler like her, who took pleasure in life. Her perfect, goody two-shoes mother.

THE NEGROPOLITAN

Benjamin, please, don't do it. In the name of Allah, Shiva, Jesus Christ, and the souls in purgatory. In the name of my blessed ears, in the name of my stomach, Benjamin, don't do it. Stop right now. Don't profane these honeyed words anymore. Don't violate. Don't desecrate. Show some respect. Genuflect and mash your nose against the floor. That's what you need to do. Prostration. Humility. Benjamin, in the name of Allah, stop reading!

Just six minutes until the end of the Arabic lesson. It's been ten minutes since Benjamin started eviscerating one of the most beautiful poems by Mahmoud Darwish, the griot of the Palestinian struggle. Benjamin is German. If his passport weren't there to prove it, his strong Bavarian accent would. Even better, he's Aryan. Canary blond, glassy eyes, diaphanous skin. Comrade Hitler would've fallen in love with his upturned chin, his large shoulders, his burly body, his chunky mouth. Comrade Adolf would've dragged the man to him and perhaps loved him more than Eva Braun. Screwed him more than Eva Braun.

Luckily, Benjamin was born after that collective delirium. His mom was an anarchist hippie, his father a Syriac philologist. That's why, twenty-five years after his first cry, Benjamin is here in my third-level Arabic class decimating Mahmoud Darwish's greatest poem. If he'd been a conventional Aryan, Benjamin would've listened to Guns N' Roses. He was an Aryan with an-archist blood in his veins, so he ended up in Tunis, in an Arabic school that was more like a synagogue, though it was always empty. Since coming here, I've only seen two policemen keeping an eye on it.

The poem the plump professor is making us read is "Identity Card. Ana Arabi." *I am Arab.* Benjamin tries giving it pathos. His accent betrays him at every letter. Everything he does is backward. The guttural sounds slip away like silk, while he brings out a certain sheepishness in the soft sounds that all Germans have when they try to speak other languages. It turns to stone in Benjamin's throat. Everything is dry and granitic. There seems to be no room for letters or their emotions. The poet's exile, his struggle, his land, are lost in the canary-colored boy's sandy cadence. Darwish dances on the architecture of himself like a dragonfly, but Benjamin destroys every emotion with his reading. He is like a caricature more than a boy. Once, I read a book in which Hitler's head had been thrown into a freezer, waiting for a perfect Aryan body to graft itself onto. Maybe the author knew Benjamin, the perfect Aryan specimen. A perfect caricature, at least. In fact, anarchic blood runs through Benjamin. Glory to Bakunin!

Benjamin, please, don't do it. In the name of Allah, Shiva, Jesus Christ, and the souls in purgatory. Benjamin, in the name of my blessed ears.

There are still three minutes left. I want to hear how this tor-ture ends. But I have a problem, and it's not an easy fix. Mahmoud Darwish still dances inside me. Despite Benjamin, I feel the rhythm of the poet's misery. I feel the pulse. It is frenzied. A de-fective drill.

I have to pee, damn. Why now? I want to hear the end of the poem. I'm holding it in. I'm trying. I feel the water compressing my intimate walls. It's violently pushing against me now. It's insistent. Can't it wait? Damn it. I give up. I have to run to the toilet, stat.

I wave at the fat professor. Sorry to ruin the magical moment, teach. I know, I'm smashing it to smithereens. I'm not a killjoy, I actually wanted to hear how Benjamin finishes destroying the poem. But I have a pressing physiological need. No *ya mu'alima*, oh teacher, I can't stay. No, I can't hold it in. I tried, but you see, I'm bending over. In a minute I'm going to pee all over myself if you don't let me go right now. She gives me a look that couldn't be any more ornery.

This hyperproduction of urine must be connected to my excessive consumption of mint tea. It's good, especially when they add pine nuts. First you swig the liquid and then you try snatching as many nuts as possible with your tongue. Some get away from me. The pine nut is cunning, but my tongue is vigilant. In the end, it doesn't lose a single one, on my word. I'm gifted at some sports. They should make it into an Olympic event. I should have multiple medals at this point, more than Sergey Bubka, the guy who obliterated everyone in the pole vault. I would be in the Guinness Book of World Records and people's hearts. Records, laurels, and glory. The pine-nut snatch would be watched more than swimming. Freestyle, crawl, breaststroke, outdated stuff. They'd use me in commercials. I'd be a heartbreaker.

But none of this will happen. I'm still single and I'm running to the restroom with a full bladder. I forgot the tissues in my purse, shit. The school's bathroom is rundown and toilet paper doesn't exist even in one's dreams. Only that damn tubing. They don't have a bidet here, they have a tube. They're doing better than the English, though. Those people don't use anything. Tunisia is still a Muslim country. They want to keep Arabs clean. During the Crusades, Roman apostles made fun of them because cleaning yourself was seen as a feminine concern. The English, who really are effeminate, don't wash themselves. They don't have bidets. They don't have mixer taps for cold and hot water. They have two lonely faucets. One burns, the other freezes. No half-measures. Tunisians have a tube instead of the bidet, a tube as long as a serpent. It's like something you'd use to water the garden. It's basically attached to the trashcan. The tube's function is simple. First, people do the usual unmentionable things in the toilet bowl, until the last drop or piece. Then they use the tube to wash away the remaining drops, and dangling residue; once the water is at the right temperature, they position the tube near their genitals and start washing. One hand holds the tube and the other massages. The tube isn't a bad invention, it's just that, barring death, I wouldn't use the one at the school. My philosophy is the same one I have for all public restrooms. I don't sit on other people's toilets. I hover above them, like a butterfly. It's hard to pee in this position. You have to exert your calf muscles, find the correct center of gravity, or otherwise you risk spurting urine everywhere. I envy the penis in these instances. You can pull it out and don't have to offset your balance.

Anyways, the school's tube could have licit or illicit uses. I don't want to know. I can't put something that has seen other people's goods so close to my own. It's incredibly revolting.

The pee doesn't let up. I feel full. I feel a blow to the groin, a faint sense of nausea. Oh God, let's hope it's only pee. I don't want to be on my period, not now. I have to go to the beach with my friends. Miranda is coming. And the piglet *gaal halouf*, the infidel. The one I like a lot, I mean. I think I like him. His name is Orlando, like Ariosto's and Virginia Woolf's Orlando. I doubt it's an easy name to have. The name of a king, or perhaps for madmen. I don't know if I actually like him. I think I do. When he's near me, I want to look at him. He seems defenseless. I want to hug and protect him. I remember the doll I had as a child, Susanna. She was all I had. Poor Susanna, she was so unlucky. She broke everything. She was always ill. I cured and looked after her. She had the same face as Mom when she came to visit me at school. Even Mom hugged her tightly. I took care of her.

No, please, not my period. I want to meet the gaal halouf today. Not tomorrow, or the day after tomorrow, today. I'd taken out my orange and white bathing suit from my bag. It's the kind of thing you'd see at the beach in Ipanema. I checked myself out in the mirror. Not half bad. A knockout, almost. He'll look at me. I'll smile at him. He'll tell me about himself. Another smile from me. He'll approach me with a trembling hand. Then, I don't know, the thing that happens in films. We'll find a nice place. We'll kiss. We'll swear eternal love. That's how it goes in the movies, right? *Titanic*, DiCaprio style. So it's important that my period doesn't start today. I have romantic plans.

The restroom seems like it's an eternity away. I run. My legs gallop at full speed. Move, get out the way, let me through. I'm about to go on myself. Really, though. Move!

There's a line, three girls in front of me. I have to hold it. At my venerable age, pissing myself would be unbecoming. I think about Miranda to distract myself. What a beautiful woman. Supple in her movements. She told me she'd join us later. She has errands to run. I think she's writing a book. Every time we stake out a spot on the beach she's bending over her pages. No one dares disturb her; she's engrossed. She doesn't know that I know who she is. I've read all her poems. I know of her immense pain. There are times when her stare goes blank. I don't like it. It reminds me too much of my own stare, of Maryam Laamane's.

The girl in front of me may have tissues. I almost dare asking her for some in Arabic. I'm not embarrassed. So what if I mess up? I clear my throat. "*Afwan*," excuse me, I whisper. "*Afwan*," I repeat, at a loss. She looks at me. Her stare makes me regress to a nonexistent Esperanto. I mix English, French, Spanish. The only thing I say in Arabic is, "*Min fadlika*," please. I don't know what language I say "tissues" in. Aramaic? "I'm Italian like you," she says. "Muslim as well. Have you forgotten already?"

But of course, I hadn't recognized her from behind. The back never corresponds to what you see in front. From behind, the girl seems like a respectable person, someone whose acquaintance or friend you'd like to be. The front dissuades you of both those things. It's true, I know her, we were on the same boat. She gets under my skin. Her name is Souad, and she's in my mabit. She's

Italo-Tunisian. She speaks the dialect well, but she's not great with classical Arabic. She's two levels below me. She's from around Turin. I don't really know why, but she puts on an act. She's no one special.

I have to pee. I need those tissues. If I don't ask her, I'll be obliged to go back in the classroom, interrupt another one of the teacher's magical moments, leave again, and stand in another line. This one is stagnant as it is. It would be a nightmare. I don't have a choice, she's all I have. Souad, the world traveler.

"Would you happen to have a tissue?" I ask neutral-toned. I privately commend myself. I was impersonal in asking the question. I don't show my emotions. I don't say to her, for example, "I dislike you," or "I think you're irritating," or "You're a pain in the ass with your fucking air of superiority." I don't say anything. I'd like to, but I mustn't forget—I don't know her. Here I cite Bersani Samuele from memory, like how others would cite Carducci Giosue. I prefer Bersani, he's more fuckable. I don't think Carducci ever was, even if someone has done it with him. I'm blasphemous. His poem about the ox was my bane as a child. It was impossible to learn. The nun punished me too. "You Zulus really have no creativity!" That stupid nun always called me a Zulu.

When I think about it, Souad does look like the stupid nun. She has the same snout, like a cuckolded pig. Souad is flat-faced. I remember her strange snout also stood out when I saw her in line at check-in for the flight to Palermo. Since then, I've wanted to say four hundred things to cosmopolitan Souad. I said, "Finally I'm going to Africa," and she said, "Tunisia isn't Africa." So what is it, then? Tunisia is on the African continent, it's still there, so it's Africa. Souad insisted, saying that they were Arab and not black, so being in Africa was only a short-lived accident. I wonder what cosmopolitan Souad wants to do with her country. Might she want to haul it to the Middle East, towed by a rope? Where would she put it? Near Assad's Syria? Or in the middle of Palestine? Because as everyone knows, Palestine is such an agreeable and peaceful place. I don't like people who want to forget the color line, the equatorial line. I didn't insist though. Geography was on my side.

She's the one I have to ask for tissues. The water sloshing in my bladder, the water my kidney is excreting, makes me do it. Residues of me. I reformulate the question, this time in the elegant Italian I express myself with only at university. The word "tissues" sounds like lacework, given my pompous pronunciation. The girl looks at me. Her black hair sticks to her head like Lego bricks. She has tortoiseshell glasses and fuschia-colored lipstick. She isn't ugly, but she looks sloppy. Her hands magnify everything. She has long bones like marble. You can see them through her skin. She has anti-reflective lenses in her frames. I'm familiar. They're the only thing I wore before permanently converting to hard contact lenses. After the hours spent in Libla, I needed to feel beautiful, alive. Hard lenses, a new coat, brand-name makeup around my eyes, and a frilly dress always helped a little. It's bullshit, I know, but they make me who I am.

I repeat my question. I think, *Manzoni must've talked like this*. I am perfect. A gentle Italian issues forth, cultured and unreal. The one I use in public offices or when I have to pay the sanitation bill. They look at me with their whitebread faces and yell, "Residency permit!" as though it were a magic spell to humiliate me. I wonder why being foreign has to be shameful. The whitebread faces distort when they press my Italian identity card, my Italian citizenship, to their noses. They don't believe it.

Souad, too, has a whitebread face. That's why I don't like her. Her face quivers. A fluctuation, a tremor at the edges of her mouth. She fixates on me like a toad. Menacingly pointing at me, she says, "You're Muslim, aren't you ashamed?" Of what, pray tell? Please, I know Arabic better than you. I'm devout, I believe, I'm interested, I read the Quran, I don't forget alms, I adhere to Ramadan and one day, God willing, I'll make a pilgrimage to the Sacred City, if I have the means. Otherwise, Allah al-Kareem will exonerate me. What should I be ashamed of, bread face?

Cosmopolitan Souad's finger expands. It's the index, but it looks like three fat thumbs put together. Repugnant. It looks like an erection. I don't like having a dick waved in front of my nose. Her threatening finger makes me uncomfortable.

"You're not ashamed?"

"Of what?" I ask her. I lost my Manzonian verve. I sound like a Tor Bella Monaca junkie.

"The tissues, idiot."

I should've cut her to pieces. I wish I was Ranma Saotome. Or, I wish I were married to Ranma Saotome. It's a shame such a handsome boy is from an anime. If I had his strength, I'd give her a lump on the head that she'd remember for the rest of her meaningless earthly existence. I let the insult slide, but what about the tissues? I wonder. She laughs contemptuously.

"You don't get it, do you? Idiot."

Here we go. She said it again. I don't like being insulted and not doing anything about it. I'm coming this close to punching her in the head and getting myself expelled. I still don't understand what the tissues have to do with anything. Curiosity prevails over rage. I wait for an explanation. She doesn't hesitate.

"Muslim women don't clean themselves with tissues, they wash themselves. You have to wash yourself with water. Do you want a squalid vagina like an infidel beast? Theirs are unwashed and stay unwashed, fool. They pee. They go around with men and they only use a tissue. We use water. We're always pure, fresh, clean."

Oh god. I can't believe it. Allah hold me back, I want to crown her head with lumps! She's giving me a sermon on personal hygiene. I can't believe it. And she's bringing religion into it. I want to respond in kind.

My stare goes through her, pierces her. I want her to feel small and useless. My hand is a masterwork. It moves as though it were the hand of Queen Victoria. Royal, glacial. A hand that knows what it wants. It oscillates and summons holy terror. Souad is scared shitless. Then the voice comes, when she's already a bundle of nerves that doesn't know what's coming next. Does she know that she's crossed every line?

"A good Muslim has to dry herself too, right? What are you doing? Do you go around dripping? You don't leave your underwear damp, do you? I mean, that's not good, for health or decency. Soaked hairs, soaked fabrics, annoying smells. You've got to think about these things. You're not going to tell me you don't use tissues?"

I see her, wan-faced. Whiter than Nosferatu. I'm winning. Triumph has a bitter aftertaste sometimes.

I'm sick of people who want to snoop around my vagina. It's mine, you understand? Mine alone, and I'll do what I want with it. Why is everyone so worried about it? Why don't they leave it in peace? What does it matter to cosmopolitan Souad, knowing whether I clean myself or not? My vagina has the right to smell bad, if it wants. That's its own business, understand Souad? You have nothing to do with it. No one has anything to do with it without my permission.

In elementary school there was that man, Aldo, who did have something to do with it. Without permission and without wiping off his shoes. He was too interested in my vagina. I was afraid of him partly because he was the school custodian, and partly because he had a fixed stare. He made me feel uncomfortable in whatever I was wearing. I didn't know how to tell the teachers that Aldo wanted to steal my vagina. When the others didn't see him, he tried caressing it, he pushed me against the wall. My heart raced. They told me that I had to listen to adults and follow their commands. I didn't like when Aldo pressed me against the wall. I should've shouted or told someone. No one ever believes kids in elementary school. One afternoon, Aldo had a strange face, he was clammy and enraged. Aldo stole my vagina that day.

The day after, Howa Rosario came and took me away. I don't know how she did it. Perhaps she pretended to be my mom. She never told me. The people at school were incompetent. They couldn't distinguish one black person from another. My belly hurt, I cried and bent over. The theft of my vagina was discovered because the sheets were soaked with blood. It flowed profusely. I couldn't hide it. I tried, but my fear of Aldo was too great. He told me he'd kill me if I mentioned what had happened. I was silent. The sheets spoke for me. Howa took me to the hospital. We pressed charges against Aldo. Mom, I imagine, was too drunk to come.

Souad stokes my rage from that time, my abiding rage. What the fuck does it matter to her how I clean myself? What do you care? Leave me in peace, Souad, you don't know anything.

My hand touches my stomach. It slips down, delicately, like plumage. The usual delusion. It's the same every time. I touch my vagina and don't feel anything. Instead of my vagina there is always that horrible emptiness.

Leave me in peace, Souad. You know nothing.

"Here, take this." This voice quells my rage. It belongs to a dark girl like me. She hands me a tissue. It's a revolutionary gesture. "Hurry up and pee, I've got to go too." It's funny. She looks like Miranda.

THE PESSOPTIMIST

In the month of May, the Shebelle River flowed bountifully in its natural bed. A conduit traveled for centuries, bringing sweet waters plunging to the south and into the furious Indian Ocean. The river was fattened by nurturing rains that fell on the Ethiopian mesa, causing a spillover on both embankments that was not always fruitful. Seeing muddy marshes in the heart of the Somali woods was no rare occurrence. That was the scratch mark of the flood, an alluvial wound that made the pastoralists cry in dejection. Immense fertile surfaces remained unusable, making the concerned populations howl in fear. The specter that wandered among the wretched was poverty—taking everything and leaving nothing—the kind that exhausts you before death. Poverty that starves and blinds you. The lands near the Shebelle were not easy. It was in those lands that Maryam Laamane imagined her life as an adult woman.

At the beginning of the twentieth century, the first banana plantations emerged there, right on the coast of the hot-blooded river. The plantations took the name of the Lower Shebelle's agricultural district. Many were still under Italian ownership, but by then, with independence, handovers occurred even there. Italians sold (at exorbitant prices) to enterprising Somali businessmen, the new sharks of politics and business who differed from the ex-masters only in complexion. Bananas were a safe business, more at home than abroad, and tempted many. Quite a few people grew rich thanks to the harmonious yellow fruit. They went around in Jeeps and built multistory villas, with a pair of consenting whores dressed in the latest Parisian chiffon on their arms.

The sweet, soft Somali bananas, with their spicy aftertaste, were easy money for the sharks. Berlin housewives, like the ones from Voghera, were euphoric over the pulp's sensuousness, the fruit's consistency. Demand increased and the floors of the villas multiplied. Growing bananas wasn't expensive. Shrewdly using the waters of the tormented Shebelle was enough. In its pursuit of death, racing toward the ocean that would annihilate it, the river left numerous traces of itself scattered about. One only needed to appropriate the redundant water to irrigate the fields. It was quite simple. With the right tools, calculations, and willpower, the bananas of the Lower Shebelle ripened and prospered.

One of the district owners was Maryam's uncle. The name on all his documents was Othman, but people preferred to call him Gurey, the left-sided, not only because he wrote with his left hand, but because, in his mind, the left was creation's natural orientation. They whispered that he had unusual communist ideas in his head, that for an owner, he treated his dependents too well. "He reads too many books that we don't understand," people said. Gurey had a snow-white beard that covered his face, a prophet's beard that instilled respect and hatred in like measure. Gurey spoke little, but that little caused the bowels of the insecure and the sloth-ful to quake. Maryam loved her uncle. Around him, she never felt the fear that turned others into jelly. Her uncle seemed like an old, good-humored man with many stories to tell. He knew everything about hyenas and the circular flights of buzzards. He could describe the wandering of ants and recite ancient stories from the Land of Punt, the ones in which the queen of Egypt, Nefertiti, took incense baths near the seething Nile. Maryam Laamane listened, enrapt, to her prophet uncle. She felt nourished by his erudition and sweet knowledge. Her uncle spoke with her frequently. Sometimes he ran his hand along her soft cheek and whispered, "Oh, little one, you look so much like my lost brother." The river prophet never spoke of Maryam's father, who died on Graziani's southern front. He never spoke of the time when they were ruled, used, and mistreated by the Italians.

It was a Sunday in May, a working day. The sun was hot and pleasant. It didn't burn one's skin with its usual demented ferocity. It had finally let up on the backs of men and banana peels. The rarified air, however, was sticky and insistent like sugar. That was Maryam's feeling at the time. It was no small thing for her to make a trip so early in the morning. The girl saw that all the farmers were busy with their tasks. Some of them had white skin. Many Italians, despite no longer being the country's rulers, had preferred to stay in Africa since it was a beautiful life for them. What would they do in Italy? A daily grind consisting of wives, office desks, traffic, and exhaust fumes. Here, on the other hand, was the yellow of the sun and bananas. Open expanses and multistory villas. Buxom women to the heart's content. They could still live the Good Life near the equator. They knew that the money and power of the West still made them rulers.

Work on that May Sunday was at its peak. Breathlessly, people tried doing as much as they could in the shortest possible time. The hands and feet of manservants and masters churned frenetically in syncopated rhythm. After the cutting, the bananas quickly passed to the harvesting center for a careful selection of clusters. The skilled labor that followed these manufacturing phases combined duty with dulcet songs. They placed their struggle in the rhyme, the sweat and pain of having to spend hours under the woodland's choleric sun.

Maryam harmonized to the words of the song. Living on a banana plantation wasn't easy. They had to face many foes. The masters, fatigue, the sun, insects, boredom, monotony, accidents. Singing freed the spirit from ghosts and *jinn*. By singing, life became simpler. The plantation masters didn't care to hear their servants' modulating voices. "Songs always carry the germ of subversion. These sons of bitches need to keep quiet!" More than one master tried muzzling the workers. The attempts failed miserably every time.

Gurey, the prophet uncle, was pleased by the music that rose from the unripe banana forest. "You can't silence your conscience, niece," he always said. Then he would smile, flaunting his snow-white beard. Gurey was a master, too, but he did things his own way. He didn't have jeeps or a multistory villa. The few square meters of his brick house were enough for him. He didn't have the megalomania of the newly rich, and he didn't want to sit like a pachyderm in an ex-colonial dwelling made of Corinthian columns and fresh lime. His brick house would do. Lunch and dinner guaranteed every day, prayer at fixed hours, and a healthy amount of sleep and leisure. He had few pretenses. He lived with the awareness that others like him were doing the same. Because of this, he'd transformed the plantation into a co-op. Some workers were also members, others had a guaranteed stipend and acquired rights. They didn't work nonstop, they didn't work like spinning tops, they weren't humiliated. No one on Gurey's plantation was barred from singing. The syncopated rhythm of the other plantations became a vigilant lullaby there. Their serenity was conducive to sleep, and their energy was worthy of the finest hours when they were strong and ready to conquer the world.

"He has queer ideas," the other masters whispered malignantly. "He'll bring them to our people, too, you'll see. Shit communist will ruin all of us with his communitarian doctrines."

When communism did arrive in Somalia with Siad Barre, it was somehow only Gurey who paid the price. The sharks that had exploited and trampled the people's rights stayed afloat and built new floors on their ostentatious villas, while Gurey lost everything, down to the last banana peel. He really was a communist, in heart and paunch, who read Gramsci and renounced Stalin, who believed in the pure genius of humanity, who had been brought up outside of the *mafioso* system that Big Mouth Siad Barre erroneously termed "scientific socialism." The loss of his plantations was a hard blow. The bananas, their golden shimmer, their fleshy softness had been his entire life. No longer having them meant no longer having a life.

But on that Sunday in May, Siad Barre was still far away. Somalia had recently become an independent state. Somalis dreamed of every possible future, and the bananas of the Lower Shebelle perfumed the air with possibility. A question about the future had brought Maryam Laamane to the Lower Shebelle. She'd embarked on an absurd journey to tell her favorite uncle about her promising future. He was the only person she felt was her friend beside Howa Rosario.

Getting off the shuttle, with the sweat from the previous night making her feel more tired than she was, her long legs took her toward her uncle Gurey's co-op. Ali Said, a shambling young man who was also her uncle's personal assistant, came to meet her. Ali Said's stride was confused, like the revolving panels she'd seen in trendy restaurants. The slight asymmetry of his glasses made people feel maternally protective, women especially. Everyone wanted to coddle the sickly-looking boy. Coddle and then fix him up with food, fragrances, and a generous, welcoming bosom. Ali Said was easy to love. In fact, everyone loved him, including the men who left him bits of the choicest meats on the communal plate at lunch. Maryam knew the man wasn't as fragile as people thought. She didn't doubt his goodness. She knew her uncle could trust him blindly. She also knew that in the hour of need, Ali Said would bare his fangs to defend himself and the ones he loved. If it weren't for Ali Said, she wouldn't have been saved from Siad's clutches. And if it weren't for him, her Uncle Gurey would've died of desperation and starvation.

Ali Said was the first one Maryam Laamane saw at the co-op that day. He told her that her uncle hadn't shown up on the plantation. "You've become a woman, Maryam, you know that, right?" Maryam had gone there because of this. She smiled as a thick, nectarous fluid flowed down her legs. A red fluid that accentuated her enchanting femininity. She smiled once more at her uncle's assistant, and then she left.

The sun had risen a few hours earlier. The work raged on and a long-legged girl found herself walking alone again on a street imbued with the bittersweet essence of bananas. The girl was wearing an outfit that was in vogue in Mogadishu, the *ballerina*, so-called in Italian because the frills of cloth recalled the fluttering tulle of classical dancers. Hers was pastel-tinted, feathery. She preferred the ballerina to the traditional *guntiino*. Maryam wasn't fond of walking around bare-shouldered and thought the ballerina suited her tastes, unpresuming and reserved. She still liked running, and the guntiino risked coming undone and leaving her as nude as God had made her. How many times had she witnessed scenes like that? How many nude women, with their shame exposed, had she seen shoddily covering themselves around Mogadishu? It was mostly young girls who had such accidents. Sometimes their naked chests leaped from the hems and oh, what shame, what *eeb*, if a boy nearby derided her. The guntiino was for older women who could tie the fabric securely, who knew how to make strong knots, who didn't frantically careen through the world. The guntiino in its marmoreal beauty was not for young girls, and it was intolerable if you had to run, scuttle, or even bend down to grab an object from the ground. It called for experience. And it was a hindrance during fights. Besides dodging the opponent's scratches and bites, one also had to be mindful that the knot at the top of the tunic wasn't loose. Nude, with shame exposed, one was more vulnerable to the nemeses' kicks and scratches. Meanwhile, the person who tried recovering would be massacred by their adversary, who benefited from the confusion the nudity created. Maryam didn't like brawling with her peers. She was a pacifist, by the book. She couldn't imagine or prepare herself for the eventuality of something like that. There were people like Fauzia Ahmed who, sooner or later, she would have to teach a lesson. Ah, how she hated that girl. She'd come this close to ruining the independence celebration for her, and Maryam couldn't tolerate that hen insulting her best friend Howa. She hadn't only insulted her, she'd also subjected her to the virginity test. What barbarity! People like Fauzia Ahmed made the country backslide. "If we were all like my Uncle Gurey or Howa Rosario, we'd be part of the United Nations Security Council by now."

Maryam dreamed big, so she preferred wearing the ballerina. The one she wore that day sent her over the moon. The style was rather particular. The classic ballerina: short dress and long underskirt, which the people called a *carambawi*, with butterfly ribbon additions that gave her a sylvan frivolity. The few pedestrians she met on the plantation path at her uncle's house watched her dumbly, as though she were an houri of paradise, descended to have her beauty admired. No one was bothersome. Women in those times were respected. They were the sisters, daughters, and nieces of the independence struggle. Eyes admired without vulgarity and everyone knew she was Gurey the communist's niece, even if she was more of a woman than the breakneck little girl they remembered. Eyes looked her over respectfully because, despite the murmurs, everyone in the Lower Shebelle respected Gurey for the coherence of his ideas.

As she negotiated the tree-lined street, Maryam was suddenly approached by a young man on a bicycle. He couldn't have been much older than her. He wore a beige, short-sleeved linen shirt, completely unbuttoned, and his breast pockets seemed inexplicably obscene to Maryam. Her eyes momentarily moved past them. The obscenity did not, in fact, lie in the two slits in the beige cloth, but in what was beneath them. Her eyes lingered on his white undershirt and black skin. The boy wore few articles of clothing, and from his pelvis down, she couldn't tell how well he was covered. The futah was duly wrapped, leaving his hairy, burly legs exposed. He was a tall boy, towering over a bike that was evidently too small for him.

For the first time in her life, Maryam felt a quickening throb in her heart. She realized, somewhat perplexed, that her heart was making noise. She hoped the boy couldn't hear it. Otherwise she would die of shame.

The boy stopped his bicycle in front of her. Maryam was shaking. The brake reverberated like an electric discharge in her stomach. Meanwhile, he watched her steadily. It was an intense stare, the kind she'd seen in films where a doctor examines a patient in critical condition. It was a mortifying, clinical exam. The menstrual blood which, until that moment, had flowed smoothly began leaking in discontinuous streams, like a drunken geyser. She felt a sharp pang at the base of her gut.

"Good afternoon, pretty young lady," the boy said in Italian.

"*Subax wanaagsan*, good afternoon," the girl replied.

"That dress fits you well. Looks like it was made especially for you—I'm glad." Then he gave her a kiss and started off again on his bicycle.

Once she arrived at her uncle's house, the girl couldn't stop looking at herself in the mirror.

"Good afternoon, pretty young lady," Uncle Gurey said in Italian.

The same words the boy said, the same words in Italian, which seemed to her especially singsong that day. The unexpected déjà vu propelled the girl into an abyss of pleasure. Suddenly, her Uncle Gurey was no longer there, replaced by the boy's unbuttoned shirt, and particularly what she had seen underneath—black skin shimmering more than the bananas. She remembered everything, every gesture and faint noise. The boy's pliable muscles moving like unembroidered silk fabric. The swish of his pedaling and the shock of that soft-lipped kiss had seemed like the chirping of a bulbul. Everything about the strange bicycle boy was marvelous. Maryam couldn't say whether he was beautiful, ugly, or just passable. She still didn't know how to judge men's beauty. She thought that boy had something of hers, as though he, a stranger, kept a part of her inside him. She didn't dare call what she felt love. It was an intoxicating loss of clarity. She felt ridiculous in front of the mirror, admiring herself in her ballerina. She couldn't help but look at herself. The green dress Howa Rosario had given her was becoming an obsession. What had the boy on the bike seen that was so special?

"You look lost, Maryam," her uncle said.

The prophet's voice snapped her out of the trance.

"Uncle," Maryam Laamane said solemnly, "I've become an adult. I have a job. I start working as an operator at the Somali telephone company in three days."

Her uncle smiled. He guessed that something noteworthy had happened to his favorite niece. He was elated. *It's time she had some secrets too,* he thought. *She's not a girl anymore.*

Maryam continued looking at herself in the mirror.

Out of respect, Uncle Gurey shut the door partway.

Maryam laughed bitterly at the memory of that May. She laughed bitterly about the tenderness she felt toward the little girl she'd been. She'd spent ten days retying the threads of something she thought was lost. Sitting cross-legged on a mat, she narrated into a recorder a past that was still very much present inside her. After ten days, she found less reprieve. She wanted to erase everything and kick the machine that collected her every breath and hesitation. She felt an increasing urge to regurgitate what used to be her story. Her happy adolescence was in those cassettes, which she'd been meticulously recording for days. The girl in the recorder's stories was pure. She wasn't the mother Zuhra knew, the one consumed by alcohol and nostalgia. These were still the blazing fifties, the mythical sixties, not quite the terrible seventies, certainly not the grievous eighties. Maryam was a little girl and she cheered for the Indians who fought haughty pale men in blue shirts. Little

Maryam was so different from the Maryam she would become as an adult. She was an incorruptible child, a fleur-de-lis impervious to the malefic radiance of jinn. She hadn't yet imbibed liters and liters of demons enclosed in a light glass. She liked little girl things: candies; Vimto, the sweet drink; colorful dresses; the delicious fresh-squeezed red grapefruit juice her Auntie Salado made for her every afternoon. Alcohol was nowhere to be found, not even in her worst nightmares. Maryam was young and people saw a kaleidoscopic future in her eyes. *I was so pure then!* she thought. She wanted to cry thinking about it, but the tears didn't fall, they were stubbornly stuck in her eyes. Her body, however, was wracked with abnormal spasms, and saltwater gushed from her forehead. Maryam sweated, feeling chills in her bones. When the spasms became more violent, she decided to leave the house. She could no longer tolerate the memory of the slight and happy girl she'd once been, nor of the dignified and uncontaminated Somalia, warless Somalia. Her pink-hued memories, like Auntie Salado's grapefruits. She shook away her chills, wrapped a green scarf around her head, put on dull brown shoes, and strung her favorite handbag across her shoulder, the confidence booster. Before leaving the house, she took stock of her most important objects. She didn't want to forget anything. The pack of Camels, spare eyeglasses, sunglasses, wallet, bus card, I.D....definitely couldn't forget that. With her black skin, it was best to be wary in an unfamiliar Italian city.

She left and caught the bus, one of the new ones with tight spaces for standing commuters. She didn't like buses. They weren't made for a sprawling city like Rome. She got off almost immediately and started walking.

She walked all afternoon, and afterward went back home to her recorder, her recollections, the frail little girl she missed so much. She'd walked for a while. Her ankles were sore and her armpits stank like fresh codfish. She ran to the bathroom. She washed, pomaded, and smeared deodorant on. After prayer and a spare evening meal, she sat on the mat again. She pressed record and said:

"Zuhra, you won't guess who I saw at Termini today: Ali Said. He came from Stockholm to say goodbye to Howa. Did you know he was in love with her?"

She hit stop. That would be enough for the day.

THE REAPARECIDA

Flaca never spoke. To make up for it, she wrote constantly, dementedly. She stooped without interruption over her papers. She didn't sleep so that she could write. She didn't eat so that she could write. She didn't think straight so that she could write. Writing had become another form of breathing. I was impressed by her attachment to the written word. I couldn't remember ever having seen her holding a pen in Buenos Aires, but in Rome she kept a thousand tattered notebooks near her bed. Quite the disarray. Cluttered things, ideas, emotions, scattered thoughts. I tried tidying up her disorder, uselessly. It was a lost battle, a Waterloo. Flaca restored her chaos, perfectly commensurate with the previous. I ended up overexerting myself—gathering and reordering—since after five minutes everything went back to how she'd had it, if not worse. At first, I went three times a week to Pablo and Rosa's house. Then one day I took Santana aside and told him, "Maybe I should be spending more time with her." And so I went to live in San Lorenzo at their place.

Our tranquil, sleepy house was on one of the many slivers of street that had been devastated in 1943 by the Allied bombing of Rome. One of our neighbors, Nuccia, the old spotted crake, told me the story of San Lorenzo's bombing. An interesting person. She was one of the tallest women I'd ever met, and her hands were

283

like those of a dwarf. "When they bombed my neighborhood, San Lorenzo," Nuccia said, "they had no idea over in Corso Trieste. They didn't realize it in Parioli either, miss." She turned red in the face and, in moments of heightened agitation, became mottled with blue. "Rome didn't want to believe it had gotten caught up in the war. We have the Pope here, everyone said, we're sitting pretty. No one will get bombed here. The world respects us because Christ is here, the Madonna, and the saints. Yes, we've got the Pope and the saints and the Christs and the Madonnas, but we also have Benito and all his terrible kind. They have no respect for anyone. Not even their own children."

Nuccia was speaking of Rome and Italy, but I always thought she was talking about me, about Argentina. It was the perfect neighborhood for veterans of pain like the three of us. *Hija*, maybe you'd like to know what kind of life I lived in those years on ancient streets. What I did, who I smiled at, how I walked. I was young, and you danced inside me—this is all I remember. The fact remains that my memories of that time are tied to Flaca, how she smiled and how she walked.

Everything was going smoothly until the day I, more stubborn than a mule, dragged her to Via dei Giubbonari, to the dance school at Madame Elsa's, in search of unattainable chimeras. I wanted the kind of normalcy that was no longer ours to have. I only wanted to see her dance. Then there was the man on the stairs. I don't remember seeing him. I just heard his voice. It was unmistakable. A youthful, striking timber that conveyed a sense of his body, the way he smelled.

I don't remember noticing him. I watched Flaca, living in her vacuous gaze. By mirroring myself in her, I realized something strange was occurring. There, my love, do you see how vague I am? I don't know how to describe the events of that time, especially that miserable day. And how can I be clear? I was the third wheel of a tragedy that I possibly could've avoided, a stupid dream of normalcy that no longer concerned us.

The boy turned around and bumped into Flaca. That's how it happened, an unremarkable, involuntary shove, like in the movies. Flaca fell down. I laughed, I remember. I laughed uncontrollably and crassly back then, in the late seventies. I should've been ashamed. Though, my laugh may have been the purest thing I've ever had in my life. Flaca was so funny on the ground with her white dress and dopey face. She was beautiful nonetheless. She seemed like the Rosa Benassi, daughter of Italians, that I knew in Buenos Aires.

He stretched out his hand. He helped her up and apologized. He whispered *Sorry* in a striking, orthodox voice and introduced himself. He had an Italian name, the kind I heard two out of three times in San Lorenzo. He said to us, "Listen to me on the radio tonight, my program is on Radio 77 at 9:30. You'll go on a journey." That made Flaca smile. She clapped like a well-fed seal. The boy vanished.

Pablo, Flaca, and I didn't have a radio. Instantly, I forgot about the boy and the radio I didn't own. I forgot about them because that's the way things were, because we forget most of the people we encounter in our lives. But Flaca didn't forget that boy at all, or his voice, or the fleeting promise of a radio voyage.

We went shopping and, at the doorway to our house, I saw that my friend's dopey face had clouded over. The rouge that she'd maintained until that moment became dirty water and her eye shadow, mixed with tacky mascara, turned into a formless soup. Flaca had a strange way of crying. She stifled herself. She shouted silently. Her deformed face was like Picasso's *Les Demoiselles d'Avignon*, Cubist and senseless. Rosa was a distressed Madonna who'd lost faith in the son she believed was God.

I was tired that day. Carrying you in the womb wasn't exactly a walk in the park, Mar. My body didn't respond to external stimuli the way it had before, as almost all my exertion doubled. Plus we lived on the fourth floor in San Lorenzo and there weren't elevators in the building. There were four flights of stairs, an infinite number of steps, breathlessness. We had groceries that day. We'd bought a lot. Memory is strange. I might not remember how the couscous I ate for lunch tasted, but I do remember how much energy it took to haul the groceries one day twenty-odd years ago. I was spent. Even though she was my Flaca, I remember her hysterical crying stressing me out. I entered the house weighed down by bags, feeling weariness and repressed rage toward my capricious friend.

"What did you do to her," Pablo Santana said, lunging at my neck. "What'd you do to her, *carajo?*"

My fury intensified.

"What do you think I've done? Who do you think you are?" I retorted.

My fury turned into worry. I walked away from Pablo and went to my crazy woman. "*¿Qué pasa, amor?*"

She gave me a hug, soiling me with putrid rouge and cheap eyeshadow. I turned pink and blue. Something of a buffoon myself. My friend cried in silence. She was mute, incapable of making noise.

"*¿*Qué pasa, amor?" I asked again, and that was when I remembered the boy and his promise of a journey. I had already dismissed him. A few kilometers, a few groceries, and a flight of stairs had come between us. He was yesterday's news, for me at least. He'd been a priority for Flaca.

I went to Pablo. I put a hand on his shoulder as a way of patching things up after our spat and explained that we should find a radio because Flaca had a new friend. Pablo and I were in a tight spot with money. He sold ducks on the streets of Rome. And me? I was unemployed, aimlessly scraping a living together in a city of exasperating antiquities. We were poor, hopeless souls. We didn't have money for a radio.

We had begun going to Nuccia's place every night at dinnertime. What beautiful evenings those were. She was lonely and our company made her feel alive. She cooked, dug up old anecdotes and, on the fairest of nights, combed Rosa's hair. Beneath the mophead, my friend had tallowy hair more beautiful than a peacock's plume once untangled.

"I had hair like that when I was young," Nuccia said. She dug in with the brush. That night, at 9:30, they turned on the radio to listen to the boy and fell silent. He had an interesting program. I don't remember ever hearing anything like it. I was in Buenos Aires before that and wasn't what you would call a radio fanatic. Mother was, however. She was glued to her afternoon radio dramas. Sometimes she would listen to them one after the other and lost the plot of each one. She never knew how those intriguing stories ended. She didn't know if Gina would marry José or if Diego would make her a widow before she could. Mother liked those absurd stories, where love was a pretext for banishing boredom. At most, I listened to songs, I listened to Gardel and sometimes to the River games. I wasn't an expert. But this boy was something else.

Alberto, as he was called, excelled at his job. He amassed words, made a shapeless heap out of them and then used them in blocks for their intrepid sounds, their overt laboriousness. He was urban baroque, Alberto Tatti, a poet of the urban ether. His program was a genuine journey. A tour of the African continent between kora and electronic sound. Today, musical Africa is very much in style. It's almost a given that you hear Cesária Évora's creamy voice or Salif Keita's regal melodies on the radio. Nowadays every cutie moves to the rhythm of griot style and delights in desert dissonances. The Tinariwen warm your heart with their nomadic guitars, or you can tear your hair out with Ali Farka Touré's overflowing blues. These days it's easy to make a feast of Africa with our virgin ears. We go in any record store and can fill our ears and pockets with trigonometric names. Angélique Kidjo, Khaled, Papa Wemba, Franco, Maryam Mursal, King Sunny Adé, Youssou N'Dour, and others whose rhythms I know, if not their names. You like continental music, too. It makes you happy, you told me once. That was shortly before our trip to Tunisia. I was astonished. You hadn't told me something so intimate in a long time. You were snuggled up on the sofa, Mar, the beige one that you've liked since you were a little girl and that I've never done away with. How could I? We were happy on the couch. We cocooned ourselves. We watched *Happy Days* and *Candy Candy*. We were mother and daughter. What were you listening to that day, dear? I don't remember. I only know that it was African. The Africa in your blood. Elias's Africa. His colors.

Listening to Africa wasn't so straightforward in the seventies, although people spoke of the motherland more then than they do now. Today people discuss it rarely and insufficiently. At the time, only about ten years had passed since 1960 jumpstarted the dance of independence. The hopes of the sixties were toned down in the seventies, but the people still believed in the possibility of creating a future on the continent. Democracies were wasting away everywhere, puppet dictators had taken power here and there, but the people hoped, they never stopped, nor have they now. Your father was also hopeful. He adored Africa. He embedded it in his fashion designs, he embedded it in his heart, and in a certain sense he embedded it in you, my love. When I see your nose, so pretty and perfect, I know the continent formed you in more ways than I could imagine.

The program drew me in. I'd already met Elias. I'd made love to him. I felt more than prepared to listen to Alberto's journey. Flaca was in heaven. When Alberto Tatti took the stage, she nearly stopped breathing. She didn't want any interference coming between her and that man's voice.

Alberto himself, I remember, didn't seem to breathe either. His ornate words followed one another in a maelstrom, one atop the other. You almost felt sorry for his perpetual absence of breath. Alberto never laughed. He never made jokes, he didn't wink at his public. He was polished and hard like a dowry chest. Serious like an old, retired Latin professor. It was a pedagogical route, a journey of initiation somewhat like following Frodo Baggins in search of the cursed Ring. Alberto was Frodo, he had to lead us, perhaps make sacrifices, and then bid farewell. We still didn't know it then. We didn't know how bad things would get.

We traveled and did nothing more. We traveled with our eyes closed.

There was a series of stops. From Oran and its nightclubs to the dusty streets of Cairo; then to Massawa to brood over the remnants of Italian occupation; a train on the Addis Ababa Djibouti Railway, and a detour in a Mogadishu that wasn't yet hellish and still smelled of mangos; then, in this order: Mombasa, Nairobi, and down to Johannesburg, which was still divided into white and black neighborhoods. We wandered in Madagascar between dumb macaques and tight-lipped Malagasy. Then we went back, always flying. We came up the coast to glimpse new ways of living on the continent. In Douala, our money was spent contemplating the ocean and then—Lord knows how, Lord knows where—indulging in a medley of other experiences. We filled our arms with Melian wax paintings and sauntered between Burkina Faso, Nigeria, and the hectic rhythms of Congolese rumba. We sat down, drank spiced tea, and waited for the griot to tell us of our deaths. Finally, we slept in Cape Verde. Or we disappeared.

Alberto was exhausted by the end of the program. We were too, since it was difficult memorizing names in a hundred different languages. Mandingo, Somali, Arabic, Berber, Swahili, French, English, dialects of a specific city, a particular neighborhood. When the program ended, Flaca clapped like a circus animal and kept going for half an hour. Pablo and I looked at one another sadly. Nuccia kept caressing her tallowy hair.

One Thursday evening, Alberto's program ended. So did the journey through Africa.

We weren't prepared for the end. No, we weren't ready in the slightest.

THE FATHER

Ultimately, it was only a heart palpitation. It could be ignored.

Majid was like that, Zuhra, he ignored things. He chilled his emotions so much that a block of ice was hot by comparison, dozing in a bikini under the sun. He chilled his emotions and, at the same time, he simmered. Your grandfather Majid was utterly cold and utterly hot inside. In permanent opposition to himself.

"Elias left a while ago and you didn't even realize it." Cutting words from Bushra, precise, not to be repeated. An absolute, inescapable fact.

Majid's questioning face, that of a once-great, failed inquisitor. An incoherent and distraught Torquemada.

"He took his bag and said, 'I'm going to Africa.'"

Africa? They were already in Africa. *My son, what have you done? Where have you gone? Why now, when I need you most? You are already in Africa. This land, this broken nose we call Somalia, is Africa. It has Africa's acacias, Africa's gazelles, Africa's smells, Africa's dreams. It is Africa, I'm telling you, I swear to you, wallahi. Why have you gone looking for Africa? Why now? I need you. I need your helping hand, your courage, your ire, which is also my own, my disguise. I need you to take revenge for me, my son. Do you understand?*

"He tried saying goodbye to you. He went to the Pasquinellis but they didn't let him in. 'There's an important guest here,' they told him, 'your father will be busy in the kitchen all day.' Elias said they were hysterical. The gaalo didn't let him enter. But you'll see your son soon, don't you fret."

Bushra took a breath. I don't know whether the woman understood how hurtful the words she threw in that poor, afflicted man's face were. She thought it was good news. Elias was leaving, living, making a man of himself, embracing experiences, forming his own vision of the world. Bushra was pleased. She dreamed of him immersed in the urban fabric of African cities. Urbane, happy, attentive. Bathed in colors and cloths.

"He told me to give you a hug and kiss. He'll come back a great tailor, you'll see. He followed Sheikh Maftuti. He'll let us know as soon as he's arrived in Nairobi."

Nairobi. He'll let us know, Sheikh Maftuti. Nairobi. Know. Maftuti. Nairobi. Departed. Africa. Journey. Nairobi. The words replayed in Majid's head. Now who would avenge him? Who?

Majid pondered revenge like a dumb dodo. Revenge. What a complicated word, Zuhra, no one really knows what it means. They tell you, an eye for an eye, tooth for a tooth. It's biblical. You have to believe what they tell you because it's written in the Holy Bible, it's the law of retaliation, something you don't take lightly. An absolute truth to consider, to act on, to live, to do nothing but repeat. Everyone is a trained parrot, skilled at repeating, but no one can ever explain. Did you steal an apple from me? I'll cut off your hand. Did you betray me, dirty tramp? I'll stone you. And you must believe in retaliation like you believe in the saliva you spat this morning. This is a strange society, they say, a counter-society. You have to defend yourself, you have to respond, you have to protect your ass and the shirt on your back. You have to shield your soul, or else they'll gobble it up with ketchup. You must. It is a moral duty to vindicate yourself, to besmirch, to wash away the endured insult. Yes, the shame, the dishonor, the ignominy, the offense, the outrage, the affront. You must carefully wash it all away. Remove the stains. Rinse off. Do it again for as long as it takes to become pure again.

Deep down, we were never clean. You can rinse and rinse again as much as you want, but the residue stays, the pain remains. Majid didn't know this. The pains were absorbed slowly, they didn't go away at all. We pretend not to know it. We play dumb. The pains transform, they become another thing. Sometimes they can be resources, improved lenses for understanding the world. But we are fools if we believe a vendetta, any old vendetta, will bring peace to our souls. Peace has other paths. It knocks on other doors.

Revenge is a baffling, vaguely useless word. Why? It doesn't quench your thirst, that's why, it doesn't bring back what you had. I don't know if Majid ever reflected on his primordial thirst for revenge. He understood there was no point in waiting. Yet wait he did. He harbored resentment because that's what he was taught as a child. He dictated his pain internally, the one that was rending his soul, which patiently trudged along after he was raped. He hadn't forgotten a single moment from that evil day. The separations, the stench of petrol, the searing sand underfoot, the hot cheap cologne, the heat of sperm between his buttocks, Famey's yells, the shots, the laughs, the farts, the military songs, the obscene cawing of the raptors, the *gorgor*, waiting for their carrion. No, your grandfather couldn't forget. It was the day he'd stopped becoming a man and had transformed into a shriveled cockroach. He had surely wished to tell Bushra, whom he loved most in the world, along with Elias and your grandmother Famey. He wanted to tell her—the singular, irreplaceable woman of his life—that as a man, a male, he was unserviceable. Majid didn't see anything ahead of him that gave him comfort. His dreams had died that day.

And yet, before that pain, Majid had been a simple man. He believed in his dreams. He wanted to have a normal life—some livestock, a piece of land, a little red cottage to view the sunset from. A few sunsets would do just fine. With his eyes toward Mecca, he would sing praises to the Lord of worlds. An uncomplicated dream. Instead, an obscene reptile ate his insides many years ago. If it had been one of those films Bushra liked, he would've confiscated the film reel. He would've rewound everything and changed the scenes he didn't like. One in particular. He would choose a different shuttle trip to avoid falling into fascist hands, into their thirst for domination. They would've taken another street. They would've been unscathed and content.

He would've married his same Famey, but this time out of love. He would've courted her, cast languid stares and sweet words. He would've composed overindulgent sonnets for her. He would've made her laugh because that's what real men do. He would've been gentle, sensual, special, in love. She also would've been in love. And on the night of their first love, he would've discovered her slowly. He would've plucked her as one does corn, ear after ear. He would've tasted her and let himself be tasted. Sweating bodies, remarkable, in unending joy. And yes, he would've married Bushra afterward. He'd have finally smelled her oils up close and the firm body he dreamed of at night. If it were a film, he would've cut out every terrible scene. He would've removed the heat of white sperm from between his buttocks and annulled the screams of his courageous woman. Famey's screams were something he still couldn't stomach. He wasn't a man—he didn't defend his woman, his pride. He was only a nigger's violated ass. A faulty, sterile thing.

These were the thoughts that crowded your grandfather's mind, Zuhra. Maybe I should tell you of myself, of what I did then. I was grown, I had made my decisions. But to speak of Majid is to speak of me. Even if my friend Hagi Nur says that I'm failing in my mission as an epic poet, I can't do anything about it. Memory does what it likes.

My father came looking for me that day. He'd just seen the man seated at his superiors' table. He'd served him quietly and looked at his neck from behind. He was fat. Brown sweat trickled down his hair. At that distance, he looked like any other man. White, hairy, fat, but normal, the kind of person often seen in Mogadishu. A man who wanted to do business, drink some mango juice, and enjoy a massage. The mistress's daughters laughed at his words. He was kind to women, especially to the young. His eyes—Majid looked at them closely—did not seem cruel. He had a distinct visage.

"You're wonderful," he said to Majid.

Majid noted that his voice was dry and woody, like an echo of the screams that had gnawed at his soul.

"Absolutely wonderful. What is your name?"

Majid did not respond. He didn't want to hear his name in that man's mouth.

"He's timid," Mrs. Pasquinelli said.

"Yes, he's our cook," the youngest daughter clarified, as though this explained the silence.

Majid had hurriedly left the house in search of revenge, toward the son who would bring him back to life. He didn't know how to do it himself. In his wounded paternal mind, he saw in Elias the possibility of payback.

He bought a gun before going back. Mogadishu at the time wasn't like it is now. Guns weren't on every corner (those were peaceful times, strange as it seems) and people weren't trigger-happy yet. But guns could be found even in peacetime. They were terrible then, too. It wasn't difficult. All it took was forking over the right amount, in the right way, at the right place. And there the gun was, beautiful and ready to kill. Glimmering and dangerous.

He placed the gun in the green trunk where Elias would stuff scraps of fabric. Elias didn't like throwing anything away. He accumulated cloth leftovers because they might be useful later. Majid put it in his trunk and prepared to tell Bushra white lies in case she inadvertently discovered his hiding place. Majid was certain that wouldn't happen. Bushra never peeked at her godson's things. That evening he ate the dinner his wife cooked. Potatoes and rice. No meat. A mediocre sauce. That was fine by him, he didn't like eating much. Feeding others gave him more pleasure. He didn't sleep that night. What was upsetting him was the nagging thought of putting another human being to death. That night, the notion of revenge showed the first sign of cracking. But it was a small thing.

The next day, he awoke feeling even more resentment. He wanted to destroy that man, that white man. He wanted to turn him into maggot food. He felt like humanity's trash collector. He wondered if a single shot in the forehead would be enough to satisfy his thirst. Would seeing the gaal's blood and brain matter dirty the floor satiate him? Surely the walls of the Pasquinelli house could use some color. After a while, all that milky white nauseated even the most rock-solid person. It made them blind and ready to vomit. The fascist's brain matter and blood could be of use on those white walls. Maybe the Pasquinellis would even thank him for that painting of human matter.

He was a fascist, a relic of the past. Didn't Mr. Pasquinelli say so at the table? "The future is with the Christian Democrats. They'll save us from the communists." Wasn't that what he said? "The fascists are useless people." By then, he said, that phase of fascism had long been over. They had done well under the Duce. That is, Benito treated people well, especially those loyal to him, but it was over. Pasquinelli wouldn't object. He was a Christian Democrat. *Kill the fascist,* he'd say, *kill him. Stain the house with his foul red blood. Go on, Majid, go on. You're a good cook. Cook the fascist, with potatoes perhaps. I'm a Christian Democrat. I was once a fascist, but that's the way it goes… It's not fashionable anymore.*

No, of course Mr. Pasquinelli would never appreciate a fresh meat stain. Pasquinelli was the kind of person who said one thing and then its opposite. In the end, the fascist was his guest. Was it perhaps just a coincidence? Majid didn't like the idea of staining the white walls of the Pasquinelli house with that sickening man's gore. The idea didn't exactly fill him with joy. It wasn't out of cowardice, and it wasn't because of the trigger. He wasn't afraid of pulling it, he would do so gladly. It was because of the pain. Would a pistol shot to the despicable fascist be enough? Would the bastard feel pain? Majid thought what he wanted was only to make him feel an unfamiliar pain, to take pleasure in it.

How could one elicit pain from someone like that? he wondered.

The thought occupied him for exactly 23 days, 16 minutes, and 2 seconds—the time it took to absentmindedly gulp down 56 bananas. How to draw pain from someone like that? Maybe he would have to strangle him, watch him slowly turn purple and perish by the second. But perhaps Majid wasn't strong enough to throw him to the ground and twist his neck. The two things required a certain amount of physical effort. If Elias were there, it would be an altogether different thing. He was strong, lean like his father, but with more fiber, a more toned musculature. And he had large, thin hands. He handled everything resolutely and delicately owing to his regular attendance at the loom. Majid shelved the idea of throttling the fascist. What if he stabbed him? Or, hell, if he poisoned him with some deadly, atrocious drug? Cyanide, strychnine, arsenic. They were all possibilities. Torturing him after drugging him was another option. He could cut off his penis, shove it in his mouth, piss on him, and set his eyebrows alight. Yes, any of those things were feasible. He could put poison anywhere, in his morning tea, in his evening snack. He was a cook. He could find a thousand and one ways.

He still wasn't convinced. They were all possible, better than a shot to the chest or head. Better than one second of anguish. Majid wanted the fascist to know why he was dying. He wanted the memory to resurface so he would palpitate while awaiting an unforgiving death. Of course he wanted to see that. But he didn't know if he could do it. The man was a soldier. He might've been trained to resist torture. Majid could rip out the fascist's body hair, nails, the tuft on his head, and still he might not say a thing. He wouldn't shout, wouldn't cry about it. He would wait for a martyr's death and die with a renewed conscience. Instead of vindicating himself, Majid risked helping the dirty fascist. By no means did he want this.

The day Majid distractedly devoured the fifty-seventh banana, the package arrived.

There were all kinds of stamps on it.

"I was waiting for you to open it," Bushra said.

He wanted to ask his wife who the hell could have sent them
such a large package, but he remembered that his son had gone
to Africa.

"Go ahead, I'm curious, chop-chop. Open it quickly, it's from
our son."

The "our" made him flinch. Ours? Yours and mine? No,
Bushra, almost all yours, almost all yours. Majid thought of Elias
in a new light. He thought of how little time he'd spent with him
and how he'd missed his spine rising toward the sky. A living plant.
Immense. Ours? No, yours Bushra, yours. They said it was she, she
herself, who'd buried Famey's umbilical cord. The first contact that
had made her a mother.

*Ours? Yours, only yours...but mine as well...yes, mine, mine,
mine, ours. Yes, ours.*

He flinched imperceptibly. Bushra spoke like an enthused radio host. The words tailed one another tirelessly, without pause.
Majid wasn't following. He was lost. He thought about revenge.

"It's from Burkina Faso, Ouagadougou," Majid read on one
of the many stamps.

"Where is Burkina Faso?"

"I don't know. Maybe it's not so far."

Majid didn't want to open the package. It would've been a
shame to unveil the secret of the scrupulously wrapped box. It was
strapped with cords and twine and slightly sticky. Covered with
scotch tape. Their son didn't want a burglar opening it. He had
been careful. Majid, however, had no desire to open it. If it was
for him, he would keep everything as it was, with all the adhe-
sive and twine. Your grandfather was often unreasonable like this.
Stubborn, an air of dreaminess. Sometimes his head wasn't quite
there, not properly attached to his body. It was elsewhere, near the

Pasquinellis' villa, thinking of how to make the dregs of humanity step outside.

Majid abruptly massacred the box, ripping at it with his nails, bruising it until there was nothing but shreds.

"Do it slowly," his wife whispered in his ear. He continued his brutal work. Was it curiosity? Fear? Anxiety? Or was the part of him that thought about how to kill the fascist bastard becoming too much for him?

It was easy guessing what was inside. Fabrics of startling beauty. The luminosity of the colors rivaled that of the sun. The package enclosed all of creation. The entirety of Africa and its hopes in a parcel. There was also a letter. I wrote of my travels. I can't recall the exact wording—every trace of the letter was lost—but it said many things. I had left Sheikh Maftuti in Nairobi and joined up with roving Zairians, a group of musicians. Madmen. From there I'd gone a long way. Mozambique, South Africa, Mali, Guinea, Ghana, Togo, Nigeria, Zaire, Burkina Faso, Cape Verde, Senegal. I'd seen many people, made friends. I'd fallen in and out of love. I swam between cotton swatches, traditional pagne fabrics, extravagant boubou, soft clays, cola nuts, and wax gowns. There was a photo that Bushra kissed again and again. In it I wore a pair of glasses, a garish shirt, and was standing in front of a loom. A textile factory. I was between three barefaced men. One was Sankara. The same Sankara who some years later would become president. Bushra thought he was one of my friends. She liked the way Sankara kept his left hand hanging. In the letter, I promised more packages. More colors.

Bushra strutted around for hours wearing the fabrics. Even Majid felt a frantic desire to wear one of his son's marvels. But he was a man. He could only watch. He went to bed upset and almost didn't tell his wife goodnight. He seemed destined to live a worthless life. He immediately asked the Lord to forgive the troubling thought. He tried holding in his sobs. Men don't cry, they hit hard, they smash chairs, throw objects, beat their fists on the table, and when they're really upset slam young girls against iron gates. Or they get revenge on their enemies. Majid dreamed of his son's outfits that night. He dreamed particularly about the yellow. The following day, he thought, he'd take revenge on the man who'd made him impotent. He would kill him.

After the morning prayer, he headed to the Pasquinellis' villa. Not to work. More than likely, he'd thought, between the sobs of the previous night, he would never cook another chickpea for those white people. He staked out a position in front of the villa because he'd decided to tail the fascist. If he wanted to kill him, he would have to know something about him. He'd need to know what he liked and didn't like doing, his routes, his breaks, his schedules. He had to know how to kill him, in what place and at what time. He couldn't leave anything to chance.

He found a spot. He was partially camouflaged. He'd wrapped himself in ochre cloth like the country's beggars, those whose begging never draws attention. Maybe people shoo them away, but no one remembers their faces, their height. No one looks at beggars.

He saw the Pasquinellis leave together, then his colleague Mohamed. No sign of the fascist. He waited patiently. Only after the noon prayer was there a breakthrough. A man exited. It was his man. The same fatness, the same egg-shaped head, the same facial expressions. He'd just left the house and was already sweaty. Wet stains had formed under his hairy armpits. His back was sodden. His soaked white shirt had a few horizontal blue lines that made his girth even more noticeable. He wore khakis and a straw hat with a black band around it. Designer sunglasses, slippers, a pink kerchief in his breast pocket. He heedlessly dragged his feet. The vainglorious man couldn't stop looking himself over.

Where could a man like that go? Majid had theories. He saw him walking toward the Catholic cathedral downtown. He had to feign devotion. Like all scum, he had to act like he knew God. The cathedral would be his first stop. It was perfect for him. The structure was a colossal eyesore. Its two towers rose brazenly toward the heavens. "A giant erection," his colleague Yousuf called it, the great fascist erection. Yousuf was spot-on. De Vecchis, one of the quadrumvirate of the March on Rome, had built the cathedral. He didn't sit well with the Duce, so he'd been sent to Somalia. De Vecchis was insane and sabotaged the country. The cathedral was a minor injury, but still a slap in the face of the Somali people. When I think about it now, in the delirium of civil war, Somalis almost miss it. Before, in peacetime, the cathedral was regarded with frustration. No one had thought to build it in harmony with the neighboring buildings. Whatever the cost, the quadrumvirate wanted to do something magnificent, monumental, something to contend with the sky and the Duce they secretly hated. Experts say that it was a faithful copy of the Cefalu Cathedral in Sicily. An erection that could've perhaps been avoided at the equator.

Majid thought the fascist would go there and search for some whore at the Indian's place. The man stretched as though he'd just woken up. Then the second man appeared, the fascist's twin. Identical in his behavior, his gestures, his stretching out to the last muscle. He was fat in the same places, sweaty under the same armpits, equally shaggy. He had on the same slippers, the same khaki pants, the same sunglasses, and the same pink kerchief in his shirt pocket. The second fascist's manner was calmer. He seemed more refreshed. He may have had fewer wrinkles, even if Majid couldn't have sworn by it. The only difference was the shirt. It wasn't white. It didn't have horizontal blue stripes. It was the opposite, Blue shirt, white vertical stripes. An inside out mirror. They took different paths. One went east, the other went. Who to follow? And where was the second fascist going? The whimsy of the situation didn't interest Majid. He didn't wonder if he was going crazy, if he was seeing double, if perhaps his rapist had a twin. He didn't ask himself anything sensible. He didn't make plans. He was occupied by what he would soon do. He was at a crossroads. What he decided would change his life forever. The gun pressed against his thigh. Revenge screamed like a maenad. He was undecided.

Who to follow? The one with the white shirt or the one in blue? He stepped toward the east, the white shirt. He changed his mind and turned the other way. He took a few westward steps, toward the blue shirt. Then he stopped. He was tired. He stopped thinking. He was about to stop breathing. Where to go? East or west? What to do? Kill, torture, or pardon? He wasn't a man, he hadn't been for a long time. He wasn't shit. East or west? West or east?

He went home. Bushra wasn't there. He'd already known she wouldn't be. She would be away all day at her sisters' house. He went in the room with the stamped package. The contents were spread on the bed, laid down every which way. A triumph of cobalt, ivory, pearls of Sahel. Violent brush strokes of blended, muted colors. Majid felt a surge of emotion. He went to the bathroom and stayed there for half an hour. He shaved everything. Underarms, legs, moustache, beard. He made himself virginally soft. He washed. He daubed himself with his wife's oils. Then he put on the outfit he'd dreamed of all night. He wondered if his son had sewn it for him. The suit was golden, stars stitched everywhere, interwoven with the sky and universe. It was a superb gown, I still remember it, *rabal* cloth embroidered with strands of raffia.

Rabal was my passion at that time. I'd found it in Guinea-Bissau. One of my friends on the street told me about the artisanal traditions of the Mandinka and I dove in, soaking up everything I could about the technique. It wasn't easy. I had to work entirely by hand at the loom with cotton yarns, and afterward I decked them with raffia or silk. I'd made the gown in Ouagadougou, on my way back from the region of Casamance in southern Senegal. I'd slept with a woman much older than me. She told me that I had to sew my first outfit in rabal for the person I loved most in the world. I had to think about that person and sentiment would guide my hand.

The golden gown was for your grandfather and Majid knew it. He wore it. He felt handsome in those reflections of the sun.

Beautiful. Unique. The east was forgotten, as was the west. He left home wearing his son's clothes, with the sun's rays enshrouding him. He left home and did not come back again.

SEVEN

THE NUS-NUS

Tunisia: low-cost, high-class Africa; Arab only on the surface. Islam suppressed and isolated. Islam persecuted. No money to be made with Islam, the whites said. No euros, no nothing. This was the money men's law. And, as always, the Arab leaders obeyed. A bribe and the nephew's got it made, the State is set in stone, despots for life. Cheers, the champagne is great. In Tunisia, everyone pretended that Islam didn't exist. Those with a veil or a beard pretended to be something else. They hid their beards in their shirt collars and their veils were the color of phosphorescent wigs. Islam was a mishap, an annoying setback. They celebrated Jesus instead. Not the real one, not the one who died on the cross in Palestine. That one made sales decline. He was a fucking Third Worlder with lice and lifelong famine, too thin for the market's tastes. No, no one was interested in that Jesus. The Jesus people liked was blond. It doesn't matter that he was born in Palestine, doesn't matter that he was Jewish. Those were mere details. Jesus was blond, authentically blond, his eyes authentically blue. Now, in the twenty-first century, someone gave him the gift of a red Coca-Cola dress. A Moschino label. Don't let that get around. Otherwise the other stylists may get offended. He no longer has a beard. He's a swaggering hunk.

Here, Tunisia, livable Africa. Africa for the right pockets, the whites, the overweight, the filthy. Africa's surrogate. A fiction, a half-joke. Like her, Mar Ribero Martino, an ongoing simulation. A pinch of Africa, a dash of Latin America, a touch of Europe. Empty, in a word. She was foreign, Mar Ribero Martino. She belonged to no one. A perennial vagabond.

Tunis, on the other hand, was a carousel on the rim of the abyss. The beards, if not hidden in collars, were strictly cut. There were no exhibitionist mullahs, no prayers spoken aloud. Yes, of course, it was a Muslim country, so what? "We have supermarkets like the French," they told everyone, proud of imitating that cruel and distant country. Someone had learned in the history books that they descended from the Gauls, straight from Asterix and Obelix. They were French. They mimicked the old masters, at least. They ate aged cheese and stuck baguettes under their arms. They even had Monoprix. *Win al Monoprix?* Where is Monoprix? Tunisians smiled at you on Avenue de la Liberté. They watched you with the flippant stare of a people compelled to be prudent, and then they explained that Monoprix was *"emsi tul w-ba'd dur 'allemin."* No one understood the directions they gave with gentle cunning. Sometimes there was an ephemeral twinkle in the well-mannered Tunisians' eyes. In some eyes more than others. A shimmer. It wasn't slyness. It was hatred. Hatred for the fact that Tunisia's land was besmirched with Western artifice. Hatred for a dictatorship that had devoured their rights, their dreams, their belongings. But it was only a shimmer. The violence had to be sedated for a while yet. It would come soon enough.

Everything seemed too calm in livable Africa. Even the Indian figs that rained impertinently on your head on the street seemed like part of some exotic comedy. The people themselves were like elements in a horrible, mystifying screenplay. One expected to see *Casablanca*'s Bogart/Rick materialize from the void, with the same cocky guise and legendary mackintosh. Her too, Ingrid, the smiling Swede, the one who made Hollywood swoon with her eyes, and who would soon steal Magnani's man...one expected to see her in the white man's Africa as well.

Mar was lying down on her twin bed in the Argentinian nuns' pension. She ran into the nun with the girlish face. They chatted, spoke about the city. The nun complained about loud music. *"En mi pueblo...allá en la Argentina, no había ningún ruido." Ningún ruido*, no noise. This city, though, especially from her room, was nothing but stratified noise. Annoying noises, sounds from a disco. The dated songs of Donna Summer and Gloria Gaynor. Shakira came on more than once. For every Gloria Gaynor, at least three Shakira hits. Mar was sure of it, she could've done a detailed data analysis. She stayed in her room to study. She'd learned the names of colors. *Abiad* white, *aswad* black, *ahmar* red. Learning classical Arabic was like studying mathematics, it was all a game of slots. One had to find the pattern and repeat it. It was like cloning, but adding a shade of difference. Each word wasn't the exact copy of what came before, sometimes it could mean the opposite. They were kind of like people: patterns, slots, fade-outs, differences. She was beginning to like that strange language. She also liked the fraudulent city. Naked on her bed, books open, alone with her thoughts. The soft wind blew away from her. The wind was coy, smitten with the coffee-colored body that offered itself. Mar was focused. She tried thousands of times to repeat the colors she'd learned to pronounce that very morning. *Abiad* white, *aswad* black, *ahmar* red, red, red like her mother's hair, *aswad* like her father's skin, *abiad* like the hole her child ended up in forever. Mar recited and got distracted. She thought about too many things at once. Her naked body stirred unconfessed desires within her. She put on a T-shirt and washed her face. The wind was fairly dissatisfied.

Mar heard the voice.

The muezzin's call to prayer. Usually, she didn't hear anything, only indistinct sounds, grousing, Shakira. Now, for a few seconds, the radios ceased. It rarely happened—a moment of pure silence in Tunis. The muezzin's voice was beautiful, precise, and convincing. Mar was happy she wasn't naked while he summoned believers

309

to join others in devotion to the Eternal. She was glad she wasn't lacking in respect for those strangers.

Mar realized that not even this Africa was the real one. There was something beneath, more intimate, and that was where people hid their own dreams.

Tunis didn't seem like anything. It wasn't Africa, it wasn't Europe, it wasn't the Middle East. It was everything blended together. A scrawl with traces of light. The shadows were numerous, the questions inexhaustible. Mar sensed a desire for change in the air, the subtle tension created by a dearth of freedom. JK explained it clearly. "We're sitting on a pressure cooker here. People don't know whether to blow up or not. They just don't, you know?" Mar didn't know. She didn't understand anything. She looked JK in the eye and thought he was beautiful. His eyes were almond-shaped. That precise, sharp slant, like a knife slit. He was tall. Long bones. High cheekbones. He was like an archer from the Tang dynasty, an enormous statue from the Terracotta Army. She liked him. He was funny. You could talk to him, and he didn't have that powdery white complexion that made her lose her mind. Pati was all baby powder. She didn't get any sun, she didn't put on foundation, she didn't try enlivening herself with showy clothes. She was an unchallenged domain of black and white, an obsolete emo kid, an aesthetic she couldn't pull off anymore. Everything was black in Pati's wardrobe. Everything black in the *nécessaire* for her makeup, everything black even among her junk jewelry. The blackness put her moribund skin in relief.

Mar felt like a zebra. Not one of those whose every stripe was distinguished from the other by a clear dividing line. She wasn't a traditional zebra of the African savannah. Mar felt like one put in a washing machine, so every white and every black was tarnished by the nuance of the other. An undertone. A comma of color. She didn't like being that way. She was nothing. She wasn't black. She wasn't white. Only sort of red. And her hair was a nuisance. Her bangs ruined her life.

Who knows if Elias, the man who'd made love with her mother only once and impregnated her, who knows if he had defiant bangs like hers. In the only photograph she had of the man, Elias smiled but didn't look up. She couldn't see his hair. He was wearing a New York Yankees baseball cap.

She'd made love with JK the night before. It had been pure coincidence. His Asiatic charm had nothing to do with it. JK didn't leave anyone indifferent. She'd seen those bimbos from Milan at the party languishing behind him with dazed expressions.

"I heard," one of the bimbos said, "that the Great Wall isn't the only big thing in China."

Between gasps and giggles, the others devised plans to fuck the beautiful little man with the politician's name.

Mar didn't know at the time that four hours later, she would make love to him. It was a wonderful party. She was dancing. Her mother danced, too. And Katrina was kind, sort of crazy, and by no means like Patricia. A volcano of ideas, not depression. If she weren't so white, fuck, if only she weren't so white…she would be perfect.

"*Sabes, nena,*" every conversation began. The *nena* made Mar go ballistic. She wanted to forget how she'd melted like wax at that evil word. "*No llamarme nena, por favor…*" Call me what you will, but not *nena*. She didn't say anything. It wasn't appropriate. They weren't close enough; they weren't even friends. Only strangers, whom destiny had delighted in bringing together for a moment. When Katrina said *nena,* or when the light struck her, accentuating her paleness, Mar remembered Pati, the woman who'd possessed and humiliated her. That diseased love. Her child. She remembered wanting to vomit. The machinery above her. She never forgot it.

Life seemed deadened by this strange African land. She felt at home because in fact it was no one's home, not even for the Tunisians. For them less than everyone else. They couldn't make anything of their lives or their bodies without Ben Ali's permission.

Before making love to JK, though, before being consumed by evanescent passion, before orgasming and asking herself what the hell would happen next, before any of it, she'd gone to that party and dealt with the aftermath.

The party. A pretense. The Serbian from the *mabit* was going home—a small town forty kilometers from Belgrade. She'd been in Tunis for twelve months. Twelve months working as a porter in the student residence. Twelve months sorting bars of soap and towels. Twelve months smiling and giving keen tourists a first impression of the city. She'd spent twelve months talking with everyone, people from the neighborhood and those from a world away. Her Arabic was flavored with crass undertones. She could spew obscenities that would make a longshoreman blanch, but it was considered proof of dedication to her studies. She was basically Arab. Blonde, but Arab. Respected because she'd become like them. The same gestures, words, and looks. No judgement. And now the lightly freckled blonde was returning to her tiny Serbian village. They celebrated her farewell. Everyone knew she wouldn't come back. The crooked streets of that battered neighborhood knew it, as did the few bare trees and the rigged car engines.

They partied for days, everywhere. Tea with friends, coffee on Avenue Bourguiba, neighborhood couscous, a special massage at the hammam. Gifts, thoughts, best wishes. Even the Westerners, the students from the mabit, not to be outdone, prepared a party worthy of a 1950s TV movie. They decked out the student atrium with red and blue banners and paper flowers and made treats early in the afternoon. Everyone tried recreating dishes from their homeland. The Italians and their pasta, Spanish paella, a Portuguese soup, a Turkish chicken. Alcohol. A corpulent Norwegian procured a surprise stash. He knew one Mahmoud who worked in a supermarket. Mahmoud had promised that, in addition to the standard junk, he could also snag some of the good stuff. Next to the useless Tunisian beer, there were also some auspicious bottles of white wine.

Mar knew she was an intruder. She didn't live in the mabit, but she felt good there. She thought about the pension, the silence of its corridors, the Argentinian nuns who roamed like blue specters on the balcony. She thought about John Paul II's picture, Papa Ratzi's absence, Ben Ali and his pudding face, unavoidable even in that religious abode.

Mama Miranda was also an intruder, but she seemed to know everyone. She was wearing green, her color. It was a pretty green, glowing incandescently. The people were nearly blinded by it.

"You're so beautiful, Miranda," the enthusiastic, infantile voices commended.

Everyone knew Miranda. No one knew her, Mar Ribero Martino.

Mar felt lonely. At home, but lonely. At first, the fake Pati wasn't even there. She was the only one she knew, the person with whom she hoped to start up some kind of conversation. She was possessed by an idiotic desire to yell "I'm her daughter! I'm Miranda's daughter, *carajo.*" If everyone knew that she, the tomboy with the ripped jeans and white tank top, was the daughter of the beautiful woman in green, would they perhaps be less indifferent?

She was invisible. Enraged, she fished around in her Peruvian handbag for a half-empty pack of cigarettes. She still had five. Maybe that would be enough for the evening. She made a move for the exit. There, too, as in her convent school, smoking was prohibited. A large man ordered her to halt.

"No," he told her. No what? Mar wondered. "No," the big man repeated, shaking his head. Mar was confused. Why no? Why not? She wanted to leave and get away from a festive atmosphere she didn't belong to. Ready with alibis, she wanted her Marlboro. She wanted to poison her lungs. She wanted a lot of things, but instead this man was preventing everything. She was about to shout and make a scene when a voice from behind explained, "Don't open the door—he's afraid all the neighbors will come to the party. That happens when people hear music here."

Mar turned toward the voice. She was a beautiful, curly-haired girl, jet black with fleshy, sensual lips. They'd stood in line together for a bathroom at school. She'd seen her a few times in Miranda's company.

Mar extended her hand. "It's a pleasure to meet you, I'm Miranda's daughter."

The sensual-lipped girl also extended hers. She squeezed Mar's hand tightly, almost crushing it. "I know, you're Mar. I'm Zuhra Laamane."

The girl's skin was soft and smooth. Her teeth bone-white. She twirled and laughed, dancing. Mar watched her for a while. Then she saw her struggle with the chicken on her plate. Everyone was at the table. The Serbian, the students, wayfarers, passersby, intruders like her.

Miranda's green shone in the half-dark room, which was spruced up like a sad whore. *Enough, Mama, enough. You're beautiful, Mama. Special. Too much for me. Can't you see that I can't take it anymore? I can't stand you. Have you never understood? You're a volcano, Mama, a volcano to me, and I'm so weak. I'm escaping. From you, from me, from everyone. I escaped from my own child. Mama, please. Enough.*

Enough!

The black girl kept struggling with her chicken. She was stripping it poorly, nibbling at it pathetically. A battle to the last blood. Pati also used to fight to the end with chicken. She did it with pasta, too—her eggplant fusilli. She inhaled everything without tasting its flavor, then hunched over the toilet to vomit. She'd seen herself bent over so many times. If only she'd known that then. She, Mar Ribero Martino, never vomited. She ate for pleasure. Maybe that's why Pati had wanted the child, to make her vomit as well.

Mar snatched the plate from the black girl. "I'll cut it, but after I do, please eat everything. Taste the flavor."

THE NEGROPOLITAN

I am bent, semi-unconscious, over a toilet. Sweating, hair clinging unnaturally to my neck. My left hand slightly trembling. I'm
buried under mounds of hallucinations. I feel horrible, downright
vile. In my fugue state, I've become the protagonist of a film. I
don't know which one. I missed the opening credits. But I'm the
star, I'm sure of this. In my delirium, I dream of marquee headlines
at the Hollywood theaters that hosted the most effulgent stars
on celluloid. I am honored by dark-skinned blacks, black *aswad*
(Muslim or otherwise), in Harlem's mythical Apollo. I'm honored
by *bianchi*—white men, pale, ass-pink faces—in some other theater, nowhere.

I'm honored by yellow faces, too, dark brown faces, olive
faces, technicolor faces. I have everyone at my feet. Don't worry,
I washed them. And even if my Genevieve slices reeked, you all
would adore me just the same. My fetor would be an exquisite jasmine oil. Nausea a tantric orgasm. You could do nothing less than
love me. I've gone inside now. I am the radiant star, the *estrella*, the
big star, the only big star of this shit show of a novel that is my life.

They adore me in Bollywood and Cinecittà. They adore
me in Torpignattara and Tufello. Like Gloria Swanson, I auda-
ciously barged into most people's consciousness. Thinking she's
about to shoot a film, she majestically descends the staircase in

Sunset Boulevard—she's killed William Holden, he's rotting in the pool—but she doesn't realize that all she's doing is falling apart, that all those people want to see her end up in handcuffs like a common thief. They want to see her convicted, without lace or knots, without makeup. She doesn't know, she'll never know that she's become a petty thief. Gloria lives on a set, which imprisons her inside her own head. They don't call her crazy. She isn't. They don't call her anything at all. They simply bask in her.

She sees herself cloaked in visions and diamonds, with every politically incorrect thing the world has made. Back to a time when people don't think about the rights of seals or foxes. Fur is a status symbol. Racial segregation is widespread in the United States. The tenacious Rosa Parks, our black pioneer, hasn't yet planned to sit in the same seats as the whites. I don't know how old Malcolm X is. He still wants to integrate himself into neoliberal society. He doesn't know yet that he's destined to deconstruct the system. Malcolm was straightening his hair. In America, the negroes stank of hair burned by white people's chemicals. Gloria, meanwhile, walked down the stairs, a queen like few others, in the subconscious. I am like her, eternal and abandoned.

Except I'm not descending anything. My set doesn't seem to be a big one. I don't have a balding butler. Paparazzi flashes don't blind me. I don't have the rotting cadaver of William Holden. No stairs, no stilts, no void, no nothing. Instead I am bent, semi-unconscious, over a toilet. Sweating, hair unnaturally clinging to my neck. My left hand slightly trembling.

This happens to me when my soul is in bad shape. I shake. Doctor Ross said it's normal in cases like mine. It may be normal, but it hurts my soul every time.

I look like a Greek tragedy mask. My face is so solemn that I might just stand and do a military salute. I inspire fear. I don't feel like myself, but like someone else. Older. More experienced. Someone who deserves respect. More formal. More serious. So serious that for a second I mistake myself for Professor Rinaldi...

It's been a long time since I've thought about her. Maybe I never did. Not even in school. She was there, she was a part of the décor, like the blackboard, the chalk, the map of our beaten up *Bel Paese*. Rinaldi taught history and philosophy. She always had snot in her nose. She was in love with one of our classmates, Bertolotti Gianluca, one of the many small fries. She was taken in by a worthless adolescent. Whenever she asked him a question, Professor Rinaldi lamented. Bertolotti was a dumbass, but she really wanted to give him a good mark. The most she could give him was a *D-* on Plotinus. Professor Rinaldi was very glum when she gave him tests. I always thought she was a bit of an imbecile. She had allergies. Partially to pollen, which explained the mucus, and partially to men, which explained her crush on Bertolotti.

I have many eyes on me now. They've never seen a woman convulse. Their stares make me uneasy. Their lingering eyes bug me. Their eyes are ball-shaped, spherical, like a toad's. It's been a while since I've had so many eyes on me. Until thirty minutes ago, I hadn't known that I'd end up center stage. I didn't know the tremor would return. It happens when my soul is forlorn.

Today I feel sick as a dog. I left with a boy and he kissed me. In theory, I should be happy. But I didn't like his mouth or his hands. He stopped kissing me when people walked by. They could've been *shurta*, the police. Orlando didn't want to get chewed out. The shurta make a fuss over kissing. Kissing on the street is forbidden. You can get into serious trouble if you're a foreigner, bigger trouble if you're Tunisian. Orlando kisses badly. He's not romantic and his breath is raw, but I didn't want to make a bad impression. I wanted to go on the date. I insisted. I was cruel on the beach. I had a nice swimsuit on and my period spared me.

I couldn't admit that I was wrong. My summer crush was a mistake. Now I avoid him.

Tonight at the party the tremor started. Once again I let someone touch my body who shouldn't have. Orlando's kiss reminded me of Aldo and the elementary school. Orlando isn't

Aldo. Orlando has bad breath, but he's a good boy. He turned into Aldo in my head. He brought the fear back. He hurt my soul.

I'm thinking about my mother. I wonder if she's ever loved someone. Mom, why have you never told me about my father?

If I had a normal family, if I hadn't gone to boarding school, if Aldo hadn't come to work sweating that day, maybe I'd like Orlando's kisses now. I feel guilty.

I was conceived in the seventies. In technical jargon, I should say that my mother Maryam Laamane had intercourse with a person of the masculine sex and begot me. A biblical fornication. She was also married, she told me, to the man who gave her his sperm. But, damn, if only she'd let his name slip. She didn't let a miserable vowel out, not a hint of that unimaginable sound.

I learned about fathers in school. Before that, I thought only Maryam Laamanes existed. Sure, there were people in the background during those first years of my life. I remember a green parrot that obsessively screeched the word "blond." It didn't say anything else. It belonged to the owner of the apartment where we lived in those first years in Italy, in the Nomentana district. I remember nothing else. I want to remember something. I want to remember my papa and not the stupid parrot that kept dreaming about some unattainable shade of yellow.

I thought children came out of their mothers' heads. I thought they were their mothers' dreams. Someone at school explained to me that it took two to dream. Two dreams and not one. I was small and none of my companions had learned about the birds and the bees. We still believed in a world of colorful fables. I believed it at the time. It didn't last long. I grew quickly. Too quickly.

Well, in the seventies, Maryam let a man's schlong skewer her. She couldn't have enjoyed it at all. Surely not! I can't see Mom enjoying herself. Even if I could imagine it, she can't. They took away her clitoris in Somalia. They do it to everyone. Stitched her up like a roulade. Somali women like roasted things.

Not me. The pendulum is still inside me. They did stitchwork in my head. In the end, the result is the same. I don't take pleasure in anything.

Now I'm the big star in the scene. I'm still bent over the toilet. There are other actors, but I'm the protagonist. How many of them are there? Hey, I tell the others, you can't steal my scene. What I'm saying is, move out the way, fuck. I'm the big star. The scene is mine, goddammit! Mine alone. Don't you see me hugging the toilet? You think I'm doing this for fun? This is the climax, the culmination, the peak, the reason why people pay the ticket price. There aren't many scenes like this. Gloria descending the stairs, Marilyn's flying skirt, Audrey looking into Tiffany's window shop, Denzel reading the Quran's opening sura. You get it? You can't be here. Only I can be here. Now get, go away and fuck you, okay?

What does it mean that I'm unwell? What does it mean that you won't leave me? Are you all my friends? What does it mean that you are all afraid I'll die, that you feel my heart leap, my guts heave, my mouth grimace? Tell me. I don't get it.

Who are you? I see a pale woman. She looks dead. I saw her in my mabit. Deader than the suicides Ophelia and Virginia Woolf. Pale like the women in Pre-Raphaelite paintings. This little cousin of Morticia lives in the mabit. She's Spanish. One night she made us paella, which was shit, too much chili pepper, too much salt. It was godawful. You can get it better at the supermarket, you can buy it beautifully prepared in the freezer and stun your friends with special effects. Then I see the masculine mulatta, the half-black lesbian, the one who gave me the tissue when the fake Muslim Italo-Tunisian bitch said that absurd thing to me about my pussy and its maintenance. And then there's *her*. Oh yes, I would share a million and one scenes with you, dear sweet poetess of my heart. You would be my celluloid Scheherezade. You and I, friends forever. Oh, Miranda. Your face is drawn, your hair messy. A beautiful green dress. You are the best dressed, the best coiffed, the best of the best dolled up whores in this shitty city. You're a whore, I know it, you know it, all your readers know it.

You said it in *Calle Corrientes*. How did you say it? *Puta virgen derrama sangre en la calle, virgin whore spills her blood on the street / puta virgen quema en su pesadilla, virgin whore burns in her nightmare / puta, virgen, mujer, muerta, Amen.*

It's in your first book, my favorite. They didn't understand what kind of monster it was—poem, prose, or delusion. It was like me on paper. Sometimes people don't really understand what I am either. We're colleagues, you know that Miranda? I wrote a few stories under a pseudonym. Some people read them. I'm a badass intellectual, like you, like Virginia Woolf. I don't care if it was five nerds who read me. I wrote stories, that's good enough. Stories of strange women. I scrape by at Libla, you know. I earn a living, a subsistence. Remember this Miranda, everyone remember: I'm a badass intellectual.

It seems like serious work if I associate the word "income" with the word "Libla," but serious jobs no longer exist. My generation took it in the ass. I was born in the seventies. Maryam Laamane allowed a blind spermatozoa passage into her kingdom. The spermatozoa entered her ovum by chance. I think it took the wrong road. I was happenstance. My birth, the spermatozoa that followed the wrong road, my mother who went to bed with a man. I can't see my mother sleeping with anyone besides herself. People born in the seventies are losers by nature. We grew up with the myth that studying led to permanent employment. The truth of the '00s, though, was somewhat different. Depression, barrenness, abuse, profit at our expense, at the expense of our bodies, our minds. Exploitation.

I'm a stocker. I go from one department to another. I put anti-shoplifting devices on CDs and DVDs that other people buy. Lovely things pass through my hands. I'm tormented. Sometimes an unexpected kleptomania takes hold of me. I want to steal and get fired. Yes, steal, and get caught by those security guard boys. There are a lot of security personnel in Libla. It doesn't seem like it. Normally you see the three at the main door and don't know about the silent (or almost silent) group that spends day and night in the store, watching over the merchandise as it sleeps. They pretend to be customers. They pass calmly from the nonfiction section to the children's books. When their minds stop working, you see them with some improbable book in hand. An avidly leafed-through astrophysics treatise, or something photographic. Artistic desires? No, pornographic. Many photography books are on the cusp of good taste. Everything exposed, everything violent. But if I buy them at a newsstand they call it pornography? The Japanese are masters at this, better than the Americans or Europeans. The Japanese have a special flair for fishing around in the dark. I wonder if virgins exist in Japan. I wonder if Akane, whom Ranma Saotome has to marry, I wonder if she's really a virgin like she says. Ranma is a cartoon, we could never be together. I love him, but he's made of paper. I can't come that way.

I've lost my patience. I'm tired. Clinging to the toilet for no reason, sweating. Maybe I smell, I don't know. I can't control my armpits. They feel sticky.

It's my scene. Me, the toilet, the light, the sweat. Lights, camera, action.

Ladies and gentlemen, a star is born. A *najma*, an estrella, a star. A larger-than-life star, the only big star in this fucking world.

I've had an epileptic fit, Miranda explains.

The girl, the semi-black butch lesbian asks me, "Is it the first time?"

Distorted sounds come out. It's my voice, it seems. My new voice. I recognize it. I sound like an awful dubbing of some horrible *Lord of the Rings* orc. I don't speak. My throat is dry. My face hurts. My cheekbones, teeth, lower jaw, upper jaw.

I hear the half-black girl's voice. "So…you've never had anything like this happen before today?"

Affirmative. I make an up-and-down movement. They'll understand that it's a *yes*. They turn me over like a newborn. They put a damp rag on my face. Miranda sings. I know that song. It's from the Chilean Victor Jara, "Alfonsina y el mar." Victor. When the soldiers took him, they cut off his hands, his beautiful musical hands. Then they executed him. A tear falls down my face.

I don't like when people see me cry.

I don't have epilepsy. But I do have fits, sometimes, as though I were epileptic. They told me that it's because I tend to tighten up. The therapist told me that "it can happen to girls who…" Wait. Stop. I don't want to hear anymore. I know what happened to me. I don't want to start this chapter. Do I always have to go there to protect myself every time I'm unwell? I'm tired. We've been talking for a year, Miss Therapist. You're a legend. Without you I'd be dead, but what's the point of bringing it up? My stomach is upset. I have diarrhea. You're making me speak ill of my mother. I know, she's not perfect. She's something of a child. But I love her. I can't stop loving her. You're not asking me to do this, are you, Miss Therapist? That's a relief. I have to admit that Mom deserves some of the blame if… I mean, do I really need to accuse her? Don't ask me to do that. You're stronger than me. I can't do it. My mother is a little girl and she cries. She cries like an infant. I'm the mama, I'm the strong one, the one who doesn't cry. I can't deal her this blow. Oh, Miss Therapist, Mom never has to know. I can't. Don't ask me to. I'm the strong one. If she sees me cry, she'll collapse. Please, don't make her cry. Don't make me cry.

I remember the details. I've had one of my worst episodes.

My body is funny when it acts up. I'm like a breakdancer from the eighties. Shakes and spectacles. Shakes and enthusiasm. I never twitch the same way twice. Every part of me twitches in its own way. My body is a frenzied orchestra, a jazz orchestra, a jam session. Voice, tenor sax, trumpet, piano. She sets the tone. The voice for me is always Dinah Washington. I see blacks on the dance floor and whites watching enviously. A black woman, when she gets going, doesn't need instructions. My inner self feels the rhythm. It believes in it. It lets go. We dance a wild lindy hop.

I read about the lindy hop in Malcolm X's autobiography.

Before becoming Malcolm X—a proud black man, a black Muslim negro like me, with the gift of speech—Malcolm was somebody else. More foolish, less sophisticated, certainly more frustrated. Malcolm burned his hair and danced the lindy hop. He says the same word. There's a hop in the middle. And yes, he made hairy pussies prance, they always gave him a little something in return. White pussies, too. Even then sexual tourism existed, you just had to go to Harlem or some other black ghetto in the city. These days you go to Jamaica or Cape Verde. The same pimps. And in Tunisia, here, where I've had my episode, where they built this cursed toilet, there are sexual tourists. I think my friend Lucy does it, too—but that's impossible. Not her. For her, it's love. It's love for the others as well. But does love exist when economic power is in the middle? Damn Lucy, you too? Why?

My fit and I are seasoned dancers. We haven't danced together much, but now we know the moves. I do a little move, a wobble, and it comes behind me. We dance facing one another, moving in a circle, a few sidesteps and then improvisation. Malcolm had done it with Laura, that woman who, had she never met him, maybe wouldn't have fallen to ruins. Malcolm was terribly sorry to have pushed her to the abyss. Malcolm wasn't Muslim yet. He hadn't gone to Mecca. He made mistakes. Don't blame yourself, Malcolm. My mother also made mistakes with me. Do I blame her? And does she blame me? Do I perhaps blame myself? Yes. That's why I think I'll always have these fits. I howl into the silence.

We dance. We tremble. The twitch extends from my hand to my chest, to my stomach, to my face. Oh yes, the fit goes there too. My face deforms. The makeup liquefies. I can't close my mouth anymore. My tongue curls. I manage to bring my hands to my chest. I ask for help. They don't hear. Maybe they don't understand.

Mar is here, the half-black butch. She's beautiful for a dyke in pants. I like her. I learned at this party that she's Miranda's daughter. Miranda is here too. I feel hands, hers, taking me. Someone comes in. I see a death glow. I'm afraid. Is it the Grim Reaper?

No, only Morticia from the mabit. She's helping. She tries taking my tongue out. They tinker around with me. I can't believe it, I'm letting those hands touch me. Did they at least wash them?

I allow myself to be touched by dirty hands. I don't mean the women's hands that are busy with my body right now. The horrible hands are different. They're a man's hands, may God curse that son of the serpent Iblis. They are Aldo's hands. Now I know. It's the memory of Aldo that caused the fit. Today, when Orlando kissed me, I should've said *that's enough* because I didn't like it. I'm still like I was when I was a small girl. I still don't know how to shout. I don't know how to save myself.

The lindy hop dies out in an aborted leap. The fit worsens. It gives me the cold shoulder. It spits in my face. It leaves me. I'm powerless next to the toilet. The hands left me. They weren't the dirty hands, I know. I apologize to these industrious women.

I remember what happened now, what happened before the lindy hop, before this senseless fit. I let myself be touched. The hands were absolutely filthy. They belonged to the pig *halouf*.

Didn't I like that boy?

No, the halouf has nothing to do with it. Those hands are much older. I was small and the hands profaned me. I heard an echo in the halouf. I was afraid that my pleasure might transform into that echo. I gave up on the halouf. I gave up on love. I fled.

But didn't I like the halouf? Didn't I like the white boy earlier?

I don't like him anymore. I never liked him. It was an illusion. I feel dirty. I want to cry, yet I'm condemned to laugh.

Mom called me before the party. She simply said to me, "Howa Rosario is dead." I didn't cry, though I wanted to. The things I want frighten me.

THE PESSOPTIMIST

A boy entered a girl's heart. A romantic story of longing stares and caresses.

It's this story that Maryam Laamane tells her daughter, Zuhra.

Maryam was sitting on a wicker mat in front of the recorder. Zuhra, her daughter, was temporarily studying in another country. On the tape, the dispersed traces of a life.

The mother and daughter didn't know one another well. Only obligatory exchanges between them: the smell of the uterus, breast milk, admonishing stares after a prank.

Interactions between them were few, and those few very out of focus. Since she was a teenager, the daughter had seen her mother lost in a bottle of straight gin. A mother overcome by the foul odor of exile. A mother who, in that new country, Italy, had abandoned her principles and dreams. The mother had suffered much. She knew she'd made others suffer. While Maryam pursued memories and gin, the daughter slowly rotted in elementary school and suffered the worst pains of any hell.

That ludicrous period had passed. She had to rearrange the melody of the present. Now mother and daughter are getting to know each other little by little, centimeter by centimeter. Life was a novelty, and often the occasion for a grand party as well.

This was why the mother recounted to her daughter her sole,

devastating infatuation. It was motivation for her sweet girl to believe that, soon, even she would fall in love and feel the stars dance inside her little stomach.

The daughter was wounded, like Howa Rosario in her time or many women today. Someone, without permission, had violated Zuhra's intimacy. Sexual molestation. Carnal violence. Words that circumscribe a chasm, fear bordering on repugnance. Maryam Laamane could not forgive herself for this. Back then, she, the mama, didn't know, didn't suspect. Zuhra's gaze, a gaze which never watched the horizon, worried Maryam. "Allah al-Kareem, spare this girl the shortcomings of love." The mama cried in silence. "Allah al-Kareem, make sure she doesn't become like my friend Howa, who was never warmed by human arms." Sometimes the woman saw Howa's same stubbornness in Zuhra. This concerned her.

In these moments, her maternal guilt grew to the point of paroxysm. She hadn't paid attention. She'd been a stumbling drunk around Rome and someone had stolen love from her daughter without her knowledge. It wasn't easy now making that same daughter believe the stars could dance inside her stomach again. Maryam Laamane wanted to try, she wanted to feel like a good mother again, or at the very least she wanted to be useful to Zuhra. That was why she sat stone-faced and cross-legged on the wicker mat. It was a battle position. She began narrating into the recorder about a girl and a boy, about their love and the stars in their stomachs. She wanted to make Zuhra understand that the miracle could also happen to her.

So then, a boy entered a girl's heart.

It was the seventies. Young people around the world dreamed of every possible future.

"I hastily made a promise to Howa Rosario. Not just any promise, Zuhra. Not something you swear lightheartedly."

Maryam promised her best friend that she would marry the son of the seamstress Bushra in her place. He was her nightmare, the seamstress's son. Poor Howa didn't sleep at night. She was no longer herself when she thought about that man and the impending marriage. As a little girl, Maryam didn't understand her friend's fear, but as an adult she thought no one should force a woman to do what she didn't wish to do.

"If you don't like it, tell him. Period. No one is forcing you."

Howa, though, had already demonstrated that sometimes a woman's will didn't have any authority when placed in a dangerous situation. Her stepfather had taken her virginity, her nose, and the best years of her life in one go. Who could assure her now that it wouldn't happen again? Howa didn't trust people anymore. She learned at her own expense that a woman's life is always hanging by a thread. This thread could snap at any moment.

Maryam didn't quite understand her friend's resistance to the marriage. She didn't know about the stepfather, nor how devastating violence could be, not yet at least. She only knew that all women, to her knowledge, enjoyed getting married. The thought of being a queen for a day inspired girls' fantasies. Being well dressed, revered, pampered. They dreamed of long processions of women ushering the bride-queen to her throne at the wedding, incense and oils and a huge reception, hip bumps that told the bride the secrets of the first night. The thing everyone talked about was the ceremony; the ones getting married hardly mattered. The important thing was having a lovely wedding. That's how people thought of it everywhere.

The first time she offered herself as a sacrificial lamb, Maryam's tits hadn't yet sprouted—she was only a tyke. She didn't own a flask yet. She was a small, childish reed who ran freely beneath the falcons and butterflies. Her gratitude for the crooked-nosed woman made Maryam Laamane promise oceans, mountains, hills, and a marriage she didn't want.

The girl still hadn't seen much of life, but she knew how to console those she loved. She knew that pain was assuaged immediately with honeyed words. She promised what she felt she had to promise. She promised to be the wife of an unknown man in her friend's stead. She was a lamb to the slaughter, like Isaac, on whom the venerated father was prepared to bring down the ax of devotion to the one and only God. Her friend Howa didn't comment on the gesture. She limited herself to smiling.

"I promised, Zuhra. Do you understand how unprepared your mother was? I promised on the most precious things, on my honor as a woman. I promised, do you understand? I was doomed. I couldn't back out. I was destined to become the wife of the seamstress Bushra's son."

The thought of the randomly encountered boy, the boy with the beige linen shirt and futah, came to dominate Maryam's thoughts. He'd made Maryam understand how foolish and excessive her promise was. No friendship could ask for the sacrifice of love. Howa hadn't asked for anything. Maryam had been impulsive and reckless in her decision.

Why had she promised? Maryam couldn't say. Maybe she'd screwed herself over because her friend was so sweet. She couldn't remember the first time someone was sweet with her. Her aunts loved her and old Gurey did as well. But in Howa there was an unequalled tenderness that filled Maryam like a wineskin. On that first of July, Howa Rosario became the most special friend in her life and, in a certain sense, the surrogate mother the girl never had a chance to know.

They told Maryam she'd only drawn a little milk from that distant, unknown woman. Maryam was weaned hurriedly. The reason was contained in the agony of a loss. The death of her beloved husband on Graziani's southern front exhausted her mother's womanly sap and accelerated her demise. The liquids in Maryam's mother dried up in her body. First her milk vanished, then her menstrual blood and, gradually, without anyone realizing it, her other vital fluids as well. Maryam Laamane's mother died of dryness. Parched by pain. Her life ended in a hostile land, on Graziani's southern front, where her husband, adored like few others, lost his life because of a weak white man's impudence. On July 1, 1960, Maryam felt she'd found a new mama: Howa Rosario. A woman who also knew how to be a sister, a friend, an accomplice. Her name was Howa like the first woman of creation and her friendship was a fantastic dream to Maryam.

But nothing, not even the most intense friendship, is comparable to love. Maryam Laamane was by no means prepared for that and, when it arrived, she felt swept up by a cyclone.

"I didn't even know his name..."

She'd seen him on a deserted street where the bittersweet, spurious odor of bananas reigned. She'd seen him for hardly any time at all, but already she felt like a part of him.

"If I don't see him anymore, I won't think about him," she said to herself.

The days, despite their implacable passing, couldn't make the memory of the fleeting encounter fade. The boy and his futah were pieces of her heart.

Maryam began behaving strangely. She stayed silent for long stretches of time. Often, to distract herself, she watched the concentric flying of hawks. She didn't dream about chasing after them anymore. She felt off course, incapable of following the dream of their flight. She looked at her feet, prisoner's feet, anchored to a land binding her to a life she didn't want.

At night, languor clenched the base of her gut. She wanted to touch herself to calm the tempest. Her hand slid beneath the sheet. She touched her pubic area quickly, then every night pulled her hand back. The stitching was under there, which had caused her such pain. She remembered it still, the day she was infibulated. Afterward, she couldn't pee correctly for days. An incredible pain. Now she wanted to tear out the stitching, put her finger there, and appease her misery. But she wasn't alone in bed. She slept with an older cousin who complained about her tossing and turning. She had to be attentive. Everyone knew it was the *jinn* that guided girls' hands to their forbidden areas.

Maryam, at that peculiar point in her life, had begun touching herself briefly, like a thief, fearing the jinn and shame. Maryam shut her eyes and tried visualizing the boy with the linen shirt. She would never confess it to anyone, but how she wished it were his and not her own hand touching her forbidden areas. That was when Maryam understood the meaning of many scenes she saw in Hollywood films, which no one had ever explained to her. Now she understood the meaning of the beds and crumpled sheets, the closed doors after the protagonists walk through them hand in hand. She understood why the soundtrack crescendoed when the camera panned away from the enamored couple and zoomed in on a solitary window. She understood why Doris Day told so many tales whenever she saw a bed, why people made up stories and said they had to stay in because they'd suddenly gotten the chickenpox. Maryam understood everything now. It had something to do with her languor, her pubic hair. It was somehow tied to her.

Her aunts watched her benevolently, whispering, uttering a truth that seemed too obvious to Maryam to be true. "*Wa qoqday*," her aunts said. "She's growing, she's weathering hormonal storms. May Allah give her comfort, it will pass, she'll get through. It happens to everyone, men and women. They go to bed as children and wake up as adults. Isn't that something?"

In those quiet days, the only relevant development in her life was her work at the Somali telephone company. She'd earned the position of telephone operator. It was one of the tidbits of news she wanted to share with her Uncle Gurey, so she went to the Lower Shebelle. She wanted to tell him that she'd become a woman, that she finally got her period and a job.

Getting it wasn't easy. She'd fought like a lioness and stood out. Two years had passed since Independence Day, when Maryam Laamane introduced herself to the telephone company recruiter. It was February 1962. She'd covered her many curls with a light *garbasaar*, the only concession to Somalia. For everything else, Maryam and her colleagues were dressed in Western style: long black skirts and white blouses. She'd received word of the recruitment from Ruqia, the hothead, who poked her nose (and ears) everywhere. In Mogadishu, Ruqia kept tabs on the gossip. Ruqia the hothead, with her gaudy lipstick and those long teeth. She looked like a rat. She wasn't nice to most people, but Maryam thought she was harmless. She was among the first acquaintances to die when civil war broke out. "Her heart stopped when the first mortar shells fell. She talked about other people and their lives because focusing on her own was too arduous a task. When she did, the fear carried her away." They called her a hothead because every time she had a fresh piece of gossip, she ran from one end of the city to the other like a nutcase.

When Maryam arrived at the telephone company, she saw a slew of girls dressed like her. The same black skirt, the same white blouse.

"There were only five spots, Zuhra."

Maryam thought the world hadn't changed much. Everywhere and at every point in time there was the same racket. Job positions were few and the candidates were numerous. Maryam smiled thinking of how electrified she felt in that moment. She would've given anything to outdo the other skirts like her. She started praying and bartering with God about her future. She promised to fast, give to charity with her first paycheck, to not go to the cinema for a week, to help Auntie Salado the following Friday, to climb stairs leading with her left foot. Her promises to God became ridiculous acts of superstition.

"You'll wonder, Zuhra, why so much trouble for a miserable job? It was only a call center. We put the city in touch, we didn't advertise products like you all do today. But yes, in the end it was just a call center. Like the one in EUR you hate so much. Hmm, how to explain it? That was a job for us. It was enough. We were content having very little."

Maryam only knew that she wanted the job very much. It meant being free, paying for her own groceries, the movies, clothes, helping her aunties. She wouldn't be a snot-nosed child anymore, but a respected woman in her family. It's true, she would've liked to continue studying, but going past the seventh grade was expensive. She knew the important things now. There was no need for anything else. For the essential things of life, she had the cinema. She would learn the rest there.

Suddenly, a powerful voice caught the girl's attention. It came from a white-haired man. Looking at him, no one would've paid him any mind, but his thundering voice was famous throughout Somalia. It was Mr. Sabrie, the hunchbacked national radio DJ, the man with snow-white hair who seemed like he had thousands of years behind him. He'd become a DJ in old age. Before that he'd been a storyteller at local parties. With independence, he started doing the *ogeyisiis*. Everyone in radio did the ogeyisiis sooner or later, though no one had Sabrie's pathos. The ogeyisiis was the national broadcasting station's most followed program. They searched for missing people in the city. Mogadishu was huge and people disappeared. Some in love. Some in pain. Some in mass graves, consumed by envy or ferocious beasts. Years later, when she was in Italy, Maryam saw *Chi l'ha visto?* on television. She smiled weakly. People from the Third World had already done a show like that. Textbook avant-garde.

Every day, Sabrie described noses, illustrated eyes, and drew mouths with the pencil of his words. He never had enough time to describe the people who'd disappeared in minute detail, so he used erratic brushstrokes of words to convey the sense of a person, their essence. In that way he was able to be precise telling stories that had no semblance of precision. Then, like everyone, he transitioned to music and newscasts. He also brought marriage celebrations to life. Oh, how he loved the *aroos* parties. He wasn't as good as his colleague Roble, the DJ everyone dreamed of being, but he didn't do half bad. He got by rather well.

He was the one corralling the girls in the telephone company forecourt. He leased his voice for a few shillings and it wasn't unusual to find him in the most extravagant places in the city. Sabrie didn't look around. Seeing faces didn't matter to him. He had been called only to make an announcement and hardly cared about the rest. Sabrie had a price; looking around wasn't included. He carried out his obligation, announcing to this crowd of Eve's daughters the start of the long struggle for placements. They obeyed like sheep.

"*Assalamu aleikum*, sisters. Get in line to sign up for the examination. Do you have a pen? A sheet of paper? Your ID?"

Maryam blessed the name of God and started writing. Thou shalt not look at other people's papers, it's a well-known commandment, the fifth, common to all religions of the Book. Thou shalt not rob thy neighbor of her destiny. If you deserve it, work will come to you, you'll see.

"We did a dictation exercise in Italian, my Zuhra. Italian was still the official language of the Somali state, despite our independence."

Maryam remembered how fluid her handwriting was in those days. Her *O*s and *M*s flowed smoothly on the serrated, horizontally-lined page. The dictation told the story of Marco, a boy from the Apennines who made a long journey to find his lost mother. "Marco, my love, brought me great fortune. I was the best. I began working three days later."

She reveled in her work. She had a kind of omnipotence about her, connecting the city, its mouths and its many ears. Then there was the matter of secrets. The operators knew everything about everyone. Who betrayed whom, who swindled whom, who usurped whom. They became guardians of discretion. They knew the sycophants, the adulterers, and the conspirators by name, surname, tribe, telephone number. This information was confidential. No one in the telephone company disclosed what they knew. It was an unspoken rule for those who took the job. Open ears and adroit hands to manage connections, but mouths shut, clamped like a virgin's hips. The operators were respected in the city. Everyone knew how reliable their discretion was.

It was a great job, Maryam knew it. Part of her was happy that the Somali phone operators could count her among their number. She was honored to be one of those revered and pampered women. Yet only part of her was happy, a tiny part. The other, bigger part, the more substantial part thought about how sad her life would be beside a man she didn't love, the seamstress Bushra's son, whom she had to marry because of a reckless promise.

Bushra's son was a mystery. No one ever really saw him. He didn't live in Somalia then. He went around Africa soaking up the teachings of the best tailors on the continent. The last time someone had gotten wind of him, he was in Mali, gleaning the secrets of oilcloth. Nobody could tell her whether Bushra's son was pleasant or not, or what he looked like. Not only could no one say whether he was handsome or ugly, but the details they had about his anatomy were fragmented and confused. The color of his eyes wasn't known, nor was the length of his hair. The same applied for his body: hair, torso, arms, face. "He was always hunched over his damned sewing machine and no one ever saw his face!"

Howa Rosario wasn't much help. She'd seen him only once. In her fear-stricken memory, Bushra's son was a monster, understandably. Maryam Laamane asked herself what it would be like being married to such a man.

The *Istunka*, the bludgeon fest, changed the course of history.

The idea of attending the event brought a smile back to Maryam's face, and she became chatty again. As the song Maryam heard many years later on the radio in Italy went: *You can't be serious at seventeen years old.* Like the teenagers in the song, Maryam's glass was full in those bygone days. She liked this Têtes de Bois hit. She recalled lost sensations. At seventeen, she fantasized about a kiss, forgetting that she'd never given one. A kiss, in her eyes, was a soft touch on the bicycle boy's lips. Like any other seventeen-year-old, Maryam dreamed of serial romance novels and the enamored star in her stomach trembling from forbidden emotions. The bludgeon fest briefly made her forget the seamstress Bushra's son and the promise she made to Howa. For a little while, she went back to being seventeen and dreaming.

It was Uncle Gurey's idea to go. Maryam, forcing her aunties to consent, joined a group on its way to Afgooye, where the spectacle happened every year. She convinced her cousin Hirsi and his partner, Manar, as well as the ever-present Howa. Hirsi had a used Fiat 500 that he'd bought from an Italian. He'd paid for it with the sweat on his forehead. The motor was inserted rather poorly, but Hirsi was good with luxury vehicle mechanics and in no time had transformed a living carcass into a beautiful, efficient machine. Hirsi whistled while he drove. His wife was mute, rarely speaking, but when she did say something it was earth-shattering.

"You know, Bushra's son got back three weeks ago," she said. "Maybe he'll come see the stick-fighting. I'd be curious to see him. I barely remember his face anymore."

A withering silence fell over the tiny 500. Howa began quietly sobbing. Maryam Laamane, for her part, bit her lower lip. It began to bleed.

THE REAPARECIDA

I switched beaches. I'm not at Carthage Amilcar anymore. Carthage wasn't bad with its voyeuristic boys, squealing girls, and an ocean fouled with baguettes and plastic bags. But now I'm no longer there. I switched beaches. I seem to have switched lives.

Mar, you smiled at me early this morning. I was blown away, and a bit worried. It had been a while since I'd seen you wake up early. You thought, so you told me, that it was right out of a Kellogg's commercial, an urban legend. You thought only alarm clocks and cellphones *cock-a-doodle-dooed*. But it was true, "It's actually fucking true," you said. You went downstairs to see the rooster. The owner of the bed-and-breakfast showed it to you. You ran onto the terrace to share your discovery. "It has a red crest," you shouted. You woke Zuhra up and made an adorable, girly face. I hugged you and you didn't push me away like you usually do. It was lovely feeling your warmth again, dear. Smelling your skin, your scent. I was reminded of when I breastfed you as Flaca watched us, rocking her body. Flaca sang us the Dylan song, the only one that stayed with her from her past life.

I'm no longer at Carthage. Now I'm at Mahdia. Silence is king here. There are people, but they don't make noise. They're like silent film actors. I'm Buster Keaton among mute marionettes. They move in the same way as people in Tunis proper do, but without the mayhem, without the hellish car horns, deafening music, chattering emptiness of the big city. I think it's because of the dead.

I could've sworn I saw them tonight. I wasn't afraid. On the contrary, I was curious. It may have just been the power of suggestion. Zuhra says she also believed she saw ghosts. "They don't have chains and sheets," she said, "they're only our shadows." What a strange girl Zuhra is. Sometimes she reminds me of my Flaca, especially when she's arched over her notepads. The same look of discovery. It was a strange night of pestering thoughts. I think it was partly because we all slept together on the terrace. I've never slept on a terrace, not even as a child. When the bed-and-breakfast's proprietress proposed it to us, I was about to respond uncivilly. Zuhra's friend—that whimsical shiny-haired Italian—stopped me. Lucy held me back. Her hand was so firm that I was afraid to think of a reply, much less say it. Lucy took the situation into her own hands and we ended up on the terrace.

"It's romantic," Lucy concluded.

"But we're alone," Zuhra tried complaining.

"Better that way."

We weren't alone on the terrace, though. A blond Swiss couple was there, as well as a French teacher, a Spanish adventurer, and a pair of Lebanese schoolboys. We occupied one corner and started chatting. I watched the stars and noted, simply, that I saw them. You never see stars in Rome anymore. I remember I did see them in Buenos Aires. When I was little, Ernesto and I gave them absurd names. In Buenos Aires I saw the stars, I surely did.

This city is a gem. Outside the city limits (I still wonder how far) are massive pleasure resorts. People go there, they say in *Routard* or *Lonely Planet*, to find tranquility. People come to meditate, rid themselves of worry, wisely idle away. I came here because you told me to, Mar. Who told you? Could I have told you and don't remember? It could've been a coincidence and no one told anyone. Perhaps the dead called us. They gave the best spot to the dead. The cemetery faces the ocean. Tombs clutter the beach and to swim you must pass them, greet them, honor and converse with them.

I'm having a good time with the dead and telling them the story I'm telling you, Mar. I'm trying to be sincere through and through.

In Rome, in the seventies, we went to Ostia to swim. Pablo Santana liked diving into the water. He was a good swimmer in Argentina. I think he won a medal at some youth tournament. Pablo had a chiseled body. Even today it's not bad. I still find myself looking at him with desire. He couldn't be mine. His pureness verged on the sacred. He was a knight, one of those who searched for the Holy Grail and had to be uncontaminated before being conceived. He could've been Flaca's, if only she'd been in her right mind. Now that I think about it, he was Flaca's, though she didn't know it.

When Alberto Tatti's program ended, our collective psychodrama began. The first night, no one had the courage to tell Rosa that the African voyage ended where it began, in Orano. She was expecting to move inland, to eat more Senegalese *mafe*, swing to the rhythms of Congolese rumbas. Instead, Alberto finished. He'd wished his audience happy listening to the Radio 77 programs and bid farewell. Very formal, with almost no warmth. A cold goodbye, hardly African. I remember being upset by it. How? I said to myself, after all that energy and sweat? How, after all those lost trains, lost ferries, accumulated kilometers? How, Alberto, do you say goodbye to us like that? Weren't you thinking about us, the people who were with you all this time, who supported you, your disciples? Weren't you thinking about Flaca, who waited for you as one waits for the singular breath of life?

Even Nuccia was troubled by it. She didn't expect such a brusque conclusion. She wasn't familiar with Africa, but she used to tell us that "My Renato waged war in Africa," at which point she'd get kind of quiet. Once each of us started thinking about other things, she'd remember to say, "That son of a bitch Mussolini sent us there. What wrong have these Africans done to us?" She'd take a tissue from the sewing basket on her lap and dry her bright eyes. "My Renato, he wanted to die in Africa. He told me that when the war ended, he would buy us land; we would keep our own beautiful farm and live happily and in peace. But only as equals, not superior like Benito wanted. We would be like everyone else. Africans ourselves." Her weeping would come at this point and never cease. Tears gushed down her cheeks like a swollen river. In a choked whisper, she'd say, "He wanted to die down there, Renato, in that city on the sea. Instead, he died in Rome. Poor Renato. August 13, 1943. Casilino-Tuscolano. They bombed the train that was bringing him back home."

Maybe Alberto's voice brought her closer to her Renato. Sometimes when I go to Verano to bring Nuccia flowers, I tell her stories about that time. I get emotional and cry. It's different, Mar. It's not crying over an unknown tomb. It is a cry of tribute to the people I knew.

The first night without Alberto was terrible. We looked disfigured. We didn't take our eyes off Flaca. In the end it was resentment that killed her. Resentment and nothing else. Rosa was like that, she took everything with graceful indignation, the pride of the disowned.

When Alberto's program ended, all her repressed pain wiped her out. The program had been a hiatus of unthinking happiness like the *khamaseen*, the gasping desert wind that reunites, blowing softly upon ruined loves. The man's extravagant voice, the metallic sound of his sighs, the saliva he spat impishly with every guttural sound. You were a stupid hiatus, my boy. A useless magical khamaseen. The first night without Alberto was pure fury. Flaca thrashed like an injured grass snake. Her entire body shook and she spumed at the mouth. It was like this for three nights. Then she began crying in her odd way. I couldn't stand it. You couldn't hear a sob; she was like a silent film. She was only the expression of pain, air trapped in lungs, suffocated breathing. It was eerie not hearing Flaca cry. You saw her in tears, but soundless.

On the seventh consecutive day of crying in front of Nuccia's spent radio, I decided I should go look for the DJ. I was fat. A ball of fat, umbilical cord, amniotic fluid, and you, my fetus, my daughter. Time was running out and my anxiety was full-blown. Today, Alberto's radio tower doesn't transmit anymore. Back then it was at a crossroads in Prenestina, before you get to Centocelle. Dilapidated premises, dust, piles of dumped newspapers, the stench of marijuana, posters of our Ernesto Guevara on the walls. Closed fists, Black Panthers, De André and, strangely, an Indian ink portrait of Eleonora Duse. A stray image in my mind. My bright-eyed father speaking at the table about that actress on the wall. He liked Duse. My mother, I remember, was jealous of the diva.

I saw a man with a white moustache and green eyes. A handsome man, I think, too old to be in a place with those young idealists. "Pardon me, do you know Alberto Tatti?" The moustached man took his eyes off the newspaper he was reading and settled them on me. I fixated on his paper. It was talking about Argentina. An entire article. *Milagro*! Close to the front page! I don't know what got into me, but I snatched the pages from the moustached man's hands and began skimming the lines like some demon. I was forward with him, rude. It didn't matter to me one damn bit. I scanned the lines in a trance. This was all that mattered to me. The lines in my trance.

I read the article's lede and cried. It was an article about us, our Argentinian hardship. I didn't think anyone in Italy knew. Things were different abroad. They'd shown interest in the Netherlands, and in Sweden they spoke a great deal about us. Pablo Santana told me that even in the hostile land of the United States, some people suffered alongside us *desaparecidos*. No one made a sound in Italy. The muteness offended me. Carajo, we were practically all Italians in Argentina, our mothers, our fathers, our grandfathers, our friends. How could Italy ignore us? She was in the blood of our mistreated bodies. Didn't she give a flying fuck? It didn't matter to her if we were her brothers or sisters. It didn't matter to her if we came from the Apennine or the Alps. It didn't matter if the colors of our football teams were taken from the historic crests of marine cities. She didn't care, the bitch.

Seeing my country's name in an Italian newspaper warmed my heart. I still remember the spreading heat. I didn't apologize to the green-eyed man. I focused on the name of the newspaper. I would've done somersaults to buy it off him. The man said, "This is a new paper, seems interesting. Rossana Rossanda and her people run it. Did you know that the split…" And he got wrapped up in an explanation of Italian politics that I tried to follow. This constantly struggling newspaper is forever going under. It's one of the few things we have in common, you and I, Mar. We're constantly struggling, always sinking. Eternal dreams of rebirth. I know you buy the paper because you can't go without your art film gurus. Me, though, why am I so fond of it? Why do I still buy it? When someone asks me, I reply, "Because they were there." That's enough for me.

The man told me that Alberto was in Africa, near Timbuktu. I was envisioning ancient manuscripts and legends, Tuareg wisemen and talking camels. I thought about hippopotami. Yes, those fat water pigs. Elias, your father, liked hippopotami. He thought they were forthright and mighty. "I would like," he once told me, "to live on a hippo's back." Later, this made me think. I wonder where he is now, the strange man whom I loved for one night only. When I think about him, I see him curled up on a hippo's back. That's why I wanted to go to Mali last summer, whatever the cost, you remember? But I didn't. I didn't have the courage. I wanted to look for your father. I'm sure he's there now. As sure as I am that blood flows in my veins and that Mali, my love, means hippopotamus.

In any case, Alberto Tatti was in Timbuktu. Far from me and far from Flaca. I was paralyzed in front of the man with the moustache. My heartache made the newspaper sheets drop to the dusty ground. I couldn't move. I wanted to be a butterfly so that I could fly to Timbuktu and drag that man back by the neck. "Come back, we need you. Flaca needs you." I had about ten empty cassette tapes in my purse. I wanted the DJ to record anything, a replay of his journey through the African metropolises. A personalized program that could placate Flaca's resentment.

"Can I leave him a message and some tapes?"

"Well, yes, but we don't know when he'll be back, ma'am."

"Maybe he'll be back in time."

I said this and felt my heart catch in my throat.

Maybe in time. Maybe…

I grabbed a piece of paper I found on a wobbly table where red ants mindlessly roamed. You were kicking quite a bit. Did you feel my sadness, love? You didn't let up. My shortness of breath exceeded expectations. I threw myself onto a seat and wrote a letter to Alberto Tatti, addressed to Timbuktu. Then I gave everything to the man with the moustache and went away as I'd come, with empty hands. My back was killing me. I felt how close your birth was. Six days later you decided to come, *cariño*. You had a pretty little head and so much hair stuck to your neck.

Resentment killed Flaca. Only resentment, my love. We should've known she wouldn't make it much longer, from the moment she took off Marilyn Monroe's white dress. Her decision was unexpected. It was the day you started making funny faces. She took off her outfit that very day. Suddenly both of you shocked us. Female telepathy. For a moment Pablo and I were happy. Now I know, there was nothing joyous in that decision. The clownish attire, the white dress that Billy Wilder had chosen to iconize Norma Jeane, was the umbilical cord that tethered Rosa to the land of the living. It was ridiculous, but such is life. When she took it off, Pablo Santana and I rejoiced. It seemed like a return to normalcy, to her former life.

The day you made your silly expressions, the day of Norma

Jeane's adieu, Rosa Benassi, daughter of Italians, took a long, humid shower. Everything in our San Lorenzo hovel was fogged by the scorching humidity that came from our tiny bathroom. Rosa walked out without a wig and without clothes, entirely nude. Her pubic hair was a vibrant red. I couldn't believe it. I'd never seen hair that color. I'd forgotten that in her past life, Rosa Benassi had been red like Tiziano's Madonnas. Pablo Santana got an erection. It was unavoidable. It wasn't desire. It wasn't anything. Only astonishment at seeing her there, like the first woman of creation. It was a hymn to her beauty. I also got an erection. Where, I don't know, but I had it. My imaginary penis straightened toward an imaginary sky. She wasn't embarrassed by our reactions. She walked past us and shut herself in her room. She'd left Marilyn's white dress in the bathroom, between foggy glass and water vapor. When she came out of the room, she was someone else. Not Rosa. Not Marilyn anymore. She was someone else. She vaguely resembled her dance instructor. A bun on her head, a brown cardigan, and a black skirt. A desert tan undershirt. All of it mine. Everything was big on her. Flaca was terribly haggard. I had had you for a while, Mar. My clothes were oversized. Flaca danced inside my clothes, but she wore them with an ease that made you think they'd always been hers.

Pablo and I were happy about her transformation. It seemed like she was putting her head back in place. Pablo proposed cooking some rice. He was great at making rice with saffron, one of his grandmother's specialties, he said. We left him in the kitchen to fiddle. Then Nuccia came. She wasn't happy. I saw it from the way she bit her bottom lip. "It's not a good sign," she said. Pablo and I downplayed it and reassured her. Nuccia combed Flaca's tallow hair that evening. She loosened the bun and made her a beautiful Indian braid. Flaca didn't react. Immobile, stuck in the space her body occupied. Absence of movement. This didn't concern us much. She'd taken off Marilyn's dress. That was the sign we were waiting for. We were imbeciles, patent idiots. We didn't know that it was already too late.

Those were difficult months. My pregnancy, the end of Alberto's program, Flaca showing no signs of life. Pablo was nervous. They sold even fewer ducks. We were in a disastrous economic situation. I saw Pablo headbutting the wall some nights. I saw him exhausted from the thousand things he did for us. One day, he came to me and said, "I found a job." I don't know if you could've called it work—it was exploitation. Twelve hours in a shoe factory in Cisterna di Latina, an odyssey, a massacre. Pablo left home with a smile and at night, worn-out, attempted the same smile he'd had in the morning. "Are you tired?" He never responded. It was a question I didn't need to ask. It was as predictable as the response. Still, I asked every night. Every night I hoped he would say to me, "I'm destroyed." Every night I dreamed of hugging him, massaging him, and telling him, "As of tomorrow you're not going there anymore." Pablo was stubborn then and even now when our halcyon days have passed. He's a hardhead as few others are. I longed for his body on those nights. I wanted to forget my anguish, I wanted to forget Flaca and her exorbitant pain, which I was incapable of processing.

Sometimes Rosa watched the spent radio. Nuccia ended up letting her have it. We never turned it on. Alberto wasn't there anymore. There was no point in listening to strange voices that weren't his. Rosa glanced furtively at the radio, worried about an imaginary betrayal. She needed someone's voice, but she felt indebted to Alberto for his marvelous trip. She didn't cry anymore. That was a relief. I couldn't stand her soundless tears.

Our lives followed an unvaried routine. The only unusual thing was you, my love. You cheered us up with your discoveries, your cries that became language. Watching you was fascinating, and you also enchanted Rosa, occasionally. I was happy you two crossed paths, despite everything. Nuccia was a big help. She took Flaca every Wednesday and Friday to dance on Via dei Giubbonari. Actually, Flaca didn't dance. She sat in a corner to watch other people's bodies keep to the melody of their own souls.

It didn't matter to the instructor whether Flaca danced or not. She knew her story and attending to her wasn't a burden. She was pleased. "One day she'll dance again," she told me, and I almost believed her. She was a good woman. I think she loved Rosa. She was Hungarian. She had been deported to Auschwitz. "She'll dance again, like I did," and she gave her a helping hand.

One day Rosa stopped going to Madame Elsa's. She didn't leave home anymore. We tried convincing her by telling her how beautiful the Roman sun was in spring. Nothing could be done. She stayed home. She played with you, Mar, and spent much of her time watching the extinguished radio to listen for the lost man's voice.

At some point, I don't know when, she began washing things. She washed, cleaned, scrubbed, rinsed. She spent all of her time absorbed in these activities. She meticulously sifted through herself and her surroundings. It was an orgy of scouring that no one understood. At first, I welcomed her new mania. Rosa didn't stink anymore, thanks to her humid, scorching showers. Before, when she had that Marilyn dress, she reeked of everything: cauliflower, excrement, pain, menstrual blood, sweat. The white dress turned orange from being worn so much. Pablo and I followed her like exterminators. We tried making the air around her less polluted. We appreciated that change, I admit. We bought her new dresses and she put them on. She spent a lot of time in the bathroom, and when she came out the air smelled of talcum powder and lavender. Being with her was pleasant, not as embarrassing as it once was.

When she stopped leaving the house so that she could wash herself, that's when I began worrying. I saw her obsessiveness and didn't like it. Even washing her hands was a ritual at that point. It was impossible to measure, on average, how much she washed her hands or her feet or her ears or nostrils. Everything was a purification ritual. You knew when she went in the bathroom, but not when she left, to the point that attending to her body wasn't enough. She had to wash everything else on top of that. Us. The apartment. She became the queen of sponges and detergents. It was a war against germs, mites, bacteria. She began making specific requests to us for detergents, sponges, and other contraptions for the house. She wrote long, exhaustive lists and we said, "Ma'am, yes ma'am, it will be done." We bought everything.

We thought it might've been a way to return to normal. We should've taken her to the doctor, though, a psychotherapist. Madame Elsa would tell us, "You can't keep her in the house." Pablo and I didn't have money for a psychotherapist. We didn't really have money for the detergents she asked for either. We were in bad shape. A psychotherapist, where? Someone on Via dei Serpenti told us there was an Argentinian doctor who helped compatriots and gave preferential treatment. "His name is Antonio Puig." They gave us his number. The secretary told us he'd be back in a month—he was on vacation. We had to wait.

In the meantime, Rosa's delirium extended to soaps as well. She looked at them lovingly, reverentially. They were the unsung divinities of the house, the principal focus of her ritual along with the drying rack. Rosa spent so much time cleaning that damn thing. The delicate balance of her mind stood on a clothes rack. It was perhaps among the appliances nearest to her heart, destined to collect clothes recently taken from the washer, destined to sustain all the cleanliness of the world. She rubbed it with care after every load of laundry. I knew it was a bad sign, but when she hung the wash out to dry, I would watch her for hours. She was meticulous, exact. Everything had a dizzying iconographic effect. It combined the colors of the clothes, their form, their weight as well. It was perfect, sprawled out as in a watercolor exhibition.

Her work with the washing machine was considerable. Without it, Flaca was lost. Today, washing machines are sophisticated. They do everything themselves, remove stains, choose the best setting, guide you like a child. In the seventies, the washer was still inconvenient, not at all sophisticated, and if you didn't operate it properly, it could ruin your favorite outfit. In the seventies, every good washer needed a good captain, a direction, a route to follow. Rosa was a captain without equal. Sometimes I would find Flaca zoned out in front of the thing. She spent hours gazing lustfully through the window. She watched the filth disappear and turn into ghosts. The washing machine window was her life beginning anew.

She took strange precautions. Her mind assaulted her with unpredictable dangers. Everything was filthy, everything could attack her, everything was insidious and seamy. She slithered slowly along the walls of the house, particularly when she carried food. She was careful at corners, believing them to be deceitful. Soiled crossroads. She looked at us suspiciously. She studied our cleanliness levels. She examined our collars, shirt sleeves, the density of dandruff in our hair, the length of our nails and our breaths. At the table, she tried claiming the seat furthest from the bathroom. She checked that everything was neat, from the silverware to the tablecloth, and subjected the food to a close analysis.

She'd also developed a fixation for handles. In our dump there weren't many of them. How many doors did we have? Three? I don't remember anymore. Regardless, they underwent thorough scientific evaluation. The quantity of bacterial microorganisms was assessed. Nothing was left to chance. The handles might have been touched by how many people? By us, certainly, and those who'd paid us a visit. People who had touched other objects, other people. It was a circle of dirty people, dirty things, infected lives. The handle had become, for my Rosa, the quintessence of bacteriological risk. A cause of death. Contamination was certain. This obsession of hers scared me. I wanted to see her again in the ridiculous Marilyn dress. I wanted to hear her sing Dylan. She didn't sing anything anymore. Her voice had been swallowed by a hermetically sealed pit.

After the discovery of the handles, I decided to read what she wrote. I read it for days. I was devastated. That's when I knew. My Flaca wanted to clean herself on the inside. That's all she wanted.

It was too late to save her. Resentment stole her from us in the end. And it was an awful end.

I didn't find her. Pablo did. He told me he'd smelled a wrathful scent, an aggressive odor of carnivorous flowers. He went into Rosa's room. Each time he entered the house, he went to check whether Rosa was well or not. He saw her empty bed, perfectly in order. On it, a blue plush bunny, the one Nuccia had given her for Christmas. Flaca adored the plushie, she never left it. On the ground were drying, circular green stains. Stains that outlined solar systems and potential worlds. The stains were concentrated at the foot of the bed like puddles. It was there that Rosa lay, in a green sea. From her mouth, pale liquid ran down her face. She was gray. Comatose. The autopsy revealed that she had guzzled liters of disinfectant.

My Flaca wanted to clean herself on the inside. That's all, *carajo*.

A month after Rosa's funeral, a package arrived. It had a stamp from a post office in southern Rome. Inside were ten cassettes. Alberto Tatti had recorded his voice. He'd done us a favor. He'd been too late coming back from Timbuktu or wherever the hell it was. I didn't listen to the cassettes. Alberto Tatti was of no use to me anymore. I threw them in the trash and didn't think about him again.

THE FATHER

"It's obvious that she killed him," said an old man with henna-colored eyebrows.

"What about the body?" asked an erratic boy.

"The body? She made it disappear, no? Is she or isn't she a dirty witch?"

Majid had disappeared. For the people in the neighborhood, Bushra was the only culprit. All blame fell on her.

Bushra wasn't concerned about these rumors. She was used to being accused. She was worried for Majid, though. He'd left without taking anything. No money, clothes, food. In the first week of his absence, Bushra was still hopeful. She hoped to see him materialize in front of her. She hoped to fill her ears with his eloquent silence. She peered out at the world, longing for his winding steps on the sand.

She liked the ritual quality of their chaste nights. She daubed herself with unguents and essential oils, he watched her with one eye, the left, and pretended not to be stunned by his woman's beautiful shapes. Bushra never completely resigned herself to a sexless marriage. And every evening, the hope of becoming Majid's woman flourished inside of her. Just before he disappeared, the woman had serious hopes. One of his hands had settled on her breast. It was brief, but for Bushra it may as well have been the preface to a dream. The hand on her chest was followed by a game with the wires of her wavy hair, then a massage, a kiss. If he hadn't disappeared, would he have finally been hers?

He vanished, and no one had the slightest idea where the cook Majid could've gone. She asked everyone in those early days. Poor Bushra ran to every corner of Mogadishu, following hearsay, recapitulating events that never occurred. Even the Pasquinellis, her husband's Italian employers, groped around in a murky darkness.

Bushra did not give up. Every night she sprinkled herself with unguents and waited, ready to make love. When the nostalgia became too upsetting, she spread hot tears around her. It wasn't a cry, but an exorcism. In her days of solitude, only Elias's letters— my letters—gave her comfort. I traveled, Zuhra. I was a curious young man. From Mali to Conakry, Guinea by way of Liberia, I tried imbibing the Africa that was rightfully mine. Everywhere I went, people looked at me and laughed. "You're not African," they said to me, "you have a white person's nose." I laughed harder than them. "The whites don't have good noses." In their eyes, Somalis were Yemeni or white, basically something else. To them, we Somalis were something other than African. I never agreed. I said that we were the Horn and that Africa was plural, that there was diversity in everything, but also convergence. When I was young, I got caught up in heated debates. While I was adrift in fabrics, colors, debates, and passion, my mother, Bushra, silently suffered my father's absence.

Papa took one thing before leaving. My outfits. Bushra couldn't find a logical explanation for this, but she was pleased. Although I'm not sure how, this fed her hopes of seeing him again in this lifetime.

While Bushra suffered, the neighborhood around her conspired.

A strange coincidence, or snide fate, would have a mysterious fever epidemic strike the neighborhood. The tribulation was blamed on Bushra. She had become the *qumayo* to everyone, the witch. Some whispered that she was Arawelo come back to life. Some called her this on the streets and Bushra closed up like a clam. She suspected that the name, which came from a fable, would bring her nothing good. Arawelo was a woman who killed men that didn't pleasure her. She castrated children and imposed the power of her vagina on Somalia. Then one day, like a dictator, she was killed by a relative. Uli Ual saved himself from castration. He had grown up in secret and, once he was older, decided to kill his grandmother.

Death wasn't enough. Her body was cut into pieces, burned, and strewn across Somalia. No one wanted the cadaver to reconstitute itself and terrorize men from the great beyond as well. Her ashes were strewn around the country. Arawelo's tombs were everywhere. But she grew again in every woman. Was not the pendulum perhaps one of Arawelo's manifestations? The clitoris was cut from little girls so that they wouldn't become like that dirty, rancid old woman. The clitoris was buried far away or fed to the hyenas. Its ashes strewn around Somalia. Men feared her for their virility's sake and buried the clitorises far away. Someone had forgotten to cut Bushra. She hadn't had to suffer a cutting. She was loose like a little girl and her pee had never caused her to suffer. Her sisters had brought her to the infibulation, but they'd forgotten her. She was so silent she could've fooled a hyena that hadn't feasted for seven days.

The neighborhood knew about Bushra's clitoris. They knew that she wasn't like the others. They knew she was whole. Everyone thought the woman was insatiable, constantly famished, gluttonous. The neighborhood had condemned her for this.

"She killed her first husband, Hakim. She cast a spell on him and he ended up under a vehicle."

"And now," the neighborhood voices said, "who knows what terrible fate she's brought upon that poor man Majid. *Meskeen*... Allah have mercy on his soul."

Majid was dead to everyone. Many thought he'd died horribly.

"She stabbed him in the heart."

"She gave him deadly herbs to drink."

"She sucked his soul night after night."

"She let jinn kidnap him."

Everyone had a colorful version of Majid's death to tell. Details weren't lacking and the stories of invented deaths became more real than the most awful nightmares.

Before the fevers, people had feared Bushra. No one, however, was prepared to admit it openly. They still acknowledged her before the fevers. They still said, "Good afternoon" or "Assalamu aleikum." But the fevers changed everything. When she walked on the street, Bushra heard the treacherous rustling of serpents moving behind her. They were the hisses of lies. The bifurcated tongues of fear. Bushra passed and four-dollar exorcisms spewed from the mouths of gossipmongers. The people gripped rosaries, shouted, *vade retro satanas*, *a'udhu billahi*, turned away, spat on the ground. They considered her the daughter of Iblis. A few old men struck her with their rosaries to banish the devil they thought she'd become.

It was all because of the fevers. A scapegoat was needed, someone to denounce for their suffering. The fevers were abnormal. They commandeered your stomach and you couldn't eat anymore. You shut yourself in the bathroom and shat to the last scrap of your soul. Then delirium. The fever carried people to the mountaintop. From there, the precipice. Some died. Usually children.

The neighborhood was desperate. Someone had to do something. There were no medicines or doctors. People hoped and prayed. Someone said they had to make a sacrifice. They had to kill the demon, the cause of their ills. They went to Bushra's house, my mother's house, with pitchforks and bloodlust. They wanted more than anything to see her dead. Her body would be quartered and burned.

Bushra lived outside the world. She only thought about Majid.

"*Ya hubbi*, my love, where are you? *Soo noqo adigo nabad ah*, return healthy and unscathed."

Years later, Hibo Nuura would sing this prayer of Bushra's. This was the eighties, when men left Somalia to seek temporary fortune in Libya. Libya wasn't yet the hell where migrants from the South dreamed of a sea crossing that would carry them to the West or to death. There was work in Libya. Somalis set off in search of ephemeral fortune. Some became rich and returned to Somalia to build villas for themselves.

Fluffy-haired Hibo Nuura sang the hopes of amorous women. Soo noqo adigo nabad ah: come back healthy and unscathed. If Bushra had known that song she'd have sung it at the top of her lungs. But it hadn't yet been written.

For now, she sang a different song. She anointed herself with oil and love and she waited. When they beat forcefully on the door to kill her, Bushra opened it impulsively. She wasn't aware of anything.

Luckily, it was Elias arriving. His journey was finished.

He wanted to open a boutique. Africa had rewarded him with its colors and he wanted to give them to Somalia.

He stopped the hatred and kissed his mother, trembling like a fledgling.

Outside the door, an evil death. It did not enter their house. He saw it enter the house next to theirs.

The next day, the neighbor's oldest daughter died. It was a terrible end.

Zuhra, I'm happy I came when I did that day. Bushra didn't deserve a terrible death. I deflected my mother's destiny with an unforeseen return. To thank me, she got it in her head to find me a wife. She didn't want to see me loveless, like her. Bushra still sprinkled herself with unguents every night. She wouldn't dare be unprepared when Majid made her his.

EIGHT

THE NUS-NUS

"There's nothing I wouldn't do for you." The words seemed to come from a horrible soap opera, where all the women are fair-haired and the men are buff.

Her hair was not fair and she was not at all buff. Nevertheless, the maudlin words were addressed to her, Mar Ribero Martino, sullen and disinterested Mar who detested the sugary melodrama of false television romances.

The authoress of these archaic, flustered words was now three meters from her. The same Mediterranean beach, in the same small African town, with the same sunlight striking their bronzed faces. Around them, the pacific solitude of the dead, laid to rest in pink tombs. Three meters, Mar was just three meters away from an outmoded ponytail and giant sunglasses. A ponytail she'd once known so well, and which she'd loved for what it could have meant for her, had the two of them stayed together. In her agitation, Mar couldn't think straight.

Seeing Vittoria again as though it were the most normal thing in the world wasn't part of her vacation plans. She called this poised, inviolable seraph Vicky. Mar felt like a hunchback, an old camel that wanted to disappear, *desaparecer*. Everything warped beneath the weight of Vicky's big, self-assured eyes. Mar was shocked by her red veins, swimming in a pellucid white sea.

They seemed to pulsate like fresh water serpents. An apparition? The whiteness blinded and destroyed her. Cursed, cursed white. She didn't know how to resist. She was a wreck.

"I wonder if she'll notice how I've changed," the girl thought. Vicky's milky eyes fixated on her shamelessly.

The woman didn't seem to detect Mar's inner turmoil. Mar sat Indian style, eating a popsicle that oozed a sweet, syrupy strawberry preserve. Her hands were sticky. She wasn't given a hand in greeting. Mar didn't extend hers either. The woman shook and wriggled her limbs, jumping with joy, her wings spread in salute. Her whiteness cleaved the torrid air. The ponytail swung around happily or, who can say, in despair from not having seen one another in ages. Mar wondered if she was experiencing one of her weird dreams, in which the past and present were a single concoction.

She was tempted to pinch herself like they do in cartoons. Instead, she stood up. She put her face in front of the other woman's, looking at her inanely. The ponytail had changed so little. Her cheeks were as full as they'd ever been. Even her eyes were the same, hopeful, guileless. Her mouth was the color of molasses, tinged with syrup and preservatives. Vicky seemed like a little girl. She was still fond of her.

How many years had passed? Two? Yes, two already. Mar shouted at her the last time they were together. She remembered it clearly. She'd said contemptible things. They were in downtown Rome, in Piazza Augusto Imperatore near the 913 terminal. Spring was nearing. The skaters weren't infesting Ara Pacis yet. The air was unreal and granular. When evening descends, Rome is unstable. The two of them were wide-eyed, imaginative, at the start of a melodrama. Mar Ribero Martino was fulminating, deformed with rage, shrieking indecencies to the stars. She was crazy and alone. Vicky cried. They both felt impotent, useless. "There's nothing I wouldn't do for you, Mar." In exchange for the girl's devotion, Mar threw her against a gate, then against a wall. Soundless, incomprehensible strength. She hurt her. Premeditated? Maybe. Her intractable desire for Vicky was putting up a fight. Desire for her body, her gentleness, her nebulous sense of the universe. Mar wanted to strangle her desire. Strangle Vicky. Strangle herself.

"There's nothing I wouldn't do for you," the girl with the ponytail said. She cried as she spoke. Her tears followed beaten paths, quietly wetting her cheeks and soft lips. She believed what she was saying. It was love, a passing moment, possibly a simple lack of intelligence. Mar wanted to tell her things that were just as sweet and asinine. She hurled her against a wall because she didn't know how to handle her love.

She started up her gray Honda SH. Her silhouette sped nimbly through the city's night traffic and she didn't look back at the girl she'd slandered. The stars withdrew from the sky. Mar spat at the lusterless stars, swearing like a truck driver. She didn't look back at the woman she desired. She couldn't look at her. Pati was waiting at home. Pati, who had enchanted her with her whiteness and her malaise. She couldn't love Vicky, or her outworn ponytail. Vittoria was too good. Pati the sick, the unbalanced, was at home. Mar had to stay with her, deep in the inferno that she fed daily. One day she'd tried explaining her relationship with Pati to Vicky. "You can't tell," she told her, "but I'm under a spell." The girl smiled. But she understood nothing. And how could she? Vittoria was healthy. She had a perfect constitution, an intact brain. Mar was hung up on Pati and her sickness, her craziness. Enchanted. Her brain was amorphous pulp.

And now, two years later, she'd found Vicky again in Mahdia. Two years since the shouting, the curses, the threats, and that woman, the same Vicky with the same cheeks, was standing in front of her on a Tunisian beach. Mar had no defenses.

Vicky wasn't crying anymore. Her hair was longer, with undertones of red. She was prettier. Mar wanted to flee.

Mahdia had been one of Miranda's ideas. She'd looked at her daughter. "You come too." It was an order. Mar was tempted to stand at attention or make a Roman salute. She didn't do any of this. "OK," she said. She looked bored and fed up, but she was excited. Miranda was always sentimental with her, amenable, but now she was giving an order, a direction. She liked when her mother was dedicated to her role as parent. Tunisia was doing her a lot of good.

There would be three of them on that trip. Zuhra Laamane, the Afro-Roman, would come with them. "We have to get her mind off things," her mother said. Mar agreed. It was strange having the same opinions as Miranda, but in Tunisia, this was happening too. Zuhra had had an ugly seizure two nights before at the Serb's party. She was in dire need of peace and good company. Mar thought of herself as a good friend for the girl. Something of a sister. Looking at her sometimes, she saw part of her own life. Even in Zuhra's despair she saw herself, especially in Zuhra's tremors. They had the same nose, the same hands. Zuhra was a little bigger, but she seemed so small and defenseless. Yes, Mar felt like a wonderful companion for the girl.

She sent JK a text explaining that they'd see each other once she returned from the trip with her mother. *I miss the way you smell*, he replied. *Have a good trip*. She also missed the way JK smelled, like the mango juice she would buy at the souq in Piazza Vittorio. Acidic, intense. Who knows what would happen between them when she got back. Who knows if it was right to keep seeing him. JK was a man. She'd never lasted with men. She'd never even lasted with women, for that matter, only Pati. That was another thing altogether, irrational dependence. The darkness of her night, her fado. A perpetual, attractive torment. Patricia's white skin left unsightly traces of madness that Mar couldn't stop pursuing. She hated white. It blinded her.

"Can I wash your hair, *abbayo*?"

"*Abbaio?*" Mar asked. She'd just woken up and didn't recognize the voice. She didn't understand why someone would want to bark first thing in the morning. She only wanted one thing in the morning: dark, boiling liquid in her mouth. Coffee, rarely tea, that she could swill. No sugar, just black coffee in a soup bowl.

"*Abbayo* means 'sister.' It's Somali. Your father's language. Miranda told me your father was Somali, like my mother."

Mar remembered where she was. Her mother had planned this trip. Together with Zuhra they'd taken one of those run-down buses that lurches at every pothole, and beneath the searing noon sun they'd started looking for a hotel where they could rest. Everything was full. Bed-and-breakfasts were bursting at the seams. The (very few) luxury hotels, too. Roaming. "How about we sleep on the beach?" she'd proposed. The evil eye from her mother. A new search, an uncertain outcome. Then a miracle, which first appeared like mockery. One hostel offered a terrace for sleeping on, at least, and a bathroom with a shower. It was a strange set-up, but they accepted it because being able to sleep with only the stars for a roof was a fine thing.

Abbayo? Evidently it had nothing to do with dogs. It was Zuhra Laamane's delicate voice, the strange girl who already felt like a part of Mar. She was kind. Mar wondered if it was because of the silly way the girl had of speaking. She stacked her words and sounds on top of one another and made people laugh. It was like hearing a tantalizing radio program. She was a very happy girl.

"My hair?" she asked. "But…"

"It looks like a mannequin's hair, abbayo, it doesn't seem real."

Mar didn't know what to say. "Can I get coffee before?"

"Yes, abbayo, there's no rush. I'm here. I'm gonna go to the tombs anyway. It's beautiful there, have you been?"

"No." She said no more. Mar was afraid of tombs. They reminded her of Pati's whiteness and the redness of her blood, which she'd wanted to see.

"You have to, abbayo. It's relaxing and, well, it's nice being between the sky and sea, thinking that they've given you the most beautiful spot. Yesterday I saw a strange Arab woman there. I want to see if I can find her again."

Mar went to the communal toilet. She shat liquid. Since she'd been in that country, her crap had basically become water. "It's because of the spicy grilled salad, *salata meshweyya*. Our stomachs aren't used to it," she'd told JK. She missed her Chinese man. His hair was smooth and wavy. She liked burrowing between his hands. JK told her stories. Zuhra Laamane did the same. With Pati it had been only silence and fury. JK laughed even when he made love. "I'm a Highlander from the same tribe as Duncan MacLeod, I'm Scottish, an immortal." Highlander. JK always said he was immortal. "Don't you all say that the Chinese never die? And that for some reason you're never able to attend our funerals?" Highlander, from the Scotsman's tribe, the sempiternal Duncan MacLeod. Ah, how she wished her small-eyed man were truly immortal. He was human, alas.

"Are you positive people die in China?" she'd teased him once after lovemaking.

"Aw, don't tell me *you* believe that horseshit about Chinese people never dying! Why should we have to die? Chinese immigration to Italy is a new thing. My parents are barely fifty years old. Why do they have to die? I'm only twenty-seven. Why should I have to go?"

Why did JK have to die? She pulled him closer. *Don't die, JK.* She pressed him against her chest like the plush rabbit she had as a child. Oh, if only her almond-eyed man really were a Highlander. She missed him. She felt the echo of his elongated laughter and muddled words ringing in her head. They spoke of Chinese funerals in the suspended moments after love. "They're very colorful," JK told her. She remembered that she was the only colorful one at Pati's funeral, where otherwise white dominated. An abominable color.

She took a cold shower to harden her muscles. She didn't have a shower cap. She tried not getting her head wet. Hadn't she promised Zuhra she'd let her do it? Her hair reassured her, flattened as it was like loose cables. Straightening her hair in Tunis and washing it in Mahdia meant one thing only: fucking up all her delicate work. Her unkempt hair was frazzled like Pati's. She'd wear it like that after massacring it with a flat iron or a disgusting product that burned her skin. Afterward, she was guaranteed to look like a beautiful Barbie. Mulberry and negroid, but Barbie. She touched the twine on her head and felt as though she were in a barbed-wire nirvana. "You'll go bald if you keep burning yourself," Miranda told her. Her mama had made an odd, disappointed grimace, which bordered on resentment.

Grimacing is easy for you, Mama. Your hair is soft, a wave, mine is like a cricket's, prickly, irregular, senseless. Pati's frazzled hair and milky reflections made some kind of sense.

Me, Mar Ribero Martino, do I make sense? I am fruit of the Third World. A black father, my mother the daughter of terroni. *Pigmented with stains of slavery and spoliation. I am conquered land. Earth to be walked on. Colorless hybrid fruit. Uncategorized. A half-blood that belongs to nothing. My blood is contaminated. Confused. There's too much of others in me. Nothing is wedded. Heavy buttocks. Small nose. Prickly hair. Overflowing pubic hair, of a dark brown hue that doesn't have the dignity of black. Big eyes. Tiny mouth. Brownish skin. Long neck. I don't understand myself. I feel like an illegible scrawl. I want to be white. Like Pati. I want to be blindingly reflective. Instead, fatigue seeps from my skin. Half-blood. Semi-negress. I'm ashamed. Not dark enough for the blacks. Not light enough for the whites. I speak like Zuhra Laamane. I'm ungrammatical. I'm piling words. Just like Zuhra Laamane. Having spent so much time with her, I'm adopting her speech patterns. She wants to wash my hair, did you know that Mama? Because abbayo, I know, loves me very much. That's how you say it, right?* Abbayo… *I like this word, I feel like it unites us. Oh, Zuhra, don't wash my hair. I'm not like you at all. You are black, beautiful, light of the sun, proud of yourself. I am a scrawl. Don't wash my hair. Let me live my life with this mop on my head. Let me live with this odor of burned skin, burned head. I am a half-blood. Leave me be with my obsessions. I'll never attain the white that blinds me. I'll never attain the black I do not know. My father, a photo, is the black man to whom I owe this color. Maybe he was a beautiful man. From that one photograph Mama has, I can't tell. He's wearing a baseball cap. I wish I'd known him. He would've told me that black is beautiful and I would've believed him. I believe even now that nigger is beautiful. Maybe I shouldn't say nigger, but black. It doesn't matter to me, you taught it to me, abbayo Zuhra Laamane, that no one should be afraid of words. Nigger is beauty. But half-nigger? Semi-nigger? Semi-white? Semi-pale? Semi-nothing? I wish I'd known Elias. I'm indebted to him for the sperm that created me.*

Mar put on her country-style jeans and went to the pink tombs of Mahdia. She slipped away stealthily; she didn't want Zuhra seeing her. She didn't want her hair washed. Like a fugitive, she wandered toward the city, minding the colors. The blue of fishermen's tombs, the violet of the sky, the gray of her pearly skin.

Seeing Vicky among the tombs really did seem like a healthy hallucination. She often saw Vicky's silhouette when she went places. She'd been seeing it everywhere for two years. It showed up in the most unlikely locations. There wasn't a day when she didn't think about Vicky. She saw her in the hot soup she made to stop colds, in the eyes of abandoned dogs, between the lines of a real estate ad, in dish detergent foam. Infinitesimal, she promenaded in her thoughts. Infinitesimal yet gigantic. She hadn't seen her in two years. It was reasonable to think that the Vicky standing among the pink-blue tombs of Mahdia was just the umpteenth hallucination. It couldn't be her in flesh and bone. The real her.

Mar didn't believe in coincidences, but when she moved closer to her, she could do nothing less than believe her sense of touch. She didn't pinch herself. She stretched out her hand toward the woman she hadn't seen in two years. Her skin was textured and lightly damp with sweat. She was human. Real, authentic. Not a dream or projection.

She touched her lightly. The last time they'd seen each other, Mar had thrown her against a wall with soundless strength. She'd wanted to hurt her. She'd wanted to destroy her and make her disappear, make her invisible to the world, her own world.

Here, among azure tombs, she touched her softly. A feather landing on that body which, just two years and a few ounces earlier, she'd attacked with wanton violence. She touched her softly and felt a shiver pass from her fingertips to her brain and loins.

"Did I hurt you badly that night, Vicky?"

The woman looked at her. "You may have done the greatest harm to yourself."

Mar felt like crying and she did. She never cried.

They went to get a coffee. Both were tired of mint tea.

"How's Pati?" Vicky asked.

"She killed herself," Mar said dryly. She didn't add anything else because the waiter arrived.

They only made strong Turkish coffee, but the waiter was frank when warning her. "No espresso, Turkish, *ladeed jiddan,* strong *jiddan.*" They ordered two, and apple-flavored hookah.

"Now I'm trying to survive," Mar said when the waiter went away.

"I understand," Vicky whispered.

"No, you don't understand. I'm rediscovering colors now. Pati's whiteness blinded me."

Again, Mar couldn't hold back the tears.

Vicky placed an arm around her shoulders.

"I'm happy you're recovering, friend."

She meant it.

Empire Hair Relaxer No Mix Crème. Super version for tough hair. It could soften pig bristles. Mar used it constantly on her chaotic head of hair. It was a drug. Without it, she would slip into withdrawal, directionless. Her hair wasn't exactly kinky, but Mar thought it had tedious, fickle curls. As far as she was concerned, her hairs were anarchists. They obeyed no laws. "They respond to atmospheric changes in their own way," she noted. She said they didn't only change according to the season, but also according to the vagaries of the day or even a ruined temperament. Humidity was harmful, a natural disaster, a biblical catastrophe. A variation in the water level could make the girl's passable existence catastrophic. The worst thing for Mar was that they grew outward. Pointless head fur.

Miranda hadn't helped her much with controlling the forest that sprouted on her head. No help, inappropriate advice, embarrassment. As in infancy, so in adolescence. Miranda couldn't tell the difference. She didn't know how to be a gentle wave. Mar, however, saw the difference. She saw the waves. When Miranda's head shook, she looked like a L'Oreal ad. She was silky soft. *Because I'm worth it*, she seemed to say. "And am I worth it, Mama?" Mar asked. She tried imitating her, shaking her head, but she wasn't silky. Everything stayed still, a singular block, like a toupee.

When Mar was younger, Miranda sometimes said to her, "I envy you, *hija*, you look like Angela Davis." Mar didn't know if her mama was messing with her or if she was dead serious. She knew nothing about Angela Davis. No one—not even her mama, who always brought her up—had told her that proud woman's story. Maybe she would've grown up differently if someone had told her. As a little girl, Mar watched the other little girls with envy. She dreamed of a Japanese manga bowl cut. She was the only one in her class in elementary school with a wig of curls on her head. The only one in section B with a false mophead.

"Can I touch it?" was a common question. Hands violated her head, inopportunely. Custodian hands, teacher hands, friendly hands, familial hands. Everyone planted the seeds of their Eurocentric curiosities in her. They touched her as though she were a species on its way to extinction, a savage forest animal. She was a human beast. An example, not a person. She was lucky she wasn't born in the nineteenth century, because back then human exhibits really did exist, zoos where ferocious beasts and inhabitants of the Afro-Asiatic colonies were dished out to the curious and the do-nothings.

> *Lo and behold…ladies and gentlemen, children and dogs. Only here, in the Zoological Garden of Paris, the* ville lumière, *will you find authentic Eskimos and Nubians in their natural state. I, Geoffroy Saint-Hilaire, director of the Garden, can also promise you real Australian cannibals, males and females, the one and only colony of this savage, strange, disfigured race, the most brutal ever found in the interior of the overseas territories. Only here will you find the basest level of humanity imaginable. Only here, beings in their natural state.*

The *village nègre* were incredibly popular—circuses where humanity was reduced to a feral state, where the dignity of the other counted for naught. She would've been placed in a nice cage, Mar thought. A nice cage with a wad of straw and a water bowl. Maybe they would've spared her the chains, but surely they'd have exposed her breasts because she was, in the end, only an animal, a thing, a good-for-nothing half-caste. If she'd been a woman of the colony, of her unidentified father's Somalia, the whites would've used her as an orifice to forget their boredom and nostalgia. She would've been like Elo, that disgraced woman she happened to encounter in the pages of an awful Italian novel for a literature exam at university. *Elo…a worthless slave who must submit her body when the white man has carnal desire.*

Yes, they would've revealed her breasts because she was only a thing, a nothing. Her nude chest wouldn't have caused a scandal. The forest on her head would've excited the public—so strange—the ideal fantasy for unconfessed masturbators. They may have also made her wear some necklaces to create a tribal atmosphere. She would've been a *mãe-de-santo*, an officiate of *candomblé*. A pagan witch who incited fear, but not too much. They would've pointed their fingers at her like they did with the Nubians, the Senegalese, and the Laplanders. "Natural humanity," they would call the beribboned women of the Belle Époque. She wouldn't have lifted her eyes. She would've meekly watched the ground. They would've made her do all the circuses and expositions. She would've been hailed as the undisputed queen of the 1889 fair together with the Eiffel Tower, which had been built expressly for that occasion. A supreme attraction, star of the village nègre, alpha female of the four hundred indigenous extras. Afterward, in 1900, she would've held court, she would've astonished the tens of millions of visitors they say went to gape at other human beings equal to them in every way, save for the misfortune of being enslaved.

Mar was from another age. In hers, the zoos were more devious. They were in the mind, and hadn't disappeared at all. People didn't often tell you that you were part of an inferior race anymore. You soon found out that the races didn't exist. Now they told you, "Your culture is too different from mine. We're incompatible." The zoos transformed into immaterial enclosures.

Mar watched Zuhra with the can of Empire Hair Relaxer No Mix Crème. She was worried. The creamy nuisance had been her lifeline that whole time. Since she'd known Pati, her hair had grown used to being chemically treated. It was a ritual. A thorough cleaning, good nutritive conditioner, straightening cream, hair dryer, flat iron. There were waiting times to respect, movements to follow. It was a ballet, a military drill. Mar was rigorous. She calmed the flurries of her confused heart by vanquishing her exuberant curls. She'd done solid work in Tunis. She'd been doing a good job for years. Her hair was smoother than Pati's, more tousled than her mother's. It was straight, a line, a border. When she shook her head, she felt her hair crackling. Initially, her head burned like hell. She wanted to scratch as though she had head lice. She got used to it. She got used to the burning smell, the tickle of chemistry. She got used to making her crown of hair flutter. *Because I'm worth it.*

Zuhra Laamane was holding the can. Vicky had gone with her to the bed-and-breakfast. Vicky laughed and gabbed. Her presence made Mar happy because she was about to rue the day she'd said yes to Zuhra's impromptu offer to wash her hair. She needed a supportive friend so that she could recover the peacefulness of that morning, when she'd stuck her face in a soup bowl full of black coffee. Vicky's presence helped her look ahead, *seguir adelante.*

"I'm going to be thinking about you!" Zuhra threatened. It was love, but it sounded sinister to Mar.

The Empire Hair Relaxer No Mix Crème ended up in the garbage. Vicky laughed. Zuhra dragged Mar onto the balcony. She had bucketfuls of shampoo. Mar was relieved to see the same deep-cleansing shampoo there. She wouldn't have to give up her ritual completely.

Zuhra made her sit on a wooden chair eaten away by time.

"Lower your head." It wasn't an order, just a request for cooperation.

Mar watched the world in ruins. Her world in ruins. Zuhra's hands were energetic. They shook her hair as if it were laundry consumed by unconquerable filth. Zuhra Laamane didn't want her to be overcome by that filth. So she shook and shook Mar's hair, she shook and revived it. She massaged and practically created it. The drying was similarly energetic. And to say that Zuhra didn't seem strong! Mar remembered the Serb's party, how Zuhra had resisted all the women trying to help her. Her body was powerful, and so was her will. Mar realized that for Zuhra to coexist with her trepidation, with her ghost, she had to be strong, energetic, powerful.

Mar prayed to a God, her own, that she might be touched by her new friend. Then came the hot, roaring wind of the hair dryer. She felt a cyclone of ringed hair on her head, Zuhra's hands making whirligigs. She liked the girl's touch. Her fingertips ran across her head like olive oil on a summer salad. It was thick and delicate. Strong, extra virgin. Heaven knew what Miranda would make of her hair when she saw her. And heaven knew what JK… no, he'd love it, definitely. Mar looked steadily ahead. She saw white. Pati was there. She was wearing the dress she had on the day she killed herself. Mar didn't recognize it. Evidently she'd acquired it after her, after their story. It was a white dress with a red rose in the middle.

Pati never wore feminine clothes. She was a pants and jackets kind of gal. She braved winters wearing turtlenecks, often devoid of color, and in the summer she lost her imagination and wore black T-shirts or, at most, gray. This dress was stunning. It was a wedding dress, Death perhaps the bridegroom. Mar didn't think about marriage. White was the color of funerals in the East. It was the only proper attire for death. Now Pati was in Mahdia, watching her from the terrace, Mar Ribero Martino, who was happy among her friends. Mar realized that the white no longer blinded her. The dress's red rose radiated outward, covering her stomach. Was it perhaps her blood that she wasn't able to see?

Pati didn't speak.

Mar saw that she had a baby boy in her arms. He was very small. Almost invisible.

Mar touched his head. She thought about how his hair was more tallowy than Miranda's and how the smell of burned skin annoyed her. She closed her eyes and saw the blended colors of his skin. A mélange of white and black, red and yellow. Mar smiled. Her child had the same hair as her, the same forest. She thought he was beautiful. Soon he would come back to her. She had to get ready.

THE NEGROPOLITAN

Fin. Kaput. The end. Roll credits. Drop the curtain. Eighteen months. Eighteen months until the end of the world. At least, that's what this paunchy woman is saying.

She says the world will end in eighteen months. That means I don't have much time to get myself back on track, fuck a man, buy a house, and eat a Sicilian *cassata*. My days are numbered. I don't want to die without an orgasm. I deserve it. I've earned it. Eighteen isn't a great number. It doesn't mean anything. It's not a month, it's not the hours in a day, it's not the seconds in a minute. It's meaningless. But the fat woman said exactly that, eighteen months till the game is up, Control-Alt-Delete and see ya later. *Khayama*, end of the world, *Apocalypse Now*. In newscasts they say that between tsunamis, the greenhouse effect, and global warming, we're fucked. The Arctic Sea won't be around anymore in 2050. Humanity might disappear soon after. We're all *desaparecidos* in eighteen months, then. There's not much time. I need an orgasm, ASAP.

She didn't say eighteen in Italian, the woman, she said *dix-huit,* in French. The bottom line is the same. She says she's the kind of person who makes predictions, and she heard the news directly from her kind-souled husband Karim. He never lied to her. "He was a saint," she reiterated. Or a great actor, I say. Men pride themselves on knowing the truth. I sort of pity Karim. This poor Muslim Christ, not even his body has been found. Burned to death at his workplace, over there in France. He came back during the summers loaded with knick-knacks. He always brought her a beautiful imitation leather handbag, she told me. He worked in an awful place in Mistress France. A place where two out of every three died. Poor Karim became human meat confetti, shipped by general delivery to Tunisia. The woman wrapped her husband's confetti in a shroud and buried him beside the sea, here in Mahdia.

I try consoling her. I place a hand on her shoulder in sisterly fashion, whispering a couple of *Allahu Akbar* and even a *fatiha*, seeing as I'm here. I don't know all the suras by heart, but everyone knows the fatiha, even me, and I'm not very good! It's the first sura, the most intense. All the beauty of Islam is in the fatiha. I try to be more comforting, I put my soul into it. I act like my teacher Morabito when she explained times tables to us. Morabito was the only good person in my childhood. She was patient and it didn't matter to her that I was black. She didn't call me Kunta Kinte like the bitchy custodians. I was just the dirty nigger to them. They didn't see anything else about me. "Not even bleach can make her clean," they said. They were hicks—dumpy and jealous of my beautiful mom. I act like Morabito, my voice becomes a veil. It enshrouds and protects. I look at the big woman and deliver my pearl of zen wisdom: "Well, this is a great place to live in eternity." I try saying it in French. I don't know French at all, but I try, I improvise, I emphasize the accent. They say eternity, *éternité*, almost the same way as the Italian, *eternità*. So I hope the message got through to the woman. I analyze her face. She seems to understand. She smiles.

Then she goes silent. Is she thinking about Karim? How long has it been since you've had a good fuck, sister? Was Karim good in bed? If you're mourning his loss, we can at least hope that he was good, sweet, and gentle. Otherwise what are you doing coming to his tomb? What are you doing putting pebbles on top of the tomb if he was a bastard? Did he hit you? A handbag every summer won't do it, sister. Courteousness is key. Remember that. And in bed, is Karim…am I hounding you again? You're blushing, you're not responding. Here it's like in Somalia. People don't say anything and then leave pebbles when they visit tombs. The Jews do it, too. I saw it in *Schindler's List*. Christians, however, leave flowers. Chrysanthemums. People always leave something. Sometimes themselves. A trace.

I want to leave some thoughts. I've placed myself right here. When I saw the cemetery I said to Mar and Miranda, "Go ahead, I'll catch up." They'll be soaking up the sun on the beach now, the two brazen women and their off-white friend who follows them everywhere. I certainly don't have to tan. I'm already dark enough, and anyway it's too nice here. When they proposed this trip to me, I didn't want to accept. I wasn't studying a lick of Arabic anymore. They'll surely shoot me down. I might get rejected, but the idea of giving up doesn't sit well with me. I wouldn't want to be worse than Benjamin, the Aryan German. His enunciation is shit. At least I know how to say the *'ayn* divinely. That's why I wanted to lock myself in the hostel, alone with the Veccia Vaglieri grammar book. But Mar insisted. A stubborn half-black girl. And here I am, towed along by the might of a mother and her daughter to Mahdia, this oasis of silence.

It's awesome here, I must admit. I like Mahdia. I'm glad I was dragged along. The driveling vendors are the only downside. They eat you up if you ask them anything. The fat woman tells me the guys are from Tunis, they aren't from around here. But everyone is from around here, I say, even those guys. If you live here somewhere, you're ultimately a part of it.

Mahdia is entirely pastel. Dainty. *Nu baba*. Open-air cafes, provisional markets, the blended smells of jasmine and fish. The sea salt permeates you, and for a moment you have the luxury of thinking about nothing, simply feeling your body. You feel your whole body in Mahdia. You like it, too. I like myself here. I have time for myself in Mahdia. I'm not like those vendors. I don't run around in Mahdia. I don't get stressed. I don't get angry. I don't take the Lord's name in vain. In Mahdia, people sit down and wait. When I saw this cemetery I said to myself, "Now I'm going to settle down here, I'm going to wait too." For what? I don't know. An epiphany. My own self. It's beautiful here, a cemetery on the sea, tombs which look out at the water. They're facing Mecca. The sea is inside them. Leaving the most beautiful spot to the dead is a treat.

Miranda and Mar are about to tan and talk. Mother and daughter. I envy them. I want to be here with my Maryam Laamane. Maryam is a beautiful woman. When I get back I want to tell her. Mom, I want to tell you that you're gorgeous. You have great boobs, Ma, and a nice ass too. I only got the ass from you. It's round, compact. I guess my tits could've been a little less surreal-looking. Mom has perfect tits, though. I'll tell her when I get back to Rome. Now I'm thinking about Howa Rosario. I can't believe she's dead. She won't shake that perfumed rosary of hers anymore. They would've buried her in Prima Porta. There's a lot of greenery there. I don't know if it's pretty. Howa wanted to be buried at Sheikh Sufi in Mogadishu, where the tombs are blue, but she ended up in Prima Porta. I missed her funeral. Mom says it was "typical," that Somali funerals are always "typical." You can never tell if people are actually sad. They never want to be seen crying. They have to come to terms with nature, Mom says, so they lock themselves in the bathroom to cry and act strong in public. To dull the pain, they tell stories, about death, about their tribes, or they mention the tales he or she told when they were alive. Men pig out at funerals. *Mufo* is never lacking, nor a good hot tea. And of course there are pots of beans and roasted coffee. The men stick everything in their giant mouths without thinking twice. The women, on the other hand, cook. They work so that they won't linger on tragedy and so their cries stay at a red light. Each one in solitude chooses her response to pain.

I once saw Somalis cry. I saw them cry together. A scene that hit home. I had just left Libla. I'd changed places with another stocker like me, Iris. I ran through the city center. Arriving stunned at Campidoglio, I couldn't catch my breath. I immediately started crying like everyone else. I had been overwhelmed by irrepressible suffering. It was the *tacsi*, the funeral. The mayor was officiating. Rome wanted to salute the bodies that didn't make it over to walk its ancient streets. Thirteen coffins in the middle of the piazza. Thirteen anonymous Somali corpses shut inside. All of them adventurous boys who had tried reaching the dream of a better life in a shabby dinghy. All of them dead without seeing that much yearned-for Lampedusa up close. The coffins were a concession to the West. Tradition entails that we bury them like Jesus Christ, like Karim, in shrouds. We are Christs, not chicken feed. The coffins in the piazza were draped with Somali flags. The flag's star struck me that day. How much have you suffered, my star? Everyone cried. There was no food. Just coffins and flags, the mayor and speeches, women beating their chests. The urge to vomit momentarily returned, but I didn't do it. I looked at the star and didn't do it.

I cried for Howa Rosario. Howa was my friend. Uncompromising on many things, but still my friend. For instance, she didn't like men, but she knew I liked them and tried showing it to me in her own way. Once, when my mom wasn't at home and we all lived together, I hung a picture of Tom Cruise from *Top Gun* in my room. Howa, I remember, looked at him askew and said, "*khaniis*," which means "fag." I whined. Tom wasn't a fag. He got loads of women and one day soon he would marry me too. We'd take a nice trip to the Maldives and have many little children, at least eight. Howa was unmoving. "Khaniis." Gay people were okay in her eyes, she just didn't want me falling in love with one of them. "You have to face the facts, sooner or later. You can't just fall in love with gays and impotents. Take that poster down." I took it down for five days before hanging it again. From there, I believe, my love life began swerving dangerously toward chastity. That's also why I'm among the tombs, to ponder how not to be a virgin anymore. Am I? Technically not. That is, my hymen is broken. But I am a virgin, of course. I never made love to anyone. Something went in my vagina, yes, but I swear I'm a virgin, *wallahi*. In my mind, the hymen is intact. I've never made love. It's not that I didn't want to, even after all the unwelcome intrusions. I grew up and began feeling desire. But I'd missed the train. I didn't know the *ABC*s of love. What they say about the *ABC*s is a scam. You have to know them if you want to fall in love and receive it in return. They explain what to say and what not to say, moves to make and not to make, how to move your mouth to say, "I want you," and how to move it to say, "Back off, you piece of shit." They also explain how to stand or sit. You'll notice trash that isn't trash and advances that aren't advances. They even explain how to handle telephone calls: him first or her? There's a heterosexual and homosexual version for every piece of advice. Tips on texts and dates. How to give kisses. How to caress. When to undress. When to say, "I love you," "I like you," "You drive me crazy." Everything on orgasms, on the *G*, *W*, *X*, *Y*, and *Z* spots. Everything on pleasure. Mine, yours, and ours. They explain how to feel free, how to believe. I lost my copy of the *ABC*s. Now, page by page, I'm copying other people's versions. I copy from glances cast on the street, words whispered in subway cars. I copy the pages and at night commit them to memory.

Howa lost her *ABC*s, too. She told me one night. She'd suffered the same intrusions, the same violations. "Do all of us Somali women have this bad luck?" I asked her. "It happens to many women," she said. "All over the world." Her mouth warped strangely when she said "world." It was a global misfortune and she thought it unjust.

I'm sitting among the tombs. It's peaceful here. *Saalam, Shalom.* Lovely peace. A slight wind blows from the east and the sea expands my soul. The chubby lady isn't there anymore. No one speaks to me about Karim's confetti. I'm sitting beside a tomb covered with pebbles. This person was loved. Everyone who walks by leaves a pebble.

In this country, in this language, you love in one hundred ways. *Hubb* is the word they use the most, the one they teach to us foreigners. But there are one hundred ways to love, the woman told me before leaving. One hundred ways to suffer. To hope. *Wasab*, passionate love, *hiyam*, limitless love, *lahf*, painful love. Arabic is a methodical language, which is why I like it so much. It is a language that, through wrought-iron grammatical structures, can fully photograph the reality that surrounds us and allow infinite possibilities of crossing gazes. With the alphabet, it photographs the moment of an encounter, the scent of a desire.

I try reading the name of the pebble-covered tomb's owner. The name is written in rough Arabic characters. A lopsided cursive, not those clear, round shapes in the grammar books. I only recognize the first letter, a *meem*, which you read like the *M* in Italian. The *meem* didn't solve the tomb's riddle for me. Man? Woman? Young? Old? Probably a child. I make conjectures, but it remains an anonymous tomb. I'm sitting next to it by chance. That's always how it is. My attention rests on the pebbles. Some are strangely shaped and maybe that's why I sat here. Despite the lack of information about the tomb, its owner, and the pebbles, there's something I know without really knowing it. The tomb belonged to someone who left a mark. There is a halo of encompassing love which it is impossible not to see. I want to leave the same trace here, but not in the distant future. Here, now, right away. The same contrails of love.

I still can't see inside this contrail. When I think about it, fear consumes me. Fear of being able to see, of not being able to. Of being happy, of not enduring the pain. Fear, fear, fear, and more fear. I exist without living. This is why I don't taste the flavors of kisses, this is why I don't feel the beating of my heart, this is why I still have panic attacks. Fear blocks each of my senses before I can activate them. I'm like one of my colleagues I met years ago, as I was plodding from one precarious job to another. He joylessly cheated death with quick flings. He was cruel with the women. He drowned them in poisonous liquids and uneasiness. He amassed one after another, like the colorful marbles that every child loves playing with. He never tasted these women's flavors. He spoke with me about it, though. I wasn't his type. He didn't play seducer with me. He treated me like a man sometimes. Did he understand before I did that we were suffering from the same illness?

My colleague had a glut of possessions: a house in the city, one in the countryside that he boasted about quite a bit, a dog he hated, two children he spoiled, a lackluster wife who drove him crazy, and many ideas that people mistook for geniality. On closer inspection, you saw that he didn't have anything. He had only a horrid life typical of the Muccinian bourgeois. He had big beautiful eyes, though. One thought they could contain the world. But they were a bluff. A cataract of fear blocked his view and maybe his veins as well. The fear made him craven.

The Buddhists say that we have room to contain pain. Every human being has places for the greatest pain, the one that blindsides us. But no space exists for fear.

I think of my colleague again. I haven't seen him in years. I wonder if he killed his dog, if he's still a coward. He told me that sooner or later he'd wring the dog's neck. "People suffocate me," he said, "and the dog more than any of them. It's another thing I have to take care of." But it was the fear he had to kill. Poor dog...

Perhaps I should also kill my fear. I have to do it with my own two hands. They'll change things, I feel it, my hands will give and receive, give and receive, constantly moving. Kind of like in that old Ben Harper song, *Now I can change the world with my own two hands, make it a better place with my own two hands*. Sometimes I forget I have so much strength inside, and hope, and happiness. I forget that man conquers everything with his intellect and with his own will. We conquer with our own two hands. My Somali women can change their own futures with their own two hands. They will do it, I know they will.

By all appearances, they have nothing. They don't have clitorises. They don't have Mogadishu. They don't have peace. They don't have… Maryam Laamane has me, though. I love her. I love you, you know that, Maryam Laamane? I think of you. Do you think of me? And when the pilgrim arrives, Mom, you'll tell me whether he's the one or whether I'll have to wait for someone better. I don't want to be afraid anymore.

Now, standing before this most beautiful tomb, I seem to have finally grasped a fragment of the truth that has eluded me. It's like in the fifth Gospel, the apocryphal one by Thomas the Apostle: the Kingdom is inside you all and beyond you.

Yes, inside me. Far from fear.

The fat woman told me that the world will end in eighteen months. Only eighteen.

Not for me. I was just born, by this most beautiful of tombs.

THE REAPARECIDA

I came to Mahdia, where I'm finding great peace these days, thanks to you, my daughter. You were the one who dragged me along, even though I proposed it. Your enthusiasm convinced me that it'd be the right destination. We brought one backpack between the two of us. There were two outfits inside, two pairs of pyjamas, two toothbrushes, some makeup, and I stuck the kisses I never gave you inside, dear. I wanted to give them to you all at once at the station while we were waiting for the school group we'd planned the trip with. Besides us and our friends from the Arabic school, the Tunis-Mahdia bus carried a conventional little Tunisian family. The children squealed, the mother shouted unenthusiastically, and the father tried taking a disinterested nap. I was sitting between him and his large wife who, when she wasn't shouting, tinkered with an evidently new cellphone. The woman smelled like jasmine. Everyone in this bizarre country smells like jasmine. Even I smell like that bright flower here. And they say I usually smell like pain, like chrysanthemum.

My kisses, the ones I'd kept for you, complained in the meantime, crammed in the bottom of the backpack. I wanted to cover your dry face with their motherly heat. But it was too soon, I had to wait a little while. To distract myself, I pushed them down even further, cruelly. It wasn't time yet. First I had to finish writing you everything, telling you everything, freeing me once and for all from the shadows of the past.

We slept, ate, talked, we strolled around town. Early this morning, I saw you heading to the beach with a white-looking girl. With silent steps, I followed close behind you all. And now we're at the ocean, together, but distant. The girl dove immediately into the water. She vanished for some time. Finally she left us alone. You and I, Mar. A mother and her daughter. I looked around and only saw tombs. I was prepared. Maybe you had told me about this cemetery on the sea. For a while, tombs had been a destination for me. I carried them on my back like a turtle with its shelter. They're my home, my pain, but in some way they're also my greatest comfort. They've always been there, since the days when I cried on unknown tombs to ease the pain of Ernesto's loss. I carried you in the womb, Mar, and I cried inconsolably in a Roman cemetery. History had split apart. My cry was an attempt to put it back together.

It is very beautiful here in Mahdia. We're together, and the tombs peer out over the sea, like in that Serrat song, *A mí enterradme sin duelo entre la playa y el cielo*, bury me painlessly between the beach and the sky. Because there is no pain, no *duelo* in seeing the ocean every day of the year. You can survive death that way, believing that it's temporary. But Flaca is in Prima Porta, in Rome, and there's no ocean there. There death is certain, definite, irreversible. Unlike in Mahdia, there's no possibility of living again in the echo of the waves. I never would've expected to see someone die in Rome. People do other things in Rome. One dreams of making love in Rome, or marrying in Rome, or kissing the Pope's hand in Rome, even though I would never kiss the hand of a religious figure, not even the Pope. I no longer trust them. I don't like devout people anymore. At least not the ones in high places.

In Buenos Aires, many bishops knew about the desaparecidos. They knew that people were tortured in the heart of the bustling city. They knew of Esma and the other detention centers.

The apostolic *nuncio* played tennis calmly with Admiral Massera, and his fraternal friendship with the soldiers was well known. I've never been devout. Jesus seemed nice enough to me, a hippie with outlandish ideas, a streak of hooliganism or communism in him. Kind of like Flaca, like Ernesto. Jesus was next to them when they were debilitated in the *villas miserias*. I thought Jesus was blond. It turns out he had the face of the disinherited—our face. In Buenos Aires and in the rest of Argentina, almost no one in the church who mattered resembled him. They were vipers, not people. They committed torture in a way befitting a Christian and assassinated with the Our Father on their lips. Then there was the other church, the one my friend Osvaldo belonged to. He was in the villas miserias with Ernesto. They skinned Osvaldo alive in Esma. His unheard screams, only imagined, still roar inside me.

You plunged into the Mediterranean. I stayed alone between rocks and tombs. I started reading to pass that interval of solitude.

"Our men," the newspaper on my lap read, "are only caricatures." It was an article on the femicides in Ciudad Juárez. A young Mexican woman ravished, brutalized, killed for Lord knows what reason. A macabre game, perhaps. Every word in the article reminded me of Flaca's notepads. After her death, Santana and I found them throughout the house. Some writings, some scribbles, some drawings, some colorings. Every page was full. A few were surprisingly lucid. I wish you'd met her, my love, but it didn't happen. I can only reconstruct her words for you:

I'll choose death, Flaca wrote, *I'll ingest liters of corrosive detergent. I'll be gray when they find me, with rivulets of disinfectant on my face. Coma, hospital, and tubes ending in death. One end. Not the only one. I was finished some time ago. Since the day they loaded me in an unregistered Ford Falcon and separated me from Ernesto. He'd given me a Dylan album the day before. We made love after eating a cream cake. We were clueless. We should've been keeping watch, and instead we moaned the entire afternoon and almost through the night. We were*

young and, in that season of life, death doesn't seem like a likely alter-
native to happiness. Our friends, however, were on the edge of nervous
breakdowns. No one believed the organization could save them any-
more. The organization was no longer there. It was dissolved, liquefied.
I kept believing in it. I thought it would take care of us and let us
escape. We celebrated my birthday that day.

Only three days earlier, Marisela, a Montonera friend, had told
me, "You're crazy, Rosa. Haven't you realized where you live yet?"
Where did I live? In Buenos Aires, no? Marisela shook her head.
"Buenos Aires has changed, my friend." She had been in shock since
she'd seen a pair of glasses swimming in a pool of blood. The collective
had to meet. Marisela was someone who, as the hours and minutes
wore on, always got us fighting. That day she was half an hour late. In
the meantime, hell broke loose. The Fords sped crazily up and down the
block. Everything was in chaos, utter pandemonium. People, objects,
dust mites, everything in motion. Gunshots rang out. Marisela hid in
a courtyard. Someone let her inside. That was something that never
happened at the time. Shortly before entering the unknown house,
Marisela saw the collective director's glasses swimming in a red sea. She
was afraid, but she was able to communicate. I was senseless, though.
When they came to take me and Ernesto, I thought maybe it wouldn't
be as bad as they said and that people tended to imagine the worst. I
had the cyanide capsule with me. What could I do? Swallow it dry? A
heroic death? Like that hippie on the cross, Mary's son, who died for his
friends, who died for perfect strangers?

I wasn't able to swallow it. They made me spit my capsule out. No
martyr for the cause.

Mahdia. Me, you, and a white girl on the beach. Me, reading about
the femicides in Ciudad Juárez. Me, who can't see any difference
between Buenos Aires and Ciudad Juárez, who can't see differences between Flaca's pain and Maya's pain, the girl in the article.

"The medical report on Maya's death was clear," the journalist wrote. "She was a mixed-race girl, twelve years old, who was

beaten, strangled, and raped by two mercenaries. Bruises were present on the thighs and torso. Her right eye had been struck with a sharp, pointed object. At the time of her death, she wore a teal tutu and a T-shirt with a smiling Donald Duck. Cigarette burns were found on her skin."

Cigarette burns, like Flaca at Esma. She'd written it in her notepads. But it was the *picana* that replayed obsessively in every description, every lived excerpt.

My first picana wasn't at Esma, she'd written. *It was in another place. Maybe at the air force base... I don't know, it was somewhere with piss-colored walls. An awful place. Or perhaps I thought it was ugly because I was afraid. I remember the walls and a gargantuan space that seemed like a stage. It was like the stage of the Rosario Theater, where I danced for the first time. I did Odette there, the stage adaptation. My knees trembled and I forgot how to stay en pointe. I was sixteen. My instructor, Mrs. Gloria Campora, flicked me twice on the cheek and said, "Fool." I danced divinely. A splendid Odette.*

I pined for Mrs. Campora in the piss-colored place. She wasn't there. There was only me on a grimy stage, me and an excessive number of brutes. They shouted disconnected phrases. Daughter of a whore, filthy Montonera, commie piece of shit. Floodlights blinded me, but they put a hood over my head nonetheless, the infamous capucha. *They bound me everywhere. I was nude and exposed. My pubic hair, my fear, my breasts. Afterward, they screamed more violently. It was a classic script, violent thugs shouting obscenities. A horror film.*

They removed the capucha. It was the perfect moment to unleash my fear. The spectacle was predictable: someone with an open fly and an erect penis on full display. Multiple rape threats. Being raped didn't matter to me. I was more worried about the contraption I saw near the torturers. They put a shade over my eyes so I couldn't see. I felt a hand. A hand that sweetly stroked my hair. Terror. Something I didn't expect. No one yelled anymore. Just that sweet hand on my hair. "If you talk, nothing will happen to you." I didn't expect the hand, the whisper, the pleasing voice. It was a beautiful, fake voice, like a radio broadcaster's. I was afraid.

What could I have confessed? I didn't know anything. I worked in the villas miserias. I danced. They wouldn't have believed me. They wanted names, dates, places, plans. I had nothing to give them. Wooden table. Me on top of it. Nude, always. Tied, always. More insults. Another table. The sensation was like wire mesh. They splashed water on me. Those sons of bitches wanted to make me feel more pain with every electric shock. They kept giving it to me, like a cutlet in oil. I sizzled everywhere. Bowels, eyes, nose, vagina, lips, torso, big toes. I lost my senses. When I awoke, they began again. It was one session, maybe the longest. They threw me in a cell. "Don't drink," they said and left me there for a while.

There was a guy, a man, or maybe a ghost. He didn't speak. He shook. I thought I would've preferred being raped. At least I expected that. When it happened, months later, I didn't feel much pain. I was almost cooperative with the green, the soldier who climbed on top of me. In the cell that first day, I heard the screams of the others tortured after me. I also heard the shouts of my companions as they were subjected to their torture sessions. I never entirely got used to it. It's horrible hearing a man slaughtered. I was alone in that piss-colored place. They took the trembling man immediately. I had no one, not even that ghost to take my hand. At Esma when I was in the sótano *there was always a shoulder I could lean on, someone who supported me in our absurd predicament, in the moment when they slaughtered another human being. I felt powerless. I couldn't save anyone. I couldn't save myself.*

I liked remembering Flaca's language. A savory language. Her Spanish flowed from the heights of the Andes, contaminated. Adulterated with the sweetness of Cervantes's dialect. It drifted like a comet between confused and intact letters. Like you, Mar, Flaca was a puzzle of sounds. And maybe like me. We speak the language of the frontier, of continuous crossings. How many languages are within us? Do you know, my sweet girl? I can guess, but I don't really know how many languages we're made of. Certainly the ancestral Indian language is inside us, the language of Coatlaxopeuh, of fertility. Then there is the language of history, Spanish exported with blood and deceit. But in our mouths it changed. I feel it. We refined and animated it. It is no longer the language rolled up by the compact consonants of the world's beginning. It becomes air and stars, sun and moon. It becomes flesh. It lives. It becomes something else, a secret language spoken since childhood, a language to communicate with the angels.

How many languages did Flaca speak? In the end, not even she knew anymore, my poor friend. She sputtered. The tragedy made her permanently lose the ability to speak with any coherence. In moments of calm, she wrote in her notebooks. They held her mouth open, my poor Flaca, and poured sperm and cigarette butts inside. She wrote it in her notebooks. She often drew her mouth filled with trash. It was as though they had cut out her tongue. When she spoke in Rome, I struggled to recognize her. I had to watch for a while to make sure it was truly her. It wasn't my Flaca from before, from more beautiful times. It was an altogether different woman, someone I didn't understand well. The bastards had stolen her sounds. They had robbed her of everything. Poor Flaca couldn't even shout or condemn. *Con cara fea le han cortado su alma, su voz. No tiene voz, mi Flaca.* With hideous faces they ripped out her soul, her voice. She didn't have a voice anymore, my Flaca.

Now I, Miranda, your mother, a woman, write. I transform my cry into a language, into rebellion. Before, I was out of focus. Your mother, Miranda, the poetess, was blurry. Almost useless. I couldn't see myself or make myself seen. Now that I've told you about Flaca, my greatest love, my image reappears. I am here, a *reaparecida*. I feel magisterial. Soon your mother will give you all the kisses she crammed into her backpack.

Our path, yours and mine, must now face the sun.

THE PESSOPTIMIST

Vehicles cruised on the street toward the *Istunka*, the bludgeon fest.

The street was filled with Mogadishu's people. A blaze of vans, Fiats, Land Rovers, *hajikamsin*, public buses. People were gathered like ripe grape clusters and happily overflowing on poorly tarmacked roads.

"Think about it, Zuhra, the Italians boast so much about having paved the streets, but in all honesty they're like big blocks of Swiss cheese. Like everything else they made, I mean. From Mogadishu to Afgooye, the holes were little more than pitch."

The memories rolled through Maryam Laamane's mind. A determined, emphatic, poignant stroll. Sitting on the wicker mat in Rome, in 2006, Maryam could still make out the sound of the seventies, the sound her shoulder blades made every time Hirsi's modified 500 went up against one of the holes the Italians hadn't cared to plug.

It was a great trip, except her cousin's wife, Manar, almost ruined it with an announcement about Bushra's son.

Yes, a decidedly good journey had brought Howa and Maryam to the Afgooye Istunka. The fresh breeze that entered through the small car windows cooled them, and belting their favorite songs wasn't a bad touch. Maryam Laamane liked music, but her tastes were different from those of her friend. Howa preferred the Italian melodic school. Maryam, on the other hand, was all about syncopated, modern rhythms. She liked the Americans. She liked Sam Cooke and Wilson Pickett. Their voices didn't sound foreign to her. She didn't understand anything they were saying, but she figured her skin couldn't have been that far removed from those notes.

Maryam mangled more than she sang. She mumbled the basic melodies and made up the words entirely, but the girl gave it her all. In her own way, she tried repeating everything her idols said. She imagined herself with them, in a rhinestone dress on a gilded stage, in front of many perfumed people who were there to see her. The theater in her dreams was always the Apollo in Harlem. There was a large photograph of that theater in the record store near the American embassy. Maryam was fascinated by it. When she was sad, she only had to think about the Apollo to make her smile again. The owner of the store, the only guy in all of Mogadishu who sold imported records, had told her something and Maryam engraved it on her heart: "That's where they make dreams, girl. The dreams are black like the color of our skin. Free dreams. Do you know what that means?"

Those were times of independence and still no one knew what being free truly meant. Maryam shook her head, clutching the vinyl she'd just purchased to her chest. The owner merely smiled. Concerned, Maryam wondered why the hell he didn't explain it to her. The owner had a nice long, pointy beard. He stroked it casually. "It's all in a *yeaah!*"

Maryam was perplexed. "I didn't catch that," she said.

"You are free only if you say *yes, yes, yeaah*, without anyone telling you to. Do you understand? When you hear a *yeaah* in a song, put your whole heart into saying it. That's your liberty. Remember that."

That's why every time she muttered, "Bring It on Home to Me" she shouted all the song's *yeaahs* with exaggerated fury. She liked that song because of the love it contained. Years later, in the dark ages of Siad Barre, when her husband was persecuted and they were in the government's bad graces, humming the song was all she needed to stop feeling pain and to believe in life again.

She and Elias were still together. He called her *Darling* and she told him *I love you*. The dictatorship formed around them. When they lived in Somalia, the dictatorship had been christened "scientific socialism," then after their exile, Siad Barre's socialism had miraculously become "capitalism," aided by a retinue of corrupt Italians and Americans. That was the age of the Garoe-Bosaso expressway, when Somalia was doused in toxic waste. The dictatorship changed form, but not substance. There was too much suffering from the start. To resist, Maryam sang her freedom in a *yeaah*. She sang for Elias and Zuhra, too.

On that muggy day in the seventies, Maryam didn't think she'd have to deal with a frightening military dictatorship. Maryam didn't think anything. She didn't know, for instance, that she would marry the son of the much-feared seamstress Bushra. She didn't know that she would love him more than she loved herself, that she would have a daughter named Zuhra, that labor would last forty-nine hours, that exile was waiting around the corner, that those impertinent *jinn* in Rome would cast a malign spell on her with a transparent bottle, that when she was old she would participate in Alcoholics Anonymous meetings, and that thanks to a therapist named Rosanna she would save her life and her daughter's as well. Her mind was free that day, like the full-throated *yeaahs* she sang.

Manar didn't know any songs and was irritated by the girl's explosion of notes. Howa joined in with the Sanremo harmonies of Gianni Morandi and Rita Pavone. Italian spilled from Howa's lips in words that were clear, crystalline, uninflected. Howa's voice was trained. Reading the Holy Quran aloud had given her lungs the dignity of an operatic soprano. The devotion that shone through her voice quieted the entire audience, Maryam Laamane included. Even if the material was profane Sanremo diddies, the sacred erupted resolutely from Howa Rosario's throat.

As she sang of love holy and profane, Hirsi's 500 arrived at its destination after an hour and forty-five minutes. The women aired out their sweaty clothes once they'd stepped outside. Their thighs were freed from the glue of perspiration and the many hours spent in Hirsi's ride. A sudden and suspect breeze cooled them. Maryam felt it nip at her vulva. She liked it.

"They say there are jinn hidden in the wind," Manar said nastily. She had guessed the meaning of Maryam's semi-open mouth. The girl took off her hat without saying anything. Embarrassment warmed her cheeks. She felt like a fire.

"The jinn love young girls' virginity," Manar added maliciously. Jinn or boys?

Maryam's mind was in turmoil like her heart. Bushra's son had returned from his continental tour. Soon she would have to meet him—she already hated him—and soon she'd be forced to marry him. She'd promised her friend Howa. It wasn't like her to renege on her word. The lip she'd bitten moments before started bleeding again. Maryam tried stopping it with a tissue. The seamstress Bushra's son would be her future.

Maryam decided to focus on the present and the event they were about to attend. Her heart beat quickly at the thought of an unanticipated encounter. She wanted to track down the bicycle boy in that throng, the one who had taken her senses away with his unbuttoned, provocative, beige linen vest. "He is my present," Maryam said to herself. She began whistling something in the style of Nat King Cole.

Afgooye, the city of cut tongues. There was a story about that city. They said that Mohamed Abdulle Hassan, the one the English called "Mad Mullah" and who Somalis called master, *saydka*, had wanted to punish the betrayal and impertinence of the citizens in that pigsty of the world. He'd cut their tongues out. Neatly, mercilessly. Saydka didn't want to hear impertinences anymore.

He wasn't the kind to take a joke. He'd fought the English and Italians, he had thick skin. Saydka was against imperialism, but also against those who opposed him. The people in Afgooye stopped talking for some time. Later their tongues reappeared in their mouths like flowers, more cautious and wary. No one spoke nonsense in Afgooye anymore. The memory of Saydka and his sharp blades was too fresh to be forgotten overnight.

The Istunka took place on the periphery of the city, on the river's left bank, in a land beaten by the searing sun. The trees were few, but those few were swarmed by the newly ravenous masses. Under every frond were automobiles, carts, men, women, children. Everyone wore strange wet rags on their heads. There were also three ambulances and a heavy security force. Everything was set for the fest to begin.

The festival revolved around the cane fight, the actual Istunka. Two contending teams had to battle it out in a melee using bludgeons of smooth, light branches. The group that made their rival retreat won. On the first day, none of the contenders could call themselves victorious. The goal of the fight was to make the enemy retreat, but initially they settled for a few meters. Two and a half hours wasn't enough to declare a winner. At least three times that duration was needed. The first day was about making calculations. The teams evaluated the weak points, the strong, the trump cards, the unpredictables, the certainties.

It was also on that day that Maryam Laamane searched among the trees and parked cars for a boy with a beige linen shirt. The canes began filling the scorching morning air with their powerful hisses. From ten o'clock to one, it was open war. The first minutes were brutal, blows, blows, and still more blows. There were no rules, save that of marking one's territory with brute force. In the opening minutes, members of the strongest group bared their chests and bragged. The brutality never lasted long. The weaker group slyly pulled back until they retreated. The short break allowed them to reconsider their strategy and come up with a plan.

There was an etiquette to follow for these first offensives. The strongest managed to avoid humiliating their enemy. The weakest avoided humiliating themselves. For this reason, the retreat was always accepted without issue on both sides. Rare were the cases when the winning group chased the losing group down. Someone would've had to attract serious animosity for this to happen. These few meters were enough to declare a ranking. One didn't have to totally humiliate the enemy. In the long run, this could be counterproductive. It wasn't a given that the winner of the first few minutes was the winner of the entire competition.

The Istunka, despite the use of brute force, was a highly strategic competition. Blows were never delivered at random. Every move had a purpose in the game's dynamic. The second half hour was dedicated, not by chance, to the rematch. Often it was in this phase that one could guess who would win the interminable struggle for power. One could even assist the clamorous turnabouts. In the dry heat, fatigue was quickly evident and strength alone was no longer enough. In the minutes that followed, mind and strategy took over.

The competition ended right before the noon prayer, only to resume again the next day. Like gluttons, everyone ran to show devotion to Allah and consume the food their stomachs demanded.

Afgooye was notable for its restaurants in the *tukul*, where they served *bamia* and goat meat with hot rice, a specialty that made people lick their lips. Maryam Laamane adored the coconut *bisbas* that was served as a condiment. Coconut-flavored bisbas was her passion. The mixture of spices gave her courage.

People gathered in the tukul, but they were lucky if they found a free space. They were good-mannered as they ate and drank hot, spiced tea to aid digestion. They had to hurry, for the best part of the fest was coming up. After all the rice and goat meat, Maryam Laamane felt heavy and weary. Her eyelids were closing.

As soon as she'd shut her eyes, the boy with the beige shirt passed in front of her. He wasn't wearing the futah that day, but khaki pants and a white bush jacket. He was buttoned-up, his hair parted to one side and his wide forehead plain as day. His eyes were hidden by a pair of dark glasses.

Hirsi signalled to the boy with the beige shirt. Maryam Laamane plummeted into a fantasyland. The boy approached the table.

"Manar, Howa, I'd like to introduce the son of Bushra the seamstress, Elias Majid."

Howa quaked. Maryam didn't wake up from her daydream. She would've been happy to discover that her love and her sacrifice were one. Without knowing it, she'd fallen in love with the promise she made to Howa Rosario.

"When you were born, Elias was holding my shoulder. He was with me for all forty-nine hours, and when the *umulisso* saw your little head, I remembered the Istunka, the day your father and I decided to marry," Maryam Laamane said into the recorder. In that moment, the woman was hit by a wave of odors. It was her uterus fighting to free the girl. Zuhra didn't want to leave that warm uterine bed. She was doing just fine inside her mama. Outside, it seemed too dangerous. "You weren't wrong, my treasure." The climate in Mogadishu wasn't the best. The military dictatorship was in full swing. Nothing would ever be the same again.

At the time, Elias hardly worked. His models, his fabrics were considered subversive by the proletariat order. Too sparkly and brilliant, too fluttery and with too many rhinestones. Capitalist decadence. Imperialist waste. In little time, the Somali textile industry and artisanal designers began adjusting to the rigid state. Everything became uniform and devoid of imagination. Divisions and standardization. Homogenous molasses that made most people's stomachs turn. Mogadishu became the city of walls. The boys of the Ubax youth circles had to learn to be good patriots. They marched. The great Proletariat had advanced. In the Ubax circles, they learned to pose theatrically. They learned to be stopgaps of global communism. They learned to be an eyelid of Marx, an eyelash of Engels, a lip of Comrade Mao, or the tip of Lenin's nose. They sang around the world and came home tired of posing as the revolution's useless joints.

Elias didn't like being a joint and he certainly didn't like sewing those uniforms. He felt his art dying every minute. For the art, and partly because he was about to have a child, he joined secret opposition groups to the Barre regime. They felt conned by the word "communism." They'd read Gramsci, they'd believed in Fanon's struggle, they missed the years of the SYL, the youth league in which everyone reveled in their freedom from colonialism's yoke. Elias had even invented a song about Howa Taqo, the woman who died during an anti-Italian demonstration. An arrow had pierced her. Her heart was lacerated. She continued running for her independence, although the arrow was lethal. Howa was his heroine, and when there were hot spells at night, Elias dreamed of stitching together the most beautiful dress in the world for her. A burial dress. A dress she could wear on Judgment Day.

When Elias joined the plot, Maryam Laamane had intuitively known that her husband was in danger and that they would throw him in prison. She was too heavy to move. The girl—she always believed she was carrying a girl in her womb—kicked spiritedly. Maryam was in the final trimester; her water was about to break, but she wanted to run like when she lightheartedly followed dreams and the flights of falcons, when she was a straw of a girl. Back then, she could run like her heroes, the *alibesten*. She couldn't anymore. She was too heavy. She simply called for others. She sent for Auntie Salado, the tough one who almost never smiled. She was always by her side during that unusual period. Her husband, though, was lost in conspiracies and political delusions.

She didn't think delusions could transform her Elias, so curious and sweet, into a dry, mean vegetable. But that's what he became. And she, Maryam Laamane, was heavy with child. When Elias came to her door, Maryam realized she hadn't seen him in twenty days. He slept in his boutique and dedicated all of his time to the conspiracy. He wore a beige shirt, like the first time she'd laid eyes on him. He hadn't shaved that day. His beard had grown rebellious and randomly from his pointed chin.

"Labor started a few minutes ago. The umulisso was called."

Elias squeezed her hand. Elias's hands were sweaty and slippery. Maryam felt a tremendous contraction. She let go of his hand. She burned. It wasn't a good sign. Was she losing it? Maybe her daughter was in a rush to get out and meet her papa so that he could see her at least once. Maryam had never thought about it until then, but it was true. The girl was coming before her time so she could meet her father. Yes, she was losing it.

"They're looking for you, Elias. You have to go."

"They mentioned Italy to me," he calmly replied. Short breaths. Curt words. Veiled glances. Contractions.

"I'll wait until she's born." He took her hand. This time it wasn't the fire that Maryam was expecting, but a soft, firm grip. She knew it well. It was the same one that had won her heart that day in Afgooye in the seventies.

Maryam spoke into the recorder. Through it she hugged her daughter, Zuhra. These stories were the maternal love that she, Maryam Laamane, hadn't had the chance to show. With her thoughts and words she went back to the distant day when her and Elias's fates united. That day, Maryam was awakened by the sound of an alarmed Howa Rosario. They were in Afgooye, the sun was hot, the seventies were being sold and lived like a myth around the world. Maryam tried recounting everything she felt into the recorder. She wanted to tell her daughter every detail of her splendid love. She wanted to tell Zuhra that, despite the embitterment afterward, taking a chance on that emotion was worthwhile. She wanted to convince her daughter, outraged by her negligence, that when the moment was right, men could be some of the most miraculous creatures.

Maryam dozed off and Howa tugged at her. The coconut bisbas and rice had calmed Maryam's digestion. Howa Rosario's tugging was anything but calm.

"Wake up, dummy, wake up."

Maryam opened one eye eventually, slowly. This irritated Howa, who yanked her even harder.

"Hey!"

"You won't believe who just came to the table. It's him, the seamstress's son!"

Maryam, who had never seen him, felt curiosity and terror.

"He asked us to dance."

The people, satiated by treats from the *Koonfur* region of the country, transitioned to the afternoon songs and dances. Between the women's *buraanbur* dances and the chitchat, there was nothing but babble in the city's grand plaza. Young people were waiting to parade their lust in dance. Maryam waited to get a glimpse of the man with the beige shirt. With her other eye she cast a sidelong glance at the seamstress's son, whom she would soon marry.

She dreamed of the moment when her gaze would rest lecherously on an unfastened shirt. The *kabeebey* on display, the young people's dance in the Lower Shebelle. A dance in which men and women, between jokes and bantering, searched for one another, found one another, loved and hated one another. It was all in a rhythmic turn. Dressed in their traditional wear, everyone got in a circle, men and women alternating. Each man had to have a woman on both sides.

At the center of the circle, two boys kept the rhythm on medium-sized drums next to a couple of guitarists and a boy banging pieces of iron together, whom Maryam couldn't see. The circle moved, the people sang and clapped their hands. In the circle, along with the musicians, there was a dancer. Her body moved to the beat. The woman was in the center of the circle, which shook with music. She brandished her buttocks and breasts. She coiled her arms like sliding serpents. The woman was like the waves of their ocean. The entire circle was rapt. Then the music suddenly stopped and so did her undulations. The dance ended with the girl moving and delicately resting her hand on the shoulders of the chosen dancer. He would enter the circle next and move as she'd done. Men and women cherry-picked their partners. The kabeebey was a game of seduction. Maryam had a burning desire to dance.

"You're too young," Howa Rosario said.

Manar stayed Howa's hand. She gave Maryam the green light.

"She has a pretty dress on," Manar said. "She'll be well-received in the circle, she'll find the man she's looking for in there, and they'll dance."

After the dance she would look for the seamstress Bushra's son and offer herself as his spouse. A promise was a promise, she couldn't back down. She at least wanted to give the boy with the beige shirt a dance, a dance of untainted love.

The boy with the beige shirt took her hand. His grip was soft and firm. He was asking her for the things every girl desired: marriage, a wedding, security, love, children, status.

Maryam was sad.

"I wanted to run far away and follow wherever it was a falcon went."

Maryam explained her friend's story, her promise, to the beautiful stranger she wanted to marry. "The seamstress Bushra's son will be my husband. I can't do anything about it."

He gave her a kiss and whispered his name. Maryam left with that name lodged in her ears: Elias.

"Think, Zuhra, no one had ever told me that the seamstress's son was named Elias Majid, no one told me the details of my marriage. I only found out eight months later, when they'd already given me as a wife to the seamstress's son who, as far as I knew, I'd never met.

Elias came to our gate every day. And every day I shooed him away. Everyone laughed then, especially Howa Rosario. She always said, 'My friend, you don't have to sacrifice yourself for me. It's stupid to sacrifice love.' But I was stubborn."

When the *nikah* came, the marriage contract, Maryam Laamane waited for her husband in the nuptial room. He hadn't shown up all morning. The people had partied, eaten, drank. Many had given her their best wishes. She felt like she was at a funeral. "I missed my falcon friends. I closed my eyes in my room and saw the scenes of my kabeebey again, that interwoven dance he and I did in the circle of young people in Afgooye." That day at the Istunka had been one of her life's best. Lying on the bridal bed, she wondered if this night would be the worst.

Suddenly, the door opened and Elias appeared in a cloud. At least it seemed that way to Maryam Laamane. He wore the same beige shirt.

Maryam ran toward him.

"Elias, please, take me away. I know you came to save me. Please take me away from here."

"I can't," he said, holding back his laughter.

"You can't? Where did your courage go?"

"It isn't a question of courage, you know, it's that I've just married you. I want to be alone with you now. My mother, Bushra, told me the party was fun. A shame I missed it."

"During labor, I thought again of those scenes from my youth. Of how different Somalia was. Us young people playing at seduction and dancing. Young people today don't have time to dance. The war has eaten up their dreams. After forty-nine hours, you came out of me. You made me suffer for forty-nine hours. You didn't want to leave my warm uterus. When you came, he looked at you. He caressed your bloody neck softly and lovingly.

You were so small, Zuhra, and already so loved. His hand slid over you and over me. A plane was waiting to take him to Italy. We would see him again, but by then our life together was done. This is why I lived, dear Zuhra. It was worth it."

Yes, living is worthwhile, whatever the cost. And so is loving more and more. Maryam Laamane pressed stop. Fragments of her were now engraved on the tape.

The memory of her friend Howa Rosario had accompanied Maryam in that epoch of memories and stories, but now the woman felt she had enough strength to run by herself. There were no falcons in the Roman skies. She couldn't see the stars very well at night. Rome was dark and sometimes terrifying. But her daughter, Zuhra, would be there to illuminate her universe. Even without her friend of a time long since past, Maryam Laamane knew that she would be okay.

THE FATHER

Everyone wanted to know about Majid and Bushra.

"Where did Majid go?"

"Did he come back to Bushra?"

"Did they ever make love?"

"Did they die in the end?"

"The end, how did it end?"

Dear Zuhra, perhaps you wanted me to tell my story. You may have wanted to know what your father did, which places he visited, how many people he met, what routes he traveled. I know I told you another story. I couldn't help it. I was a failure. A designer of nothing. I was incapable of properly loving the women who loved me. I was incapable of sharing my days with you, my daughters. I regret the lost time, though I don't regret putting you two in this world. I wanted to show you that your story as a woman is tied to a more ancient story. I don't know if it will be useful to you. Something in me hopes it will be. I digressed, I know. I've never been good at telling stories. I can't do anything, really. But I love you, daughter of mine.

Bushra, Majid, Elias. One story. My own. Yours, too, my daughter. Everyone's story. Memory.

"Only lice are treated that way. You squash them and forget them."

Bushra was speaking with a cousin who lived in Italy. She was old and wrinkled then, my Bushra, not the energetic woman you've heard of to this point. She was in a puny public telephone booth. Majid still hadn't come back to her. It was 1990. She hadn't heard from her cousin in years. Yet in those twilight days, as she waited for civil war, Bushra tried talking to her relatives abroad. Everyone, no exceptions. She wanted to prepare her family who had gotten out for something devastating. Not even she was adequately prepared. Her cousin was very worried.

"On the BBC they say a civil war is about to blow up. Oh god, abbayo, how will they do it?" The cousin's lament filled the small booth with anguish. Bushra didn't think she could bare it for a minute more. That insufferable woman pushed too hard and, despite Bushra's weight, she made herself small and invisible. She had to end the phone call. She had to find an excuse. She said goodbye to her cousin in a rush, "Bad signal…a bad signal." Myriad justifications, the line, groceries to get, fear.

When she left, she saw eyes watching her suspiciously. All the eyes in Mogadishu were like that then. No one trusted the stranger next to them anymore. You glimpsed tomorrow's enemy in each person's face. Itching for revenge. Leery eyes. Once, like everyone else, Bushra enjoyed going to public places. There were phone booths that connected the world, lines that let you feel like part of a complex universe. You could speak with the entire world at the post office. Moscow, New York, Kuala Lumpur, Bamako, Rome. You could send big packages and pick them up from the post office too. The trafficking of dreams. She picked up Elias's fabrics, mine, and the cassettes Maryam had recorded. That place made her feel alive. And like most people, Bushra didn't have a telephone in the house. She wasn't rich. What did she need one for? No one would've called her. Majid least of all. He had vanished long ago, a man in pursuit of his own destiny. Bushra wasn't resentful. Rather, she waited. Sooner or later they would meet again. When she needed to call someone, she went to the post office and spent her pretty shillings, but there was nothing else to say except, "Thanks be unto God, *Alhamdulillah*." What did she need her own telephone for? She had thousands at her disposal. She was never short a phone line and the globe stretched out at her feet. What more did she need?

Then things changed.

Elias didn't send her fabrics anymore. Maryam stopped recording her voice on cassettes, her lovely voice telling Bushra how strange Italy was, how they treated Somalis, how the fruit of her loins, Zuhra, was turning out. Oh, how she missed the voice of that madwoman Maryam Laamane. The girl recounted many things on her cassettes. She did it for her, Bushra, who didn't know how to read or write. She would've liked reading and writing. Listening to Maryam was a little like being at the cinema. The stories chased one another drunkenly. And she drank of the life Maryam Laamane had tasted with her own lips.

Then one day, no more cassettes from Maryam. No more cinema. Nothing, *eber*. Maryam was abandoned by Elias. The standard script. The son following in the father's footsteps. The son abandoning a woman as his father had done. The son with a pain too great to share, like his father. Farewell, wife. Farewell, marriage vows. Farewell, life. Maryam Laamane alone in Rome, Bushra alone in Mogadishu. No more fabrics from Elias. No dreams from Maryam. At first Bushra wondered: "Is my son dead?" The speculation hardly convinced her. Elias, she felt, would die after her. He couldn't precede her. He was a good boy, Elias, but not an angel, and only angels precede their parents in death. God loves them too much to leave them suffering in this immense ocean of pain. When she didn't get Maryam's cassettes anymore, she knew the girl was suffering. *She doesn't have my nerves*, Bushra thought.

Once these absences were solidified, she only used the post office for sporadic telephone calls, a useless refill of words. The post changed radically for Mogadishans too, not only for Bushra. It wasn't a benign place anymore, but the back end of a taxing wait.

You spoke with foreigners because, while everyone else watched, hope led people to pack their suitcases and leave Somalia, potentially forever. The post office regurgitated people every day. That day, though, more than most. There wasn't much time, not much time at all until war. The eve, the countdown to upheaval. Everyone stood in line in front of those tiny booths. Everyone was strung out and alienated. Those were the last days of peace and, in the days preceding the chaos, the most perceptive people sought an escape route from a horror no one wanted to imagine. The watchwords were tickets, visa, plane, life. Everyone was hooked up to a telephone, trying to contact a relative abroad who might somehow fix the situation for them.

"Lice, we're only lice," Bushra said to her cousin and hung up.

The Mogadishans' movements, Bushra thought, had become distillated frenzy. They all ran toward a possible salvation. They tried saving their own skin. Bushra, despite the torment dogging her heart, was the only one not to have changed her stride. She was old and walked slowly toward the threshold to her home. Mogadishu floundered around her. The people's discordant steps upset her delicate stomach. Only she, an elderly woman, kept her stride as before. A peaceful gait. Bushra looked like a cripple. She may well have been. She shouldered her way forward, as though wanting to challenge life, but maybe she was too well-behaved to do so. She hid, dancing as she did. When she walked, Bushra did one of the city folk's tribal dances. She pushed against the wind. Her shoulder thrusts took her places. Still, shutting the door behind her was always a relief.

The city, that haughty phoenix on the sea, had been in this state for a few months. Barre had tugged the rope of power too hard. He had risked more than he should have. No one warned him that the Berlin Wall was in shambles, the Soviet Union had dissolved, the needle was no longer tipped in favor of the black world, and that soon someone would give it to him in the ass, the whole thing and without vaseline. Barre slumbered in his villa, deluding himself into thinking that he was still somebody. Only the Italians still paid their respects. There was still food to be scavenged by collaborating and, as you know, some Italians really like eating. Big Mouth and his ilk didn't know that they were already fucked. Barre didn't want to know that Somalis hadn't been afraid for some time.

On the day the Manifesto was signed, all cards were laid on the table. The Manifesto. Their Manifesto. The one all Somalis had in their hearts.

Bushra saw that sheet of paper for the first time one afternoon in May 1990. A thorny-haired boy named Juje chucked it by the *garees*. Bushra knew the boy well. He was from the same *laf*, from her same tribe, the same blood and bones. Bread of her same *qabila*. She'd seen his parents marry and then argue. She'd seen him crawl and then walk.

The paper the boy was waving in the wind with rabid pride was the Manifesto, a document written in Italian by 114 of Barre's opponents, who were requesting that the government step down to pave the way for democracy's return. The Manifesto. Their Manifesto. No clan, only nonviolent struggle, hope. The country's intellectuals shouted, the great elders, some of whom had worked for the nation's independence and were active in the SYL. Among the signatories were sultans, qabila leaders, imam, businessmen, and yes, some soon-to-be looters.

Bushra looked at the boy. She didn't know what to say. The people were tired of bowing their heads. War was seconds away. The boy had large, watery eyes. They contained vistas of pride. It was from watching, for the first time, so much rage in such a tiny body that Bushra knew banishing Barre would be easy. Getting them all to agree, however, was a titanic enterprise.

In July, the boy died in the stadium massacre. He'd gone like many young people to watch the start of the football championships. This was a time when inquiring eyes, the damned *jawasees*, regime spies, had invaded the city. Juje was the first in a long list of the dead. He'd gone to see his friends play football. Many young people, a lot of testosterone. More whistling than necessary. Mixed mutterings. Barely whispered slogans. They didn't yet have the strength to say the word *liberty*.

Bushra remembered the stadium massacre. She'd supported the head of that boy's mother. It spun without end, oh it spun, the poor mother's head. She shouted, "Allah, my child! Allah, my boy!" There is nothing that can match the strength of a woman who wants to stop the powerful stride of death. At first they thought it was a celebration. They had seen colors in the sky and heard noise in the background. The little children at home thought it was fireworks. Only the boys' mothers understood. Only the mothers cried. The boys' whistles and dissent in the stadium were heard throughout the city. But only the mothers knew they wouldn't come back again.

Was it you, Juje, who interrupted the president's speech? Was it you? Yes, maybe it was. You'd read the Manifesto. You believed in it. You couldn't listen to Big Mouth spew his lies anymore. You couldn't take it anymore, could you, Juje? Was it you who hooted at the president? You'd read the Manifesto. You believed in a better Somalia. His minions shook with anger. Their fingers on the triggers shook too. The Red Berets brought fire down on those boys. Aim, shoot, *bang*. And another: aim, shoot, *bang*. Again: aim, shoot, *bang*. Brain fragments on the bleachers. Blood on the walkway.

How many died with you, Juje? How many? The bodies were taken away. No one knew the exact count of the massacre of innocents. The first, not the last. Then the people who wrote the Manifesto were targeted, one by one, their sympathizers too. And those who had only crossed their paths. In July, Ismail Jumaale Ossoble died. He'd created the Manifesto. His friends cried loudly. They surrounded the airport. "We mustn't let them kidnap the corpse," they shouted. "They won't stop us from attending his funeral." All of Mogadishu wanted to be there. They defended the corpse. The Red Berets could've kidnapped it and thrown it to the warthogs of the Savannah. Bushra remembered going to the funeral. She saw heads to the horizon. She sobbed.

Three days later, she went to pick up Maryam Laamane from the airport. Maryam had alerted Shukri, a neighbor with a phone, that she would be arriving. Bushra wasn't surprised. "She wants to stop suffering." Maryam had strange signs on her face, lines of premature old age. Bushra didn't say anything to her. She caressed her head. She was pleased by her company. "Mogadishu has changed," was what she told her goddaughter.

Mogadishu was blind. There was an evening curfew. The regime's minions had the city in thrall. The rest of the terrors were thought to be bandits and ghosts.

At the end of the year, Bushra began hearing the hyenas plot.

She was sitting on a *gember*, shut in her house with people from her laf. She was sitting next to Maryam, who was on the prayer mat rattling off fatiha for everyone.

"Tomorrow, the hyenas descend upon the country," she said.

No one heard her. She'd spoken in a low voice.

The hyenas…she hadn't heard their strident calls since childhood. As a young girl, when she was bored, she listened to their conversations carried by the wind. She'd learned everything about their plans. In the densest forest, knowledge of the scoundrels' language was a gift from Allah. You could save the livestock and yourself. You slept calmly and contentedly. Every night Bushra heard the agitated words of those lowly beasts. Every night she would misdirect their cruelty. She'd warn her father and the others in the qabila. She'd lived in dense woodland since she was small. The hyenas were the bane of her daily existence. When the hyenas caused no more problems, she went to the city to design clothes and get married. No more hyenas.

That evening, at the end of the year, she heard these harsh voices again. They had returned. Without a doubt, they'd come back. They would descend on the city the next day.

She heard their plans. She heard their betrayals. She smelled their vile odor.

"Oh no," she shouted, "leave the children alone! Take whatever you want but don't touch the children."

The relatives who were with her in the room shook their heads. They thought she was insane. "*Waa ku dhufatay*, she's going crazy."

"No, friends. I'm sane. I'm well. I swear it. But the hyenas are returning. They are great in number. They'll hurt the children."

Someone reminded her that she wasn't in the woods anymore. They were in Mogadishu, the city, the capital, the one and only Xamar, and hyenas had never been spotted here. They told her to put aside once and for all her wood-dweller's language: that was what had caused Somalia to backslide.

Only Maryam approached her, asking, "How many hyenas are there?"

"Many, my love. Too many to count. They're not like the ones from before. These will never stop killing. These ones are never satiated."

"I understand," Maryam said.

"What? What do you understand, my girl?"

"Power is a woman who doesn't share."

Wardhiigley was shelled. Their house was taken by cannon shot. Their home was in the same neighborhood as the presidential residence. They paid the price for an annoying proximity. Power does not share. There can't be too many lions in a pack. Only one leader, one guide. So the leaders thought. No one wanted democracy anymore. Everyone wanted to become the new Big Mouth. Only power, force, and blood. The Manifesto was forgotten and with it, its ideals, all of its hopes.

Bushra heard the hyenas plotting every night. In every laf, a conspiracy. Games to double-cross the tribes. They were accused of nepotism, despotism, plots, and intrigues of every sort. Everyone looked after themselves. Weapons and devastation went hand in hand. Meanwhile, the city died. Meanwhile, the children suffered.

"Where are you going, Bushra? You can't go outside," her relatives enjoined. She was getting fed up. "I'm old, nothing can happen to me." Lame, she traversed the empty streets of her lost city. Big Mouth Siad Barre had gone away, exiled to Nigeria. And then he was stone dead. The rest of the city followed his lead. They were all dead by then. Blood continued flowing in their bodies out of sheer inertia. Siad had won. *Divide et impera*. He'd infected many people with his greedy thirst for power. With his cancer.

Bushra walked among the ruins. She saw horrors.

She saw a boy on the ground. Face covered in blood and sand. Torn uniform, a gaunt body. Wearing government colors. They had just shot him, a mortal wound. He should've been taken to the hospital right away. Instead, he was surrounded by militants with masked faces. One said, "I'll finish him, friends, leave it to me."

A woman in uniform skeptically approached the quasi-cadaver. "What's happening here?" she asked him. The boy began reciting the Quran. He was dying and nothing else came to mind. He bonded with those last words, that last *bismallah*. "What are you doing here, where are you from?" The boy did not have eyes to look. He barely whispered, "I'm from Puntland, but I'm not a government worker. I did it for the money. The militiamen here are paid well. Please, brothers, don't kill me. Please…*waa lai siray*, they tricked me." Then darkness. End.

The hyenas yelped in laughter. "Yes, more blood. Kill each other. More blood, Somalis. For us, we feed on it. You're all so stupid. That's fine by us."

Bushra realized that seeing people die wasn't like in the movies. On-screen, people closed their eyes, let their head dip to one side, their hand to the other, and left themselves exposed to the camera's eye. Dying was easy on film, child's play.

"Is he dead?" Bushra asked. She didn't know why she was asking something with such an obvious answer.

"You don't see it, *ajuza*. You don't see that his brain has tarnished my new shirt? Ajuza, fool."

"Why did you do it?" Bushra insisted.

The hyenas surrounded her. "Kill the old woman. She asks too many questions. We don't like her. Kill her."

The man, who was the same age as Juje, pointed his AK-47 at the old woman's forehead.

Bushra looked at him inquisitively.

"Leave that woman alone. She's not from the Marehan tribe. Leave her be. She's from your own laf, you can't kill her…," a voice said, emerging out of an indistinct chorus.

Was it the hoarse, high-pitched voice of a woman or a man? Bushra looked in that direction. A sundress. She recognized that dress. It was hers. It was one of the ones Elias had sewn with waxed cotton in the Congo. She was very fond of that dress. She hadn't been able to find it. And to think that she'd searched everywhere. Here now, after so many years, she saw it on Majid. It was the voice of her husband, her lost friend. Hoarse voice and shrill notes. The voice of a man and a woman.

The cold iron of the AK-47 stayed on her forehead, but the bloodlust had cooled. The boy was ashamed of frightening a woman from his clan. It was possible that she'd even cradled him as a child.

"Take that old woman away. We don't want you old people around here. Next time we'll kill you."

Majid, dressed as a woman, took the hand of his wife of long ago. She was flooded by his abnormal warmth. The hand, the heat of that man-woman, made her mad with desire. She didn't think it was possible at her age to feel it. The hand told her a story. A bus in the desert and a smell of ancient war. An evildoing and a shackled love.

"Let's go to Elias's house," Majid said to Bushra.

Bushra responded affirmatively and they walked down a path that neither of them could fully see.

This is where I end, my love. I don't know how to tell you the rest. I'm still waiting for my parents. I'd like for you to meet them when they arrive.

EPILOGUE

Mom speaks to me in our mother tongue, a noble Somali whose every vowel makes sense. Our mother language. Frothy, blunt, intrepid. In Mom's mouth, Somali becomes honey.

I wonder if my mother's native tongue can be my mother, if Somali sounds the same in our mouths. How do I speak this mother language of ours? Am I as good as her? I doubt it. Actually, I know I'm not. I'm not on Maryam Laamane's level

No. I, Zuhra, daughter of Maryam, am distant from every nobility. I don't feel like an ideal daughter. I stumble uncertainly in my confused alphabet. The words are twisted. They reek of asphalt streets, cement, and the margins. Every sound, in fact, is contaminated. I try all the same with her to speak the language that unites us. In Somali, I knew the comfort of her womb. In Somali, I heard the only lullabies she sang to me. I dreamed my first dreams in Somali. But then, all the time, in every conversation, word, breath, the other mother peeks through. The one that breastfed Dante, Boccaccio, De André, and Alda Merini. The Italian that I grew up with and which I hated at times because it made me feel like an outsider. The vinegary Italian of neighborhood markets, the sweet Italian of radio broadcasters, the serious Italian of university lectures. The Italian that I write.

I wouldn't know how to choose any other language for

writing, for casting out my soul. Written Somali isn't the same thing. It can't be, not for me. I barely know how to write in Somali at all. Some words, perhaps, but I screw up the script. Written Somali has a very unusual history. It was born in 1972, they say. Or maybe 1973? I don't know the exact date, but I do know that it's still very young. Mom doesn't know how to write it. She got out before Barre's literacy campaigns started.

What a horrible man, that Siad Barre! He killed, molested, tortured. Many remember him only because he introduced the Somali alphabet. "He gave us a written language," a handful of demented people tell you with foolish enthusiasm in their dry mouths. They forget the harassment, the hardship, the homicides, the threats. They only remember the alphabet. "The warlords killed even more than he did. In eighteen years of civil war, they've carried out far worse massacres." But Barre was the one who signed off on the first dirty massacres with the red of Somali blood. Accursed Siad paved the way for today's disaster. Somalis forget that the speech of the written language was born before Siad Barre. He gathered the fruit of other people's labors. In the alphabet's case, he appropriated other people's things.

Maryam Laamane doesn't know how to write this Somali in Latin characters, which Siad pickpocketed from others. She writes in Osmanya. My mom's Somali is spoken. Her Somali is made of history, poetry, music, and singing. When she writes—it happens rarely—she only knows how to do it in characters that no one remembers. She learned it when she was little in the cultural resistance meetings her older cousin, the patriotic one, dragged her to. She was a small girl then, and she entertained herself by tracing squiggles on squared sheets, like some pathological tic. The young Somalis of the League chose these characters to write their language and sign off on their new independence.

Maryam told me the story of Osmanya. She says that the first characters, curvate as snakes and folded like an ox tripe, were more adapted to the richness of Somali sounds. "All these white people's square letters, they're not fit for us. Latin characters aren't made for our lexical richness. The *T* with its toughness, the *S* with its serpentine hiss. You can't trust them or their letters. They won't carry what we say, think, or stow away. They betray. They are foreigners."

My mother is pregnant when she speaks. She gives birth to that other mother, her language.

I enjoy listening. She makes me travel in the deepest part of her. I want to stay quiet forever, simply listening. Attending the birth of a mother who begets my mother. I also have to speak and, each time I do, my voice pronounces falteringly. I hear shrill sounds, my own. I plug my ears, disgusted at hearing my shaky voice. I want to cry every time, but I refrain.

Mom likes my mix of Somali and Italian, she says that it's my language. I'm still ashamed of it, though. I'd like to be flawless in each. When I speak one, the other emerges shamelessly without an invitation. Continual short circuits in my brain. I don't speak, I mix.

Now, my mom is in front of me. We're sitting face-to-face. I got back from Tunis the other day and want to give her a full report of the trip. Howa died and we haven't spoken about it in person. I'm happy we can talk about Howa and Tunis here, in Mom's comfy home in Primavalle. The atmosphere is sweet and relaxing. Scientific studies show that the best air in the capital is in Primavalle.

My mom's house is penny plain. Like all the houses of diasporic Somalis it is practically unadorned. The painting of Mecca is the exception. The whiteness of the walls blinds me. I'd like to see a Renoir on one of the walls, but there is only whiteness with glimmers of devotion here and there. Multicolored fabrics only on the armchairs. A triumph of sensual delight that I sometimes can't explain.

Mom watches me, scrutinizes. All she needs is a microscope to vivisect my soul. I wait for her to say something.

Until now, we've talked about nothing. Tunis, its streets, its fears, its thousand follies. I gave almost a full account of my vacation. I didn't tell her everything. A daughter's censorship. I didn't tell her, for example, that I fell in love with the wrong man again. I didn't tell her that I had a nervous breakdown. I didn't even talk about Miranda. I didn't want her to be jealous of that marvelous woman. I did show her how much headway I made with classical Arabic, though. She smiled and clapped, my Maryam Laamane. She had a soft spot for classical Arabic. Like all Somalis, she was in awe of the language of worship. I threw in a small sample of the Tunisian dialect. "Do you see," I wanted to say, "how good your Zuhra is?" But I didn't say anything else. I waited for her second round of applause and went silent.

She was quiet, too.

"Yesterday I spoke with Sabrie's widow." Linear words, which my mother said in one go, breathlessly.

This was the signal I was waiting for. The serious conversation I was expecting.

"I hadn't seen her in a while, you know? She's very fat now."

I laughed. *Very fat* wasn't the right descriptor for Sabrie's wife. I'd call her elephantine, and Howa Rosario would've backed me up. Between the two of them, Howa was the one without reservations. Mom, though, was always politically correct, even when she drank gin early in the morning.

"So?" I ask. "What did she tell you? Can it be done?"

The words leave me, wobbly as gelatin. Anxiety eats me alive. Our pointless conversations of a short while ago seem prehistoric.

"So?" I press.

"She gave me a telephone number, someone named Abucar. He started the work recently, but he's honest, she told me. She trusted him with her niece and now the girl lives in Sweden."

Oh, yes, Sweden. I dreamed of Sweden because of my cousins Abdel Aziz and Muna. I dreamed of that perfect welfare country. There, Somalis could access everything, have a house, money, school paid for. Somalis there had a chance. Mom and I often spoke of Sweden as a solution for my cousins. Abdel Aziz and Muna were young. They couldn't stay at my house forever. They couldn't spend their entire lives reading Jehovah's Witness magazines and watching TV. They couldn't stay for so long in the blind Italy of Bossi-Fini. They had to venture elsewhere.

Italy is no longer welcoming for anyone at this point. This applies also to those who were born here. When I came back from Tunisia, my cousins were a favorite topic of mine. Finding a solution for them, a solution for me. Finding them a life, a life for me. If this meant paying a soul smuggler to drive them around half of Europe, so be it. Was it illegal? No more than it was tossing toxic waste in Somalia or feeding civil wars and insecurities to plunder the riches of African countries, as the West did. The word illegal didn't make sense anymore. Not for me.

"Are you all right, Zuhra?" my mother asked in the other mother, the sweet Italian of radio broadcasters.

Am I all right? In what sense?

"Your face is tense, dear, and the words are coming out of you like a brook."

Really?

"It's like…"

Like what?

"It's like you're happy."

Happy?

"How can I be happy, Mom?" I tell her. "Howa Rosario is dead. I miss her. How can I be happy when she's not here? And I can't sleep with this mess about my cousins having to leave illegally."

"But you are," she said in her mother tongue, categorical, absolute.

What can I say? How can I justify this untimely happiness? It was true. Mom read me like an X-ray. I was happy. It was because of the dream I had after getting back from Tunis. In the dream, I gave birth. My stomach was bigger than that of Sabrie's widow and slightly disc-shaped. In the dream, Howa Rosario had a perfect, luminous nose. She helped me breathe. My contractions became more painful and came closer together. I don't remember what happened after that, how I gave birth, how much I screamed, if they performed a C-section. I don't know anything. I only saw the result. Instead of a child, long iron rods. They looked horrible, they were heavy and some were rusty. I looked at them and felt a burning sensation in my stomach. Howa was there next to me, though, smiling. Her smile and her perfect nose gave me courage. I didn't ask, "Where is my child?" I knew that something else had come out of me. I remember asking, "Where are we hiding the umbilical cord?"

I was fine when I woke up from the dream. Sweating, but with my heart beating at a normal pace. Seeing Howa's gorgeous, perfect nose made everything okay. I touched my stomach and felt light as a butterfly.

I told my mother about the dream, as it had happened to me. Partly in our mother tongue, and partly in the other mother.

"Mom, you should've seen the awful tubes I had in my stomach. They were made of rusted iron. I touched them quickly. My fingers brushed against them. I was afraid to touch them for too long, you know? It was the fear of letting myself understand what had happened. I didn't give birth. I expelled. That's why I don't have an umbilical cord. I don't have to hide anything. After, when I woke up, I touched my stomach, and I touched my vagina. I felt so light! I went beyond Babylon, do you understand? Beyond everything, to a place where my vagina is happy and in love."

Beyond Babylon was a phrase I'd invented in high school. I'd been on my period. I knew nothing at the time about physical education. I was sitting in a corner with the other menstruators, two girls in the grade above mine. They didn't speak to me much. Few people spoke to me in high school. I was fat, black, standoffish.

I certainly wasn't the social queen. I was the example not to follow. Suddenly, I don't know which one of the two said something about Bob Marley and Babylon. She said that Babylon was everything bad that could exist in the world. White trash, vomit, disgust, pain. I suppose that in my mind's silence I thought, *I'd really like to live beyond Babylon.*

Beyond...

"I have something for you, Zuhra. A gift, let's call it," Mom said.

I was about to tell her that it wasn't my birthday. Mom was like that with me, she often bought me underwear like she did when I was a child. All those pairs of underwear embarrassed me.

"*Hooyo*, I don't need underwear, I have enough, really. Give them to Muna, she'll need them there where she's going. She could use them on the trip."

"It's not underwear."

She placed a colorful envelope on my lap. It wasn't closed. Inside, some audiotapes. I took them out one by one, slowly. I felt like I was being invited on a trip backward in time, to an age buried by the rhythms of life, by progress, by music downloaded from eMule. I remember that audiotapes weren't all that great for listening to music. The sound quality was poor, but in school they were passed around faster than word of mouth. I listened to so many tapes as a teenager, oh my God, so many! Tons of compilations, and my friends and I marked our favorite songs with heart shapes and asterisks.

At home, too, a bunch of tapes played. We received the words of a coarse-voiced woman from Somalia. Maryam Laamane never let me listen to those tapes. She didn't want to. She locked herself in her room and rudely distanced herself from me. Every once in a while, she forgot to close the door and I eavesdropped. I remember her crying to those cassettes. She cried like a storm. I eavesdropped until I couldn't take it anymore. I was small and didn't understand anything about those messages, those characters, and like a breath of wind the words in my mother language slipped swiftly away from my ears.

The tapes made me so nostalgic. They reminded me of my small self in front of the radio, my favorite station, searching for sounds to fill my soul. I adored the shape of cassettes, rectangular and contained. It gave me a sense of security, even of love. I trusted the cassette. Putting it in the recorder to listen was a ritual. The sound, despite all that rustling, was pleasant.

"Once, dear, you asked me if it was nice being with Papa."

I hold my breath.

"I didn't know how to respond. I can't really tell you how it went between me and him, honestly. But there's a response in these tapes. One of the many possible."

A response? An attempt? I'm shaking. I touch the cassettes with my ringed index finger.

"Is Papa in here?" I ask.

"We're inside," Maryam Laamane said.

We. What a marvelous word.

To: alice.balambalis@hotmail.com
Cc:
Subject: I'm going to a party!!!! Should be fun

Hi Alice, Abdi Nur! Your Zuhra here. Things haven't changed much where I'm at. What's the word among the igloos? I know there aren't eskimos where you are in Sweden, but when I think about that place, brr, I think of ice and those semi-spherical little houses. They look claustrophobic on TV...but I wouldn't know! From your messages, it sounds like you like the freezing cold and, like you say, the Swedes are super warm people... You can meet up with Somalis there, apparently. Ah, this diaspora! We're everywhere...but nowhere, in the end.

It's crazy hot here in Rome. I want a scholarship to get

out of this absurd heat. Rome is grand, but I can't stand it in the summer. It literally burns you alive!!

I don't have a ton of new things going on. Well, I might have one. Tonight I'm going to a party! If I tell you what kind, I already know how you'll respond, "That sucks! You call that a party?" So first I'll tell you what's gonna be there. A lot of guys, apparently (fuckable ones between their 30s and 50s), a filthy rich buffet, African music... I know, I know, no one says "African music." I'm black too (even if I'm Italian) and I know these things about Africa, sweetie. Everyone tells me I'm a go-getting intellectual, so show some respect :) and don't be so fussy, okay? Even if you're right, African music is too generic. You can't put Libya together with Madagascar at all. What I'm saying is I know that only whites talk about Africa without qualifying, but it's to abbreviate, OK? I didn't abbreviate and I'm still getting lost in turns of phrase.

So, to make it short, like Francis Bebey we'll say there's gonna be music. A.m.a.y.a. African modern and yet authentic. LEZGO! Sekou Diabate is DJing. He's a mother lode, a reservoir, not a man. There will be Senegalese dancers too. Good!! We Puntlanders like to bring our big butts and dance the niiko. Everyone thinks it's only a traditional dance, but to me it seems like what it is: women who make love (but with who? Among themselves? That's what I never understood about the niiko and Somalis). Thank goodness no one realized it...that we have sex, that is. I'm going to be standing on the sidelines, I'm not shaking my ass in front of other people.

Are you ready to hear it? I'll tell you what the party is for. Brace yourself. It's to commemorate the 50th anniversary of Ghana's independence. It's already been 50 years!! It's slightly before we got it too and, slowly but surely, the whole continent. It's been roughly 50 years since we were all declared free. But are we actually?

If I look at the map I'd say not really. Have you ever tried? If you look at Europe, you'll see lines and borders all jagged and curved. If you look at Africa you only see clear, straight borders cut with an ax. You see right away that they were made at the white man's table, where we just bowed our heads, as usual.

In the end, maybe we shouldn't celebrate. No niiko, no amaya, no Sekou. Fifty years of freedom in ruins. Whose fault? The whites? No. And so who if not them? It's easy to hate the whites, it may even feel good, but it's pointless. We have to take our share of the blame too. It's true, I know... first the Cold War...then the World Bank...then the arms trade, the trash trade, the children's organs trade, and trades for the fresh meat of women in whorehouses. The whites have their hands in it, sure. Arabs too. Now it seems that even the Chinese are involved. The Chinese have always had a stake in Africa, but the West is only now realizing it. They always see things late. They think things exist only after them. Everyone is involved, no one's left out. Africans are at the heart of it too. Siad Barre, Bokassa I, Omar Bongo, Idi Amin Dada, and Mobuti Sese Seko weren't white at all. I don't think. Amin Dada maybe, but I don't really think of him as white...

Anyway I bought new shoes for the party. You'll never believe it, they have heels! I want to feel like a woman tonight. A cabaret singer. I loved the shoes from the moment I saw them. A thunderbolt. Shock to the system. They used all their seductive power. I couldn't resist. I was prancing in the heels, drooling. I found them on Ebay. Yes!! On Ebay! I don't know how they ended up there. Leather clogs, pointed, in soft faux fur, with spotted pony details. Original Docs, box included (!!), drawstring dust bag, and warranty. Used, but still perfect, like in the photo. They came in three days. I'm wearing them tonight. Also because, dear (BRACE

YOURSELF), my pilgrim arrived. Yes, the one I was waiting so long for. He arrived unexpectedly. The shoes are also
to celebrate his arrival. I've got to be careful, though. Mama
Africa won't want me if I share her party with someone else.

Kisses, my friend, and don't freeze up there.

Yours always, Zuhra

CLICK, SENT.

Suspenseful minutes. The girl closes all the programs. She clicks
the *X*s. She's like a pianist, running quickly over keys of ebony and
ivory. At a certain point, darkness. The curtain falls. The computer
shuts down. First it announces, flashing, that the darkness is about
to submerge the light. That afterward, there will be only blackness.

She created that obscurity. She is pleased. She stands. She has
a stomachache, cramps gnawing at her lower gut. She'd ignored
them while typing the message to her friend. But the letter is finished, the computer is off. She has no more excuses for postpon-
ing. The bathroom is in the back of the house. The house almost
doesn't have a back. It's small. A squirrel's burrow. It is Saturday.
She bought many newspapers. She buys an armful on Saturdays.
All the inserts are there. They cost more. Saturdays are very colorful. She grabs one at random. She goes into the bathroom and slips
out of her underwear. She doesn't look at them. She doesn't like
them. She sits. Her stomach hurts. She starts leafing through the
magazine. She hopes it can help her with her work. She flips. Too
many interesting articles in the insert. She doesn't want to start
reading them. Those are best read at the writing desk. Perhaps
even underlined and analyzed. What do you want to learn while
you eject the residues of yourself? She flips, flips, flips. She needs
one of those gossip magazines, where the faces are fake and the
romances only a frontispiece. She feels overwhelmed. She cannot
expel. Undecided on the reading, she flips again. The photographs
are moving, the colors a *métissage*. She is struck by something

unforeseen. A flame. She fixates on the center of that heat. It's a picture of a man in a Hawaiian shirt. She begins to read.

The man tells of a frog. The man is from Burundi. He's a story collector. There are those who gather pears. Those who, exploited, gather tomatoes. This man, however, places words into his sack. He shares them so as not to lose them. During the harvest one day, he found a small frog. It had fallen in a bucket of milk. Surely it would drown. Dead without anyone knowing. But she, the frog, did not want to die. She hadn't yet lived. She hadn't yet fallen in love. So she starts to think. She thinks for as long as she can. "I like my life," she says to herself. Yes, she liked her life, more than anything else. It was then, after this thought, that the frog began flapping her legs. Slowly at first, then faster. She doesn't want to die. She hasn't been in love yet. Her legs churn. Fast. Faster. They kick as hard as they can. They float. The milk stirs. It dances. It wobbles. A tumultuous wave. The frog kicks. She sees that, on the surface, a dense, crude substance has formed. Less watery. It's butter. The frog thinks, "Maybe it will save me." She starts kicking hard again, fiercely. The milk dances and totters. More tumultuous waves. More butter. It goes on like this for a while and, finally, all the milk becomes butter. The frog stops kicking. The butter is solid. A tall mountain. The frog leaps on top, *hop, hop, hop*. And she leaves the bucket. Saved, finally saved! The small frog steps happily into her life again, as though nothing had happened.

The man from Burundi often speaks of this frog, the magazine says. He gathers stories. The girl forgot where she was sitting. She traveled with that man. Without realizing it, she has evacuated. She sets the magazine down. Goodbye, and thank you to the man from Burundi. She still has cramps. She looks down. She looks for where she tossed her underwear. She lifts them. Stands. They're dirty. A wet, expansive stain. It looks like a star. Perhaps it is.

Her star is red. Somewhat damp, but beautiful. It emanates light. A menstrual star that shines only for her, infinitely. The shapes scatter. The star broadens. A constellation. Inside the constellation, her woman's story. And within her story, the story of others before her and others after. The stories entwine, at times converging, often searching for one another. Each one united by a color and a feeling. Her cramps diminish. Expulsion feels good. In one moment the constellation dissolves. It vanishes, leaving a ring of red. And if love in Rome is that way? An undertone of red?